STRIPPER!

A Natalie McMasters Novel

By

Thomas A. Burns, Jr.

STRIPPER!

Stripper! Copyright © 2017 by Thomas A. Burns, Jr.

Cover designed by Thomas A. Burns, Jr. with CreateSpace Cover Creator

Front cover image used under license from Shutterstock.com

This book is a work of fiction. Names, characters, places, and incidents either are products of the author's imagination or are used fictitiously. Any resemblance to actual persons, living or dead, events, or locales is entirely coincidental.

Thomas A. Burns, Jr.

Printed in the United States of America

First Printing: April 2018

ISBN-13 978-0692102701

ISBN-10: 0692102701

To Terri, the love of my life, who believed in me and supported

me when no one else did.

Table of Contents

Chapter 1.

My living room is like the inside of a space station, festooned with cameras, boom mikes and lights on poles. So many people are crammed in here that I'm sure we're violating several fire codes. Their body heat coupled with the heat from the lights and other electronic equipment has raised the room temperature to half past sweltering, even though all of the windows are wide open to accommodate the power cables running to the moving van that now occupies our lawn. My roommates, Kwan and Fields, have wisely decided to stay on campus for the evening until the show is over.

The technician who's applying my makeup has to continually blot the sweat from my forehead to keep it from ruining his work. I see in the mirror that he's spreading a deep pink liquid on my lips with a small paint brush. He brushes my long blonde hair until it's straight and neat, then leans back to critically survey his work.

"You'll do," he says. "Sit over there on the sofa." He addresses a technician. "Tell Roderigo she's ready."

To say I have butterflies in my stomach would be a gross understatement. I'm about to be interviewed by one of the most famous, most hunky, and most controversial TV personalities in the country, who's come all the way from New York!

He makes his entrance, a small entourage of nubile females fluttering around him like a cloud of butterflies, ready to serve his every whim. OMG! He's even better looking than he is on TV, with his trademark steel grey hair, well-coiffed goatee and pencil mustache. A rush courses through me as he favors me with that famous toothy smile before taking a seat next me on the sofa.

He seems to sense my anxiety. He takes my hand and massages my palm with his thumb. It relaxes me a little.

"Ready?" he asks.

I nod.

He lets go of my hand, makes a gun with his thumb and index finger, and points it at the producer, then fires it by dropping his thumb. A flunky clicks a clapperboard in front of us. The sharp crack makes me jump.

Stripper!

"McMasters interview, take one."

"Good evening, America! This is your host Roderigo Hernandez with Miss Natalie McMasters, a college co-ed and the heroine of the day, who saved a young woman's life from being taken by a vicious sexual predator. As her reward for putting her own life in jeopardy, the District Attorney is convening a grand jury as we speak, to indict Miss McMasters for breaking and entering and quite possibly for first degree murder." He turns to me. "Natalie – can I call you Natalie?" He doesn't seem to notice my nod. "Natalie, can you tell us briefly how you found out that Mr. Randall Leighton was holding this young woman as his personal sex slave in the basement of his home?"

I explain that I'm working as a private detective trainee for my Uncle Amos while I'm in school. Most of his business comes from dogging insurance scofflaws, waiting for them to do something for the camera that shows they're not hurt as badly as they say. Randall Leighton was a builder who claimed he hurt his back on the job, and he had a disability policy. The insurance company hired Uncle Amos to verify that the claim was legitimate.

"Our usual procedure is to watch the subject for a few days, to see if he does anything that is inconsistent with his alleged injuries."

"Such as," prompts Roderigo.

"Oh, carrying a heavy trash can, yard work, that sort of thing. Once I even got a picture of a guy working out on a rowing machine in a gym after he'd claimed he'd thrown his back out." Roderigo smiles for the camera. They told me during the pre-interview to be sure and include that nugget.

"So you watched him for several days and became convinced he had a woman in his house. Why did you think so?"

"Because he bought too much food for one person, for one thing. And he bought women's underwear and bubble bath. It was a small house and I could see inside. There was no sign of a woman."

"How did you know that he just didn't like to wear women's underwear in the bathtub while he ate?" I'll bet that line will get him a big laugh.

"I didn't. But I was pretty sure he had a woman in there."

"So you decided to break into his house and find out. Why didn't you just call the police?"

"Because I had really skimpy evidence, and no prospects of getting any better unless I went in. If I was right, I couldn't just leave her there."

"You couldn't just leave her there," he repeats, "even if it meant the end of your college career and prison if you were wrong." He gazes at the camera with that heartwarming look of his. "People, that's what we call courage on this show! What happened next, Natalie?"

I tell him how I lured Leighton out of the house that night with a ruse, then broke in upstairs, only to find nothing but a heavily secured basement that I couldn't get into. I went back outside and managed to break a basement window, and found an elaborate love nest, complete with ropes, pulleys and whips.

"But no girl?"

"Not at first. But I knew that she had to be there somewhere!"

"And where did you find her, Natalie?"

"Under the bed, in a box like a coffin with air holes! She was eighteen, maybe twenty, naked and had all of her hair and eyebrows shaved off. I could see the scars from the whips on her body."

Roderigo just stays silent, and lets that sink in.

"And then what happened?"

I tell him how Leighton came home before I could get the girl out of there. And how I fought him.

"You fought him! How tall are you, Natalie?"

"Five one, and I weigh less than a hundred pounds."

"I'd never ask a lady how much she weighs," he says in an attempt to relax me. It works. "But your adversary was a construction worker who weighed over two hundred pounds. What happened next?"

"What do you think happened? He beat the shit out of me, threw me on the floor. He kicked me and he broke two ribs." Belatedly, I wonder if they'll bleep the "shit".

"So then what did you do?"

I must be very careful here. I tell him how the victim joined in the fight when she saw that I was losing, but that she couldn't overcome him either.

8

Stripper!

"But she got him to turn his back on me. That's when I grabbed the machete…"

"He had a machete!"

I nod. "It was in the cabinet with the whips. I grabbed it, stuck him, and he went down. I found out later that he was dead."

Well, that's it. I've just admitted on nationwide TV that I killed a man in his own home. The DA should have no problem getting that indictment now. But it's a lie. I didn't kill him. The girl in the box did. But I figure that she just doesn't need any more grief or notoriety.

"And you finally called the police, and they came and arrested you instead of giving you a medal. That's our America for you, people! No good deed goes unpunished!"

Later, all of the TV people are gone, and the house is silent again. I'm lying wide awake in the dark. It's still hot, but my old window air-conditioner is laboring noisily. The phones are turned off because they won't stop ringing. But you know what? Most of the callers are saying that I did the right thing!

The next few days are totally awesome. The post office has to dedicate a truck just to deliver our mail. Many of the envelopes have checks inside for my legal defense – five, ten, twenty dollars. I never do find out the final total. The grand jury returns an indictment for breaking and entering and manslaughter. Then I hear that the computers in the DA's downtown office were forced offline by a DDoS attack. People are flying in from all over the country for a rally for me in front of the courthouse. I don't go, but I do hear that it jams up the traffic in the capitol all morning.

My day in court is very short. The DA rescinds the indictment. She has to. She knows that she'll never even get elected to dogcatcher in this town if she there's a trial. Such is the power of the media!

A week later, the furor has died down somewhat. I'm sitting in the back of Econ class only half-listening as the prof drones on. It's late spring and the air conditioning is off, so the auditorium is baking from the heat of the students' bodies, and smells of deodorant and sweat. The events of the last few weeks have taken their toll – it's been increasingly difficult to pay attention in class.

The prof stops lecturing and addresses a student in the front of the room. "Miss McMasters, can you tell me some differences between the Keynesian and Chicago schools of economics?"

A female voice replies, "Yes I can, but my name isn't McMasters."

I strain to see the woman who spoke, but there are too many tall people in front of me.

Mercifully, class is soon over. As I'm filing out of the auditorium in the crowd, a voice behind me says, "Hey, McMasters! I'm tired of people thinking that I'm you!"

I turn to see who spoke. It's like looking in the mirror. She's about my height and has long blonde hair cascading half way down her back. She's way cute! I've noticed her in class before, but until now, I didn't realize how much we look alike. I grope for a response, but I'm speechless.

"I'm Becca Chapman," she says. "I've been wanting to meet you since you were all over the news. Gosh, no wonder the prof made that mistake. We could be sisters."

"Becca, you can call me Nattie. And you're right, we could be sisters."

A snide remark reminds us we're blocking the exit. Becca pulls me aside into a row of seats. "I really don't mind being mistaken for you." she says. "I kind of like the attention."

"I don't like all the attention I've been getting since my interview with Roderigo. All of my profs know me and call on me all the time. That's why I was hiding in the back of the class."

Becca smiles at me - she has dimples just like mine. "This is my last class. How 'bout a drink at Max's?"

I want to, but since I've lost my job, I'm totally broke. She sees it on my face. "C'mon! My treat!"

I decline again – I'm embarrassed to have to take charity. But Becca's not hearing it. She gets that petulant look that I have learned to use, and I find out it works on me too! So we take off across the quad.

Max's is your typical college bar. Been there forever. Everyone knows it, so there's no sign. You open the door and go up a narrow flight of stairs that are bowed in the middle from countless feet. It's cool in the stairwell and the light from the single bulb is muted and casts your shadow on the stairs. As you open the metal door at the top, the hubbub of voices, the clatter of glassware and the aromas of yeast and alcohol engulf you. Max's is one big room with a square bar in the center and tables scattered about the perimeter. There's no table service – you just elbow your way up to the bar and tell Max what you want. Luckily, it's still early and the place is busy but not packed, so we get a table at the window overlooking Lee Street – a prized location.

"Wow, you're hardcore!" Becca says. "I don't know anybody else who drinks shots and beers."

"I got it from my dad. You should try it sometime, as long as you're just having one or two."

"I will." she says. "Back in a sec!"

She returns with a shot. I elevate mine in a toast. "To my new friend!" I gulp it down and it warms my belly and curls my toes. Becca tries to do the same but gets only half of it down before she starts choking.

"Hey, that's all right." I say. "Go slow if it's your first time."

She grins sheepishly and sets the half shot on the table. OMG, she's totally cute! Does that make me a narcissist?

We chat for a bit and I find out she's an econ major.

"Where are you from?" I ask.

"Ma…, I mean, Ohio."

My antenna vibrates. "So you moved recently?"

"A while ago," she says. "But I live here now. Where do you want to go to law school?"

I feel like she dodged my question, but hey, it's none of my business if she doesn't want to talk about it. The conversation flows into safer waters – school, our likes and dislikes in music and clothes and of course, guys.

"So are you hooked up with anyone right now?" The alcohol has made me somewhat tactless.

"No. Are you?"

I tell her about Michael. "Asshole was engaged to somebody else while he was engaged to me."

"Gee, that's tough," she says. "But better to find out before you got married, right?"

I notice that her clothes and backpack are brand name. I try to change an uncomfortable subject.

"So I guess your folks are pretty well off?"

She frowns, and I'm sorry I said it. "Not really," she says. "I'm putting myself through school."

Normally I'd have taken the hint and changed the subject again, but given my current financial state, I have to ask. "How are you doing that?" Now her discomfort is totally obvious, so I try to smooth it over. "Hey, I'm only asking because I got fired recently and I'm looking for a job."

Her eyes get big. "I thought you said on TV that you were a detective."

I spend the next ten minutes telling her the story. She's totally captivated. Her turquoise eyes stare intently into mine, making me vaguely self-conscious.

"But I did something Uncle Amos said never to do." I finish ruefully. "I made direct contact with a subject and nearly got myself killed. Uncle Amos was furious! He said he never wanted to tell my mom I'd been hurt or killed working for him, so he fired me on the spot. And I lost my only income."

"I don't believe that D.A. was gonna charge you for saving somebody's life."

"Well, technically, I did break the law when I broke into the house. People sent me contributions, but after I paid off the legal bill I did incur, I gave the rest to charity. I didn't want to profit off of somebody else's misfortune."

"Why not? Isn't that what a lawyer does?"

"It's not the same thing."

I can see that she doesn't agree, but she doesn't argue the point. "Can't you get a job at State?" she asks instead.

"Not without amending my financial aid. I've started the process, but it takes forever."

"Well, how about someplace here on Lee Street?"

Stripper!

"I've got applications in, but the other students got all of those jobs before the semester started. It's hard for me to look too far from State because I don't have a car. I was driving one of Uncle Amos', but I lost that with my job."

"What about your folks?"

"My dad passed while I was in high school. My mom doesn't really have a lot of money. Maybe she could help some, but I don't want to ask – college is about learning to stand on your own two feet."

"That's how I feel," Becca says. "Both of my parents are dead too."

"I'm so sorry, Becca." It sounds so lame.

"It's OK. It's been a long time."

I change the subject. "So how are you paying for school? Do you have a scholarship?"

She's doesn't answer for a moment. Finally, she says, "How'd you like to come for dinner Friday night? I'll tell you then."

"Hey now, I'm not looking for a free meal…"

She takes my hand in hers. A tingle courses up my arm. "I'm not offering charity, Nattie," she says "I like you a lot and I'd like to get to know you better. And maybe I can help you out."

I really like her too! "Okay, I'll come."

She lets go of my hand and I notice a long, pink scar on hers, running from the base of her thumb across her palm to the base of her little finger. "Ouch!" I say. "That must have hurt."

"Cut myself on a broken glass," she says. "It was a while ago." She pulls out her cell. "I'll text you my number."

I give her mine.

"I'll meet you after class on Friday," she says. "You can ride home with me." She drains her beer. The half shot is still on the table.

"You gonna drink that?"

She smiles and pushes it over to me.

Chapter 2.

The house is dark and lonely when I get home – Fields and Kwaneshia both have night class. I'm hungry, but the booze has upset my stomach. I check the fridge – all I've got left is some white bread. I see a fresh pound of hamburger on Fields' shelf, but I resist the temptation. I'm not going to steal food. Not yet, anyway.

I'm knocking down a ketchup and mayo sandwich with a glass of water when the phone rings. I figure it's Fields' BF, so I let it go to the machine.

"Hi. This is Danny Merkel calling Natalie McMasters. We met last month at your uncle's detective agency. You said I could call you…"

I snatch up the phone. "Hi, this is Nattie!"

I first met Danny when he was a policeman. Later, I was at the 3M detective agency when he interviewed for a job as a PI with Uncle Amos. He's way hot and has a pretty boy face you can't help but like. He's a former marine and former cop with a blonde military haircut that makes him look like an action movie hero. As he was leaving after the interview, he asked if he could call me whether he got the job or not. I said yes.

"Hi, Natalie! I hope I'm not bothering you. I waited to call – I saw your interview with Roderigo, and I heard that Mr. Murdoch let you go. How are you doing?"

"OK, I guess. It helps to know I saved somebody."

"You sure did." He hesitates. "Well I wanted to let you know that Mr. Murdoch gave me the job. I hope that's not a problem."

I fight to keep the sadness out of my voice. "No, Danny, that's great. Congrats!" Looks like I'm really on the outs with Uncle Amos, then.

"So I was wondering if you'd like to have dinner on Friday."

Damn! I already promised Becca for Friday. And I don't break promises just because something else comes along.

"I'm busy Friday, but I would totally like to have dinner with you."

"Well how 'bout tomorrow?"

Stripper!

I don't have to look at what's left of my nasty sandwich to take him up on it. I give him the address and leave the choice of the restaurant to him.

The next day is rough. Breakfast is dry toast washed down with water. Isn't bread and water what they feed you in jail? The final two slices of white bread go in a zip lock with a packet of ketchup and mayo for lunch. I know I'll be famished by the time Danny comes.

I'm not wrong. I'm waiting for him in the front room, so hungry that my stomach hurts. I keep pulling the curtain aside, checking the driveway. Mental note - do not bolt the food when we get to the restaurant. It wouldn't do to let him think I'm a charity case.

Finally, his car pulls up. It's the one I used to drive when I worked with Uncle Amos. Still, I've never been so glad to see anyone in my life. After he knocks on the door, I force myself to wait a minute before I open it.

OMG, he's totally smoking! He's wearing black cargo pants and a tight red t-shirt with a Marine Corps logo that shows off his muscles. He looks like a cop even without a uniform, which could be a big disadvantage for a PI. I wonder if he's carrying. Since he's an ex-cop, I assume so.

We make small talk on the way to the restaurant. I'm mildly miffed that he won't tell me where we're going – I hope it's not a sandwich place because I'm looking forward to leftovers. I'm pleasantly surprised when we pull up to a steak joint.

My knees go weak as we enter and the food smells assail me. Fresh bread, char-broiled meat and beer all compete for my attention as I try to keep up with Danny's patter. All I want to do is charge the salad bar.

Danny tells me to order anything I want, so I go for the 26-ounce Porterhouse. He raises an eyebrow at that, but I'm shamelessly thinking that I can leave here with a doggie bag. Then Becca will feed me tomorrow night. I have no idea how I'm gonna get through next week, though. How do poor people live?

Danny orders one of those giant fried onion thingies, and I finally get to the salad bar. Soon I've beaten back the hunger pains enough so I can make intelligent conversation.

"So you want to go to law school," he says. "Me too, but I'll have to do it at night, and take one course a semester."

"Takes a long time that way. I want to get school over with, so I can do something useful."

"That's why I joined the force," says Danny. "I helped somebody almost every day."

"So why did you quit, if you don't mind my asking."

His expression tells me that the subject is distasteful. "Let's just say that some things went down that I couldn't square with my conscience, and leave it at that," he says. He pauses, then asks, "So how did you get involved with that lunatic last month? You saved that girl's life!"

I tell the story for the second time in two days.

"I suppose it was worth getting fired to save a life," I finish.

The conversation stops when the steaks come. Danny got the Porterhouse too, so there's almost no room on the table when the giant plates and all the sides are laid out. Looks like I'll have plenty of food for the weekend.

"I wish I had done something like that." Danny says. "Saving that girl, I mean. When I was on the force, towards the end all I did was bust Internet hookers."

"That's a waste," I say.

He gets a funny look. "Not really," he says. "Those girls can get hurt just like street whores can. Your experience proves that there are a lot of predators out there. Those girls are just asking for trouble."

"But my girl was no hooker. She just got snatched by a pervert. Wrong place, wrong time. At least the hookers know what they're getting into."

"They don't have a clue," Danny disagrees. "Most of them are immature and in it for the money, or they're junkies. They have no idea how evil some people can be. And they don't give a damn about the law."

"Well, that's one reason I want to be a lawyer," I say. "Maybe I can help women like that. Get their lives back on track."

"Good luck with that," Danny says.

I totally don't like his attitude, but I'm not about to start a fight with a guy who's feeding me when I'm starving. I change the subject. Other than his jaded attitude about hookers and people in general, I find out we have a lot in common.

Finally, the doggie bags are packed and we're ready to go. Danny pushes his box of food towards me.

"You want that?" he asks. "I'm watching my weight."

I resist the impulse to say, God yes! "Sure," I reply casually. If he's watching his weight, the muscles rippling under his t-shirt tell me he's doing a damn good job of it. I wonder if he's picked up on how hungry I was.

We're both quiet on the ride back to my place – being stuffed to the gills with food and beer probably has something to do with it. It's a warmish evening, and I have to fight to stay awake as the cool breeze wafts over me through the car window. In my driveway, he gets out to open the door. The awkward moment has arrived – is he going to want to hook up?

He takes my hands in his. "I had a nice time tonight, Nattie," he says. "I can't come in because I've got to get up early tomorrow, but I would like to see you again. Can I call you?"

"Sure, Danny. I had a nice time, too. Thanks for the great dinner. Next time will be my treat." Now why in the hell did I say that, given my present financial circumstances?

He squeezes my hands, then lets them go. He gets a funny look on his face. "Hey, would you like me to talk to Mr. Murdoch about firing you? I mean, I've just started working for him, but…"

"Don't you dare!" His stricken expression makes me sorry I was so emphatic. "Look, you don't know how Uncle Amos is when he makes up his mind about something like that. You'd just get yourself in trouble without helping me at all. The best thing to do is just let him cool off."

"Okay, okay! I won't say anything if you don't want me to."

I watch from the porch as he drives away. Shit. I want to see him again – it's high time I moved on from Michael. But where am I gonna get the money to take him out? I can't even feed myself.

I go inside and put the food away. I should have enough to get me through the weekend, especially since Becca is feeding me tomorrow. I still have no idea what I'm gonna do about eating next week.

Chapter 3.

A good breakfast and lunch of steak joint leavings on Friday give me enough fuel to pay attention in class. I arrive in Econ at the end of the day. Becca is not there, but she plops down a few minutes later.

"All set for tonight?" she asks.

"Looking forward to it." I haven't had a BFF in ages and I think Becca might just be the one for the job.

"I forgot to tell you I'm a vegetarian. I hope you don't mind."

All of the meat I've been eating lately, I don't mind. Besides, beggars can't be choosers.

Conversation stops as class begins. I try to concentrate, but Becca's nearness makes it difficult. She's wearing a frilly blouse over a mini skirt and a subtle fragrance that's both flowery and spicy. She's dressed fancier than she was on Wednesday - it seems a bit much for school.

When class is over, we hop the shuttle bus to the parking lot. It's packed, so we have to stand. The swaying causes Becca to push against me and I find myself pushing back. She's not wearing a bra – her nipples are obvious beneath her translucent top.

I'm surprised to see Becca's car, a snappy red Z-car with a black racing stripe. It still smells new and the contoured black leather seats hug me like a lover. Becca hits a switch and the sun roof whirs, letting in the late afternoon sunshine.

I'm surprised again when she heads for the Beltway instead of the student ghetto surrounding campus, where I live. We drive for fifteen minutes to the north of town into rich folks' land. We roll into a posh townhouse park that reeks of money, filled with free-standing, two story white buildings with windows on all sides. The green space between them is spattered with azaleas and wisteria, and their cloying aroma invades the car as Becca cuts the engine. She parks in a spot with a plaque atop a mahogany post that has her townhouse number on it - this is about as far from student housing as you can get! Because of her reluctance to talk about money, I say nothing.

Stripper!

Each building is a separate residence. Hers is pleasantly cool as we enter; it smells of flowers and has another, earthier undertone. The outside door opens into a great room, tastefully but sparsely furnished in glass, stainless steel and black and white leather. The flat-screen TV on the wall looks wider than I am tall. There's a galley kitchen and a master bedroom off the great room. A spiral staircase in the center of the great room leads to upstairs bedrooms. The entire first floor, except for the kitchen and the bathrooms, is carpeted with white shag, which perfectly matches the yowling Siamese cat that prances up and leaps into Becca's arms.

"I've never seen a white Siamese cat before."

"She's a lilac point. They're rare," she replies as she ruffles the cat's ears. "This is Xin Niu." Becca gestures towards the living room. "Make yourself comfortable. Would you like red or white wine? Or maybe a shot and a beer?" she smiles.

I start to ask for red wine, then I think about the carpet and opt for white instead. I couldn't live in a place like this, because I just couldn't keep all that white stuff clean.

She goes to the fridge for the wine. Belatedly, I wonder if she bought the whisky just for me?

The kitchen is separated from the living room by a pass through that serves as a dining bar. I perch on a stool on the living room side while she works in the kitchen. My eyes are drawn to the perfectly sculptured legs below the hem of her mini skirt as she fixes a green salad with fresh fruit and nuts. The pancakes she fries up to go with the salad smell amazing, like sweet bread and nuts.

Our conversation revolves around school. She is aware of the elephant in the room, however. When the conversation turns to her background, she artfully steers it in another direction.

She serves dinner up on the bar, replenishes the wine, then sits next to me. The salad is scrumptious with its creamy, citrusy dressing and even better when wrapped in the crispy, golden pancakes. The wine goes perfectly with the food. I'm not much for rabbit food, but this is one of the best meals I've had, ever!

As we're cleaning our plates with the remnants of the pancakes, she says, "You know, you're the first person from school I've ever brought here. And I know you're wondering how I can have all of this and put myself through school too. I really like you Nattie, so I'm going to show you."

19

She takes me by the hand and leads me up the spiral staircase. As we enter the upper hallway, a light, triggered by a motion sensor, comes on automatically. She stops in front of a closed door. She seems tense and anxious. WTF? Is she dealing, or cooking meth? What have I gotten myself into?

She opens the door and the overhead light flashes on. OMG! It's a huge, gaudy red and white bedroom redolent of perfume and musk, like a girls' locker room. Venetian blinds conceal the windows. A heart-shaped bed dominates the room's center and is flanked by shuttered lights on poles at the corners. An opaque, garish green screen hangs behind a raised platform next to the door. There's a settee on one side of the platform and a pole that extends from floor to ceiling on the other. An elaborate computer system occupies a desk on the opposite side of the room.

"What is this place?" I ask.

"It's my studio, Nattie." She makes a little bow from the waist. "Meet Kira Foxxx, interactive dancer extraordinaire!"

Becca explains that she's been "working" as an exotic dancer on the Internet since she started school. She began with just a webcam and worked her way up to this system. I'm amazed as she points out the tiny cameras on the wall, focused on the bed and the green screen, which is similar to the apparatus used by TV weather forecasters. It can display backgrounds ranging from a tropical beach to a steamy nightclub interior. Everything is computer-controlled by an unobtrusive handheld remote that Becca uses while performing. Microphones and speakers strategically positioned around the room allow her to hear and speak with her clients.

"It's interactive dancing," she explains. "My clients tell me what they want, and I do my best to oblige." She opens a drawer to reveal an array of sex toys, making me blush.

"How do you get paid?" I ask.

"In advance, of course!" she smiles. "I take Visa, Mastercard and AmEx."

I'm stunned, trying to take it all in. "Why are you showing me this?"

"Let's go back downstairs, and I'll tell you."

We return to the living room. She gets us another round of wine, then waves me to an easy chair while she gracefully sinks down on a beanbag. A tremor goes through me as I see her reclining there. What's happening to me?

20

Stripper!

"You know, when I first realized how much we look alike, I thought we could be related, and I wanted to get to know you. Now that I have, I know that I like you. A lot. You told me you're having money troubles so I wanted to ask if you would join me in my business. We could do a twin act. We would clean up!"

The warmth that I'm feeling suddenly chills. Without thinking, I blurt out, "No way!"

"That's exactly how I felt when I got started – I wouldn't have done it, except that I wanted to go to State, and it was the only way short of hooking that I could make enough money."

"But it is hooking..." I begin...

"No, it isn't!" she says adamantly. "I never have sex with my clients. I just perform for them."

"But you know what they're doing when they're watching..."

"No, I don't! I can't even see them, and what they might be doing doesn't concern me. They're just paying for my time. If they tell me to do something I don't want to, I just say no and give them their money back. And this is way better than dancing in a club! No lap dances! They don't even know who or where I am."

"Did you ever work in a club?" I ask.

"For part of one night, and that was plenty. This pays a lot better and there's no pressure for me to do anything I'm uncomfortable with. Will you at least think about it before you say no?"

"But I want to go to law school..."

"...which will leave you destitute for most of your working life. Listen, besides you, the only people that know that Becca Chapman is Kira Foxxx is my ISP, and they could care less. Heck, we look enough alike that someone who saw one of my performances might even think I'm you."

Now there's a disturbing thought.

I sip my wine for a minute, then I smile and ask, "So did you ever have to give someone their money back?"

"A time or two. And no, you don't want to know why!"

"I'll think about it," I say, "but the answer is very likely going to be no."

21

"Do you think it would help you make up your mind if you watched me perform?"

OMG! Did she just say that?

"When?" Did I just say that?

"How about right now? If I turn on the phone, I'll have a client in five minutes."

The wine probably has something to do with my response. "I guess so."

"Then let me get changed."

She disappears upstairs. I sip my wine and wonder why the hell I'm not out of here. I like sex as much as the next girl but it would creep me way out to put on a show for some guy that I can't even see.

A few minutes later, I hear "Nattie, I'm ready." I go on up. Becca is seated in a mesh chair at the computer. She's wearing a red babydoll nightie open in front with a black microbikini beneath. Her perfect legs are sheathed in black fishnet stockings and she's sporting a pair of four-inch heels.

"This is the master control center," she says, indicating the computer screen. "It controls the lights, the cameras and the green screen."

She opens a drawer and takes out a smart phone, clips it into a stand on the computer monitor, then activates it. "My business line," she says. "It won't be long…"

A few minutes later, the phone chirps.

"Sit there." She points to large pillow on the side of the room. "They can't see you there, but don't move until I tell you."

She taps the smartphone screen.

"This is Kira." I'm amazed at the sexy timbre in her voice – she doesn't sound like the same person.

"There you are!" a masculine voice replies. "I was afraid you weren't going to be around tonight."

"I'm always here for you, Stud."

"Will you do it for me, Kira? What you did last time?"

22

Stripper!

"Are you sure that's what you want, Stud? We talked about my doing something different."

"I know, Kira, but right now, I need you to do what you did last time. Please?" he whines.

"OK, Stud. Put the money in the piggy bank, then Kira will take care of you."

She watches the computer screen for a moment, then goes over to the drawer with the toys. I can tell the moment he can see her, because her bodily motion changes from a normal walk to a sensuous glide. She removes a small toy from the drawer and holds it up. "Is this the one you want?"

"No! You know which one. The big one!"

She smiles at me, then removes the desired toy. "This one?"

"God, yes!"

She slowly steps up on the raised platform, wiggles out of her bra and panties for the camera, then reclines on the settee wearing only the babydoll, the stockings and the heels. I can't tear my eyes off her body!

I really can't describe the next fifteen minutes, except to say that I never knew that you could do so much with just one toy! Stud tells her what he wants, and she enthusiastically obliges. By the time she's finished, I'm soaking wet, and my whole body tingles.

"Did you like that, Stud?" she says, breathlessly.

"God yes!"

"Kira's got to go now, but she'll be in tomorrow night. You call back and we'll talk about some other things I can do for you."

"Kira, no, wait…"

She looks directly at me, then at the phone. I cut it off.

She rises from the sofa and stretches languorously, as if totally unaware of her nudity. The glaring spotlights have turned the room into a steam bath and her pungent scent suffuses everything. Fascinated, I watch as beads of perspiration roll from between her breasts down over her stomach.

"I just made two hundred and fifty dollars in twenty minutes," she says. "If I had worked all night, I would have made nearly a thousand. Still think you don't want to join me?"

"I don't know…"

She comes to me. The odor of sweat, sex and perfume that she exudes is intoxicating, and my eyes are fixed on her breast, with its jutting nipple. She reaches over and brushes my hair.

"Nattie, we could have a lot of fun together, and make lots of money, too. We could easily get double my rate for the two of us. What do you say?"

I don't know if I want to jump out of the chair and run out of here or take her in my arms. I gently remove her hand from my hair.

"I really don't know, Becca. And even if I did say yes, I would still need time to get used to the idea."

Her eyes reflect her disappointment. "I guess you would," she pouts. "Let me take a shower, then I'll take you home."

She stops by the door and looks back at me. "Sure you don't want to join me in the shower?"

OMG, I think that I do! But Uncle Amos' voice echoes in my head. *Never do anything you can't take back without sleeping on it first.* "Not tonight, Becca. Please let me think about it."

"OK," she smiles. Then she's gone.

I go downstairs, help myself to more wine, and mull over the evening. I've always thought I was straight, but I can't deny my feelings while I watched her perform.

She reappears in about twenty minutes, dressed tastefully in jeans and a man's shirt. "Ready?" she asks.

I nod. Outside, the night is warm and alive with the shrill drone of nocturnal wildlife. We're silent during the drive, but it's not uncomfortable – it's really just about two people respecting each other's boundaries.

In my driveway, Becca puts the car in park and engages the emergency brake. She doesn't kill the engine. The awkward moment has arrived again.

"We'll talk Monday after class," she says. "And I want you to know that whatever you decide, I would still like to be friends."

"I want to be your friend too, Becca." I get out, then watch her drive away. The alcoholic haze makes it difficult to analyze my feelings. I give it up and head to bed.

Chapter 4.

I make it as far as the kitchen by early afternoon. Fields is at the table, drinking a cup of tea and reading.

She looks up as I enter. "Finally," she says.

I don't like the sound of that.

"What?"

"Nattie, the rent's due."

"Yeah, Fields, about that…"

"Look, I'm sorry you've had it rough since you lost your job. I've talked to Kwan, and we've agreed that we'll spot you a month. But if you haven't paid or at least have a job by next month, we're going to have to ask you to move out."

My stomach aches. What do you say to something like that? I just nod, and shuffle back to my room.

I hole up in my room for the rest of Saturday and all day Sunday, coming out only to go to the john and eat. I'm aware that when the leftovers from the steak joint are gone, I'll have no food and no money. I'm pretty sure Becca would take me in if I asked her, but I'm not sure that I could be a good dancer, even if I decided to try. And I'm not sure what kind of relationship I want with Becca. I skip school on Monday to avoid her.

Monday evening, she sends me a cryptic text.

Nattie, I've done something to prove how serious I am about taking you on as my partner. Let's go to Max's after Econ on Wednesday and I'll tell you about it.

I can't bring myself to respond.

Depression is a great thing if you're on a diet. The leftovers last until Wednesday breakfast. I know I have to get myself out of this funk, so I go to class, dreading Econ all day, but Becca's not there when I arrive. She never even shows up at all. What's going on?

Home, I check the fridge, even though I know what I'm going to find. But there's a surprise. A pound of sausage, a package of lunch meat, a loaf of bread

26

and a dozen eggs are on my shelf along with a note. *There are five TV dinners in the freezer and a gallon of milk in the door for you.* It's signed Fields and Kwan. I just stand there with tears running down my cheeks, ashamed!

Later that evening, I decide to tell Becca that I just can't join her. I like her a lot, but I'm just not ready to have sex with a girl, and it's obvious that's what she wants. So I'm afraid a friendship won't work, either.

I call, but it goes right to voicemail. She's probably dancing.

"I missed you in Econ today. We really have to talk. Let's try again for Max's. Call me."

As I'm coming out of the shower Thursday morning, Fields meets me in the hall.

"The police are here for you, Nattie. On the porch."

WTF?

I go downstairs in my robe with a towel around my hair. An officer is standing outside the screen door. People, this cannot be good!

"Are you Natalie McMasters?"

I admit it.

"Can I please come in?"

I nod and open the screen door. In the living room, she asks me to sit. She remains standing.

"Ms. McMasters, I need to ask you about your relationship with Rebecca Chapman," she begins.

Suddenly, I have to pee! "Why?"

"When was the last time you saw her?"

"Why?" I say again. "I'm not telling you anything until you tell me why you want to know."

"I'm sorry, Miss McMasters. Ms. Chapman is dead!"

Chapter 5.

I don't believe her! "Becca's dead! How?"

"Somebody killed her," the officer says.

"No! I just saw her! Where is she?"

"Her body's at the morgue."

Becca's dead? At the morgue? This is not happening! "Why did you come to me?" I ask.

"It appears that you and she were close."

"What makes you think we were close?"

"You don't know?" She sounds disbelieving.

"Of course, I don't know!" I struggle for control as I feel myself starting to go over the edge.

"You're her partner. Everything she had is yours now that she's gone."

WTF!

"When did you see her last?"

I tell her about our dinner Friday night, leaving out the aftermath, of course.

"You may have been one of the last people to see her alive. Could you come downtown, so the detective can ask you some questions?"

I totally lose it and start wailing like a child who's gotten a whipping. The officer just waits for me to cry it out. After I regain control, I go get dressed. My mind is whirling. Becca's dead, and she's left me everything? What about her family? Surely there's somebody more important in her life than me that should have her things. A more troubling thought surfaces – do they think I have something to do with her death because she made me her partner?

The ride to police headquarters is silent. The officer apologizes for making me ride in the back seat, with a screen between me and her. "It's policy", she says. But it makes me feel like a criminal, and I can't help scrunching up to get away from the window, lest anyone who knows me sees me there. Once at the police station, the officer conducts me to a featureless cinder block room furnished with a table that has a chair on either side, like I've seen in a hundred cop shows on TV. The room has a faint bathroom funk, not quite masked by the chemical smell of disinfectant. The cop seats me in an uncomfortable metal chair facing a large, presumably one-way, mirror and leaves. I don't get up to find out, but I'm pretty sure I heard the door lock behind her.

I sit there for what seems like hours. Finally, a husky, middle-aged black man in a rumpled brown suit enters. He's overweight and going bald, with a ring of curly hair like a monk's circling his head. His broad features are splayed across his face and he has a greying mustache under a large flat nose. He's got a large brown wart on his upper lip which I know is going to make me uncomfortable because I'll struggle to avoid staring at it. He introduces himself as Detective Kidd as he takes the seat across from me.

He skips the preliminaries. "Tell me about the last time you saw Rebecca Chapman."

I tell him about last Friday night, again leaving out that I watched her perform.

"You know how she makes her living." It's not a question.

"Yes." I counter with my own question. "What happened to Becca?"

"Somebody killed her."

I'm not letting him off the hook. "The police lady told me that. How did it happen?"

His stern façade dissolves, and he favors me with an avuncular smile.

Look," he says, "normally, I wouldn't tell you, because I'd be looking to see what you know. But I'm pretty sure you didn't do this. I'm hoping maybe you know who did or can help us find out." He takes a deep breath. "It wasn't pretty," he says. "She died of multiple stab wounds. And she was apparently tortured first."

OMG! I throw up in my mouth a little and swallow it back.

"When and where did this happen?"

29

"We found her Tuesday night. Dumped in a vacant lot downtown. That wasn't the primary crime scene - we don't know where that was. It wasn't at her townhouse –no evidence says she was killed there."

"How did you know who she was?"

"Oh, her ID was on her, as well as some cash. So robbery wasn't the motive."

I have to ask, but I'm afraid of the answer. "What do you mean, she was tortured?"

"As I said, she was cut up pretty bad." Kidd tells me. "A lot of it was perimortem, directed at her breasts and groin. And she had some pretty bad multiple burns. She had been tied up and raped, though we found no semen. So it was a man that did it, likely one of her johns."

That hits me all wrong. "She didn't have johns!" I explode. "She had clients! She wasn't a hooker! She was an interactive dancer!"

"Whatever." He doesn't sound sympathetic. "Women put themselves at risk when they choose to be sex workers. Do you know who any of her john… er, clients were."

"No I don't. I didn't know her that long."

His look is plainly unbelieving. "We've had no luck finding any family for her," he says. "We found some documents on her computer naming you as her partner and a will with you as her sole heir and executor of her estate. She drew it up on one of those Internet legal sites last weekend. Tell me why she would do this for you, who didn't know her very long."

"I'm sure I don't know," I stammer.

"Were you lovers?"

"No!" I explode. "She was my best friend!"

"Your best friend that you knew for what, a week?"

I don't answer him. But I know how it sounds.

He tries a different tack. "You sure nobody else knew you'd be coming into a pile of money if Ms. Chapman was dead? Your boyfriend, for instance?"

"I haven't got a boyfriend! And I didn't know about the money!"

"You had a fiancé, right?" He consults a notebook. "Michael Lamont?"

30

How the hell does he know that? "He dumped me for somebody else months ago."

"You let me know if he calls you up looking to get back together," he says.

"Michael is a total asshole, but he's no killer."

"That's unfortunate," Kidd says. "This kind of case is tough. We almost never find the perpetrator, unless we can get one of the girl's associates to give us a lead."

"She had a call-in business," I tell him. "You can check her computer or her phone records to find out who her clients were."

There's that indulgent smile again. "Ms. McMasters, I have a heavy case load, like all the detectives. We didn't find a client list on her computer. Chasing down email addresses and phone records can take a long time. We'd like to clear this up, but we have to manage our resources. If we can't get a specific lead, it's likely we'll never find the guy. Unless he does it again."

Suddenly, I'm pissed. "You mean that since you think she was no better than a hooker, you don't have the time and money to waste on her."

The smile vanishes. "I didn't say that. But I do have other victims that demand my attention."

"I wasn't aware there were that many murders in this city."

"There aren't," he admits. "And there'd be fewer still if foolish young women didn't peddle their asses online. Now, can you give me a lead or not?"

I think about Stud on the phone. His plaintive whine as he pleaded with Becca to show herself to him. Do I think he had the balls to cut her up, even if he knew who and where she was?

"I guess not," I tell Kidd.

Another heavy sigh. "Then I guess we're done, for now," he says.

"What about the partnership papers, and the will?"

"What about them?"

"Won't I need that stuff?"

"We'll have to hold on to it for a while," he says. "It could be evidence."

"Evidence of what? You said you don't think I did it."

"I don't. But I'd still like to know why a twentysomething coed who's stripping online suddenly gives everything she owns to somebody that she just met."

"If I knew, I'd tell you."

"Okay," he says. "We're getting nowhere. I was you, I'd call a lawyer about that will." He pushes back his chair and gets up. "You can go."

"Can I get a ride back home?"

"We're not a taxi service, Ms. McMasters." He walks out, leaving the door open behind him.

Great. I haven't got a dime on me, and it's at least five miles home.

It's a warm spring day and the walk gives me time to think. I'm horrified about how Becca was murdered and baffled as to why she left me everything. Is that how she was going to prove she was serious about wanting me for a partner? I think Kidd was totally right - it was one of her clients that did it. But how did that client find her? She was sure that nobody knew who she was. I'm certain that the cops are going to drop this if they don't get a lead soon because Becca danced naked online, and they don't think people like her are worth their time. Or was Kidd just lying? Does he think I did it or had it done, and he's just giving me enough rope? God, I'm so confused! I start crying again, and I don't quit the rest of the way home.

Once home, I call Gary McDougall, a lawyer I met while working for Uncle Amos. He's a laid-back older dude, forty or so. I tell him about the murder, the partnership papers and Becca's will. He says he can see me tomorrow afternoon.

I get another unpleasant shock later that evening when Kwan cuts on the evening news. Becca's murder has hit the national spotlight. The viciousness of the injuries she suffered have piqued the media's morbid interest. Worse, Becca has been identified as Kira Foxxx, the Internet stripper, and there's a veiled undertone to the report that this is the expected, if not deserved, fate that such women suffer. Somebody dug up one of the pictures from her website and cropped it to make it more or less SFW. My stomach tightens and the bile rises in my gorge again when that picture appears on the screen, because I know what's going through most people's minds when they see it - people who never even knew her. Kwan gasps audibly, then looks disbelievingly at me, as if I'm a spectre who's haunting her.

Stripper!

I have to drag myself out of bed the next day and force myself to shower. I know that I have to go and see my attorney, if for no other reason than to honor Becca's last wishes. But I really don't want her stuff. That should go to her family.

It's another nice day, so I decide to walk. Our neighborhood is single family houses built for the soldiers returning from World War II. It gradually turned into student housing after the soldiers raised their families and their kids moved out, and the University expanded. Some houses like ours are pretty well kept up while others are mostly trashed – students, especially guys, can be rough on stuff they don't own. But as cozy as our house is, it's a far cry from Becca's townhouse, which is now mine. I will do my best to find out if Becca has any family, and if I find them, I will share with them. But I feel like it would dishonor her memory if I just sold off all her stuff, took the money and forgot about her. She was so proud of the things she had accumulated, especially the townhouse, because they were a symbol of her independence. I'm not sure where our relationship would have ultimately ended up, though I'm pretty sure I know where she wanted it to. Nevertheless, she made a big impression on me in the short time that I knew her. Living at her place will allow me to keep part of her in my heart.

I come out of my reverie to find myself downtown. Gary McDougall's office is in the old city in a building that used to house a hardware store in the early 1900's, and now has a city museum on the first floor. The ceilings have been removed all the way to the roof and a skylight installed, so the lower floor is awash with sunlight, pleasantly warm and smells of books and old wood. Terraces surround the open space above, with offices dispersed around the perimeter. Gary McDougall's firm occupies the entire second floor.

I take the elevator up and find a receptionist. Gary arrives and conducts me to a conference room.

"I've spoken with Detective Kidd," he says. "He's assured me that you're not a suspect in Ms. Chapman's murder. I think he's being truthful. He's sent me electronic copies of all of the pertinent documents."

Quite a change of heart on Kidd's part from yesterday, I think.

"I've got good news for you, Natalie," Gary goes on. "Ms. Chapman put the title to her townhouse into joint tenancy, so it automatically belongs to you and probate is unnecessary," he says. "She also named you as the payable-on-death beneficiary for her bank account, which also avoids probate." I stop breathing

33

when Gary shows me the balance. I'm no millionaire for sure, but college and even law school expenses are no longer a problem. Her household items and car are also now mine, and their value is low enough that probate isn't required for them, either.

"So you can move in whenever you want," Gary says. "I'll give you a letter for the homeowners' association so they'll get you a key. Boy, you and Ms. Chapman must have been really good friends!"

"Not that I knew," I say. A disturbing thought intrudes. "Who's going to take care of her funeral?"

"I don't know," Gary says. "Her family, I suppose."

"I don't think she had one," I say. "Could you find out for me? I'll take care of it if nobody else is going to. It's the least I can do."

Gary said he would. I tell him I'll call him next week – sooner if I have trouble.

Becca's bank (now mine), is just down the street, so I go in and write a counter check for $1000. I present my ID and the teller hands the money over. It's surreal – just this morning I was wondering how I was going to eat! In an attack of extravagance, I spring for a cab to take me home.

Fields and Kwan are both home, so I go into the kitchen to tell them my plans. They're fixing lunch together – Fields is cooking while Kwan is setting the table.

"Hey guys," I say.

They both immediately look guilty. "Oh, hi Nattie," Kwan says. "Are you joining us for lunch? We might be able to stretch it for three."

"Don't bother, I can fix my own. I do want to thank you two for the groceries, though."

"*De nada*," says Kwan.

"Look, I've got something to tell you. I'm moving out. So you'll want to get looking for another roommate right away." I count out $400 onto the dining room table. "Here's my part of this month's rent."

It's obvious that they don't know what to say, so I tell them about today's events.

Stripper!

"Wow!" says Fields. "That's bizarre! It's terrible what happened to your friend, of course, but why would she leave everything she had to you?"

"I've been asking myself that all day. I'll let you know if I figure it out."

"You know, if you can pay the rent now, you don't have to leave," says Kwan.

"I'm the proud owner of a beautiful, new furnished townhouse. It would be silly of me not to live there."

"She was murdered there, and you're just going to move in?" Fields says. "Isn't that just a little macabre?"

"The cops told me that Becca wasn't killed in the townhouse – if she had been, there's totally no way I could ever live there."

Both of my roommates are looking away from me, probably because they feel bad about asking me to leave.

"Hey, guys, I totally get it. I understand that I couldn't live here without paying. And you don't know how much that food you got meant to me. I'll have y'all over for a housewarming and dinner as soon as I get settled."

"Nattie, if there's anything we can do…" Fields says.

"Actually, there is. Can you give me a ride over there tomorrow so I can pick up my new car?" I confess to guilty pleasure at the shock on their faces!

Chapter 6.

I t's Saturday morning. I pack all my worldly possessions in a suitcase and a footlocker. There's space left over. I tell Fields and Kwan that they can keep my ratty old furniture. The Z-car is a two-seater, so I tie the trunk lid down to hold the footlocker. The suitcase rides on the seat next to me. Fields and Kwan come outside to see me off. I'm sad to go – I've lived with those two since I came to State.

There's no trouble getting a key when I arrive at the townhouse – Becca added my name to the deed. The guy in the office even volunteers to help me with the footlocker – I think he wants to hit on me. I decline.

Finally my stuff is at the townhouse door. I yank off the crime scene tape like Kidd said I could and open it. I'm greeted by an unearthly caterwauling! Holy shit, I completely forgot about Xin Niu! She darts up and slithers back and forth between my ankles. The poor thing probably hasn't been fed for days. I immediately embark on a search for cat food. I find several cans, give her one and she bolts it down. I realize that I don't know squat about taking care of a cat. Great.

I haul my stuff to the master bedroom. The overhead light automatically comes on when I enter. After a moment, it winks out. As I turn toward the door, it comes on again. A little investigation reveals how it works. A motion sensor turns it on when the room is entered, or when you're moving around. If you're still, it stays on just long enough so you can find the switch to keep it on.

I look for a place to put my stuff. OMG, Becca had her some clothes! A whole dresser full of sexy lingerie – her work clothes – and another dresser full of daily attire. I assume that most of it will fit me - I really didn't need to bring anything of mine. But Becca was more of a girly girl than I am, so I don't know how much of her stuff I'll actually end up wearing.

I dump the contents of the footlocker on the bed and refill it with the lingerie from the drawer. I'm a little creeped out – I know that these clothes are mine now, but it still feels like I'm messing with somebody else's stuff.

My hand touches something hard. I push a camisole aside and find a small, semi-automatic pistol in a red suede holster. The slide is bright cranberry and the lower and the grip are black. I take it out of the holster and see that it's got a

36

laser mounted on the trigger guard with a button on the grip to activate it. I find a small card in a pocket on outside of the holster - a permit to carry a concealed handgun in the name of Rebecca Chapman, issued a couple of months ago.

My dad and Uncle Amos taught me to shoot, so I know something about guns. This one is a Ruger compact nine-millimeter. Plenty of firepower. The red dot on the side tells me that the safety is off. I click it on, then push the little button on the grip and the magazine pops out. It's fully loaded with jacketed bullets that have a piece of bright orange plastic peeping out of the tip. I lock the slide back, and another cartridge pops out and falls to the floor. She kept it ready for action! As I lay the little pistol down, I notice a thin sheen of oil on my hands from handling it.

So Becca felt threatened. She certainly gave me no inkling of that when we were together. Why wasn't she carrying when she was taken? The answer hits me in the pit of the stomach. She was probably going to or coming from school, and State campus is a gun-free zone, even if you have a permit. It's a good bet that she was attacked right downstairs in the parking lot - her car wouldn't have been here if she was grabbed elsewhere.

It is also obvious that the cops haven't searched this place very thoroughly or the gun would no longer be here. Probably not worth their time – they think she was just a hooker. I slide the magazine back into the grip and work the slide to chamber a round, then pop the magazine out again and load the remaining cartridge on the top of the stack. Finally, I shove the magazine back into the grip.

I put the pistol on the bottom of the drawer where Becca kept it, then pile my stuff on top. I know that, partner or no partner, the gun is not legally mine because I don't have a permit for it. And I can't get one until after my next birthday. But for right now, I'm just glad it's here.

I search the drawers and cabinets in the rest of the townhouse. I'm still uncomfortable about going through her things, but dammit, I know Becca has family somewhere who will want to know what happened to her. I search everywhere but her studio and I don't find anything but household stuff, bric-a-brac, paid and unpaid bills and financial statements that don't tell me anything that I don't already know.

Finally, I'm standing at the door to the dreaded studio. Regardless of how I feel, I know, I've got this to do. I take a deep breath and open the door.

The studio looks different in the daytime - just a room full of strange stuff that doesn't belong together, part love nest, part TV studio, part office. Even the odors are muted. It's dead like Becca, pining for her vibrant presence.

I look through the desk and find a locked metal box in the bottom drawer. I don't have a key, but it's a cheap lock, so a minute with a straightened paper clip does the trick.

Inside is a paper with her computer logon info and passwords, along with photos, newspaper clippings and jewelry – a diamond ring, a wedding band and a gold chain with a locket.

The photos are family shots – a thirtyish, dark haired man, a woman of about the same age and a little girl who I know instantly is Becca. She's about ten or twelve and bears an uncanny resemblance to me, even then.

The locket contains pictures of the same two adults.

The wedding band is narrow enough to be a woman's. It's engraved on the inside – MPH to BFO – with a date twenty-five years ago.

The clippings document the deaths of Michael and Bridget Hines of Brookline, Massachusetts. They were killed in a car crash twelve years ago. They were coming back from a night out, but alcohol was not involved. Car went through a guardrail. The story speculates that Michael, the driver, might have dozed off at the wheel. They left behind their ten-year-old daughter, Fiona. The article mentions that there is no other family, so Fiona is going into foster care.

It's obvious that Rebecca Chapman was Fiona Hines. But why the name change?

There's a second folder full of printed news articles about someone called Declan "Blackie" O'Halloran, a Boston mobster. His wicked ways finally caught up with him about 10 years ago and he was arrested. Like most crooks, he demonstrated his high integrity by immediately ratting out his pals. The information he gave the Feds led to the arrest and conviction of many Irish mobsters and almost to Blackie's own demise – an all-out attack on the courtroom during his testimony nearly killed him. Apparently that totally freaked him out, because he escaped custody and disappeared shortly thereafter. He hasn't been heard from since.

Blackie O'Halloran. I study his photo. He's got swarthy skin, a round, beaming Irish face with heavy dark eyebrows and a thatch of black hair. He's wearing a Derby and looks like some kind of dark leprechaun. He doesn't appear dangerous. Why would Becca be interested in him? Was she working on a college paper? Had she seen him somewhere? Was that why she felt it necessary to arm herself?

I fire up the computer. I find e-copies of the partnership papers and Becca's will on the desktop, like Kidd said. I also find out that Becca has two email accounts, one from State that contains school-related stuff and a Hotmail account for her business. In addition to her dancing, she exchanged dirty emails with her clients. Her recent activity tells me that she'd drop an email client in a week or so if she couldn't schedule a performance – dancing was obviously a much more lucrative use of her time. But there's nothing in her email that indicates that she might have met someone the day she died. It's also unusual that there are no personal emails from friends or family.

Bookmarks lead me to Kira Foxxx's web page, which is pretty much what you'd expect. Pictures of Becca in various costumes, most of them NSFW, and a couple of paragraphs extolling the experience of completely controlling your own personal exotic dancer. There's a phone number and a payment button.

Another bookmark takes me to her payment site, where I find out that I'm another couple thousand dollars richer. I shake my head – it's hard to believe there are so many guys out there who would pay that much money to watch a woman take off her clothes on a computer monitor.

I stop working for a moment. Am I starting an investigation into Becca's death? I guess so – Detective Kidd strongly implied that the police were not going to do squat because Becca was the next thing to a prostitute, and likely had it coming. That's just not acceptable!

I move on to her Internet history, which is a hodgepodge. She obviously visited web sites for school, as well as numerous free porn sites – to study her craft, I suppose. Again, I find nothing in the last week or so that sheds any light on her murder.

I dig deeper. A couple of months back, it's more of the same. Then I find a long string of searches on a site called Family Search.

She was obviously interested in her lineage. I click on one of the links in the History list.

<The requested URL [URL] was not found on this server.>

Hmmph. I switch to Google and type in Family Search. The top item in the list is FamilySeach.org, run by the Church of Latter Day Saints out of Salt Lake City. I click the link.

<The requested URL [URL] was not found on this server.>

Okay, then. I use Google to pull up a list of genealogy websites. Ancestry.com is at the top of the list. I click the link.

<The requested URL [URL] was not found on this server.>

Really?

I work my way down the list of genealogy sites. I get the same message for every site that I click on.

Something is very wrong here!

The computer chimes, indicating an email has come in. It's on the Hotmail account, from someone named Bobby. The subject line is *Turn on your phone*! Even though Becca's murder made national news because of its violence and sexual overtones, apparently not all of her clients got the message.

I'm not sure why, but I take the business phone out of the drawer, clip it into its stand and turn it on. It's only a minute or so before it lights up and chirps.

My hand quivers as I touch the screen.

"This is Kira," I say in my best sexy voice. I sound terrible!

"This is Bobby! Where you been, babe? I been callin' and callin'! I'm dyin' over here!"

I think fast. "I've been taking a little vacation, Bobby. Don't you think a girl needs a break?"

"You shoulda told me!" The guy actually sounds pissed. "I dint know where you were!"

"I'm sorry," I say. "I'm back now."

"Good. So you gonna dance for me?"

I think fast again. "I can't tonight. I just got back a little while ago. But I'll tell you what. You send me an email and tell me just what you want me to do. Then you call back tomorrow night and I'll take care of you."

Stripper!

"You know what I like!"

"Yes, I do." Not! "Write me a dirty email, Bobby. Tell me what you want me to do!"

He's not happy, but he has no choice. He begs for a while and finally gives in. I hang up, shaking. What the hell did I just do?

Kidd said he thought that it was one of Becca's clients that killed her. It obviously wasn't Bobby – he wouldn't be calling for a dance if he knew she was dead. But if it was a client that killed her, and he heard that Kira Foxxx was back in business, just maybe he might come around to check it out. It's a crazy idea that could get me killed, but it's all I've got right now.

I hate to admit it, but it was a total rush keeping Bobby on a string. He was begging me! I could have gotten him to do damn near anything I wanted.

Bobby's email comes in a little while and what he wants is not as bad as I feared. However, to give it to him, I will have to learn to use the green screen.

By the next evening, I've got it down. It's easy, really, because Becca already did all the work. All I have to do is dance for the camera – the computer does the rest. I'll be able to hear the music that Bobby hears through an earpiece, but I won't be able to see what he sees on his monitor.

I'm still having second thoughts. Bobby wants me to dance and end up totally nude. I totally don't have many hang ups about sex, but I'm not promiscuous and pragmatically, I don't think that promiscuity is a good idea. I've never been into exhibitionism, which Becca apparently was. I've always been uncomfortable about men looking at me sexually – it makes me feel like I'm being judged, and I don't like it. I'm also not much of a dancer – most of the dancing I've done has been social, meaning that I did it because it was expected of me, either by friends or some guy I wanted to like me.

So can I really take my clothes off on camera for a guy I can't even see? Come to think of it, maybe not being able to see him will make it easier – I can always pretend he's not there. I watched several strippers on the computer earlier today, to get an idea of how it's done. What I saw was not high-level choreography. I think I can handle it.

The real question is, do I want to do this? No, but I need to find the son of a bitch that killed Becca. The odds are pretty good that it was a customer, and I think that if he finds out that her website is back active again, he's going to have to check it out. So what I want doesn't matter, it's what I have to do. All right Nattie, you've made your choice. Let's give that pervert a show he won't forget!

Finally, it's time. Bobby is on the line, waiting. Per his instructions, I'm wearing a long, wraparound dress that snaps in front so it can be opened a snap at a time. Underneath is a semi-transparent bra and panties and black fishnet stockings held up with a garter belt. The stays run under the panties so it won't be a problem to slide them off.

I squeeze the controller in my hand and the music starts. Bobby sees a stage in a smoky nightclub, but all I see is the glare of the spotlight in the darkened bedroom. I close my eyes and try to imagine myself in the cabaret, smelling the smoke and listening to the low muttering of the men in the room. Do it, baby, do it! Take it off! Show me what you got! A moan emanates from the phone across the room. Apparently Bobby likes what he sees.

Mouthing the words to the song, I undulate my hips and slowly undo the dress. I imagine Bobby in his cramped little room, eyes glued to the monitor, his hand moving furiously. My body begins to tingle with an incipient sexual urge – so much for pretending he's not there! The dress is open to my waist so I slide it off my shoulders, thrusting my breasts at the camera. I'm rewarded with an animal growl from the phone. I let the top of the dress fall behind me – the sudden chill that flashes over my dripping torso is feverishly fleeting. I slide the bra straps off my shoulders, then grab the cups and inch them downward, slowly, slowly. I brush my hardening nipples with my fingers to enjoy the sensation and to hide them from Bobby. He's begging me now, he's damn near crying. OMG, what a rush! I give into him and yank hard. The bra comes free and I fling it across the room.

I strip faster, impatient to shed the stifling garments. I rip the bottom of the dress open in a single motion and fling it after the bra. I grab the sides of the panties and sidle out of them – this is the trickiest part to keep smooth and sexy without pitching myself on my face. But I manage and then I'm standing there in only my stockings and garter belt. The sweat is pouring off me and there's a deep musky odor that touches something primal within me. I begin touching myself, not for Bobby but for me! I must release this pent-up energy or I'll surely explode.

Finally the release comes, and I almost pitch off the dais onto my face! Somehow I manage to sink straight downward instead, melting into the top of the little stage like a ballerina. Bobby is long forgotten. I just lie there, enjoying the afterglow.

Stripper!

Later, Bobby is gone. I'm two hundred and fifty dollars richer, and I've made a date to dance for him again in a few days. The theatrical lights are off and the overhead fluorescent light in the bedroom glares down on me like the lights in the interrogation room downtown. The equipment stands out starkly and everything suddenly seems very tawdry. Did I really just strip for a man I don't even know and let him share my most intimate moment? Why would I do that? For Becca? For money? What am I becoming?

Chapter 7.

I dance several times for Bobby and some other clients in the following weeks. Each has his own particular fantasy. Nobody seems to notice that I am not Kira Foxxx, and no one is surprised that I'm here. As terrifying as it sounds, maybe Becca's murder was a random event after all.

I'm also going to class and studying and caring for Xin Niu. I'm around people all day, but now that I've moved, I'm alone when I'm not at school. It scares me that I'm beginning to like it.

Detective Kidd calls to tell me that the coroner has released Becca's body. Since I couldn't locate her family, I make arrangements with a local crematorium.

I get out of my car one evening and open my belt pouch to put away my keys when I feel a presence behind me. Before I can turn around, I feel something hard press into my back.

"Don't scream, don't turn around." a voice grates in my ear. "Let's go inside." I can smell the sweat, cologne and garlic exuding from him.

I do as he says. I know this is Becca's killer, and he won't hesitate to kill me. But why is he taking me into the townhouse instead of where he can do to me what he did to her?

I open the apartment door and he shoves me inside. I take a few steps and stumble to the floor. I hear the door close.

"Get up," he says. "Look at me!"

It's Blackie O'Halloran! He's older than in Becca's picture – his black hair is streaked with white. And he's pointing an evil-looking black pistol at me. He steps forward and his free hand lashes out, slapping my face hard enough to stagger me.

"What the hell do ye think yer doing?" he barks.

I start babbling. "Don't hurt me, I'm not Rebecca, I'm Natalie, please don't hurt me."

Stripper!

"I know who ye are," he says. "I'm not going to hurt youse. That was just to knock some sense into you." He gestures toward the living room with his pistol. "Get in there and sit!"

I'm thoroughly cowed at this point, so I do as he says. He pushes me into the easy chair, then slides the pistol into his jacket pocket. He stands in front of me with his hands on his hips and repeats, "What in the hell do ye think yer doin'?"

My face is on fire, and I know I'm going to have a bruise to explain. He's put his gun away, so now I'm getting pissed!

"What do you mean? This place is mine! Becca left it to me."

"Not that!" he snarls. "What the hell are ye doing dancing naked for them perverts? That's how my granddaughter got herself killed. Don't you have any self-respect?"

His granddaughter!

"Becca…" I begin.

"Fiona!" he barks. "Her name was Fiona!"

"She was Becca to me! She was my friend. After meeting you, I understand why she didn't want her old name anymore."

It's like I hit him in the gut. I see the fire drain out of him and he's just a sad old man.

He sinks down on the sofa. "Maybe yer right," he says. "Hell's bells, I know yer right! Her mom got killed because of me, so Fiona ran as far away as she could get and got rid of everything that could tie her to me. But God damn it, she wasn't raised to dance naked for men. She did that to get even with me! What the hell is yer excuse?"

The first thought I have is what business is it of yours, but what I say is, "I thought I might find the guy who killed her that way."

He looks at me incredulously, then bursts out laughing!

"Ye thought ye might find the guy… Oh Jesus, that's rich! And just what in the hell did ye think you were gonna do wit' 'im if ye did find him?"

My belt pouch is in my lap, still partly open with my car keys peeping out the top. As furtively as I can, I slide my hand inside past the keys to touch the little pistol beneath them. He notices what I am doing and I see the look of alarm

45

flash into his eyes. He reaches for his pocket and his own gun but I am faster because I've already got a hand on mine. The car keys and other items in the pack go flying as I yank the Ruger out and train it on his chest. The little red ball bounces across his shirt.

"Don't do it!" I tell him.

He stops, then raises his hands to his sides, palms facing me. Something tells me this is not the first time he's been in this situation. I must be very careful!

"Keep your hands away from your pockets and take off your jacket. Don't get up, do it sitting down."

He complies, sliding it off of his shoulders in back, much like I got out of that dress while dancing for Bobby.

"Don't even think about throwing that jacket at me. I'll shoot you right through it! Just drop it on the floor."

His scowl tells me that I accurately foresaw his intentions. He drops the jacket.

"Now push it away with your foot." He does so.

"What are youse going to do now, little girl? Call the cops?"

I won't let him get to me. "I don't know." I tell him. "Why did you kill you granddaughter?"

His scowl becomes uglier. "How could you even think I would do that?" he says.

"Oh, I don't know. Maybe it's because of all the other people you murdered before you became a rat!"

He looks like he's going to come right off that sofa, gun or no gun, so I flash the laser at him just to remind him. I totally don't want to shoot him, but I know I must if he comes at me.

Apparently he believes that I will shoot, because he settles back on the sofa. "I didn't kill her," he says. "I came over here to find out who did."

"You said her mom got killed because of you. What did you mean?"

"My daughter and her husband were killed because of something I did. One of my competitors was trying to take some of my territory. There was some

46

shooting, and his son got killed. So he got even by killing my daughter and her husband."

"Did you kill his son?"

"Jesus, I don't know! Maybe. There was a lotta shootin' goin' on."

"What happened to Becca after her mom and dad died?"

"I couldn't take her to live with me. All I had was her and her mother, and her dad had nobody. So they put her in the system. After Bridget got killed, I knew I had to take down the guys that done it. So Fiona got foster parents in another city, courtesy of the U. S. Marshals. I didn't even know where she was until I saw on the news what happened to her."

"So she was in witness protection?"

"Not really. I don't think that nobody never told Fiona that her parents were murdered. It was an accident, as far as she knew. After they almost got to me in that courtroom, I figured that I was the best one to take care of me. So I skedaddled."

"So if you didn't kill her, what are you doing here?"

"What the hell do ye think? I want to get the bastards that killed my little girl!"

"I mean, why come to me?"

"I was on that disgustin' website of hers, hoping to pick up a clue about who might have done it, when I realized it was active again. So I came over here to find out who was running it. Jesus God, you could be her sister!"

"Why did you stick a gun in my back?"

"Ye get used to a certain way of doin' things after a while," he said in a reasonable tone of voice. "So what are youse going to do, call the cops?" he asks again. "I don't think I can let you do that."

"What are you going to do about it?"

"I can make you use that gun. Maybe ye'll shoot me and maybe ye won't, but at least I won't have to go to prison. I'd get killed in there fer sure!"

Is he bluffing? I think I'm gonna have to do something way stupid!

47

"Look," I say, "Becca was my best friend. I really don't want to shoot her grandpa. So if you'll give me your word that we can continue this conversation without guns, I'll put mine away."

"Sounds good to me."

I swallow hard, then I get the holster out of my belt pouch, slide the little gun inside and put the holster back in the pouch.

"I'm just going to get my coat," he says, then moves to do so. I can't stop him now.

My heart comes out of my throat as he picks it up and puts it on.

"Can we start over?" he asks. "My name is Declan O'Halloran. I'm Fiona's grandfather. It's good to meet youse, Natalie."

"Did she know who you were when she was a kid?"

"Yes and no," he said. "I visited her a few times a year when she was little. I don't think her folks ever told her how I made a living."

"Well she knew before she died." I tell him what I found on her computer. "I thought she got the gun because she was afraid of you."

"She had no reason to be, other than the dancing," he says. "Once I knew about that, I would of had to put a stop to it. Now that she's gone, I hope I can get you to stop it. Why do ye do something that disgraces you like that?"

"It doesn't disgrace me. It's my choice, as it was hers."

"Look, I've run girls like you. I know what this kinda thing does to a girl…"

I cut him off. "Forced them, you mean! Forced them to do things they didn't want to do. Becca danced because it made her independent of people like you. She wanted me to join her, because she knew I was going through a rough time and she wanted to help me out. I never did get the chance to join her, but I can sure as hell dance in her memory."

"But people will think…"

"I don't give a damn what people think! Did you, when you decided to be a gangster?"

"That's different, its …"

Stripper!

"You're right, it's different. I don't hurt anybody, and neither did Becca. That's more than I can say for you. Who the hell do you think you are, coming in here, lecturing me, hitting me?" I've got myself so worked up I want to pull my gun back out!

He's quiet for a minute, then he asks, "She danced because she wanted to? Not because of me?"

"Yes. She didn't even know who you were when she started dancing. She found out later. And she was proud of herself, proud that she was making a living, proud that she was putting herself through school, proud that she wasn't beholden to anyone."

He smiles. "That sounds more like Blackie O'Halloran's granddaughter!" The smile turns into a frown. "But I still don't approve of it."

"It's really none of your business," I say. I wonder how many people have talked to Blackie O'Halloran like that and lived?

He puts both hands on the sofa and pushes to get up. He really is an old man.

"Look," he says. "I'd appreciate it if youse don't say anything to the cops about me. I'm gonna nose around, see what I can dig up." He cocks an eyebrow at me. "Kin I call you from time to time, to see if ye find out anythin' about Fiona's murder?"

"Sure," I say. "I want to get this guy, too,"

"Ye need to stop that goddamn strippin'. Yer gonna get yerself killed!"

"We'll see." I tell him.

He heads for the door. I walk him out.

He puts a hand on the knob, then turns and says again, "Jesus God, you could be her sister," he says again. "Do you mind if I come around once in a while, just to talk?"

Against my better judgement I say, "Sure. I think I'd like that."

He opens the door, starts to step outside, then stiffens. As his hand darts to his jacket pocket, a cascade of muffled spitting sounds erupts and he staggers back into the hallway, his shirtfront dripping crimson!

Chapter 8.

I don't even think. I tear through the living room as those spitting sounds hurry me along. A picture on the wall explodes, showering glass everywhere as the frame tumbles to the floor!

A CLANG! reverberates through the tubular frame of the circular stairs as a bullet ricochets. I wrench the bedroom door open, slam it behind me and lock it. I know that will only buy me seconds. I dive behind the bed and kneel. It's poor cover, but better than nothing. I jerk my pistol out of the pouch and shine the laser on the door. The ceiling light winks out. There's a pounding on the door and half a dozen bullets whizz over my head. Then the door explodes inward! The overhead light flashes on.

The guy in the doorway stands out starkly in the glare, dressed in a black hoodie and a white Guy Fawkes mask. He's got a suppressed pistol a foot long. He's frozen – the flaring light has apparently disoriented him. I get a shot off. OMG, it's loud! It blows a chunk out of the doorframe. He ducks back outside. After a few seconds, the overhead light winks out.

The light strobes on again as he rushes in, his gun stuttering like a balloon running over the spokes of a bike wheel. I let off three more shots. One hits the doorframe, one blows a hole the wall and I think the third one connects. Something burns my shoulder. He disappears again.

The smell of gunpowder lies heavy in the air. "It's just a matter of time, you know!" His voice is muffled by the mask.

"Come on in, and we'll see!" My voice is steady, belying my terror.

The room goes dark again.

A 9mm will go straight through the drywall in a place like this. Keeping my finger off the laser switch so he can't see, I aim at a spot to the right of the doorway about chest high and squeeze one off, slowly. The report is immediately followed by a scream!

The muffled voice from the hallway says, "Shit! Nobody paid me to do you!"

It's quiet again, except for the tinnitus.

Stripper!

Time passes. Is he trying to wait me out? Maybe. I wait, still petrified. My shoulder burns and I feel something running down inside my shirt. I know I've only got three rounds left, so I resolve not to fire unless he charges again. Surely someone has heard and called the cops. There's no way I'm moving until they're here.

It's an eternity before I hear "Police!". Then, "Holy shit! There's a body here!"

A shadow appears in the bedroom door. The light pops on and I see a cop, his gun levelled at me.

"Put the gun down and show me your hands!"

I drop the gun on the bed and obey.

As I'm marched out in handcuffs, I see that the townhouse is a disaster - holes in the walls, and blood all over the white carpet in front of the bedroom door. Blackie O'Halloran lies dead in front of the outside door in a much bigger pool of blood.

Naturally, the cops arrest me and charge me for having an unregistered gun. Uncle Amos once told me that if I was arrested, the worst thing I could do is talk to the cops. So I don't. Bye, bye law school!

Later, down at the cop shop, I'm back in the little room where I first met Detective Kidd. My shoulder wound has been bandaged. It's only a crease, but two inches to the right and I would have been dead with a bullet in my throat. The door opens and Kidd enters.

"You've been busy," he says.

"I want my attorney."

"Now hold on," Kidd says. "We know you had Rebecca Chapman's pistol, who had a permit for it. It's obvious that you recently found it and were gonna turn it in at your earliest convenience. How my doin' so far?"

"Pretty good," I say. Maybe there's a chance I can get out this, after all!

"We also know that you didn't kill Blackie O'Halloran, because he was shot with a .22 and you had a nine. We also dug a few more .22 slugs out of the wall in your townhouse, so it's pretty obvious you were defending yourself from the guy that shot Blackie. If you tell me what happened, I'll talk to the D.A. about dropping the gun charge. I'm pretty sure she will. This ain't New Jersey, you know."

Kidd even hints that I might want to get a permit to carry on my own after my next birthday. "In the meantime, we'll have to confiscate the gun," he says.

I think about it for a minute. If I tell him, I'll be admitting that I had a gun in my possession and no permit, but that's totally a slam dunk anyway because the cop saw me with it. And Kidd's been decent to me, at least up to now. So I tell him the story.

"It seems like the guy in the mask was the one who killed Becca, and he probably did it to draw out Blackie, who was his real target," I finish my statement. "Poor Becca!"

"Well the guy who killed Blackie got away," Kidd tells me, "but you got a piece of him. He was most likely a pro. We've got security footage of him from your apartment complex, but the hoodie and the mask make it impossible to identify him. He was also smart enough not to park in your lot – must have left his car nearby and walked into the complex. But we'll get his DNA from the blood outside your bedroom and the shell casings from his gun that he didn't have the time to clean up, thanks to you. It's likely he's in the system and we'll find him. Anything else you can tell me that would help identify him?"

"I don't think so. Average height, average build. He was wearing a hoodie with the hood pulled up around a mask like the guy in *V for Vendetta* wore. I can't even tell you his hair color."

"Any peculiarities at all? Voice? A limp?"

"The mask muffled his voice. If anything, it was a little high, but he might have been trying to change it. I didn't notice any limps, but he might have one now that I got a piece of him." I smile with satisfaction.

Kidd changes the subject. "So I hear tell you've taken up Becca's line of work?"

"I only did that to see if I could get the guy who killed her to show up," I say. "And there's no way I'm going back to live in that townhouse now that somebody's been killed there. So my dancing days are over." I sure hope that Kwan and Fields will take me back!

Stripper!

"That's a good thing, Natalie." Kidd says. "Even if it wasn't Rebecca's dancing that got her killed, no good can come of it. I'm glad you've seen the light."

I don't agree with him, but I don't argue.

The D.A. had enough of me last month, so she declines to prosecute the gun charge. I tell Roderigo and the other venues when they call that I won't be appearing on TV again. Law school is still in the picture!

They didn't get a match to the killer's DNA, so he's still out there, but Kidd said it's unlikely he'll come after me since I can't identify him. I hope he's right.

I have to hire professional cleaners to make the townhouse salable, but when it sells, I'll get the price of law school three times over. Yay.

So everything turns out pretty much OK, if you discount the fact that my best friend was horribly murdered by a psycho. We only knew each other for a few days, but we formed an incredible bond. There's an emptiness in my chest that just won't go away, and I find myself unexpectedly crying every day. But it will get better. It has to!

Chapter 9.

I'm standing on a smoky nightclub stage in a tight, wraparound dress held together with snaps over sheer black underwear, stockings and heels. The smell of smoke and sweat makes it hard to breathe in the skin-tight attire. The spotlight glares in my eyes but the room is dark, so I can't see the audience. But I can hear them – the low muttering of men in the room.

"Do it, baby, do it! Take it all off! Show me what you got!"

The band strikes up a spicy number. Mouthing the words, I slowly undo my dress, a snap at a time. When it's open to the waist I slide it off my shoulders, thrusting out my breasts. I let the top of the dress fall and a sudden chill flashes over my dripping torso. I slide the bra straps off my shoulders, then grab the cups and inch them downward, slowly, slowly. I brush my hardening nipples with my fingers to enjoy the sensation. I yank hard! The bra comes free and I throw it into the crowd. The muttering erupts into cheers and catcalls.

The scene slowly changes. I'm in a long, featureless hallway, completely nude. A man staggers past me, his shirtfront spurting scarlet. As he falls to the floor, I know I must run, or I'm next!

The silenced gun spits behind me. I feel the bullets tear into me!

The scene fades out and in again. I'm suspended by ropes tied to my arms and legs over a dirt floor. There's a puddle of blood beneath me. Little splashes pop up as more blood drips into the pool. I watch a little red rivulet snake down between my breasts, run onto my belly and drip into the rapidly spreading puddle. Terrified, I realize the blood is coming from a hole in my chest!

I avert my gaze. Not three feet away, there's another nude girl, hogtied with ropes from the ceiling. She looks like me! Her torso gapes open and her insides hang out, dripping into our shared lake of blood.

I wake up, screaming, bathed in sweat.

This can't keep happening! I've been having this nightmare for a couple weeks, not every night, but often enough that I'm beginning to dread sleep. The last few nights, a couple of boilermakers and a Benadryl before bed afforded me a dreamless slumber, but tonight I took nothing. I know that I can't keep medicating myself forever without serious consequences.

Stripper!

It's been about a month since Becca's murder. Things have changed. I wanted to move back in with Kwan and Fields, but they'd already found another roommate. So I had the townhouse professionally cleaned and stayed here. Even though I had the rug replaced, I swear I can still see a shadow on the carpet where Blackie fell.

In a morbid mood, I saved a square of the carpet with the killer's blood on it. You never know…

I've found myself increasingly alone the past few weeks. School has gotten way more intense. Uncle Amos finally relented and gave me my job back, but he hasn't had much work for me. Danny is also working for him and that's been a little awkward. Danny and I haven't resumed a relationship as anything more than co-workers.

I come home from school at night and try to study, but it's hard to concentrate. I start going to bed early and lying awake for a long time before sleeping fitfully.

The dream began a couple of weeks ago. Naturally, it scared the shit out of me but the terror went away after I was awake for a while and I didn't think much more of it. A couple of nights later, I had the same dream again. This time it bothered me all day. I'm no psych major, but I know that recurrent dreams are a sign of serious problems. Then I had the dream for the third time that very night. That's when I began resorting to booze and drugs to get an uninterrupted night's sleep.

My bedside clock says 5:40. Shit! Too early to get up and too late to go back to sleep.

Midmorning in chem class, I'm so tired, I've hardly heard a word. I do hear the prof say that he's handing out our midterms at the end of class. There's a ball of ice in my stomach.

I take the folded-up exam from him. I don't even have to see the grade –the reproach is in his eyes. I wait until I'm in the corridor before I unfold the paper where no one can see. It's worse than I thought. A 45 – that's an F in anyone's book!

If chemistry was the only class I was failing I wouldn't worry too much. Truth is, I'm failing all of them!

Later, I'm in the library. I know I should be studying, but every time I crack the book, I start to nod off. So I decide to check email instead.

An email from State at the top of the queue gets my attention. It's marked urgent.

Dear Ms. McMasters:

> Your midterm reports indicate that you are to be placed on academic probation for the remainder of the Spring semester. If your situation does not change by the end of the semester, a hearing will be held to consider whether you will be allowed to enroll for the Fall semester.

> An appointment has been made for you for tomorrow at 9 a.m. with your academic advisor, Dr. Sherman Applegait. You are strongly urged to keep this appointment. If you cannot, please log into the Counselling Center and reschedule at your earliest convenience.

It's signed by the Dean of Students.

I know that I have to keep the appointment. I just can't let them kick me out of school, not after all the shit in my life – anyone would be doing badly if all that happened to them! But I don't like Dr. Applegait. He's a weaselly little man who stares at my tits every time he sees me.

My phone dings and another email pops up at the top of the queue. The subject line reads, Meeting at 3M – 5 p.m.

3M is Uncle Amos' detective agency. I'm still just a trainee there. I can't get a license of my own until I've completed two thousand hours working for a licensed PI - about a year of full time work. But I can't work full time because Uncle Amos told me that if I drop out of school, I'll have no more job. I'm pretty sure that also applies to flunking out.

Somehow I get through the rest of the day, then I drive out to the 3M office. I'm thankful that the weather is still spring like even though it's getting on towards summer – with the sunroof open and all of the windows down, I feel almost human as the wind swirls around me.

The office is also Uncle Amos' home – he lives upstairs and the office is downstairs. I park around back. Uncle's pickup is in the yard and there's another new, gaudy pickup that I assume is Danny's. The little grey surveillance car is there too. I'm the last one to arrive. Great.

56

Stripper!

I enter the kitchen through the back door. The sharp coffee smell tells me that the pot has been sitting on the stove for hours and reminds me how tired I am. Good. It will probably tear up my stomach, but it will keep me awake. I grab me a mug before heading toward the front of the house.

I head down the hallway into what used to be the living room. The afternoon sun is streaming through the three windows that face the street. There are two desks along the back wall, both occupied.

Uncle Amos is at one desk in a typical pose – his chair rocked back at an alarming angle and his feet on the desk. He's as Southern as grits, biscuits and country ham, all of which he consumes way too much of. He's not a lot taller than my 5'1" but he's easily double my weight. He's not quite sixty and I constantly worry that he's not going to make it there if he doesn't stop with the fatty food and the cigarettes. He has a broad, likeable face topped off with a shock of pure white hair. It's a great face for a PI – it makes people just naturally want to tell him things. He's wearing his usual cheap, wrinkled seersucker suit with the collar open and his tie pulled halfway down the front of his shirt - I don't think I've ever seen him with it done up properly. Magnum P.I. he ain't!

Danny is sitting upright at the other desk with an open file folder in front of him, looking annoyed.

I flop down in an easy chair facing the two desks.

"Bout time you got here, Nattie," Uncle Amos says.

I look at the clock on the wall between the two desks. "I'm five minutes early," I tell him.

"No, you're ten minutes late," says Danny. That clock's slow."

"Whatever. What's this about?"

"We've got a new job," Danny says. "We need to coordinate the surveillance."

I am miffed. "You dragged me all the way down here for that? Why couldn't we do that by phone, just like always?"

"Now, Nattie, don't be that way." Uncle Amos says. "Danny thinks we need to start bein' a little more bidnesslike and I agree with him. There's no harm in havin' a meeting when we get a new subject, just so we all have our ducks in a row."

"Fine." There's no use arguing with guys when they want to be businesslike. "So who's the subject?"

Danny takes a piece of paper from the folder on his desk and scrutinizes it seriously.

"The subject's name is Robyn Carlson. She's a waitress at the Kitten Club, a strip joint near State. She's filed for workman's compensation, claiming that she threw her back out carrying heavy trays and her employer is contesting the claim. Should be a quick job, no more than a few days, just keeping tabs on her to see that she doesn't go out bowling or to the gym."

Danny hands out pictures of our subject. She's a thirtysomething, rather plain-looking brunette.

"I suggest we maintain surveillance from 6 a.m. to 10 p.m., for a total of sixteen hours a day," Danny says. "Broken down between the three of us, that's a little over five hours a day. Three or four days should be enough to tell us if she's faking."

"That seems like a lot," I say. "We typically only watch subjects during the daytime. There's no point in sitting in a car watching the outside of a house at night."

"The point is that we get paid for our time, Nattie," says Danny. "Our business is growing and we need the revenue."

Hmmph. The only growth in "our" business was when Uncle Amos hired you, Danny. That's why we need extra money.

Uncle chimes in. "I agree with Danny on this."

Fine. I'm not going to win this one. Men!

"Danny, you take the early shift from 6 to 11. I'll take 11 to 4. Nattie, you can have the graveyard shift. You can study in the car like you always do."

I do not miss how the extra hour was foisted off on me, but I say nothing.

"We'll keep in touch by phone for the handoffs like always," says Uncle. "We'll start in the morning. I guess that's it for this meeting."

"We also need to discuss the new website, Amos," Danny says.

Stripper!

A website? For Uncle Amos? He's kidding, right?

"Let's put that off for right now, Danny." Uncle says. "I've got some feelers out for a website designer, like you suggested. I'll bring you in on it when I've got somebody to interview."

"You're getting a website?" I ask, unbelievingly.

"Danny thinks we need to get 3M in step with the new millennium. I guess it's about time."

I leave quietly, shaking my head and Danny follows me out back. As I reach my car, I hear his voice behind me. "You doing OK?"

I turn and face him. "Why wouldn't I be?"

"You just seem a little off, is all."

"I'm sorry you had to wait for me to get your meeting started," I say, not really meaning it.

"It's okay. You weren't that late." He hesitates, then continues, "Look, I hope you don't think I'm trying to take the boss' job from Amos. I just really want our business to be successful."

That makes me smile. "You couldn't take Uncle Amos' job if you wanted to, Danny. He wouldn't let you. And really, I'm fine. School's been a bear lately, that's all. It will get better." God, I'm totally lying through my teeth!

"That's good," he says. "You know you can talk to me about anything that you need to."

I don't think so, but I don't tell him that. "Sure, Danny." I turn toward my car again. "Call me tomorrow." I get in the car and shut the door before he can reply.

Somehow I make it back to the townhouse without falling asleep at the wheel. I open the door and I'm immediately assaulted by five pounds of yowling Siamese cat. That would wake anyone up! Xin Niu runs ahead of me into the kitchen and jumps six feet straight up to the top of the refrigerator where her empty bowl is.

I can't look at Xin Niu without thinking of Becca. I still haven't sorted out my feelings for her. Apparently, she didn't have the same problem with me.

The townhouse is still not home. Becca's ghost haunts the halls. She must've totally had her heart set on me as her partner to give me title to all of her stuff. Did she have a premonition of her death?

No wonder I'm so fucked up!

I can't bear the thought of that nightmare again, so I grab a bottle of Heinie and a shot of Turkey. I know I should eat, but I'm just not hungry.

A couple of boilermakers and two Benadryls later, I drag myself off to bed.

Chapter 10.

I awaken to the high-pitched beeping of the bedside clock. OMG! 8:20! How could I not have heard that?

I rush frantically to get out the door. It's a righteous twenty-minute drive to campus and you never know how long it will take to find a parking spot. I cannot be late for this meeting with Dr. Applegait.

I'm in the car when I realize that I could have considered my wardrobe choices a little better. My jeans are way too tight and my Gojira t-shirt is old, worn and tight as well.

Dr. Applegait leers at me when I walk into his office, ten minutes late.

His office is the archetypical old fossil prof's abode. It smells musty and it's way hot, likely because the single window behind the old lecher's desk is shut. The other walls are lined with bookcases crammed with double rows of books. Books bury the single table in the office and more books are piled on the floor. He's cleared a space on his desk for a file folder that doubtless contains my life history.

He's left a path to the wooden armchair facing his desk. As I sit, my t-shirt rides up, exposing my belly. Now old Applegait is positively drooling.

"It speaks poorly of your attitude towards your academic career when you can't be on time for a meeting to discuss your future at this University, Ms. McMasters," is his opening salvo.

He can't tear his eyes away from my chest.

"I'm sorry, Dr. Applegait. Things have been difficult for me lately." I don't like his tone, I don't like his attitude and I don't like him ogling me like a porn star. It's way different when I'm dancing on camera and I can't see the guy. But I realize that if I want to stay in school, I have to work with this man. Unbidden, I launch into a recital of my recent life events. Despite my best efforts, tears are running down my cheeks when I'm done.

To give him credit, Applegait seems somewhat less interested in my anatomy than he was before he heard my story.

"That's quite a tale, Ms. McMasters. Unfortunately, as far as your academic eligibility is concerned, the University must remain objective. However, that is not to say that we cannot offer you help with your personal issues. I would suggest two things. One is that you begin seeing someone in our Counselling Center immediately. The other is that you consider taking incompletes in your courses and a leave of absence for at least the remainder of the semester. That will keep you from being asked to leave the University because of your grades. You will be allowed to re-enroll in the fall when your personal issues have been seen to."

"But what will that do to my chances for getting into law school?"

"I can't say," he replies. "But I can tell what your chances will be if you suffer academic expulsion."

I agree to Applegait's plan. What choice do I have?

He pushes books around on his desk until he finds a phone, then calls the Counselling Center and has a brief conversation.

"You're in luck," he says after hanging up." Dr. Feiner can see you tomorrow at ten." He writes the name and phone number on a post-it and hands it to me.

He tells me that I'll have to go to the Registrar's office to do paperwork for the leave of absence. "I suggest you go today, right now, before any more poor grades come in. I'll call while you're on your way and authorize it." He finally looks into my eyes instead of at my tits and says, "I wish you luck, Ms. McMasters, I really do. I hope to see you back on track in the fall with all of this behind you."

You know, I think he means it. But he's still an old lecher!

I spend the next couple hours at the Registrar's office filling out the forms required by the bureaucracy to temporarily withdraw from school. All the while I'm worrying about how Uncle is going to take it. He expressly told me he'd fire me if I quit school. Uncle is not callous, but he is old school. He thinks that people should take care of their own problems and not expect others to give them special treatment. That's totally how I feel too, but dammit, taking care of my problems is what I'm doing! Surely he'll see that and let me keep my job while I work things out!

It's midafternoon by the time I'm through with the Registrar. I'm lightheaded and somewhat nauseated. I realize that I had no dinner last night, just booze and drugs, and no breakfast and no lunch today. If I don't start taking better care of myself, I'll never beat this thing! I head out to Lee Street for a late lunch.

Big state universities are pretty much the same no matter where you go. They're cities unto themselves. They have a downtown (the campus), the rich folks neighborhood where the professors and the Greeks live and the dorms and student ghetto for the proletariat. And there's the commercial district – that's Lee Street – the strip adjacent to campus where the University bookstore is, along with shops that sell everything from college gear and upscale clothing to comic books and drug paraphernalia. There are loads of ethnic restaurants, sandwich and pizza joints. I'm headed for one of those.

I almost lose my cookies as I emerge from campus and the food smells hit me. I grab a light post to steady myself as I'm waiting to cross the multi-lane road. I glance at the row of shops and restaurants across the street to decide where to go and my eyes light on the doorway that leads to Max's. I haven't been back there since the day I met Becca. I briefly consider it – they do serve sandwiches and snacks in addition to drinks and I wonder if going there would help me deal with her death. Then I think it would just give me an excuse to order an afternoon boilermaker, which I definitely do not need if I'm going to be on stakeout until 11 p.m. I opt for the pizza joint next door.

I barely taste the pizza, but as I eat it, the hollow feeling subsides. I check my phone. Holy shit, it's after three. The stakeout! I punch up Uncle's number.

He gives me an address not far away. I head over to an apartment complex parking lot. I see his car there in a visitor space. As I pull up next to it, I hear his whistle. There's a gazebo that sits by itself in a small field nearby. He pokes his head out and waves me over.

"This is not the best surveillance situation I've ever seen," is his greeting. He indicates a building across the parking lot. "The subject's place is on the top floor. Her windows are on the right. She's been in all day, far as I can tell. I thought I'd be conspicuous as hell sitting in my car, so I camped out in here."

Apartment complexes are a pain in the ass for surveillance. With an upper floor apartment, unless the subject is outside, you have no idea what they're doing. The blinds are down on the windows. She could be up there working out on an exercise machine for all we know. There's no yard to work in, no trash cans to carry. And the parking lot is generally fairly busy, so there's ample opportunity for one of the residents to spot somebody hanging around who doesn't belong.

"Can she get out of there without you seeing her?"

"Unfortunately, yes. The entry to the building is open front and back and you can't see the stairs from here. But that brown Chevy over there is her ride and she hasn't been near it. So I think she's still up there."

"Have you checked the pool or the tennis courts?"

"No, because if I did I could come back and find her car gone. Why don't you go do that now, then come back and take over for me?"

I pull out her picture and give it a hard look, then head out. Ten minutes later, I'm back.

"She not there," I tell him. "So she's either upstairs or we've lost her."

"Well, we can bill the client in either case," Uncle says.

When did you get so mercenary? I think.

"Get you a book to study," he tells me. "I'm gone."

I decide now is not the time to tell him that I won't need to study for a while. So I go the car and grab my iPad. Back in the Gazebo, I pull up Ralph Ellison's *Invisible Man*, which I was supposed to read for a class. Just because I'm out of school doesn't mean I can't keep improving my mind.

The book is hard to get into but that's good, because it keeps me looking away from the screen to Robyn's building. The sun is just setting when I see her emerge and head for her car. I shut down the iPad and head over to mine.

I let her get out of the parking lot before I start up because I don't want to be on her tail while we're in the lot. Too late I realize that my bright red Z-car is not the ideal surveillance vehicle. I'm hoping I can spot her when I get to the road.

Sure enough, as I pull out of the driveway I see her hanging a right a block away. I step on it, take the right myself and there she is. I settle in for the drive.

She gets on the beltway heading into town. Tailing her is a snap because I can keep a couple of cars between us without fear of losing her. After a while, she gets off the Lee Street exit and turns towards State.

Traffic is sparse on Lee so I stay about a block back. A red light stops her and I have no choice but to come up on her bumper. I'm not worried because I'm pretty sure that she hasn't seen me until now.

Stripper!

The light changes and we roll. I have to follow her more closely now because it would be obvious if I dropped too far back again.

Just before we get to campus, she hangs a left on a side street. Right beside the Kitten Club. Don't tell me she's going back to work!

The Kitten Club occupies an entire block and looks like it used to be a warehouse. A windowless brick wall that was once white faces Lee Street. It's illuminated by a bright green and fuchsia neon sign on the roof that sports the club's name in cursive, flanked by a dancing cat who's very obviously female. The parking lot, where the club's entrance is, is around the back behind seven-foot privacy fence, likely because many of the customers don't want their cars spotted here. As I pull through the open chain link gate I see my subject walking across the parking lot to the entrance.

I know I have to follow her inside, so I hunt for a space. The parking lot is amazingly full for early Tuesday evening, so it takes a few minutes to find a hole.

The club entrance is a windowless metal door. A sign handwritten with a magic maker proclaims *You must be 18 to enter! No drugs! No guns!* There's a large white guy in a tank top sitting next to it on a three-legged stool. He looks like a pro wrestler or a biker, with his long hair tied back in a ponytail and spiked leather bands around both wrists. He's got his feet propped up on one of those angled, metal cellar doors next to his chair. Looks uncomfortable as hell.

His eyes run down and back up my body as I draw near. "Lookin' for a job, sweetcheeks?"

"Maybe," I reply.

He swings his feet off the cellar door and gets up from the stool. "Less see some i.d."

Really? I look that young to you, sleezebag? I pull my wallet out of my hip pocket and flash my driver's license.

"Yer good, babe." He pulls an ink pad and a stamp from his back pocket to stamp my hand.

"Why do I need a stamp? Is there a cover charge?"

"Nuh-uhh, not for the ladies. It just means I've seen yer i.d. You want a drink, they'll check it out with a black light. Saves time. By the way, I'm Jesse."

I do not care what your name is, sleezebag. I hold out my hand and he stamps me. As I move toward the entrance, he says, "You might want to keep yer wallet in yer front pocket inside. Just sayin'."

So maybe he's not such a sleezebag after all.

The first thing that hits me as I step inside is the noise. It's so loud, it's palpable. Eighties disco music with a driving bass line so amped that it goes right inside your head. OMG, I'd go nuts if I had to spend hours in here!

The second thing is the smell. Booze. Perfume. Sweat. A faint tinge of weed. And underlying it all, the unmistakable odor of sex.

Naturally, it's dim inside, so I pause in the foyer to get my bearings. The place is cavernous – it looks like the second floor has been ripped out. The large room is indirectly lit with red and purple lights hanging on flat black metal tracks twenty feet up. White spotlights illuminate both ends of a bar along the right wall to make it obvious that it's there. Three runways extend into the room from a narrow stage on the back wall. Six or seven girls, all pretty much nude, are bathed in silver pools of light and writhing on poles set along the runways. The customers sit at tables between them. Waitresses, wearing little more than the dancers, weave in and out among the tables, carrying pitchers of beer on trays. Now I see how Robyn could have hurt her back.

The left wall is totally taken up by alcoves, separated from the main room by wooden doors. They remind me of the confessionals in St. Philomena's where I spent a lot of time as a kid. I see a dancer sit down on the stage, slide off onto the floor, then matter-of-factly take a customer by the hand and lead him to an alcove, likely for a private lap dance or something more.

I scan the place for my subject. The low light and the surprisingly large crowd makes it difficult to spot her, but all I need to do is to find a fully clothed woman in a mostly male crowd. I spot a couple, but neither one is Robyn.

A waitress apparently notices my hesitation. "Lookin' for a job, honey?" she asks. Why else would a woman come into this place? Becca told me once that she danced in such a club just for part of one night. Now I know why! I wonder if it was here?

I shake my head no and head for the bar. I'm not totally keen on putting anything into my mouth that's been in here but I don't want to stand out anymore than I already do.

Stripper!

There's only a few guys sitting at the bar, probably die-hard alkies, because they're paying more attention to their drinks than to the girls.

A bartender comes over and places his ear right next to my lips. I decide that a complicated order isn't going to fly in here. "Beer!" I yell, drawing a look of reproach. Surely I couldn't have hurt his ear. He reaches into a cooler behind the bar and withdraws a dripping bottle that he wipes with a nasty bar towel before he places it in front of me. It's a seven-ounce Corona. He holds up four fingers. Four bucks for a seven-ounce beer? I guess sex sells.

The bartender is a tallish, lanky guy in his mid-thirties. He's got straight black hair, a pencil mustache and a heavy five-o'clock shadow. He's got a wicked scar that starts under his right eye and disappears in his beard. He's wearing a white apron over a black and mauve striped shirt. What a fashion plate! He's sporting a gold name tag. Valery. Funny name for a dude.

He takes the five I hand him and puts down the beer that he's holding in the same hand. I smile at him but get nothing back. The five goes into a cash drawer and he withdraws a one. I notice that he's only using his left arm. He flips the one on the bar in front of me, then goes about his business.

I wipe the top of the bottle neck with my fingers. Who knows where that bar towel's been? Then I twist off the cap and take a swig. Yep, it's Corona all right.

Again I look for Robyn on the floor. No luck. Gee, maybe she'll pop up and grab a tray of beer, making my surveillance superfluous. Can't claim workman's comp if she's hustling tables. I turn back to the bar just as a door near the end opens and she comes storming out, making a beeline for the exit. I chug the rest of my expensive Mexican brew and follow her.

Because of low lights inside the club, I stop and squint in the floodlights outside. I don't see Robyn – I belatedly realize that I neglected to see where she parked before following her inside. Nothing to do now but get to my car and hope that I can spot her.

As I hurry to my car, she appears from between two other vehicles and blocks my way, glaring.

"Okay, honey! Who the hell are you and why are you following me?"

"I'm not following…" I begin.

"Bullshit! I picked you up on Lee and I remembered seeing that red car of yours in the parking lot at my place. Who are you and what the hell do you want? Don't make me ask you again!"

Have I mentioned that I'm only five one and less than a hundred pounds? Robyn has at least six inches on me and I can see the muscles rippling in her neck and arms.

She stalks toward me, forcing me back against a parked car. "Look, Shorty," she grates, "you're gonna tell me who you are, or I'm gonna hang you up by your ankle, take your i.d. and find out! What's it gonna be?"

"Kira? Kira Fox?"

Hearing that name shocks me more than Robyn's threats ever could. I turn to see a bespeckled guy in his twenties approaching us, his eyes fixated on me. He turns on Robyn.

"You leave her alone!" he simpers at Robyn like Sponge Bob. "You just leave her alone or I'm calling the cops!"

Even though this guy looks like Robyn could mop up the parking lot with him, his sudden appearance has taken her aback.

"OK, Kira Fox!" she says to me. "I'll find out where you live! And if I ever catch you following me again…" She doesn't need to finish the threat. She marches off into the forest of cars.

I turn towards my rescuer. Like I said, he's a scrawny twentysomething, a little under six foot, with a black buzz cut and huge black glasses. His face is pimply and he's got a couple of open sores. He's wearing a bright pink Kitten Club t-shirt over a pair of cargo pants. He's looking at me uncertainly.

"Kira!" he calls me again. "It's you, right? You look different somehow. It's me! Bobby! I'm so glad to see you! I thought something bad happened to you when you didn't answer my calls. Who was that bitch?"

Bobby? Who the hell…? OMG! Bobby was the first guy I danced for as Kira Foxxx. I have got to get rid of him and get out of here!

"Are you gonna be dancin' here now?" he asks, his face full of anticipation.

"I don't know," I tell him. "They're giving me an audition. I was just going to my car to get my outfit. Why don't you go back inside and wait for me?"

He still looks uncertain. "Who was that bitch?" he asks again.

68

"Just another dancer. I think she's scared I'm gonna get her job." That makes him smile.

"Now go back in and wait." A second. "Maybe we can have a drink when I'm done, Bobby." His face glows like the sign on the roof.

"Okay!" he says. "See you soon!" He damn near falls down as he whirls around and scurries back into the club.

As soon as he's gone, I make a beeline for my car. Seconds later, I'm driving down Lee Street, faster than law allows!

Later, I'm in bed, wide awake. I don't dare drink or take anything. What a day! I'm not in school anymore. I screwed up the surveillance and I'll have to tell Uncle before he goes out tomorrow. And I left poor Bobby hanging. He may be a creep but he surely has his own problems - he didn't deserve that! He likely saved me from an ass whipping.

I'm way scared. My life is falling apart and I can't stop it!

Chapter 11.

I finally fall asleep, only to be jolted awake by the dream. No more sleep after that!

At six a.m., I send Uncle a text to call me before he goes out. He does, and he's not happy with what I have to tell him. Thankfully though, he doesn't blame me.

"I shoulda taken that red car of yours and left you with my heap," he says. "Did she look hurt to you when she braced you in the parking lot?"

"Just the opposite," I tell him. "She looked like she could kick my ass, then run a mile!"

"Well I'm sorry, but I'll have to take you off the case since she's seen you." Great. There goes my paycheck. "We'll get you back on the next one. But you can't use that red car for surveillance anymore."

He's right. There's nothing more to say.

My appointment with the counsellor is at ten. I dress more conservatively than I did for Applegait, in jeans and a looser t-shirt, with my hair up in a bun.

I'm surprised that I don't feel tired while driving to campus. Maybe the thought that I'm going to see somebody who might help me is staving off the fatigue.

Dr. Feiner's office is in the Counselling Center, a red brick building in the old part of campus. The buildings ring an oval courtyard rimmed with stately oaks in which students lie on blankets studying or run about chasing a Frisbee. As I approach the building, I can't help looking for anyone who might recognize me. Why is it such a problem for me to seek emotional help?

Before I can see Dr. Feiner, the receptionist gives me a stack of forms. I've been enrolled at State University nearly eighteen months, and they still need all of this information? I complete the forms as fast as I can, reading only enough to know what goes in each blank. Twenty minutes later, I hand them to the receptionist, who accepts them wordlessly.

A few minutes later I hear, "Miss McMasters, Here's Dr. Feiner."

Stripper!

Dr. Feiner is strikingly beautiful, although she's dressed pragmatically in a white lab coat over a business suit. She's in her thirties, about five eight and voluptuous, to say the least. Her high cheekbones, black hair worn in a bun and coppery skin make me wonder if she doesn't have native American blood. She takes my hand in greeting and looks into my eyes as she does so – hers are such a deep brown that they're almost black. Her ready smile relaxes me. She leads me back to her office.

Even though the building is old, her office is furnished in contemporary glass and stainless steel. Surprisingly, it contains few books. The room smells of leather and flowers but there's an underlying muskiness - she's obviously made an effort to fight old building syndrome but there's only so much you can do. A comfortable-looking black leather armchair faces her desk and the obligatory daybed is beside it, also in stainless and black leather. Her framed diplomas inform me that she's an M.D. and Ph.D. from Johns Hopkins – I guess I could do a lot worse for a counsellor.

She waves me to the chair, as she takes her own behind the desk.

We exchange pleasantries and she asks a few general questions – my age, where I'm from, what I'm studying.

Suddenly I blurt, "You've got to help me with the dreams! I'm scared to sleep!"

Her smile vanishes and she becomes totally serious. "Tell me about the dreams, Natalie."

I begin hesitantly, then the dam breaks. I tell her about the dream, about Becca, about the murders and my stripping online. When I pause for breath, she holds up a hand to shush me and picks up the phone on her desk.

"Please cancel my ten-thirty and eleven o'clock," she says. "I'll let you know about the eleven-thirty in a little while." She comes to take my hand and leads me to the daybed. After she's made sure that I'm comfortable, she takes a form from a filing cabinet and returns to her desk.

She consults the form for a moment and then says in a clinical tone, "For the rest of our interview, I want you to keep the shooting in your apartment in mind as I ask you some questions about how it may have affected you. I'm going to ask you about twenty-five questions. Most of them have two parts. First I'll ask you if you've ever had a particular problem and if your answer is yes, I'll ask you how often you've had it since the shooting. Then I'll ask how much distress or discomfort that problem may have caused you."

Suddenly her clinical tone changes, becoming soft and gentle. "Natalie, I know that some of these things will be difficult to discuss. You can decide how much you want to tell me about a certain thing, but please realize that the more I know about how you're feeling, the more I can help you. If you find yourself becoming distressed as we go along, please let me know and we can deal with it. OK?"

I feel like a little girl again. "OK," I say.

She takes me through a detailed account of the shooting, then drills into specifics. She asks about the dreams, of course, but as she probes, I realize that other things have been happening too, like my inability to concentrate, my growing sense of isolation and my fear that the killer will return, which have been causing me to look for threats when I enter a room or exit a building. We also talk about Becca's murder. She seems surprised when I tell her that Becca made me her partner and that I'm living in the townhouse. I feel myself starting to shut her out when she asks about our relationship.

"Why do you think that Becca decided that you should share all of her things and her money, Natalie? Doesn't that seem strange to you?"

"Yes, it does," I admit. "I totally don't know. I was as shocked as anyone when I found out."

"I can only think of one reason," she says. "I think Becca had fallen in love with you."

I begin weeping uncontrollably. I know that she's right!

She lets me cry it out, then brings me a box of tissues from her desk.

"Do you want to take a break? Go to the rest room, freshen up a little?"

"No." I tell her. Let's get this over with!

"Then close your eyes and relax. Go to sleep if you want to. I have a little paperwork to do, then we can continue."

The next thing I know, her hand is on my forehead, stroking me awake. I grasp it, and gaze into that beautiful, elegant face. She attempts to withdraw, but I don't want to let her go. She frowns, and I release her hand.

Stripper!

She asks if I want something to drink. When I say yes, she leaves. I briefly consider bolting, but I know I need to fix this. She comes back with cans of Coke for both of us and places mine on her desk, motioning me to move back to the chair from the daybed.

When we're settled, she says, "Well, I have some good news for you."

"I could totally use some."

"Natalie, you're experiencing post-traumatic stress disorder. The good news is that your case is a mild one, and eminently treatable."

"PTSD? I thought that only soldiers got that!" I realize how dumb that sounds the second it's out of my mouth.

"Anyone who's experienced a traumatic event can suffer from it, even if it doesn't involve violence. Given what you've experienced lately, it's not at all surprising it's affected you."

"What about the dream? Can you do anything about it?"

"I am going to prescribe some medication to help with that. Now, it may not work right away and if it doesn't, you must gradually increase the dose according to the instructions I will give you until it does. Whatever you do, no more alcohol, either to help you sleep or socially."

I nod. I was getting worried about the drinking.

"Now I don't think it's necessarily a bad thing that you're living in Becca's townhouse. I know that there are unpleasant associations there, but I think that confronting them will serve you better in the long run than avoiding them will. I also think it's good that you've dropped out of school for a while. However, I don't want you just sitting around brooding. Do you have a job?"

I realize that I've told her nothing about my work for 3M, so I go into that now. "But it looks like I'm on hiatus for a while." I tell her about the debacle in the strip club parking lot last night, leaving out my encounter with Bobby. "Since the subject knows me, I can't be on surveillance with her anymore."

She purses her lips as she thinks. Her face fascinates me – I purposefully look away from her as she's thinking because I don't want to offend her by staring at her.

"Do you have a significant other that you can confide in?"

"No, ma'am." I hesitate, then I tell her about my ex-fiancé who became engaged to me just so he could screw me.

She shakes her head in sympathy. "You certainly have been kicked around lately. And please don't call me ma'am. Doctor will do if you feel a need to be formal, but I prefer Rebecca."

"I hope you don't mind, but I think I'll have a problem with calling you that right now."

"I understand," she says. "The man who shot at you that got away?" she asks. "Do you feel like he might come back for you?"

"Yes and no," I say. "The last thing he said to me is that he wasn't being paid to kill me – that I was too much trouble to mess with."

"And how did you feel after hearing that?"

"Good, I guess. But now the cops have his prints and DNA, even though they don't know who he is. That might totally piss him off."

"It might at that," she agrees. She pauses, then says, "You tell me you're a private investigator. Is there any way you could help the police to find him? I'm not suggesting that you go after him yourself, mind you. But it's good therapy to face those things we're afraid of."

"Maybe. I'll think about it."

"Good. Well, I think we've done all that we can today. I'm giving you a prescription for a drug called Prazosin." She writes on the pad on her desk, then goes back to the file cabinet and withdraws a paper and couple of small boxes. "Here are the instructions for taking it," she says as she hands them to me, "and some samples to get you started until you can fill the prescription. It should stop the nightmares when you reach the right dose. Now remember, no drinking! It's dangerous with this drug. And don't take it and drive, at least until you know how it's going to affect you. It will stop the dreams, Natalie. You just have to give it a chance."

"Yes ma'am, I mean, Rebecca." I say.

She smiles. "See? Not such a problem after all." She turns to her computer and makes a few mouse clicks. "Today is Wednesday," she says. "I'd think I'd like you to come back Friday so we can see how you're doing, then again on Monday. After that, if you're stabilized, you can start seeing less of me."

Stripper!

"I don't mind how much I see of you, Rebecca."

She takes a couple cards from her desk drawer and fills them out, then pushes them across to me. "These will remind you of those appointments."

She puts her arm on my shoulder as she escorts me to her office door.

She looks into my eyes again as she says, "We're going to beat this, Natalie. What you've been through would overwhelm most people. Don't be ashamed."

God, I could get lost in those eyes!

Chapter 12.

The little bit of sleep I had in Rebecca's office makes me feel wide awake, so I decide to go to the 3M office to talk to Uncle. I'm not looking forward to this conversation, but I'm trying to take what Rebecca told me about facing my fears to heart. I hope that Danny isn't there, because I don't think I'm up to sharing my troubles with him right now.

I'm in luck. Uncle Amos' pickup is the only vehicle in the yard. I grab me a cup of coffee and find him in the office.

First thing he does is apologize again for letting me use the red car on the Robyn Carson stakeout. I feel as responsible about that as he does, and I tell him so.

"But that's not what I came to talk to you about. I wanted to tell you I've taken a leave of absence from State."

He bristles. "Nattie, I told you…"

I stop him with an upraised hand. "Listen to me before you get mad!" I tell him about the problems I've had since Becca's death and that I'm going for counselling. "As soon as I get myself straightened out, I plan to go back to school."

His face is serious. "Well now, do you need a leave of absence from your job, too?"

"That's exactly what I don't need, Uncle. You know that I've come into some money recently, so I'm not relying on what you pay me for my living. But my counsellor told me it would be bad just to sit around. She told me it could help me if I made an effort to help the cops catch the guy who killed Becca."

"That's the last thing I want you doin'! It's dangerous as hell…"

I make him talk to the hand again. "All I'm talking about is some internet research that will hopefully help me recall some things about him that I can pass along to Detective Kidd. This guy is a pro. Becca and Blackie O'Halloran can't be the first people that he's killed."

He still doesn't look happy, but he says, "Well, I guess that will be OK. But you get any leads, you tell Kidd! No chasin' them down on your own."

"Believe me, after all that's happened lately, that's the last thing I want to do."

"Good," he agrees. "But there's another problem. Since our current subject knows you, you can't be involved in any more surveillance."

I look around at the office. Papers and files are piled on the tables and chairs, even on the floor. Uncle claims that he knows where everything is, but I know that I'm looking at a twenty-year accumulation of detritus.

"You said that after you get your website, you want to computerize everything. Does that include this mess?" I indicate the effluvium with a broad circular wave.

"Well yes, eventually."

"Then why don't you let me come in here and start sorting and filing this junk. Once that's done, you can go through it in an organized way and decide what you want to keep and what you want to toss. Then we can address getting it digitized."

"That would take you all day, every day for a while, right?" I can hear the reluctance in his voice. I know that the business is running on a shoestring and hiring Danny on has likely stretched his resources thinner.

"Look, Uncle, I know you pay me by the hour, but I'm not trying to get extra money out of you. I have what I need right now. You decide what you think I'm worth and pay me that. And I'll take care of the mess. It will get me out of the house and give me something to do."

Relief is evident on his face. "Sure Nattie, that'd be great!" He extricates himself from behind his desk and finds his hat under a pile of papers. "Look," he says, "I need to go into town and check on a few things. You can stay here and get started or go home."

"I want to give Detective Kidd a call before I go."

He leaves, and I wait until I hear his car fire up outside before calling Kidd. After the ritual small talk, I ask him if any progress has been made on finding the shooter.

"Not really," he tells me. "The DNA analysis on the blood came back, but it wasn't in CODIS. So we can't trace it to any other killings he might have done. Same thing with the gun. The bullets we dug out of your wall were .22's and the shell casings told us the gun was a .22 magnum. But there was no ballistics data in NIBIN, so we couldn't link the gun to any other killings. This is one careful man."

"A .22 doesn't sound like a professional's weapon," I say.

"Oh, but it is!" Kidd disagrees. "A .22 magnum has terminal ballistics nearly as good as a .380, and very little recoil, so it's really accurate. Even if it's not suppressed, it makes less noise than a bigger gun. And he likely had 25 or 30 rounds in that pistol when he started shooting. Blackie was nailed eight times! If the noise from your gun hadn't attracted attention, you wouldn't have had a chance."

"Well, how many people own that kind of gun?"

"It's hard to say. They're somewhat rare. But there's no national gun database – the sales records are kept at the individual shops and there's plenty of those in the city. Besides, a guy this cautious probably didn't buy the weapon legally anyway. Also, he's a pro who knows that he left shell casings behind. The odds are he got rid of the gun later that same night." He hesitates, then asks, "Are you sure there's nothing else about this joker you can tell us?"

"Not really. He was average-sized – maybe a little tall and skinny. His clothes were ordinary –Dockers and a plain long-sleeved shirt. He was wearing one of those full-face Guy Fawkes masks, like the Anonymous guys wear."

"Hair? Eyes?" I could tell by his tone that Kidd wasn't really into this. We'd been over it all before.

"He had short dark hair, I think. And I never saw his eyes while he was shooting at me."

"OK, Ms. McMasters. There's a reason that these guys are professionals. You've done humanity a service by getting us a sample of this one's DNA. He'll slip up eventually. They all do."

No, they don't, I think. That's the reason these guys are professionals. Kidd hangs up.

Suddenly a wave of fatigue hits. I consider going home, but I'm hardly fit to drive. There's a spare bedroom upstairs. I'd better go and find it!

Sometime later I wake up, wooly-headed. I took one of my pills before lying down. I don't know if it was the medicine or sheer exhaustion, but my sleep was dreamless.

Stripper!

A glance out of the bedroom window tells me that it's dusk. I wander back downstairs, looking for a cup of coffee. Uncle Amos is not in the office, but cooking odors permeate the house. I follow my nose to the kitchen and I find Danny, frying a hamburger.

"Hi Nattie," Danny greets me. "Amos told me you were asleep upstairs before he left. Want a burger?"

Suddenly, I'm starving. "That sounds great!"

As Danny goes to the fridge, I consider telling him about what's going on with me. I decide that as my co-worker, he has a right to know. Of course, I don't tell him everything…

"Wow, Nattie, I'm sorry I didn't realize how much your friend's death affected you." he says when I've finished.

"Why don't we eighty-six the burgers and let me take you out for a proper dinner?" Danny says.

"No sir! After our last dinner, I told you next time was going to be my treat." God, that seems like another lifetime.

The glare of headlights in the driveway heralds the arrival of a car. As it pulls into the back yard, I see the bubble on the roof. A police car.

The door opens and Kidd gets out. He approaches Danny and me as we stand on the back porch.

"What's up, Detective?" Danny asks him.

Kidd looks directly at me.

"I need you to tell me why you were following Robyn Carlson last night," he says.

Chapter 13.

K idd, Danny and I are sitting around the kitchen table with coffee that's been reheated way too many times.

"I need you to tell me why you were following Robyn Carlson last night," Kidd repeats.

I counter with a question of my own. "How do you know about that?"

"Because she told me."

This makes no sense! "She told you?"

Kidd sighs. "What I'm about to tell you doesn't leave this room," he says. "Her name isn't Robyn Carlson. She's a police officer, working undercover at the Kitten Club. That shithole is a hub for drugs, guns, vice and all sorts of other lovely things. I am her handler, and when she checked in last night, she told me that she was followed to the Kitten Club last night by a short blonde chick named Kira Fox. Now where do I know that name from?"

I glance at Danny guiltily.

He continues, "She was supposed to meet me this afternoon. She didn't. When she misses a check-in, protocol says that I go to her apartment to check up on her and if I don't find her, the whole department is alerted. I went over there a little while ago, and I found bloodstains."

Holy shit! I was following a cop! No wonder she spotted me.

"Bloodstains?" Danny says.

"There wasn't a lot of blood, but I found it in the foyer. I wouldn't be as concerned if it was the bathroom or the kitchen, somewhere where somebody would normally cut themselves."

"What's her right name?" I ask Kidd.

"You don't need to know that."

I tell him about our surveillance. "I know you said this information about Robyn is confidential, but we have to tell Uncle Amos about it," I finish.

Stripper!

"Of course," Kidd says. "When she hurt her back at the club, we thought that she should file workers comp so as not to arouse suspicion. We actually wouldn't have gone through with it. We were transitioning her out of there and she would have been compensated for her injury through the department. We didn't anticipate that Horaz would hire a PI to investigate the claim."

"Who's Horaz?" Danny asks.

"Judd Horaz owns the Kitten Club and we think he's one of the major drug dealers in the city. It was him that Robyn was investigating. She went down there last night to bitch him out for blocking the claim, again just to stay in character."

Maybe that's what Kidd thought, but she looked pretty pissed to me when she came out of his office, more than she should have been about Horaz denying a claim that she knew she'd never collect on anyway.

A thought lurking in the back of my mind suddenly coalesces. "Wait a minute! She was investigating this Horaz, so she gets a job as a topless waitress at his club to get inside? How is that any different from what I did to find the guy who killed Becca, for which you raked me over the coals?"

As soon as the words are out of my mouth I regret them. Danny looks at me, puzzled.

"It is different!" Kidd says. "She's a trained police officer."

In for a penny, in for a pound. "I'm not talking about that." I press him. "I'm talking about you pointing the finger at me for what I did!"

Kidd has the decency to look at the table as I glare at him. Danny still looks clueless. Finally, Kidd says, "All right, so you do what you have to, to get the job done. But that's not what's important right now. Right now I need to find my officer."

"I'm sorry I can't help you with that," I say.

"We terminated our surveillance after she made Natalie," Danny says. "It's a shame, because otherwise we might have had somebody at her place when whatever happened went down."

Kidd looks glum. "Well, that's it then. You can tell Amos what's going on and that your operation is finished." He rises from the table.

"Can you let us know if you find her" I ask him.

"Need to know," he says again, and heads outside.

After he's gone, Danny looks at me obviously puzzled. "So who is Kira Fox?"

I give him the short version, leaving out my extracurricular activities. The murder of Blackie O'Halloran made the news, as did Becca's murder, but Kidd managed to keep my name out of it by keeping the media focused on Blackie.

"That's the first I've heard that you were there when Blackie's shooting went down," Danny says. "But did you mean about what you did to find the guy who killed your friend?"

I can lie, I can tell him to mind his own goddamn business, or I can tell him the truth. I opt for the latter. When I'm done, he's regarding me strangely.

"Well, I guess it's getting late to go out tonight," Danny says.

It's pretty obvious what changed his mind.

"Yeah, I'm totally wiped," I tell him. "I'll give you a rain check."

When I get back to the townhouse, I take another pill per doctor's orders and fall asleep. The dream is mercifully absent again. I'm awakened by a rough tongue in my ear and the sound of purring. The room is awash with sunlight.

I look at the clock. Wow! 10:30!

I have a leisurely breakfast of cereal and yogurt. I feel oddly apprehensive – I'm not used to having a lot of time in the morning. Usually I have to shower, bolt down breakfast and rush to not be late for class. Now I realize that I can actually choose how I'm going to spend my day. I could get used to life as a dilettante!

Well, I promised Uncle Amos that I'd help him clean up the mess in his office, so I guess that's what I'll do.

Sometime later, I pull into the backyard behind the 3M office. Uncle Amos' truck is there but thankfully, Danny's isn't, and there's a van that I haven't seen before. A client, I wonder?

I walk into the office from the kitchen. Uncle Amos is standing next to a young man at the PC - both of them seem absorbed with the screen. They turn to look at me as I enter and I almost pee my pants!

"Hi Ki..., I mean Natalie!" Bobby says.

Stripper!

Bobby! What the holy fuck is Bobby doing here?

"You two know each other?" Uncle Amos asks.

Bobby and I answer at once.

"No!" I say.

"Yeah!" says Bobby. OMG! Uncle Amos doesn't know anything about my online stripping. That sure doesn't need to come up now!

"I mean, you told me that you work here with your partner Danny and your niece Natalie," Bobby says to Uncle Amos. "So who else could she be?" He winks at me.

"I'm considering hiring Bobby here to do our website," Uncle Amos says. "He was just showing me some of his work. He comes pretty highly recommended."

"If you'll pardon my saying so, computerwise, you guys are really in the dark ages," Bobby says. "I can give you a system that will make your work so much easier and let you compete with the big boys."

Something isn't right. "How did you know we were looking to upgrade the office computer and get a website?" I ask Bobby.

"Mr. Murdoch put a query for information about a new system and website on the Net," Bobby says. I look at Uncle Amos for confirmation.

"I guess that's right," Uncle Amos says, "but I didn't realize that it would actually attract people to bid on the job. I thought I was just getting information."

"Oh, a good computer monkey like me tracks those sites to identify potential clients," Bobby says. "You got to keep ahead of the crowd if you want to be successful in this business."

"Sounds like a good bidness attitude to me." Uncle Amos says. "Well Bobby, your references seem OK, so I guess the next step is to send me a bid. Then we can talk turkey." Uncle Amos slaps Bobby on the shoulder as a gesture to seal the deal.

"Owww!" Bobby squeals like a puppy that's been kicked.

Uncle Amos' face is a mixture of concern and disbelief. "Hey, sorry, I didn't think I hit you that hard."

He didn't. This Bobby is obviously a total wuss.

"Well, you did!" Bobby whimpers. "I've got a sunburn! And I'm not used to being manhandled like that."

"I'm sorry," Uncle says again.

"It's okay, I guess," says Bobby. "I guess I'll have to get used to getting slapped on the back if I'm going to do business out here in the boonies. I'll send you a bid this afternoon, Mr. Murdoch."

Obviously, I'm not happy at all about this situation. After Bobby is gone, I say to Uncle, "I'm not sure he's the right guy for this job."

"Why not? What's wrong with him?"

I can't bring myself to tell him the real reason right now. "I don't know. I just think he's kinda creepy. You didn't hit him that hard, you know."

"I didn't think I did," Uncle says. "Hell, most of them computer guys are as strange as a preacher in a cat house. You got to be to understand that mess. Let's just see what kinda bid he gives us and go from there."

Changing the subject, he says, "So I hear we had a visit from the cops last night."

"Did Danny tell you what happened?"

"He surely did. I had no idee we were tailin' an undercover cop. And I hope we had nuthin' to do with her disappearance."

"How could we have?"

"Dunno," he says. "Only way would be if somebody made her 'cuz they noticed our tail. And if we hadn't dropped surveillance, mebbe we'd a been there when whoever took her down."

Do you think she's been kidnapped?"

I think it's likely. She knows she'd have the whole force huntin' her if she didn't check in."

He grabs his hat from the rack and plops it on his head. He says, "With Robyn Carlson out of the pitcher, they ain't no money comin' in to pay fer a website, or anythin' else. I'm gone over to the insurance company to see if I can scare up any more bidness. You plannin' on spendin' the day here?"

Stripper!

"I guess."

"Well, I'll call and let you know if I get anythin'."

With that, he heads out back to his truck.

I look around the office and the stacks of files and papers strewn everywhere. It looks like a landfill! Why did I ever volunteer to straighten out this mess, and where do I start? I sigh. Same place you start anything, Nattie. Right in front of you.

A few hours later, the piles have changed from completely disordered to somewhat orderly. The work consumes very little brain power, so I've had plenty of time to think. And what's consumed most of my thoughts is the topic that I've obviously been afraid to address until now. The elephant in the room.

Am I a lesbian?

Impossible! I was engaged, for God's sake! I'm not promiscuous, but I have had a few lovers, all of them guys. I've never been attracted to a woman - that is, not until that night that Becca performed for me.

That thought takes me aback. Was she performing for Stud, or for me? I try to remember.

Just thinking about some of the things she did with that toy sends jolts of electricity through me. Did she look into my eyes as she was pleasuring herself? I'm sure she did! She obviously wanted me – she asked me to shower with her afterwards. I suddenly realize that I said no because I was pretty sure what that would turn into.

Did I say no because the thought repulsed me? Or was I terrified that I was going to like it?

Without warning, I'm crying, no, weeping! Sobs and shudders rack my entire body – I drop the papers I'm holding and collapse to the floor. I'm sucking in air only to immediately expel it again in torrents of grief. My head spins as if I'm being strangled. There's an ache deep inside, a tremendous loneliness that I can barely identify and it threatens to consume me. I feel as if I'm losing myself!

Later, I come to. Jesus, what a hot mess, lying in a heap on a filthy floor amid stacks of yellowing paper. I struggle to my feet, grateful that no one saw me. I stagger to the bathroom and look in the mirror. OMG! I could be the poster girl for a zombie walk. My skin is sallow, my eyes bloodshot, my cheeks scarlet and my yellow hair dangles around my face in matted strands, swathed with dust bunnies from the floor. I scare up some soap and water and a towel. I've got to get cleaned up before anybody sees me!

Later, I'm better. I'm still not satisfied with my appearance but the mirror tells me that at least I don't look like I'm going out for Halloween. I'd better get out of here before Danny or Uncle Amos show up. They're sure to have questions if they see me like this.

Driving back to the townhouse, I realize that I've got an appointment with Rebecca tomorrow morning. Am I going to tell her about my breakdown? I feel better now – the threat of being discovered is gone and I feel somehow cleansed, as if some evil spirit has been exorcised. I'll decide in the morning, I think.

Chapter 14.

I'm about five minutes late for my appointment with Rebecca. I slept like the dead last night and overslept my alarm. No dream! Whatever happened to me yesterday appears to have done me some good. I still haven't decided whether I want to discuss it with Rebecca.

I tell the receptionist I'm here for Dr. Feiner and she calls her. I don't even have time to sit down before Rebecca arrives to take me back.

The sight of her brings a weakness to my knees and a hollow feeling in the pit of my stomach. She's dressed as usual in a frilly blouse, dark skirt and her white lab coat, but today, her shining black hair is down instead of up in a bun, cascading about her shoulders and framing her perfect face. Even from three feet away, she smells like spring. Her bittersweet chocolate eyes touch mine.

She takes my hand in greeting. OMG –it's like a jolt of current up my arm! Did she feel it too?

Later, I'm on the daybed in her office. I'm so confused! We've been talking about the last couple days. I barely remember what I've told her. Yes, the dream is gone for now. I'm doing office work for Uncle Amos. Yes, I've thought some about the shooting, but I haven't really had any new revelations.

Unexpectedly, I just blurt it out. "I think I'm a lesbian!"

It doesn't knock a feather out of her. "What makes you think that, Natalie?"

I tell her everything. My "date" with Becca. The performance. The shower invitation. How I avoided Becca afterwards, for days, so I never got to see her alive again. Goddammit, I'm bawling again!

She lets me cry it out, then brings me the box of tissues from her desk.

"You're having a very typical reaction to severely repressed emotions, Natalie," she tells me. "Confronting one's sexual orientation can be difficult, even traumatic, depending on your background and expectations. Your difficulties have been compounded by several factors – your broken engagement, Becca's death and the violence you've experienced. It's no wonder you've been unable to resolve these issues. But you will. It will just take time."

"But am I a lesbian?"

"That's for you to decide, not for me."

"But I've had sex with guys and... enjoyed it!"

"Our culture tends to regard sexual orientation as black and white. Nothing could be further from the truth. It's a continuum, both among the population and within an individual. That's what makes it so confusing."

"So what I'm feeling is normal?"

"Normal is another bad word. It just means something that is the norm - that it applies to a majority of people. That something is normal says nothing about its worth. It's just about the frequency of occurrence. What you're feeling is what you're feeling. Period. Feel it. Don't judge it."

"You're telling me to act on my emotions without judgement? That sounds dangerous to me!"

"Feelings and actions are two different things, Natalie. I'm telling you to trust yourself. You are basically a good person. You'll know it if you're about to take an inappropriate action."

I'm not so sure about that, but there's no point in arguing with her. I realize that I've said nothing about my feelings for her, very deliberately. I wonder if she knows?

It's just a little after eleven when the session is over. As usual, Rebecca gets up to walk me out. She places on hand on the doorknob and the other on my shoulder. The current flows again.

"Let me leave you with this for today," she says. "You are a strong, capable young woman. You've been through a great deal, but I think it's nothing you can't handle if you'll just recognize what your issues are and face them head on. No more sweeping them under the rug. I want to see in a week and I'll expect to hear about the progress you've made in resolving your sexual orientation issues. And keep taking your medicine and call me if the dream comes back." She opens the door and ushers me into the hallway.

As I walk down the stairs into the courtyard, I feel drained. It's a beautiful spring day with the smell of flowers and new mown grass in the air and the students are taking full advantage of it. There's a Frisbee game in progress and others lie about on blankets watching, talking or studying. I see two young ladies occupying the same blanket with their hands on each other's shoulders, their foreheads touching as if in a mind meld. Are they lesbians? Or just good

Stripper!

friends enjoying each other's company? One suddenly pushes the other away – she falls over on her back, laughing. I feel an ache within me, and I'm not sure why it's there.

I want to go back to the townhouse to bed, but I know that's not what I need to do. I promised Uncle Amos I'd work on the files.

Later I'm sorting through the mess and questioning my sanity for taking on this job. When will I ever make heads or tails of it? I hear the screen door in the kitchen slam. I smile with the anticipation of greeting Danny or Uncle, but Bobby walks in! His arm is still in a sling. Maybe too much exercise in front of the computer after the club is closed?

"Hi Kira!" he greets me.

"Don't call me that!"

"Hey, I'm sorry Natalie. Or Nattie. You like to be called Nattie, right?"

Not by you! "Natalie's fine." I tell him.

"OK, Natalie it is."

"What are you doing here, Bobby?"

"Hey, Mr. Murdoch gave me the job after I sent my bid yesterday. And a key. If I'm going to get y'all on line, I need to wire the place and load the software."

I just stand there, glaring at him. He can't help but notice.

"Hey," he says. "I don't know what I did that you don't like me anymore. But you don't have to worry. I'm not going to tell Mr. Murdoch and Mr. Merkel that you're Kira Foxxx or that you danced for me. So you don't have to be so mean."

His words take me back. He's right, I am being mean to him. And he doesn't deserve it. All the poor guy did was to call me on the phone so I could provide a service that I offered. For which he paid me a substantial amount of money. And he probably saved me from a beating by Robyn Carlson to boot.

"You know, I waited for you at the club that night until closing," Bobby says. "But you never came." He looks like he's going to cry.

Now I feel ashamed. All I could think of was getting the hell out of there, away from the club and away from him. I didn't even think about how standing him up like that might make him feel.

89

"You're right, Bobby, and I'm sorry I did that to you." He brightens up at my words. "Mr. Murdoch is my uncle and he doesn't know anything about Kira Foxxx. I suppose I'll have to tell him someday, but I'd like to be the one to decide when. Danny does know, though."

He smiles at me sheepishly. "Hey, no problem Natalie - I get it. Your secret's safe with me."

To change the subject, I ask Bobby, "What's that you're installing?"

"It's the Tor browser. It will let you search the web anonymously," he says. "I figure you guys being PI's and all, you don't want people knowing you're searching for them, or having them trace you back. This software will make everything you do on the net secure. And it will let you access the Dark Web too."

"What's the Dark Web?"

"Doo doo doo doo, doo doo doo doo!" Bobby sings the theme from the Twilight Zone. "The Dark Web is where all the bad guys hang out! Everything from illegal arms dealers to cannibals. I figure you guys being PI's, you'll want to keep tabs on 'em. So I'm giving you the capability."

He's sad and way creepy, but harmless, I think. But I need to be careful. Now he's grinning again. It's obvious that he's infatuated with me and nothing's ever going to come of that on my end.

"Look, Bobby, we've both go a lot of work to do. Let's get at it." I turn away from him and take up an armload of files.

We turn to our respective tasks. Bobby tries to start a conversation, but I either answer him in monosyllables or find an excuse to leave the room. I don't want to be nasty, but I sure as hell don't need to encourage him either. He finally seems to accept the situation and we work silently for a couple of hours.

Finally, he says, "Well, I guess I've done what I can for now. It's lunchtime. You want to go and get something?"

"Nope."

He gives up and starts packing up his things.

"I'll see you tomorrow, OK?"

"I guess so."

Stripper!

He leaves and the tension in the room goes with him.

It doesn't take long for it to return, though. Danny comes in about twenty minutes later.

"Oh, hey Nattie." I can feel the frost from across the room. Now the shoe is on the other foot.

Danny takes a seat at his desk and fires up his PC. He clicks the mouse a few times, then looks annoyed. He finally looks my way and says, "What's wrong with this thing? I can't get to the home screen."

"Search me. The computer guy was working on the system. He just left a little while ago."

"He didn't say anything about the system being down?"

"Nope." Two can play at that game.

"Shit! How the hell am I supposed to get any work done? Why didn't you check the system before you let him leave?"

I don't believe this! His PC won't work and it's my fault?

"I wasn't aware that I'd been promoted to head of IT around here."

"That's a stupid thing to say!"

I fire back at him. "One stupid thing deserves another!"

He sits there glaring at me. What did Rebecca say this morning about facing issues head on?

"I know what this is about, Danny, and it isn't computers."

He looks apprehensive. "What do you mean?"

"It's about Kira Fox."

"What do you mean?" he says again.

"Oh, please! I saw the switch flip when I told you the other night that I'd been stripping online. Killed our dinner date real fast, didn't it?"

At least he has the decency to look at the floor.

"You found out that I wasn't the sweet little Southern belle you thought, and you didn't like it."

91

I see that he's getting ready to deny it, then he changes his mind.

"You're right!" he agrees. "I did think you were different from what you apparently are."

"And?" I press him.

"And I guess I don't want to go out with you anymore."

"Why not, Danny? Why won't you give me a chance to explain why I did what I did? Did you ever stop to think about how I must have felt after having a close friend horribly murdered, then seeing an old man shot to death in my home? That I might have been just a little crazy and that maybe I needed a friend instead of a judge?"

He looks away from me again, then says, "I'm sorry for judging you without an explanation. That was wrong. But so was the stripping."

"It was the only thing I could think to do to draw out that scumbag that killed Becca. Maybe it was way stupid, but it worked. I got me a piece of that son of a bitch!"

"That you did." he agrees. He's looking at me strangely again.

"You get to decide whether you want to date me or not because I stripped," I allow. "But I think it's hypocritical as hell for a guy who'll go to a strip club or have a one-night stand to look down on a girl for making a living."

"But I don't do any of those things. The only time I've ever been in a strip club was in the line of duty as a police officer. I don't believe in one-night stands and I don't think that stripping for a living is moral. That's just who I am!"

His tone of voice takes me aback. He's telling the truth!

"How about showing your titties to catch a killer, like Robyn Carlson did? Where do you draw the line, Danny?"

"I'm not sure," he admits. "I guess I understand why you did it, even though I don't necessarily think it was the right thing to do." He hesitates, then goes on, "I guess I'd like to go out with you again sometime if you want to."

The ball's in my court now and I can slam him if I want to. "Well, how 'bout that dinner tonight? It's still my treat."

"I guess so," he says.

Stripper!

"Why don't you meet me at my place at six thirty?"

Since his PC is not working, Danny decides to bounce. I stay behind to clear up a few more files – I'm not where I need a computer yet. But now I want to see Bobby again, and soon. He's got to get our system back up and running. I realize that I don't have his contact info, but I'm sure I could find him at the Kitten Club nearly any night. I hope it doesn't come to that.

I realize that I haven't heard from Uncle since yesterday afternoon, which is a little unusual. The office is also his home, so he must have left out of here pretty early this morning to be gone when I arrived. I consider giving him a call but decide not to. He's an independent, unreconstructed rebel and he wouldn't take kindly to his niece keeping too close an eye on him.

****

My doorbell rings precisely at six thirty. Even though I know it's Danny, I peer through the peephole before opening the door – what happened to Blackie when he opened that door without checking is way too fresh in my mind. OMG! It's Danny all right, in a jacket and tie? I've changed into my evening jeans and one of Becca's less ostentatious blouses, but I'm nowhere near as formal as him.

I open the door to greet him and his hand comes from behind his back to offer me a bouquet. He got 'em at the supermarket, but still!

He reacts to my shocked expression. "Now don't get the wrong idea, Nattie." he says. "I was such a shitheel earlier that I thought I should make it up to you. Please accept these as my apology."

I don't know what to say, so I just step forward and give him a big hug, then take the flowers and go find a vase.

I decide to take him back to the same steak joint where he took me. And I drive. I can't resist showing off the power and agility of the little red Z car.

"Hey there, Jeff Gordon!" he says. "A ticket from one of my former co-workers would sure put a damper on the evening!"

I obediently slow down and move to the right.

As the hostess is steering us to our table, I wonder if coming back here is such a good idea after all. I'm a very different person than I was when Danny brought me here, half starved. Becca's gone, I'm living on my own, no longer in school and I have a full-time job of sorts. Oh, and by the way, I'm a lesbian? Then what am I doing out on a date with a guy?

As dinner progresses, I find myself really enjoying Danny's company. He's a bit of a boy scout, but he's charming and witty and undeniably hot. We order a couple of beers. As the alcohol takes hold, I'm laughing at his jokes and totally admiring his intelligence and poise. We don't discuss this afternoon's unpleasantness – that's behind us, as it should be.

As the waiter clears the remnants of desert, I'm thoroughly stuffed and maybe just a little drunk. I belatedly remember Rebecca's warning about alcohol. Too late now! I notice the doggy bag containing our leftovers.

"Hey Danny, I've got to know. Did you realize that I was starving the last time we were here, and give me your leftovers?"

He just smiles.

When we get to the car, he says, "Better let me drive, Nattie. You drank as much as I did, and I'm twice your size."

I'm immediately annoyed, but he's right. I've got no business driving.

"I'm perfectly OK," I tell him, "but I know you want a crack at the Z-car." I give him the keys.

When we get back to the townhouse parking lot, the awkward moment arrives yet again. As on our last date, he moves to take my hands to say goodnight. I let him, but before he can say anything, I say, "Why don't you come in for a nightcap?"

I lead him inside and get him settled on the sofa. Our togetherness is interrupted by Xin Niu, who is squalling about being left alone. I take her to the kitchen and get her a can of food.

I call to him in the living room. "What would you like to drink?"

"Whatever you're having."

He raises an eyebrow as I bring him a bottle of Heinie and a glass, accompanied by a shot of Turkey.

"Hey now, I've got to drive home." he says.

"Why?" I ask him and sit on his lap.

Later, in bed, my head is on his chest and he's playing with my hair.

Stripper!

"I told you I don't believe in one-night stands," he says.

"I know you did," I say as I move to kiss him.

I'm dreaming, but it's not the dream. There's music playing – that old familiar song. My eyes open. It's my cell phone, out in the living room.

Danny is dead to the world. I get up naked and walk to the coffee table where I left the phone. I look at the name on the screen.

Leon Kidd.

A cold chill sweeps aside the fog in my head.

"Yes?"

"Natalie. It's Detective Kidd. I'm afraid I have bad news."

I sink to the sofa, clutching the phone so hard my hand hurts.

"What?"

"It's your uncle. He's been stabbed. He's in the ICU at University Hospital. You'd better get down here as quick as you can!"

Chapter 15.

During the day, hospitals are cold and impersonal places at best, but at night they truly suck.

University Hospital occupies several acres on South Campus and looks like a jumble of white concrete blocks haphazardly stacked by a giant child. I want to run right to Uncle Amos' bedside, but I have to stop at reception to find out where in that warren he is.

The guy behind the counter is a little balding thirtysomething who looks annoyed that someone is making him work. He puts down his magazine and takes his time checking the computer.

"Yes, we have an Amos Murdoch in ICU," he says.

I struggle to be polite. "We'd like to see him. How do we get to ICU?"

"Only one visitor at a time in ICU. Which one of you is going in?"

"I'm his niece. I am."

"Here. Fill this out." He hands me a clipboard with a form.

"Why?"

"It's the rules. For your badge."

I try not to lose it as I fill out the form, which demands way too much information for a simple hospital visit. In addition to my name, address and phone number, they want my social and my occupation, place of employment, how long I was there, etc. I hope Uncle doesn't die in the time it takes for all this bullshit.

I'm finally done and I hand it back.

"I need your ID."

Luckily, I remembered to grab my wallet as I rushed out to see my critically injured uncle.

"Look here!" He's waving his hand above a camera mounted on the reception desk. I look that way and a light flashes. More waiting for the picture to come out. Finally, he hands me a badge on a lanyard. My picture looks like you'd expect.

"Wear that at all times in the hospital," he says. "ICU is in B wing. Take the elevator to five and follow the signs."

I head for the elevator and Danny starts to come with me, only to be stopped by the flunky behind the counter.

"Sir! You can't go up without a badge!"

"Go, Nattie! I'll catch up."

Everything is in slow-mo - waiting for the elevator, the ride up to five. The door opens and the caustic medicinal odor that permeates this place assaults me. I find ICU on the overhead sign and notice a blue square next to it. WTF? Then I see the lines on the wall – red, blue, green, yellow, orange, brown. I navigate the seemingly endless, meandering hallways, following the blue line. Eventually I end up at a pair of glass double doors labelled *Intensive Care Unit*. Of course they're locked and no one's at the counter inside.

I push a button on the wall. More waiting. Finally, a nurse in pink hospital scrubs comes. I ask for Amos Murdoch and thankfully, she leads me straight to him.

He's lying on a bed in a glass-walled room, where he can be constantly observed. He's uncovered, probably so all the tubes and wires don't get tangled.

"How is he?" I ask the nurse.

"Critical, but stable," she says. "Beyond that, you'll have to ask the doctor."

"When can I see him?"

"She makes her rounds around seven a.m. You can talk to her then."

Three hours from now.

Chilly air slaps me in the face as I slide open the door. The medicinal odor is almost overpowering, laced with an undercurrent of sweat and excrement. The room is strictly utilitarian with an uncomfortable-looking vinyl chair next to the bed. Not a place that you want to spend time in.

Uncle looks very small and terribly old in that bed. Scads of wires and tubes connect him to gently humming machines. His skin is sallow, his face is scraped and bruised and his hair is sticking out at all angles. I try to smooth it with my hand but it pops right back up again. His forehead is cool to the touch – too cool, I wonder?

Uncle Amos is my mother's brother. We didn't see much of him when I was a kid because we lived in a different city, so I didn't know him very well. When I was accepted to State, Mom asked him to keep an eye on me, which I resented at first. One day we got to talking about his work. I found it fascinating – in his younger days, Uncle Amos didn't always devote himself to exposing insurance scammers. When I expressed an interest in learning more about becoming a private investigator, he bowled me over by offering me a job! He even got me a private investigator trainee's license from the state, of which I'm prouder than I like to let on. I didn't know it then, but it was Uncle Amos' strong sense of family that was responsible for that job offer. That same sense is why he fired me when he had reason to believe I might get hurt working for him.

Standing there looking at him, precariously clinging to life by the strands connecting him to those nurturing instruments that demean him somehow, I realize that I've come to love him.

A while later, the nurse tells me that Danny is outside. She reminds me that only one person at a time is allowed back here – given the cramped quarters, I see now that the rule makes sense.

I ask her, "My uncle is not in any danger of dying soon, is he?"

"He's stable for the moment," she says. "That's really all I can tell you."

I decide to take a chance and go out to talk to Danny.

Danny is perched on a chair similar to the one in Uncle Amos' room. He looks like hell. Both of us basically just pulled on yesterday's clothes and rushed over here without so much as brushing our hair.

"How is he?" Danny asks.

I repeat what the nurse told me. "Hey, you don't have to stay here," I tell him. "I'm going to wait until the doctor comes and talk to her to find out how long he's going to be in ICU. If he's not in any immediate danger, I can always get a bus home later this morning."

"Not on my watch," Danny says. "I'll stay until you're ready, then I'll take you home." He hesitates, then says, "Look. While you were in there, I talked to Detective Kidd."

"And?"

98

Stripper!

"Believe it or not, a homeless guy found Amos in a vacant lot on Lee Street not far from the Kitten Club. He found a patrol car and told them about it. The cops found Amos' pickup parked on a side street not far away from the lot."

"Wow! We were lucky that cops were there."

"It wasn't luck. That neighborhood is a known trouble spot, so a patrol car drives around every half hour or so. The homeless guy knew it because he's usually trying to avoid the cops instead of finding them."

"When did they find Uncle Amos?"

"Real early this morning. He'd been robbed, so he had no ID on him when they brought him in. It's hospital protocol to take photos of all the John Does every day and send them to the cops to see if anyone can identify them. Kidd spotted Amos' picture, came over here to verify that it was him, and then called you."

It hurts to hear Danny refer to Uncle as a John Doe. But I guess that's what he was.

"So somebody nearly killed him for the few bucks he generally carries," I say unbelievingly. "But what the hell was he doing down there at night?"

"You think he just went to see some titty?" Danny asks tactlessly.

"No way!" I spit Danny with a glare for suggesting it. "Uncle Amos is as straight-laced as any bible-banging preacher! If he went to the Kitten Club, he had another reason, and it would have had to be a pretty damn good one."

"I wonder if it had anything to do with Robyn Carlson?" Danny mused. "I thought we closed that case."

"Maybe it did. Uncle Amos has a strong sense of personal responsibility. If he thought that our actions had anything to do with Robyn's disappearance, it would be just like him to try and lend a hand to find the person responsible."

"How could our surveillance have had anything to do with what happened to her?"

"It was me that blew the surveillance, but Uncle would feel responsible for that since I was working for him. My confrontation with Robyn in the parking lot was pretty public. We don't really know who all saw it or heard about it. If she was there undercover to investigate the club's involvement in the drug trade and the wrong people got wind of it, it could have made her a target."

"I guess that's possible," Danny agrees. "And the same people who took Robyn could have hurt Amos because he was nosing around."

"I'm sure that's what happened. This is all my fault!"

"You don't know that, Nattie! If what you say is true, then Amos had no business going down there without backup."

"You don't know him like I do, Danny. That's exactly what he would do."

"Well look, I'm sure Kidd has already thought of most of this, but just in case he hasn't, I'll mention it the next time I talk to him. Right now, let's just focus on Amos."

"I'm going back in with him until the doctor comes." I turn to open the door to ICU.

"Well, bring him out here to talk so I can hear too." Danny calls after me.

Time creeps by in a hospital, especially in ICU. The feeling of helplessness is overwhelming. But the nurse's statement has eased my fear of Uncle's imminent death, so my thoughts have nowhere to turn but inward.

Why did I have sex with Danny? Was it to prove to myself that I'm not a lesbian? I know him well enough to realize that he's a fine, honorable guy, and I guess I'm attracted to him. But is an intimate relationship what I want right now? I guess it better be, because Danny told me I'm no one night stand. And he's sure in no hurry to bolt and leave me here on my own. But what about the feelings I had for Becca, and seem to have for Rebecca? God, I'm so confused!

An errant thought intrudes. I step outside and find the nurse's station. The nurse in the pink scrubs who I talked to earlier is there.

"Can I help you?"

"That coffee sure smells good," I say.

She smiles at me and pours a cup. "You take anything in it?" she asks.

"Black is fine."

"Hope you like it. Nurses are famous for their strong coffee. Only way to get through the graveyard shift."

I take a sip and discover that she isn't kidding. I wait a beat, then get to the real reason I came out here.

Stripper!

"Look, this is going to sound strange, but I wonder if there would be a hand-held UV light around here?"

"What for?"

"It might help me find out where my uncle was when he was hurt."

She looks at me strangely, then says, "Go on back in with your Uncle. I'll check the lab and bring one if I find it."

Ten minutes later she comes into Uncle Amos' room and hands me the light. "You have to plug it in,' she tells me. "Here."

Once it's powered, I thumb the button. I direct the light to back of Uncle Amos' right hand. A vivid green caricature of a cat springs to life! He did go into the Kitten Club!

I give it back to the nurse with thanks, and she goes on her way.

Finally, the doctor arrives. She's a cute, petite Indian woman shorter than me, who looks like she's still in high school. Per Danny's request, I take her outside to the waiting room.

"Your uncle is a very lucky man," she says. "If the knife had gone in an inch to the right, his kidney would have been sliced in half and he would have exsanguinated. Even so, he's lost a great deal of blood. The fact that he's in very poor physical condition is not helping him."

"What do you mean, poor physical condition?"

"He's morbidly overweight and he has diabetes," she says. "That will slow his healing greatly."

"How much longer will he be in ICU?"

"Right now, he's in a coma, doubtless due to a combination of shock and blood loss." She speaks with that precise rhythm particular to many Indians. "I'd like to keep him here a couple of more days, until I'm sure he is recovering."

"He's not going to…" I can't bring myself to say it.

"I don't think so. But if he's here in ICU we can react quickly and aggressively to any emergency."

After she's gone, I tell Danny, "I guess there's nothing more we can do here. Let's go back to the townhouse and get a few hours more sleep. I'll come back this afternoon."

The ride is silent. Now that I know that Uncle is likely to live, my fear rapidly turns to anger at the lowlife who did this! The hand stamp proves that he went into the Kitten Club, so it's a good bet that something he saw or someone in there did this to him. By the time we pull into the parking lot, I know what I have to do. And Danny's not gonna like it one bit!

Chapter 16.

Two nights later, I pull the Z-car into the Kitten Club's parking lot. As I was certain we would, Danny and I had a terrible fight over the course of action I've decided upon. We're not speaking and any relationship we had is gone. That makes me sad, but I'm doing what I have to!

Bobby is my other problem. He knows who I am and the Kitten Club is his second home. I had to tell him what I'm up to, to be sure he won't give me away. Not too surprisingly, he was OK with it, largely because he thinks he'll get off watching me dance on a pole.

Jesse is still manning the door. There's no sign of recognition as I extend my hand for the stamp. He's probably seen a thousand girls like me go through that door.

It's early, about seven thirty in the evening, so the crowd is still sparse. A couple of topless girls are on poles, each surrounded by a little coterie of devotees. Bobby is nowhere to be seen. As I watch, a guy reaches up and offers a bill to one of the girls. She swings around the pole and gracefully snatches it, then places it in her thong. She kneels on the runway and leans down to give him a big sloppy kiss. Yuk!

Is this what I really want to do? A picture of Uncle in that hospital bed pops into my head, with all those wires and tubes coming out of him. I walk straight over to the bar and shout to the bartender, who looks like a State student barely old enough to be in here, that I'm looking for a job. He scopes me out. I've dressed for the part in one of Becca's filmy see-through blouses with a skimpy pink bra underneath, over a tight pink miniskirt, heels and stockings. His ogling makes me uncomfortable. I'll totally have to get over that if I'm going to pull this off.

He tells me to wait, then motions to the other bartender to come over. It's Valery. Again I shout my reason for being here. He nods expressionlessly and signals me to wait, picks up a phone on the wall behind the bar, holds the receiver to one ear and puts his hand over the other to shut out the blaring music. Seems like his arm has gotten better over the last week. After a moment he hangs up, then indicates a metal door at the end of the bar.

"You can go on back," he says. As I get up to go to the door, he reaches under the bar with one hand.

The metal door is just like the one that leads in here from the parking lot - gray, featureless and heavy. I push down on the handle and shove it open. Inside is a short, fluorescent-lit hallway that smells of disinfectant. The music cuts off abruptly as the door closes – only the dull thump of the baseline penetrates. There's a wooden door at the other end. As I approach it, I see an engraved gold sign - *Judd Horaz. Proprietor.* Cute.

The door has a push-down handle, not a knob, with a built-in keypad above it that contains five buttons.

I knock. No response for a few seconds, then the door opens.

The guy who opened it is barely taller than me. He's twice as wide though, and has a puffy face. A livid scar runs from just next to his right eye across his cheek, terminating at his mouth. His crew cut is so intensely blonde, it's got to be bleached. He's wearing a dark, expensive-looking suit over a white business shirt with no tie. His expression instantly changes from one of bored disinterest to anger as he sees me.

"You've got a lotta goddamn nerve comin' back here!" he says.

I shy against the wall as he clenches his fist and draws back his arm as if to hit me.

"What? I've never been here before in my life!"

He's followed me out into the hall and got me pinned in the corner. But my outburst seems to have saved me, for the moment at least. He backs off and checks me out again, and the anger leaves his face to be replaced with a sheepish grin. I'm not sure which expression I like least, the glare or the grin.

"I'm sorry," he says. "I mistook you for somebody else. Please come in." I hesitate. I bet I know who he thought I was! Seeing my reluctance, he says, "I won't hurt you. I promise. Come in." He stands aside and extends a hand.

I accept his invitation to enter the office. It's a large room, nearly 20' by 20', totally inappropriate for a strip club, paneled in rich dark wood and suffused with the aroma of pipe tobacco. It's furnished in an oriental style with garish pottery, statues of mythical creatures and a huge carved desk of gold-trimmed ebony. A tapestry hanging on rings is behind the desk, brightly lit by a lamp mounted on either side. It depicts two nude oriental women in a garden, lying so that each is inspecting the other's genitals. The detail is rich enough that I can feel myself reddening, and despite my present circumstances, it sparks an incipient sexual tingle.

The rest of the walls are lined with shelves that contain smaller sculptures and oriental pottery, many of them with erotic motifs as well. The carpet is a lush deep burgundy shag, and there's a large rug atop of it in the center of the room, also sporting nude oriental figures engaged in unabashed sexual activity. Makes sense that this guy would run a strip club.

The last of the noise from the club outside vanishes as he closes the door to the hallway. I think furiously as he moves away. I know that Becca's been here, and that the meeting did not go well. I'm crazy to know what happened, but now is not the time to bring that up if I want to get hired here.

Horaz looks me up and down like I'm a centerfold. "I'm Judd Horaz," he says. "I own this club. So you think you want to be a stripper?"

"I know I do, Mr. Horaz." The answer makes him smile.

"How come? By the way, you can call me Judd."

I raise my right hand and rub my thumb and forefinger together. He smiles again.

"OK," he says. He places a straight back chair with the back facing me and sits down bassackwards about three feet away. His eyes are level with my chest.

"Strip."

"What?" Here? Now?

"You say you want to be a stripper. So strip!"

This is the last thing I expected! To buy a little time, I say, "I thought it would be outside. You know, on a pole, with the music..."

"I need to see whatcha got before I put you out with my customers. Strip, or hit the road!"

You want the job or not, Nattie?

This is totally different than the webcam, where I couldn't see my audience, or in the heat of the moment when I was with Danny. I know that my body is being evaluated like a side of meat and I don't like it. No woman would! I struggle to put myself in a sexy mood. Not happening!

I undo the buttons on my blouse, one at a time. Judd just sits there with that penetrating stare, and his arms wrapped around the back of the chair. His face remains expressionless as I slide off the blouse and drop it on the floor. It's warm in here, and a rivulet of sweat runs into my skimpy pink bra. The skirt is next - it comes off quickly when I undo the zipper on the side. I reach for the bra clasp and hesitate. Judd's face is still frozen like one of his hideous statues.

I don't know why, but instead of taking off the bra, I grab the panties by both sides and inch them down, scrutinizing his face for any sign of arousal. I let them fall around my ankles, step out with one leg, then kick with the other foot to launch them at Judd's face. Quick as a snake, his hand darts up to catch them. There's a glimmer of a smile.

I reach back, undo the bra and flip that at him as well. I should have known that the same trick wouldn't work twice – he just lets it hit him, then shrugs to shake it off on the floor.

He gets up from the chair and approaches me as I stand there in nothing but my heels and stockings. Hands behind his back and still expressionless, he leans toward me until his face is inches from my body, then he sinks down on his haunches, taking in every detail. He's staring at my crotch now, and I hear him inhale deeply through his nose. I realize that he's done this to other girls before and he's trying to make me as uncomfortable as he can, so I steel myself and take it. I wonder if he did this to Becca, and how she reacted?

He stands up and circles behind me. I keep my eyes resolutely forward, but I know he's going through the same drill because I can feel his warm breath on my flesh.

Finished with his examination, he turns the chair around the right way and sits down. "Not bad," he says.

Not bad? You son of a bitch!

Now a leer appears on his face. "One more thing. Come over here and give me a lap dance!"

I can just get dressed and slink out of here if I want to. But that's not why I came.

I stalk towards him as sensually as I can. He clasps his hands behind the chair and raises his crotch to me. I step forward and straddle him, then inch down slowly until I'm brushing against him. Every nerve in my body is screaming for me to get out of there. But I won't give him the satisfaction!

106

Stripper!

I gyrate my hips against the cloth of his trousers. The wool tickles my genitals and is vaguely arousing. My breasts are an inch from his face. He's still grinning as he looks up into my eyes. Unexpectedly his arms erupt from behind the chair to clasp me behind my back, pulling my nipple to his mouth! I almost bolt then, but I recover, then slowly move my breasts back and forth across his face.

He lets me service him that way for a minute, then pulls my head down to kiss me on the mouth. He pushes his tongue inside. He tastes neutral, but the sick sweet smell of alcohol is on his breath ‑ it makes me want to gag. I hesitate, but then I remember the dancer outside who I saw kissing a customer, so I kiss him back. He enjoys it for a moment, then lets me go, moving his hands to my hips and pushing me off his lap. I step away from him as he rises from the chair.

"Come over here," he says, moving toward the hideous carved desk.

I follow him. My foot catches on a bump beneath the Oriental rug, and I nearly pitch forward on my face, but I manage to recover. The desk is huge, about six feet by three, with a polished wood top covered with papers and file folders. There's a crystal decanter containing an amber liquid and three matching tumblers sitting on a teakwood tray.

Judd sweeps the papers off onto the floor, creating a clear space. "Lie down on your back and spread 'em." His hands move to his belt buckle.

"No."

"What did you say?"

"I said no. I'm auditioning for a job as a dancer, not as a whore!"

"You're auditioning for a job to do whatever the hell I tell you to! Now lay down on the desk!"

"No!"

His hands leave his belt and he stalks towards me, glaring angrily, but when I remain where I am and glare back, he slowly breaks into a smile. "OK," he says. "That's exactly right. You want to make extra money hooking on the side, that's fine by me. But in my club, you make no deals for sex with the customers. You want to go home with a customer, you don't mention money while you're on the property, either inside or in the parking lot."

All business now, he sits behind the desk and removes a folder from a drawer. "Take that and fill it out after you get dressed. You can use that table over there.

Then you can go to the locker room behind the stage. Ask Nan to get you a rig and put you on a pole. She'll fill you in on the rest."

He picks up the papers on the floor and doesn't spare me another glance while I get dressed. I'm surprised that he didn't ask me to do it naked.

The paperwork is a contract between me and the Kitten Club. After my "interview", I figure I'd better read it.

"This can't be right! It says here that I have to pay you a $50 stage fee a night to dance here. I get no salary, just tips. And there's no health insurance, paid vacation or sick time."

"That's the standard contract that all my dancers sign, honey. Look at the bright side. Anything you make over that fifty bucks is yours to keep. Because you're an independent contractor, we don't do withholding, so what you tell Uncle Sam is up to you."

"And what if I make less than $50?"

"Then you're one sorry ass dancer and you need to find another line of work!"

"What about your waitresses and bartenders? They don't make tips like the dancers do."

"They're employees, not contractors. We pay 'em a wage and give 'em some bennies. And by the way, they'll expect you to give some of your tips to them – ten percent is usual. But look, a good dancer can make $1,000 a night, so a hundred is peanuts. And I'm giving you a nice, safe place to work."

Wow. That this kind of shit exists is why I want to go to law school! I don't have a choice if I want the job. I sign the contract. He says nothing as I give it to him, so I bounce and go find Nan.

The club is more crowded now. The music hits me in the face like a punch. I pray it doesn't take me long to find out what happened to Uncle, or I'll go deaf. I barely hear the hoots and catcalls from the audience as I go up the short staircase alongside the stage. Behind the curtain is another metal door. I open it and step into a brightly lit room where three naked women are sitting on a central bench with a row of lockers on either side. I shut the door and the music subsides to a dull vibration, then I approach a short black girl.

"Nan?"

Stripper!

"She's out on a pole. Should be back in soon."

"You're new?" The speaker is a skinny white girl with short black hair and fine, chiseled features.

"Yeah. I'm Kira." I had to use my real name on the paperwork, but there's no reason I can't use a stage name when I'm dancing.

"Hi Kira," the black girl says. "I'm Shalyla."

"Summer," the black-haired white girl says.

"I'm Annie." The girl on the other side of Summer is also white and has shoulder length red hair.

"So you just went through Judd's interview," Shalyla says. "I hope you didn't let him fuck you!" The other girls laugh.

"No I didn't," I tell them. "Did any of you?"

That gets peals of laughter. "Not hardly, honey," says Summer. "But you've got to watch out for him. He doesn't give up!"

We chat for a while. I learn that Shalyla is new too, here only about three months. Summer is an old timer, here nearly three years.

"What about you, Annie?"

"Coming up on a year." She places a familiar hand on Summer's shoulder. "Summer got me the gig."

I'm aching to ask about Uncle Amos, but I know it's not the time and I totally haven't figured out how to go about it yet.

Summer points to the large clock on the wall above the entrance to the showers. "Hey girls! We go on in five! Let's get dressed!"

Getting dressed is not complicated. Each girl puts on a miniscule bikini from her locker and grabs a feather boa.

"Why bother?" I ask no one.

"Hey, you gots to have a place to put the tips!" says Shalyla.

The room is suddenly filled with the thumping music from outside as three more girls enter. One is in her 40's, but her near nudity revels she's still in great shape. The second one is a dark-skinned Hispanic girl about my age, who is even a little shorter than me and has a black shoulder length hair, big soulful eyes and large, pillowy breasts with very large nipples. The last girl is drop dead gorgeous, a statuesque strawberry blonde with perfect, natural breasts– she would make the cover of any national girlie magazine. Unlike the other girls, she's carrying a see-thru Teddy and wearing only a G-string that leaves nothing to the imagination, stuffed full of cash. WTF is she doing in a dump like this?

I clench my teeth against the music as Shalyla, Summer and Annie go out. The other ladies stuff their cash inside their lockers. When she's finished, the blonde gives me a quick smile and a "Hi! I'm Kathie," as she scampers back outside. The older lady extends her hand.

I take it. "You must be Nan? I'm Kira."

"How'd you guess?" She indicates the Hispanic girl. "This is Lupe."

"Hi, Lupe." She smiles shyly but doesn't respond to my greeting.

"Lupe doesn't say much," says Nan. "We're trying to change that by helping her with her English." She gives me the once over. You're new," she says unnecessarily. "Did you bring an outfit?"

"No, ma'am." It seems like the right thing to call her.

She smiles. "Well, I reckon we can find something you'll fit into for tonight. You won't be wearing it long." She gives me a long hard once over. "You look familiar."

"I get that a lot. I must have one of those faces."

"Ever danced before?"

"Yes, on a webcam."

"Well, this is going to be a little different, then. After we get you dressed, go outside, stay behind the curtain and watch the other girls for a bit before you take a pole. Find you any empty pole and have at it. Judd tell you about the tip schedule?"

I shake my head.

"If somebody gives you a dollar, give him a peck on the cheek and stay on the stage. A kiss on the mouth is five bucks, ten for some tongue. A lap dance is twenty and up and happens in a booth. Just hop off the stage and lead him over there. If somebody slips you a Benjamin, you can make up your own mind about what you want to do."

110

She goes on. "About the lap dances. Some clubs have a no touching rule. We don't. If a customer tries to go too far when you're with him in an alcove, try to calm him down. Threatening to leave the booth generally works. Most of our customers are pretty sorry with the ladies and are just here to make a connection with a woman the only way they know how. As a last resort, there's a button you can push to alert security. Don't try to fight a horny guy off by yourself! But don't use those buttons too damn often either, or Judd will get pissed and fire you! As long as there's no sex in the booths we won't get hassled."

"What do you call sex?"

"Who are you, Bill Clinton? Naked contact with the private parts, his or yours. As long as his clothes stay on, you're pretty much okay." She hesitates, then says, "Some of the other girls might tell you they go a little further than that. If they do, I don't want to know! Just make sure that anything you do, he asks you first. If he's a cop and he asks you, that's entrapment."

I try to keep a neutral expression, but inwardly, I'm full of dread. Now I know why Becca chose to dance online! I totally don't know if I can do this!

Nan rummages through a hamper near the showers and hands me a top, a thong and a boa. "Leave the top on for a few minutes to get them jacked up. Make sure you drop it on stage – if it's too close to the edge or you throw it in the crowd, you'll never see it again. The sets are about twenty minutes long. There's a red light above the bar and another above the booths that will come on when it's time for a break. To start with, just do every other set. When you've been doing this for a while, you can dance as long as you can stand it while the crowd is hot." A beat. "You didn't bring a lock, did you?"

I shake my head.

"Your clothes will be all right in an unlocked locker. Better give me your wallet and keys, though. I'll put them in my locker for tonight. You can get them at closing time."

"When's that?"

"One o'clock. Give your stage fee and staff tip to me before you leave."

The wall clock says it's only a quarter to eight. It's gonna be a long night!

111

Chapter 17.

A s Nan advised, I watch the other girls perform before going out. They're all topless now, and all of them have different dancing styles.

Shalyla is the least experienced. The music doesn't seem to have anything to do with her moves on the pole. She just hangs on to it and makes no attempt to do anything more complicated than swing around or rub her chubby body up and down it. She's got a group of four admirers watching her avidly, but no one is offering any tips yet.

Summer and Annie are more acrobatic. Both girls have climbed half way up their poles and are doing spins, supporting themselves with their arms. They watch each other as if they're trying to coordinate their movements. When they tire, they drop to the stage and perform moves similar to Shalyla's, but it's obvious that they're more practiced and graceful. Setting foot on the stage seems to be the signal for tips – in the space of two or three minutes, each girl has smooched about half a dozen guys. Not bad at five to ten bucks a pop! None of their admirers seem to be up for a lap dance yet, though. Probably saving their money for later in the evening.

Lupe is as agile as a jaguar. She spends a lot of time on her pole – her compact body makes it easy for her to hang on by her legs as well as her arms and she has a good repertoire of spins. By the time she's through, she has several guys in line for lap dances.

Kathie is by far and away the star of the show. Unlike the other girls, she's completely nude, wearing only a gold string tight around her waist as a place to put money. She spends most of her time on the pole, seemingly oblivious of the crowd of guys on either side of the stage who are frantically waving banknotes. Her moves are smooth, accomplished and elegant – as a former high school gymnast, I can appreciate the difficultly of some of them, especially when she spins around the pole hands-free, supported only by her legs, seemingly defying gravity with her long blonde hair streaming down. When she finally descends to the stage, she gives them a floor show to rival Becca's performance with the toy on the settee, using only her hands. One guy tries to climb up on the stage with her, but his comrades grab him by the shoulders and pull him back. Finally she stands up and appraises the waving bills, plucks one from the lucky winner's hand, then hops off the stage and leads him to an alcove. She's gone about ten minutes, then returns with her disheveled Lothario shuffling along at heel. She doesn't even return to the stage – she just chooses another guy from the pack, takes his money and leads him off.

As I watch the girls and their devotees, I truly understand why Becca chose the path that she did. The little groups of guys gathered around each pole dancer remind me of wolves, drooling as they watch their prey. I so totally do not want to go out on that stage. But I can't just trust the cops to get to the bottom of Uncle's stabbing any more than he could trust them to find out what happened to Robyn. I grit my teeth and step out from behind the curtain.

At first, no one seems to notice me. Three runways extend from the stage out into the crowd and each holds four poles. Kathie has the one nearest the alcoves all to herself while the other three girls are dancing on the one in the middle. There's an empty pole available at the end of the middle runway and the runway nearest the bar has no dancers. After a moment's thought, I opt for that one.

A couple of guys notice me as I walk over there, but no one moves to meet me. I take the pole nearest to the curtain and begin slowly swinging around it, holding on with one hand. I'm still wearing my top – doesn't seem to be much point in taking it off with nobody watching. The boa keeps sliding off my neck, so I dispense with it. I'm beginning to feel like a wallflower at a high school prom, worried sick that no one will ask me to dance!

Round and round I go, all undressed and nobody cares! Then one of the guys watching Summer notices me and hits a companion on the shoulder. OMG, it's Bobby! I knew this was going to happen. He grabs his beer, gets up and wends his way through the crowd towards me, taking the table directly in front of my pole. A couple of his mates follow.

So now I've got my audience. There are four of them now, all regarding me with an expression like a cat watching a mouse. I take another couple of turns around the pole to get my emotions under control, then I stop spinning, put my back against the ice-cold pole and summon up a smile for my fans, such as they are. I begin sliding my back up and down the pole, reaching behind me for the string that holds my top in place. Naturally, the boys start clapping and cheering, but that only makes me more apprehensive. There's a club rule that no patron can set foot on the runway, but what if they do? I've never felt so vulnerable in my life! I undo the knot and slide the top off as slowly and sensuously as I can and the guys become even more animated. I hold the bra out towards them at arm's length, and they come up out of their chairs, arms extended, like little kids reaching for Halloween candy. I remember what Nan said and drop the bra on the stage where they can't get it. I hear the groans of dismay even over the booming music. I begin to understand that I'm in control here, not them.

Might as well give them a pole dance. I grab the pole with my hands, pull myself up, clasp my legs around it and shinny halfway up. My shoulders immediately groan in protest and the bullet crease, which I've hidden with some pancake, totally begins to burn. I let go with one hand and lean backwards, thrusting my breasts towards the boys, evoking the desired response. Bobby is particularly appreciative, jumping to his feet. A chill runs through me. I think that I'm beginning to like the attention!

High school was a long time ago! I find that I can only spend about two or three minutes on the pole before I have to drop back to the runway to give my aching body a rest. My landing is awkward and I nearly stumble forward toward the edge of the runway where the boys are, but I manage to recover and make the move appear deliberate. OMG, the guys are waving bills at me now! A quick look tells me that I'm faced with two fives and a twenty – Bobby wants a lap dance!

I move to the edge of the stage as I saw the other girls do and let the guys tuck the money into my thong. As the first one reaches for me, I pull back a little just to enjoy the hurt look on his face, then I let him slide the bill in. The second one cops a feel as he pays me, and I ignore it as the price of doing business. I lean down and kiss one of the five-dollar boys. He's got his hands behind his back because club protocol is that you can't put your hands on a dancer, at least not out here on the main floor. The kiss couldn't be more asexual - I can smell the beer on his breath and his lips are dry and cracked. I linger a little more over the second one because I'm dreading what comes next, and he tries to slip me some tongue. I draw back quickly and slap him, pulling it at the last second so not to hurt him. He grins at me like he earned the slap.

Finally, I sit down on the edge of the stage where Bobby is waiting with a Jackson and a big, shit-eating grin.

I'm so totally not looking forward to this. I take him by the hand and lead him over to the alcoves. There's a red light above the door of the one that Kathie's using, so I open the one next to it. The stall stinks of sweat, tobacco, weed, and urine. I see a light switch on the inside door frame with a red push button beneath it – that must be the panic button that Nan told me about. I flip the switch and a lone straight back chair is bathed in the glow of the single naked light bulb. There's also a plywood bench along the back wall.

Stripper!

As I shut the door, Bobby sits down in the chair. The door is surprisingly solid and the volume of that damned music drops off so conversation is actually possible.

"I wanted to be your first customer, Kira," Bobby says. "I hope you don't mind." He holds out the twenty.

I start to tell him not to call me that, but then I remember it's my name in this place. I take his money and tuck it into my thong.

"You don't look happy about this," Bobby says.

I try to force a smile, but it doesn't come. Then I decide to try a little honesty.

"Bobby, it's not you." Oh yes it is! "It's just that it's the first time I've ever done anything like this. It's gonna take some getting used to."

His expression is surprisingly sympathetic. "I figured. That's one of the reasons I wanted to be your first customer." He hesitates, then says, "You know that you can't not do lap dances if you want to work here, right? And you need to work here if you want to find out what happened to your uncle."

"I know it, Bobby."

He opens his arms. "So c'mon. Use me to get used to it. I promise I won't try anything too nasty." He really does look concerned. "C'mon," he says again.

I go to him, sit on his lap facing him, and put my hands on his shoulders. I see him wince, so I let go.

"No, it's just my sunburn," he says. "It's okay."

I put my hands back and grip his shoulders lightly, then begin slowly gyrating my hips. True to his word, he just sits there grinning, watching my breasts undulate in front of his face. I have no idea how long I'm supposed to do this, then it occurs to me that I've got an expert right here.

"How long do lap dances last?"

He smiles. "Never long enough. Ten minutes or so, I guess. And they usually end with a kiss."

I service him a while longer. I can feel him growing beneath my hips. Why do guys like this? It seems like an exercise in frustration to me.

I plant a long kiss on his lips. At first, he accepts it passively, then he starts to open his mouth, slowly. I think he's giving me a chance to back off. I hesitate, then I grab his face give him a full tongue kiss.

As I rise from his lap he says, "Wow! Now that wasn't so bad, was it?"

Yes, Bobby, it was very bad, right up there with the worst things I've ever done. "I guess not," I tell him.

"I'll tell everybody how great you were, so you get lots of customers. And you let me know if anybody acts up, and I'll take care of them!"

What are you gonna do Bobby? Most of the dancers in here could kick your little white ass, never mind the patrons!

I take Bobby's hand to help him out of the chair and lead him back outside.

The sharp smell of marijuana assaults my nostrils as I open the door. Bobby smells it too. He takes my shoulder and holds me back while he searches the club floor for the smoker.

"Watch out," he says, pulling me back inside the alcove, leaving the door open.

Seemingly out of nowhere, two large guys who look like tight ends from State weave through the tables, converging on one. I can see a guy sitting there with his hand cupped near his face. The smoker! One of the bouncers steps up behind the smoker's chair, grabs the back of it and pulls out and up. The chair pops out from under the smoker's ass, dumping him on the floor. The other gorilla reaches down, grabs a handful of shirt collar, and hauls the miscreant to his feet. When the smoker is upright, Bubba grabs his victim by the belt, hoists him high overhead and makes his way to the exit. He opens the door and literally throws the unfortunate customer out into the parking lot.

"I didn't want you to get involved in that." Bobby shouts. "Judd has a strict no drugs policy in the club, and he means it."

Over the next few hours I realize that this is totally just a job. Of course, I wouldn't be here if not for Uncle, but if I'm gonna find out who hurt him, I'll need to blend in. So I have to suck it up. As I dance, I begin to learn how to manipulate my audience. If I don't like what they're doing, I tone down my act, and when they're being good boys, they get a reward – I shake my titties in someone's face or briefly pull back my G-string so they can glance a snatch. I

116

even started to leave the stage at one point just to see how they'd react, and the looks of dismay were downright funny! Maybe I can get used to this.

As the evening wears on, all of the girls come out on stage for all of the sets. Nan takes the pole next to mine. Her body has seen better days, but she sure makes up for it with experience. That lady can play the guys like a violin! Part of the crowd she attracts spills over to me. I wonder if that's why she chose this spot. I see that a lot of guys treat this place like a county fair, moving from one attraction to the next.

It doesn't take me long to discover that I'm way out of shape for pole dancing. At one point while I'm trying to do a spin, I lose my grip and thump my ass hard on the stage, earning a round of guffaws from my audience. I find that I have to take Nan's advice and rest every other set. By the end of the evening I'm dancing like Shalyla, just circling the pole without even trying to climb it.

Back in the locker room, I count my take. A hundred and fifty bucks, for what, five, six hours work? After the stage fee and the staff tip, I'm barely making minimum wage! No wonder Becca chose the Internet gig!

Nan comes over with a manila envelope to collect.

"Don't worry, baby," she says. "This is typical for a first-timer. Soon you'll learn to pace yourself so you can do every set when the crowd is hot. Look, before you come in tomorrow, put on some perfume and make up. Fix your hair. Shave your legs and your snatch. Get yourself a good pair of high heels and some sexy outfits. Remember to play the guys. Try to put some life in your lap dances and word will get out. You're pretty cute and you can do a lot better than this!"

Great. My first pep talk from my stripper mom. Now there's a high point in my life!

Chapter 18.

O ver the next few days, I settle into my job. I guess it's true that you can get used to anything. While I'll never be a fan of tongue kissing guys I don't know and shaking my titties in their faces, it gets easier because I just pretend they're not there. I've always been somewhat of a tomboy and I've never liked primping – besides, since I'm way cute, I've never really had to. But I take Nan's advice and get myself prettied up before my next outing. I'm sure not at a loss for sexy clothes – Becca saw to that.

Even though I shouldn't be, I'm surprised to find out that besides Bobby, a half a dozen or so of the club regulars were clients of Kira Foxxx. Some of them I danced for, and Becca must have danced for the others. None of them seems to notice that I'm not her. They've started congregating around my pole and bringing their friends. Each night, my take improves.

I learn about my fellow dancers between sets. It's quickly apparent that Annie and Summer are lesbians and partners. There's a rumor that Lupe is gay as well, but she keeps to herself so nobody seems to know for sure. I wonder how a gay woman gets into this.

An Internet dancer never sees her clients. I guess I found that kind of performing sexy because most of it was in my head. I hate the club dancing because I don't like being touched by the guys and I don't like being eyeballed like a side of meat. Maybe it's easier for a lesbian, because it takes all of the sex out of it. So does that mean that I'm not one?

Investigating is difficult. I can't just grill the girls in the locker room. When we're all leaving to go home one night, I try to start a conversation about the safety of the neighborhood. I'm hoping that somebody will mention what happened to Uncle, since he got attacked only a few nights ago. But it seems like nobody even knows that it happened.

"I carry a tube of mace in my hand on the way to the car," says Shelby, a thirtysomething transplant from Manhattan. "Anybody who tries to fuck with me will get a face full."

Turns out that most of the girls carry some form of defense. Nan has a taser and Liz, another girl who wasn't here on my first night, has one too. Annie and Summer go everywhere together and rely on each other for protection. Kathie doesn't carry anything. "Any guy tries to mess with me, I'll just fuck him till he drops," she says. "Then I can cut his heart out!"

I'd love to tell her how well being unarmed worked for Becca. The cops confiscated Becca's Ruger, so after my first night at the club, I put a paring knife in my belly pouch and I keep it in my hand when I'm going to car after work.

Kathie is uniformly hated by all of the other dancers. She's gorgeous, intelligent and comes off as a raging nympho. She's studying engineering at State so she only works three nights a week, but she easily clears a grand a night. She exudes confidence and self-assurance, and the other girls read that as disdain for them, which might not be far from the truth. Shelby tells me that she's sure that Kathie is holding a contest every night to see which one of her lap dances will get to screw her after work. But not for free!

We see almost nothing of Judd. Valery the bartender is his straw boss and deals with the day-to-day operations. He's a weird dude. The other bartenders are State students and are always ogling or hitting on us trying to get something for nothing. Valery could care less. He doesn't ogle, he just looks right through you. The waitresses don't like him at all because he's constantly prodding them to get out on the floor and circulate among the tables, not allowing them a minute's rest. He's given them a standing order to bring at least one drink to each customer every set whether it was ordered or not, and woe betide a waitress if Valery spots a customer with no drink.

If there's trouble, Valery's two football jocks handle it. Once, I saw him sic a bouncer on a customer for no apparent reason – the poor schmuck was drinking a beer and watching me dance when Godzilla came up behind him, plucked him out of his chair and summarily ejected him. Later I found out it was a guy that Valery had banned permanently. He'd hadn't seen the guy come in, but as soon as he noticed him, that was it.

It occurs to me that Valery is the right height and build for the guy who killed Blackie. I wonder if that bad arm is due to a bullet wound? Kidd told me that the cops will have the killer's DNA. I wonder if I can get a sample from Valery for Kidd to run?

About once an evening I'll spot Judd leaning on the end of the bar, watching us dancers. When I look back again after a few minutes, he's gone. I get the impression that most of the girls don't like him. Now there's a shock! The "interview" that he put me through, he did to every girl. Nobody but Kathie will cop to having screwed him at the end, but I wonder. I also think that a couple of the girls are afraid of him, specifically, Shalyla and Lupe.

I go to the hospital every afternoon before going to the club. Uncle isn't getting any worse, but he isn't getting any better either. Nobody can tell me when he'll come out of the coma – could be days, weeks, months, or years. And nobody knows what shape he'll be in when he does come out. The best-case scenario is that it's soon, and he tells us who did it. The worst case is…, well, let's not go there. I don't ever want him to find out what I'm doing here because I know he won't understand. I hardly do myself!

I haven't been back to 3M since I started stripping, mainly because I don't want to see Danny. He doesn't understand why I'm doing this, and he said some pretty mean things to me.

So it's Friday and I'm parking the Z-car in the spillover lot as far from the club as I can get – Judd's orders are that the spaces nearer the door are reserved for customers. It's still daylight, so I don't bother with my knife. As I get out of the car, I notice another one coming into the lot – a little silver Chevy that's seen better days. I see it's Lupe, so I wait until she parks.

"Hi, Lupe!"

"Hello, Kira!" she smiles. God, that little gap in her front teeth is cute! It's cute too, that she still has a little trouble with my name.

"It's Nattie, not Kira. Kira is my stage name." Now why did I just tell her that?

As we walk around the fence into the main parking lot, I struggle to start a conversation. Lupe doesn't interact much with the other girls, allegedly because of her poor English, but the few times I've heard her speak, it didn't seem to be all that bad. My thoughts are interrupted by a couple of taps on a car horn behind us. I look over my shoulder and see a big ass Beemer pulling into the lot. Judd!

He passes us heading for his spot next to the door, and Lupe hangs back. It's obvious that she doesn't want to encounter him. But he gets out of his car and stands there waiting. She has no choice unless she just wants to wait in the middle of the parking lot.

"Hey, it's the twins," he says, obviously referring to our height.

"Hi, Judd. What's up?"

Stripper!

"How's work so far, Kira? Anything I can do to make you more comfortable?"

Yeah, drop dead, you douche bag! "Hey, it's fine, Judd. I'm doing a little better every night."

"So I hear. Hey, how's your twerking?" He points to Jesse, the doorman, who's setting up a whiteboard on a tripod next to the door.

Twerking Contest Next Friday Nite!!

Amateurs Welcome!!

$500 First Prize!!

Ladies Nite!!

Oh brother! Maybe I can arrange to be sick...

"Hey Lupe," Judd says. "Come by my office before you go home tonight."

Lupe goes white, but nods.

Judd precedes us, not bothering to hold the door for a couple of working girls. Why should he? The club's not open yet, so the music is mercifully absent and the overhead lights are up full. The place looks truly vulgar under the harsh fluorescent glare, like an old whore without her makeup. I can see that some of the floor tiles are cracked and mismatched, the paint on the wall is peeling and there are permanent stains on the tables whose nature I don't even want to contemplate. Lupe's lack of color is even more obvious in the severe, pallid brightness.

"Lupe, you OK?"

She looks at me angrily, not answering, then her expression softens a little. "Si, I mean, yes, I'm fine."

I have to press her. "What does he want you for?"

"I..., I have some papers to sign."

Obviously a lie.

"Look, if there's anything I can do..."

"No, Natalie. Is fine. Don't worry."

"I can go meet him with you."

121

That stops her for a moment, then, "No. Really. Is fine."

I give up, for now.

This is my first Friday night at the club. Fridays are traditionally Ladies Night, meaning that women get half price drinks. Big whoop. As I come out for my first set on the pole, I notice that there are more females than usual, maybe about 25% of the crowd. Some of them pay absolutely no attention to me and some scrutinize my every move – aspiring dancers or lesbians, I wonder? Some regard me with the same expression as they would have for a stinky brown substance on their shoe. Almost none of them seem to be here with a guy. As the evening wears on, the place gets totally packed, for sure exceeding the number that the Fire Marshall has posted on the wall. I try way hard to dance every set – it's my nature to try to be really good at anything that I do, even this. I get lots more lap dances, and I find that they afford me an opportunity to rest my arms and shoulders so I can spend a longer time on the pole when I return.

When the evening is over, I count my take. Five hundred and eighty-five dollars! I count off a hundred and ten dollars for Nan and put the rest in my belt pouch. I've cleared about eight hundred dollars so far at this gig, in four nights, with the big Saturday night yet to come. No wonder ladies with no marketable skills take up this line of work! Still a lot less than I could make on the Internet, though.

I find out that there's another Friday night tradition that I didn't know anything about. As us dancers are coming out of the shower, Nan comes into the locker room with a couple of bottles of cheap champagne and a stack of red Solo cups. She sets the cups in a row on the bench and begins filling them, moving back and forth from one to another, attempting to get them all at the same level. When she's done, she says "Another week in Paradise has done gone by! Drink up, ladies!"

There's a press of wet, naked females toward the bench. I bump into Annie and am rewarded with a smile! I want to bump her again, but Summer's right there and gives me the look. When everybody's got a cup, I see that there's one left. That's when I notice that Lupe is absent. And remember that she's probably in with Judd.

I scarcely participate in the banter as the bubbly is drunk. The chatter is light-hearted and nobody mentions Lupe, though I'm sure that they know what is going on. I resolve to wait for her before I go home.

Stripper!

When the rest of the dancers have gone, Nan gets her envelope to take to Judd. I follow her out and stop behind the curtain on stage. I watch as she opens the metal door next to the bar and disappears inside. A minute later, Lupe comes out. She doesn't look good.

She's still wearing her dancing rig – a miniscule silver bikini. Her gait is jerky as she approaches me. I make a quick decision and scamper back to the locker room before she sees me waiting for her behind the curtain. I go stand next to the last locker nearest the shower so she won't spot me immediately when she comes in.

Not to worry. She doesn't even look around as she comes through the door and goes straight to her locker. In the bright light of the locker room, I can see a bruise rapidly developing on the side of her face, and that her jaw is set – she's gritting her teeth to hold back the tears. She fumbles with her lock, failing to open it the first time she tries and clanging it off the locker door in frustration. She calms herself down and gives it another go, and she gets it open.

That's when I step out of concealment. "Hey, Lupe! Everything OK?"

The poor kid jumps so quickly that she bangs into the half open locker door, slamming it shut. As she wheels to face me, it's obvious that she's been crying.

I approach her with my hands out. "Lupe, what's wrong? What did he do to you?"

"N-nothing! Go away, Natalie! Everything is fine! Leave me alone!"

My mind flashes back to months ago, to a naked girl in a basement with no hair and no eyebrows. "Bullshit, Lupe! You're not fine! What did he do to you?"

"N-no…" she starts, then collapses into my arms, crying uncontrollably. I enfold her and begin rocking her back and forth to comfort her.

"That bastard! Lupe, get dressed! We'll go to the police and report this!"

She shoves me so hard that I almost go down. "No! You cannot! He'll tell them! They will send us back! Please!"

Gradually, the story comes out. Lupe is here illegally, and Judd knows it.

"He says if I no fuck him, he will tell immigration! He says he will be big hero for turning in an illegal!"

"But the police often don't turn in illegals into INS, especially when they report a crime."

"He will say I fuck him because I want to. And he's right! Is not rape if I let him do it!"

I point to the bruise on her face. "What do you call that?"

"Some men like to be a little rough with a girl."

I don't believe this! "It's called extortion, and it is rape!"

"I don't wanna take a chance. I gotta think about Eduardo, too!"

"Eduardo?"

"*Mi hermano*. He's eight. I'm all he has."

She has a kid brother? Shit.

"Where's Eduardo now?"

"At home, asleep probably."

Shit! Judd you motherfucker!

"Look, Lupe, I can't just let you be alone like this. How about I go home with you?"

Her lower lip quivers and the tears well up in her limpid mocha eyes.

Chapter 19.

I follow Lupe to a trailer park a little way from town. The place reminds me of the set of a bad slasher movie - the street lights are out and the trailers loom like dark, deteriorating hulks against the charcoal sky. My headlights pick out all manner of terrestrial jetsam – twisted lawn chairs, rotting grills, dirty trikes and bikes coated with rust, and even a couple of cars on blocks. The faint cooking scents in the air are sharp with chilies and garlic, giving the place an exotic atmosphere.

Lupe's trailer is in the back, next to a barbed wire fence that separates the trailer park from a pasture. It's a teardrop-shaped affair about twenty feet long that reminds me of the one we had when I was a kid. It was great for summer camping trips, but I sure wouldn't want to live in it. I wonder what she does with the money she makes at the club – surely she can afford better digs than this!

She parks in the yard and cuts her headlights, but I leave mine on, having no desire to stumble over rubbish on my way inside. But the headlights reveal that her front yard is uncluttered and there's even an attempt at a flower bed next to the door.

I follow her inside. She flips on the light. I'm in an immaculate galley kitchen that's barely big enough for the two of us, but it's redolent of corn and chilies. She moves into the living room beyond, which is also spotless and contains a six-foot plaid sofa along one wall with a folding dining table in front of it. The sofa is occupied by a sleeping little boy, all wrapped up in a blanket with his head on a pillow. Lupe sits down next to him and ruffles his black hair. He stirs, but he doesn't wake.

"This is Eduardo. Like most kids his age, he can sleep through anything. I put him in my bed so you can sit." She scoops him up, blankets and all, and carries him to the back of the trailer. We pass through a bathroom that's also squeaky-clean but smells faintly of sewage, probably because of a faulty septic system.

A queen-size bed beneath a large window covered with a Venetian blind fills the entire rear end of the trailer. Lupe gives the sleeping Eduardo a kiss on the forehead and lays him down, then covers him with a quilt. "It's colder back here because of the window," she says. She motions back towards the living room, then follows me out.

"Sit, *por favor*," she says, indicating the sofa. "You would like a beer?"

125

I really don't want anything, but I can see that she is anxious to please, so I nod. She goes back to the kitchen and busies herself for a moment, then returns with two seven-ounce Coronas, with a lime wedge in the mouth of each one. She hands me one and takes a seat on the couch next to me.

It doesn't take a trained psychologist to see that Lupe is distressed. The tension in her face and shoulders is evident and it's also obvious that she's immersing herself in the hospitality ritual to avoid dealing with what happened in Judd's office. I reach over and take her beer from her and place it on the table along with mine, then I grasp her shoulders firmly and look her in the eyes.

"Lupe, how long have you been putting up with Judd's abuse?"

The human contact was all that was necessary for her to break down. She begins weeping bitterly and collapses forward into my arms, burying her face in my bosom. I just hold her and rock her, letting her cry it out.

Finally, she stops crying and sits up. I go to the kitch and get a couple of paper towels, saturate them with warm water and wring them out, then I come back and wash her face with them, like my mom used to do for me when I got through crying. I put the wad of towels on the table and hand her her beer.

"Now, how long has he been doing this?"

She sips the beer. Then, "Since I start work there. I let him fuck me when we do the interview. I really needed the job."

"And how often does he call you?"

"Maybe two, three times a month. He do it to Shalyla and Kathie, too."

His own little harem. Nice!

"Are you hurt any more than that bruise? Did he force himself on you?"

"No, Natalie. Judd is a little rough, but really, I let him do it."

I think for a minute, unsure of where to go next. As much as I'd like to bust Judd for this, Lupe does have a point. He can claim it was consensual. In the current political climate, I'm pretty sure she won't get deported if she goes to the cops, but I remember Kidd's reaction to Becca's murder. The prevailing attitude seems to be that women sex workers are asking for it, and nobody is too put out when they get what's coming to them. If social services finds out that Lupe is a stripper with an eight-year old, Eduardo could easily end up in the system. It's obvious that she loves him and it would break her heart.

126

Stripper!

"So are you going to keep letting him do it?"

"What choice do I have? I need the job."

"But you've worked at the club how long?"

"Almost a year."

"So you should have some money socked away! Quit, and go get some training for a real job!"

"I have some money, yes, but I send most of it to Mexico. My *abuelo* is there. He is too old to come to the U.S. My cousin watches him, and he needs money to take care of him. And my cousin, he has kids, too."

Right or wrong, Lupe seems convinced she's at a dead end. I know that I'm not going to convince her that she's wrong tonight. I take a different tack.

"Do you remember about a week ago, an older, fat man with grey hair was at the club? He would have worn a blue and white striped suit and a tie, and an old white hat."

"No. Who is he?"

I hesitate. I can blow this thing right here. Do I trust her?

"He's my uncle. Someone attacked him and he was hurt very badly after he left the club. I was hoping you might have seen him and could tell me who he might have talked to."

"I'm sorry, I no remember him. You know how many guys are in there."

Yes, I do.

"How about a woman? She was a waitress, her name was Robyn." I give Lupe the best description that I can, having seen Robyn Carlson only for a short while.

"*Si*, I remember Robyn. She liked to talk to us dancers. She said she wanted to dance too, and she wanted to know how you learn."

"What else did she talk about?"

"She ask me what I know about some guys that Judd meet in his office. I tell her I know nothing."

"What guys?"

"Black guys. They wear clothes too big for them and lotsa bling - rings, chains, watches. I think they belong to gang."

"Do you know which gang?"

"No. I learn in Mexico not to ask about such things."

I'll bet you did.

"I've never seen them in the audience," I say.

"They no come to watch girls. They have business with Judd."

"What kind of business?"

Now she's obviously distressed again. But I have to push this.

"C'mon, Lupe! I'm not going to tell Judd what we talked about. Do you know what their business with Judd is?"

"Kathie say it is drugs."

Drugs! I find that hard to believe. Judd is maniacal about customers not doing drugs in the club. I've seen easily a half a dozen guys ejected in the week I've been there, ostensibly because they were caught with drugs. There's some weed in the club to be sure, but if you're caught with it, you're banned. I say as much.

"You're right," she says. "But I'm just telling you what Kathie said." She hesitates, then goes on, "She go to Mexico with Judd a couple of times, so she should know."

This is getting interesting! "Mexico?"

"*Si*, I mean, yes. Judd, he tell me when we fuck, if I am very good and do everything he say, he will take me one time so I can see my family."

That shit! There's no way he's gonna try to get an undocumented immigrant across the border, especially if there are drugs involved. "Lupe, he's just saying that to get you to do what he wants. Don't believe him." I can see the sadness in her face.

"And Valery runs things when Judd is gone?"

"*Si*." she hesitates, then says, "That one I do not like. He scares me."

"How so?"

128

She bites her lip as if she really doesn't want to answer. Then she says, "After I find out that Judd is fucking Kathie too, I talk to her about it." She uses the word *fuck* casually, like any other English word, and it's vaguely disconcerting because I'm sure she doesn't realize the power of that word. "I don't want her to be mad at me because she is fucking him too," she goes on. "She laugh at me, then say that she don't care, and that maybe her and me and Judd could have threesome someday. I'm no sure if she means it or not, but I say that I wouldn't like that. Then she say, 'Honey, it don't matter what you like. You do what Judd tells you or he'll send Valery after you.'"

So Valery is Judd's enforcer! I thought as much.

She changes the subject. "You know, you look a lot like another girl who came to the club one night."

Becca! "What girl, Lupe? When was this?"

"It was just after I start working there. This girl, she come in looking for a job. She go back with Judd for interview."

"What happened to her?"

"I dunno. I think she failed the interview, because she never come back to locker room to go on stage. Nobody see her leave. But she look a lot like you!"

I'm getting to know Lupe well enough by now to hear the indecision in her voice. There's something she's not telling me.

"What else happened?"

"After that night, we no see Judd for about a week."

"And…" I press her.

"When he come back, he got great big bandage on his face."

Good on you, Becca!

Lupe continues, "He call another girl back to his office that night, not me, *gracias a Dios*! He hurt her bad – she no come to work anymore after that. Kathie say that Judd get Valery to give her ten thousand dollars so she don't tell nobody what he did."

So Judd tried to rape Becca, she cut him and got away, and the bastard took it out on somebody else. I'll bet Becca's pistol permit dates to shortly afterwards.

"Lupe, I want you promise me something." She looks at me expectantly. "I want you to promise me that you won't go back in the office with Judd anymore."

Her face falls. "But he fire me if I no do what he wants, and turn me into INS."

I hope that I'm not lying to her. "The U.S. government is not going to send you back to Mexico. There are too many others like you here for them to do that."

"But what about Eduardo?"

"Does Judd even know about him?"

"No. I never talk about Eduardo at the club."

"Then it shouldn't be a problem. Since you came here undocumented, Eduardo shouldn't be on the books anywhere. Does he go to school?"

"Not yet. He no speak much English."

Oh brother. The poor kid's whole life is in this ratty trailer park!

"But what am I gonna do if Judd fires me?" Lupe asks.

Stop getting raped every couple of weeks, for starters! "Surely you have some money that you haven't sent to Mexico. How long could you get by with that?"

She thinks a moment. "Maybe a month. Maybe two."

"So that's a start." The next words are out of my mouth before I even have a chance to think about them. "And you know what? If Judd fires you, you and Eduardo could come and stay with me for a while. I have a big place, and it's kinda lonely sometimes."

She looks at me stupefied for a moment, then the tears start flowing again. "You would do that for us?"

The import of what I just said is now seeping in, but it's too late. You just don't take something like that back. "Sure," I tell her. "You've had it rough, and I'd be happy to help." I think a moment. In for a penny, in for a pound. "As a matter of fact, why wait to get fired? This nasty trailer park is no place for a little kid. Why not just don't go back to the club anymore and come and live with me now?"

She looks at me seriously. "We no want handouts, Nattie. I want to work for what I get."

"You can help me with the bills as long as you have money. But truthfully, I think it's a great idea for you to get away from Judd just as fast as you can."

"I don't know..."

"I'll tell you what. Why don't you get Eduardo and come home with me now? You can see my place and we can get some sleep before we have to go to work tomorrow. You can use my guest room. If you think you'd like to move in with me after that, we can talk about getting you out of here."

"I don't know..."

"Please?"

"OK. We come and see."

My phone tells me it's pushing three a.m., but this is still early evening for us strippers. We don't have to be back to work before seven thirty tomorrow evening. Lupe chugs what's left of her beer then busies herself gathering a few things.

"I'll drive if you want," I tell her.

"No, we'll follow you."

As we head outside and I wait for her to get Eduardo in the back seat of her car and lock the trailer, I think again about the implications of my offer. I know that it's much easier to move someone into your home than it is to get them out again if things don't work out. Thanks to Becca, I have enough money to support Lupe and Eduardo until she's able to find other work, but I don't know how long that might take or even if she'll be able to pay for her upkeep if she takes a job other than stripping. I also don't know how Judd will react if he finds out what I've done. I don't want to get fired from the club until I know whether he's responsible for what happened to Uncle Amos.

The Z-car's headlights knife through the darkness, illuminating the stark squalor of the trailer park. That's all it takes to steel my resolve. I'm know I'm doing the right thing!

Chapter 20.

I get a chance to think as I'm leading Lupe and Eduardo back to my place. The roads are clear this early in the morning, a time when most respectable people are home in bed. A light rain falls, leaving a sheen on the asphalt and creating little circular rainbows around the streetlights. When we reach the highway, I lay my wrist at twelve o'clock on the wheel and point the Z-car down the center lane.

In a word, I'm discouraged. I've gotten absolutely nowhere with finding out who hurt Uncle Amos. Based on what Lupe told me, I'm wondering if he thought that Judd might be responsible for Robyn's disappearance because she found out about the drug trade in the club, and that Judd, or more likely, Valery, tried to put him out of commission. It's a great theory, but I haven't got a shred of evidence to back it up, and I've got no clue how to get any. At the club, it's difficult to do anything but dance. I've managed to ask the other girls a few questions in the locker room between sets, but I can't address the things I really want to know without seeming suspicious. I'm beginning to see why Robyn got a job as a waitress instead of a dancer. It gave her free rein to move about the place.

What I'd really like to do is get into Judd's office when he's gone. But how? I'd be conspicuous as hell prowling about in nothing but a thong, and there's also the little matter of the keypad on the door.

We pull into my parking lot and I park in my space, directing Lupe to the adjacent space. I get out of the car and wait for her. I'm surprised to see that Eduardo is now awake, getting out of the car with his sister.

I unlock the door and open it. As usual, Xin Niu scampers up to greet me, but freezes when she sees the visitors. Eduardo immediately rushes her. Xin Niu bolts into the living room and takes a flying leap six feet up the spiral staircase, clinging to it with her front paws like a monkey. In a second, she vanishes upstairs.

Lupe is aghast at her brother's "bad" behavior, and grabs him by an arm, spewing reprimands in Spanish.

"Whoa, that's all right. No harm done! Xin Niu's not used to company. She'll come around in her own good time." I hope!

Stripper!

We try to calm down Eduardo. I search through the kitchen for something appropriate and find some milk and cocoa, so I offer to make him hot chocolate. The offer is gratefully accepted. While the milk is heating I get Lupe another beer, and me a boilermaker.

The chocolate gets Eduardo sleepy again, so when he's finished, I show Lupe the upstairs guest room where she can bed him down. I'm pretty wiped myself and I'm flushed and tingly all over. Too late I realize that I'm not supposed to be drinking on the meds that Rebecca prescribed.

Rebecca! Shit shit, shit shit, shit shit, shit! I had an appointment with her yesterday!

I rummage through my pouch for my phone. Sure enough, there's a message with a State University exchange at the top of my recents list. I never got the call because my phone was in my locker while I was wrapped around a pole on the stage. I touch the screen to play the message.

"Natalie, it's Rebecca Feiner. You've missed your session with me today. While I hope this means that you're feeling much better, we're at a critical time in your treatment and you really can't afford to miss sessions. I've rescheduled you for ten o'clock Monday morning. Please call me ASAP if you need to change this time. As we agreed, I'll leave this message at your work as well so you'll be sure to get it."

I don't remember giving her permission to leave messages at work. It must have been somewhere in all those forms I signed. I enter the appointment time into my online calendar, along with a couple of alarms to remind me over the next couple of days.

When I've finished, Lupe has returned from putting Eduardo down. I give her a fifty-cent tour of the townhouse.

Her dark coffee eyes seem to get wider after each room that we visit. Sadly, I think that she could probably get a place like this on her own, if not for all of the money that she's been sending off to Mexico every month. I wonder if her cousin is ripping her off. How much can it really cost to care for her grandfather in a Mexican village?

Finally, only the studio is left. Almost without thinking, I lead her past the closed door as if it's not even there. I notice the slight turn of her head towards the door as we go by. She's much too polite to say anything, but I can tell she knows that there's something there that I don't want to show her.

133

Suddenly, I stop walking. What the hell am I afraid of? I lead her back to the studio door and thrust it open. The light comes on automatically, revealing the room in all its garish glory.

Lupe's eyes get wide indeed as she takes it all in. Finally she asks, "Natalie, what is this?"

"It's a room for dancing, Lupe. Online."

I carefully show her all of the features of the room, as Becca did for me. I can tell that she's puzzled by some of it, but she seems to get the general idea.

"If you can dance and make money right here, why you work at the club?" she asks.

I explain again about Uncle Amos.

We look into each other's eyes as we get it at the same time.

"I could dance here..." she begins.

"...and you wouldn't have to go back to the club and Judd!" I finish.

Then I realize all of the problems with that idea. "It's been several weeks since I've danced here, Lupe, and I'm sure that most of my clients will have left. Also, they're used to Kira Foxxx. We'll have to transition them over. We'll have to change the website."

She's looking at me expectantly. I can see that she doesn't get it.

Thinking aloud, I go on, "I don't have the skills to do that. We'll have to have help." A distasteful thought intrudes. Bobby can get an internet site for Lupe off the ground. But he's obviously infatuated with me. He pays me for a lap dance every night, sometimes twice a night, and his entire demeanor tells me that he wants our relationship to go much further. Whether I'm a lesbian or straight makes no difference, the guy just creeps me out! But he's still the best person I know to do the website. His contacts at the club could even bring in some clients for Lupe to get her started. So I guess I'll have ask him.

I say to Lupe, "You probably shouldn't do this under your real name. Why don't you think about choosing a stage name?"

"My name is Maria de Guadalupe Carmella Aguayo Ibanez. What name should I choose?"

134

Stripper!

"Well, Carmella sounds sexy. You could use that. Now you need a last name."

"I can use Foxxx?" she smiles. I think she's joking.

"No, I think you get away from Kira Foxxx and use a new name. What's Spanish for hot and spicy?"

"There are several words. *Caliente, picante, picoso, ala diabla…*"

"Carmella Picante! That's perfect!"

"Yes! *Picante* means sexy also."

We go downstairs. I offer Lupe another beer, but she turns it down – a good thing, because I probably would have had one too, and I need to get way serious about doctor's orders. A glance at my phone tells me it's almost five a.m. The dancers usually arrive at the club about 7 p.m., so it's high time to get some sleep.

Lupe and I have a discussion late Sunday afternoon. Needless to say, she danced her last dance at the club last night. We chart out a schedule for her to move in. This Friday is the end of the month and she's hasn't got a lease on the trailer, so that seems like a good date.

Eduardo is a little bundle of energy. He wants so badly to play with Xin Niu, but unfortunately, she has not come out of hiding since the interlopers arrived. It's hard to talk to Lupe when he's around because he speaks hardly any English and he's constantly chattering in Spanish. I realize what an adjustment it's going to be for me to have a little kid living here. Becca had a video game console on the TV, so we get him set up there with the volume on low.

"You really should put him in school, you know."

"I can't," she says plaintively. "I look into it. I need his birth certificate. He must have a doctor's exam and shots."

"Lupe, there are people who can help with that. After we get you moved in, we can look into it again. In fact, you should take some of your money and get some training. You can't dance forever, you know."

"I know. It's hard. My family in Mexico would be ashamed if they know what I do."

That raises my hackles. "You have nothing to be ashamed of! I can't imagine the hell you went through to get you and Eduardo here, where you didn't even know anybody! Then you found a way to make a life for him and you. And you're taking care of your relatives back home, too! I only wish I was as strong as you!"

Now I've made her cry again. "I don't know how we can ever repay you…"

"You don't owe me anything, Lupe."

Sunday nights at the club are generally slow. Some of the girls don't come in at all. I toy with the idea of not going in, but I do need to see Bobby if we're going to get the website up and running. There's a phone number and email for him at the 3M office, but I haven't been there since Uncle Amos got hurt. I totally don't want to see Danny. He disapproves of what I'm doing, and I just don't want to get into it with him.

I decide to go to club to get up with Bobby if he shows, then meet Lupe at the trailer to help her pack.

The club parking lot is sparsely occupied. Judd's Beemer is not there, and I don't see Bobby's car either.

Nan, Kathie and Liz Cleary are in the locker room. Liz is about 25, and a somewhat chubby brunette who's been dancing for about eight months. If you saw her outside, you'd never think she had the looks to be a stripper, but I've found that all kinds of women get into this business. The guys who come to the club tend to be neutral about a girl's looks as long as she'll take her clothes off. Liz is married and I wonder if her husband knows how she's earning their keep.

"… and we're going to spend a whole week in Acapulco!" Kathie is telling them. She notices me. "Oh, hi, Kira! Guess what? Judd is taking me to Mexico for a week!"

Kathie does not look like her usual, vivacious self. Her skin is sallow, and she's got a cold sore at the corner of her mouth that's obviously bothering her, because she's continually licking at it.

"Good for you!" Good for me, too! "When are you leaving?"

"Tomorrow night. We're going to grab a red eye."

"And you're coming back?"

"A week from today. I'll be back dancing next Monday."

136

Stripper!

Nan, especially, looks jealous as hell, and Liz has somewhat of a sour expression as well. I wonder if either of them has really thought about what it would be like to be Judd's sex slave for a week? As far as I know, neither has been the subject of his attentions like Kathie and Lupe. Maybe he only rapes a girl who lets him screw her during the interview.

"I'm not dancing tonight," I tell Nan. "I just came in to get up with somebody."

"Up to you," she replies. "But you should dance as much as you can until you get established if you want to make this a career."

A career? I don't think so!

The walls begin pulsating - the music is on. Bobby is usually here when the dancing starts, so I take a look. He's at his usual table.

I can't talk to him inside, so I go to his table and pluck his sleeve. He gets that shit-eating grin when he sees me. God, why does he creep me out so bad? I motion to him to follow, then head outside. I don't have to look to know that he's trailing me like a puppy dog.

I lead him around the club over to the Lee Street side to get away from the smokers in the parking lot. Here the club presents just a white brick wall covered with years of grime from the road traffic.

"So what's this about?" Bobby says expectantly.

"Not what you think." His face falls. "I need somebody to do a website." He brightens up again.

"I'm still doing the one at your office," he says. "After Mr. Murdoch got hurt, Mr. Merkel told me that I should finish it. It's nearly done."

"No, I'm talking about Kira Foxxx's website." Now his grin is bigger than ever!

I explain to him what I'm trying to do for Lupe, leaving out any mention of Judd.

"I can do that," he says. "But does this mean that you won't be dancing here anymore?"

"Not at all." I think fast. "Lupe is moving in with me and we're starting a business. I'll be dancing here, and she'll be online. We think that will be better for both of us."

"I'll tell you what I'll do," Bobby says. "I'll set you up and I'll tell my friends about her new site. I'll even give you guys a crash course in online advertising. All I ask in return is privileges on the site. No money."

I don't like the sound of that. "Privileges?"

"I get free dances. And some lap dances here." He must notice my sour expression. "Don't worry, I won't abuse it. I want you guys should be a success."

I would just as soon pay him, but I know he'll fight me if I suggest it.

"I can come over whenever you want," he says.

"Not tonight." I would just as soon that Lupe is there when he comes. "I'll call you. What's your number?"

"Give me your phone," he says. I do, and his fingertip whirls about on the screen. I'm vaguely nervous that I can't see what he's doing. I'm not happy about our new relationship, but there's not much I can do. "There!" he says, finally. "We're connected!"

Great.

"Look, I can come over tomorrow morning," he says. "No use waiting, right?"

"Something nags at me, but I brush it off. "I guess. But I want Lupe there. Let me talk to her and I'll get back to you."

"Not like you did when you let me sit around till closing waiting for you," he replies.

"That was uncalled for, Bobby. I asked you to do a website for me. I'll call you."

"Fair enough."

We head back inside. As expected, the crowd is sparse. Nan, Liz and Kathie are dancing on separate runways. Judd is there, standing at the end of the bar, arms folded, surveying his domain. My belly knots at the sight of him. I'd like nothing better than to go over there and kick him in the balls, then keep on

138

kicking after he goes down to pay him back for what he's done to Lupe. Yeah, right. All ninety-five pounds of me. Getting into his office while he's gone and getting something I can leak to the cops seems like a much better plan.

The problems that I envision with that are Valery and the bartenders and the lock on the office door. I need a plan to take care of them.

I head over to Lupe's trailer. The lights are ablaze and I find her surrounded by boxes in the living room. Eduardo is everywhere, obviously overstimulated and delighted that he's going to be living with Xin Niu. I tell Lupe about Bobby's pending visit and that she's welcome to sleep at the townhouse again tonight. She agrees, so we split the load of boxes between our cars and take them over. Lupe doesn't have a lot of worldly possessions, so we think that one more trip will get her moved in, but she'll have to put her furniture in storage until she can sell it.

We call it a night around midnight. I have trouble sleeping – I'm not used to going to bed this early. I fight the wakefulness for what seems like hours before I give up. I check the bedside clock. One a.m. I get up and head up to the studio where the PC is.

The problem of the lock on Judd's door has been worrisome, so I decide to do a little research. I find many types of push button locks of different quality. Some are nearly worthless and some are even used in high security facilities. The number of buttons ranges from four or five on a cheap lock up to twenty on an expensive model. If a particular lock sees a lot of use, sometimes it can be bypassed by examining the buttons for wear, then trying various combinations of the worn buttons until you arrive at the correct one. That can take a few minutes or a few hours, depending on luck and the complexity of the lock. I also find a video that shows that some locks can be defeated by simply clamping a fairly strong magnet on the side nearest the doorframe, which disengages the locking bolts normally controlled by the buttons so the handle can be turned freely without entering the combination.

Of course, I didn't examine the lock on Judd's door very closely when I went in for my interview. I close my eyes and try to visualize it. I'm walking down the hallway, grateful to get away from the booming music but anxious about what I'm about to do. I stop at the door. Do I really want to go through with this? I look down at the door handle, surprised that there's no regular knob. I'm pretty sure there are no more than five or six buttons, and they're not numbered.

I search Amazon for magnets. There are many choices, but the magnet in the video was a little smaller than my hand and cost about $100. I order a similar one. If it doesn't work, I'll just have to try trial and error.

My computer screen tells me it's 3:15 – a much more normal time for me to be getting to bed these days. It's amazing how quickly your life can change. Of all the possible futures I've envisioned, stripping in a club didn't even make the list. Yet, here I am. I wonder if it's even worth planning your life at all. Just going with the flow seems to work as well.

Chapter 21.

I have no idea how long the music has been blaring as I struggle through the haze of sleep into wakefulness. The bedside clock says 8:35 – I swear that I set it for 8:00. I click off the music, then I notice an unfamiliar aroma. Coffee! And another underlying scent that I can't identify.

I get up, then remember that I now have roommates, one of whom is male, so I pull on a pair of sweats over my panties. With a t-shirt on top, I'm decent.

I find Lupe in the kitchen.

"Good morning, Nattie." Lupe says. She waves to the stools at the pass-through. "Sit, and I'll get your coffee."

Get my coffee? I could get used to this!

She walks right past the coffee maker. She takes a long-handled pot from the stove and pours a stream of dark liquid through a strainer into a mug. She tips in some steaming milk from a second pot, then places the mug in the microwave for thirty seconds.

"I usually take my coffee black," I tell her.

"This, I do not think you will want black," she replies.

Lupe places the cup in front of me. It's couple of shades darker than Georgia red clay. I finally identify the unfamiliar scent. Cinnamon! The aroma immediately brings sadness. I would never even think of buying cinnamon, but Becca had a superbly stocked pantry. Oh, why did she have to die?

I take a sip. OMG! That's coffee with a vengeance – no wonder she said I wouldn't want it black. It's almost cloyingly sweet, with a nutty flavor. After I swallow, the aftertaste of cinnamon lingers.

Lupe is looking at me expectantly, obviously waiting for a complement. I oblige.

"Wow! That's a mouthful to wake you up! What's in it?"

"It's *Café de Olla*, just as my *abuela* would make it. It is coffee and cinnamon. In Mexico, we would sweeten it with *piloncillo*, but I had to use brown sugar."

Lupe's dark hair cascades down starkly over her white cotton robe, which doesn't do a lot to hide her charms. Her feet are bare. Her dimpled smile tells me that she's obviously pleased that I like her coffee and it makes her soft features glow as if illuminated with an amber flame. She's very winsome indeed, with eyes that mirror the color of her coffee, a full mouth with just a hint of an overbite and that slight, sexy gap between her front teeth, all of which evokes a rustic allure. A familiar inner tingling courses through me, and I remember the rumor going around the club that Lupe is a lesbian. I contemplate my coffee cup to avoid staring at her and take another sip of the thick, spicy brew. Now is not the time to be thinking of such things, especially after her recent mistreatment by Judd.

She seems to have noticed my interest, because she blushes and turns away.

"Would you like me to fix you some breakfast?" she asks.

"Sure." It seems like the right thing to say.

In ten minutes, Lupe places two plates on the bar, each containing three tacos. Again, I have Becca's vegetarianism to thank for the presence of the corn tortillas and the beans and spices inside, but I will claim credit for the eggs and cheese. As Lupe watches expectantly, I pick up a warm taco and take a bite. There's just the faintest crunch, then the flavor of unfamiliar spices explodes in my mouth followed by a rush of chili heat, which is instantly moderated by the fluffy scrambled eggs.

"OMG, Lupe, you're going to make me too fat to dance if you keep cooking for me like this!"

Her face falls, and I rush to reassure her that everything is fine.

Lupe wants to get another load from the trailer, but I remind her that Bobby is coming and that I don't want to be alone with him.

There's a knock about ten a.m. I open the door to find Bobby on the doorstep, sporting the vermillion Kitten Club t-shirt that seems to be his sole article of clothing. He's carrying a backpack. Against my better judgement, I invite him in. Lupe and Eduardo are on the sofa in the living room, playing a game on Lupe's phone. Lupe rises as we enter, giving the phone to Eduardo.

Bobby precedes us to the spiral staircase and ascends. He waits for us at the top, and I lead the way to the studio door. I unlock the door – we've installed a padlock to keep Eduardo out. The light flashes on as I open the door.

Stripper!

Bobby stands transfixed. "Wow!" he says. "So this is where it happens!" I swear there's a hint of reverence in his tone.

I go in and log on to the Kira Foxxx website, then relinquish the chair to Bobby. He's all business as he rapidly clicks through the site.

"You realize you're still getting requests for performances?" he asks.

I shake my head. "I haven't really bothered with the website or the phone since I started dancing at the club."

"You should," he says. "Don't blow off your loyal clients like that." He clicks some more, then says, "Well, you're obviously going to need a new website that features Lupe, but we can use the old Kira Foxxx phone number and payment accounts. I can also set things up so that anyone who tries to go to the Kira Foxxx site will automatically end up at the new site."

"Sounds good to me," I say. "Lupe will be using the name Carmella Picante."

"I like it! We're gonna need lots of pictures of Lupe, too. Hey, I'd be happy to take them!" he says expectantly.

I'll bet you would. "No, Lupe and I can do that. But you can put them on the site."

He frowns. I've obviously dashed his hopes. Awww.

He produces a thumb drive which he inserts into the computer. "Well, let's look at some website designs and see what you like.

My phone chimes. I look at the screen. Rebecca Feiner. Shit! I had an appointment with her this morning!

I don't want to deal with Rebecca right now with Bobby and Lupe here. I let it go to voicemail. I'll call and make amends later.

For the next half hour, we review various website designs. One pops up that closely resembles the current Kira Foxxx website. Suddenly it hits me.

"You designed the original Kira Foxxx website for Becca, didn't you? Why didn't you tell me?"

He looks guilty and scared. "You never asked me."

"Then you must've know I wasn't Kira when you met me in the club parking lot that first night?"

"I wasn't really sure at first," he says. "I mean, I heard that something bad happened to Kira, so I called and called, hoping she would answer. Then you answered, and you danced for me. I was so happy! I figured the media had got it wrong like they always do. When I saw you in the parking lot, I knew you weren't her."

He has the mother of all dumb looks on his face. Exactly how many brain cells have you burned out on meth and booze, Bobby?

"Where did you meet her?" I ask.

"At the club, of course, that first night. She had gone in for an interview with Judd. She came out in a hurry and she didn't look good. She ran out into the parking lot. I followed her. Found her next to her car, fumbling with her keys, trying to unlock the door, but she couldn't because she had a bad cut on her hand."

I remember the long, pink scar on Becca's hand that I saw on our first date at Max's.

"She was bleeding like a pig – no way she was going to drive. So I asked her if I could take her to the emergency room, and she said yes. She got stitched up, then I brought her back to get her car. I offered to drive her home, but she said she could drive as long as she wasn't bleeding all over the place."

"So how did you end up doing her website?"

"I guess I must have slipped one of my cards into her purse," he says. "She called me up a few weeks later."

"So you have been here before."

"No, she didn't live here then." He waves a hand to indicate the studio. "All she had when I set her up was a cheap apartment, a PC and a webcam." He pauses, then continues. "I tried to get her to go out with me, but she didn't want to. She said she didn't want anything to remind her of the club. So I started calling her to dance online. I don't know if she knew it was me – I didn't tell her, and she didn't ask. Told my friends about her, too."

I can't help but feel sorry for this pathetic little man, who can't seem to have a relationship with a woman outside of a strip club or online. And it bothers me that he knew Becca, even though she had little to do with him.

Stripper!

We have just settled on a design when my phone chimes. The screen informs me that call is from the University Hospital. My heart skips a beat as I thumb the button.

A staccato Indian voice is in my ear. "Ms. McMasters, it is Dr. Chowdhury, Mr. Murdoch's physician. How are you this morning?"

"I'm fine."

"Good. I'm calling to tell you that we will be moving your uncle out of the ICU this afternoon. We will be putting him in a standard room."

"That's great news! When are you going to move him?"

"I can't give you an exact time, but he should be downstairs by five o'clock. You can see him then.

"When will he be awake?"

"I can't tell you that, either. We will be bringing him out of the coma over the next few days, but he will wake up when he's ready to."

"That's wonderful! Thank you so much for calling, Doctor!"

"You're welcome." She hangs up.

I share the news with Lupe and Bobby.

"Look, I guess I've got what I need to get started," Bobby says. "I can get everything else on the net. You guys just send those pictures when you get 'em and we'll be ready to rock and roll."

After Bobby leaves, I think about the rest of the day. Lupe has told me she's got a couple more loads to bring from her trailer, so if I go along with her, we might be able to finish moving her in one run. After that, maybe we can see about getting some pictures of Lupe.

I don't see any reason to dance at the club tonight. I'm not ready for my incursion into Judd's office and frankly, I could use another night off. Hopefully my magnet will come tomorrow, then I can plan my raid.

In about an hour I'm tooling down the road in the Z-car following Lupe and Eduardo out to the trailer. It's a gorgeous day. Spring is rapidly becoming summer, so the air is a little heavy, but it's hardly oppressive at seventy miles an hour with the sunroof open. There's a lot to be said for night work. My days are my own, much more so than when I was in school, and I've seen my earnings at the club increase steadily. I despise the kissing and the lap dances, but Becca found the perfect solution for that. Maybe a partnership with Lupe dancing online isn't such a bad idea. The thought takes me aback – am I seriously considering stripping as a career? What happened to college and law school? Maybe the time for that is after I get old and fat...

We're back at the townhouse by three thirty. We did it! Lupe is totally moved out of the trailer. I really can't help her put her things away, but I can and do keep Eduardo busy playing games. His English is poor; he keeps asking for *el gato*, but Xin Niu has made herself scarce since Lupe and Eduardo have been here. I know she's been coming out at night and when we're not here to eat and drink because I've had to replenish her supplies, but she's steadfastly refused to associate with the intruders. Well, she's just going to have to get over it!

I do remember to call Rebecca to apologize for the missed appointment, but I get voicemail. I ask her to please reschedule me and promise that I won't be a no-show again.

Finally, it's time to go the hospital. I've already got my badge, but I still have to show my i.d. at the reception desk and get the new room number. I head up there. God, I really hope he'll be awake so he can tell me who did this!

I step out of the elevator and check the sign on the opposite wall. Uncle Amos new room is about halfway down the hall. They've already moved him - he's lying in bed with the sheet tucked up under his chin. And there's another visitor. Danny!

Chapter 22.

I haven't spoken to Danny since we had the fight about my going undercover at the club. He made it crystal clear that he would have nothing more to do with me if I did that.

He's looking at Uncle Amos with a solicitous expression as I enter. He glances up and his face hardens. Fine. I totally don't want to be here with him, but I won't let him keep me from Uncle's side. It would be stupid to just stand here in silence until somebody leaves, so I speak first.

"Has the Doctor been here yet?"

You could cut the air with a knife. Danny obviously doesn't want to answer, but he apparently realizes the banality of silence as well as I do.

"No," he says finally. "An orderly brought him. I asked about the Doctor, and he said she'll come in a little while."

I think about going to the far side of the bed to put it between us, but then I think *Screw it!* - I won't let him control me like that.

I have to move the stand that holds the i.v. out of the way so I can stand near Uncle's face. Danny moves to accommodate me. I almost don't recognize Uncle. He's pale and gaunt –he's lost considerable weight, probably because he hasn't eaten in more than a week. Ruefully, I think that it will probably do him good to lose that weight if he comes out of this. Of course, he's going to come out of this! He has to!

I ruffle his hair. His skin is cold. Is that a bad sign? The heart monitor shows that his heartbeat is regular and his blood pressure is low. Maybe that's a good thing.

Danny's cold look has disappeared, replaced by one of concern. I try to start a conversation.

"Have you heard anything from the police?"

Again the look that tells me he totally doesn't want to talk to me. Then finally, "No. I called Leon Kidd a couple of days ago. He hasn't called back."

"Are you sure they're even working on it?"

147

"Yes, I'm sure!" he snaps. "I used to be a cop, remember? They probably just don't have anything yet. Investigations like this can take a while. You just have to get over the immediate gratification thing and accept that fact."

"And what's that supposed to mean?"

"It means that things don't always work the way they should, or the way you want them to," he says. "An adult realizes that."

I feel the blood rushing into my face. "So I'm not an adult?"

"You're sure not acting like one. What do you think Amos would say if he knew what you're doing? This kind of crap is the reason he fired you. Are you going to tell him what you've been doing when he wakes up?"

"What I tell him is none of your goddamn business! I just want the animal who did this caught, and if the cops can't or won't do it, I will!"

"You just don't realize how immature that sounds, do you?"

I start to retort, but it dies in my throat. I have a nagging suspicion that Danny is right.

Apparently realizing that he's cracked my armor, he goes on. "How is Amos going to take it when he finds out you've been taking your clothes off in a strip joint? Have you been doing lap dances too? What else have you done? Is it worth destroying your reputation and your honor just because you haven't grown up enough to let the police do their job?"

He should have kept his mouth shut while he was winning. "Maybe it's just that we have very different ideas about what reputation and honor are, Danny. Some of us are willing to settle for whatever life dishes out, and others have the spunk to make it what they want it to be. That's how Uncle Amos is. You'd know that if you really knew him. Thanks for helping me make up my mind. Yes, when he wakes up, I am going to tell him what I did to find the guy who hurt him. He's not going to like it, but he'll understand it after he thinks about it. That's because he's a lot more of a man than you are!" I really shouldn't have said that last, but I'm mad!

Danny's face is so red it's positively smoldering. He inhales to yell, and I hear the door creak behind me. Somehow, he manages to stifle the outburst. I turn to see an orderly in scrubs, a cap, and a surgical mask pushing a cart into the room. The top is covered with a cloth and there's a bunch of i.v. bags on the bottom. I turn back to Danny, thinking that maybe I should apologize for denigrating his manhood, then I see the fear leap into his eyes.

"Get down!" he screams. I turn back to see the orderly drawing an enormous, horribly familiar pistol from under the cloth. I don't even think. I just go for him with my claws!

He backhands the gun like a tennis racket, catching me under the eye. I collapse as if my legs suddenly turned to paper.

The shooter puts three or four rounds in the prostrate form of Uncle Amos, then shifts the gun back to me. I see nothing but the tiny hole in the silencer, as big as a water main. Come on, motherfucker! Shoot me and be done!

The gun moves out of my field of view as Danny goes for him. It spits again then Danny is on him, forcing his gun hand toward the floor. Another spit and Danny goes down, taking the shooter with him. Danny's face against the white tile of the floor fills my entire field of vision.

Silence descends and I roll over as the gunman disappears into the hall. The blackness is still there – all I can see is a tiny circle of light. I clench at the bed and haul myself to my feet, intending to chase the shooter, but I notice a scarlet stain swiftly spreading across the bedsheets.

OMG! I wrench open the door and scream for help! The tunnel vision makes it impossible to see where the shooter went – it gradually subsides as hospital personnel converge.

The next half hour zips by like a madcap joyride. White-clad people hustle me out of Uncle's room, throw me on a gurney and wheel me to another room. I remember trying to fight them off, but more toadies grab my hands, holding me so I can't do violence to anyone. I feel the sharp prick of a needle.

Later, I come to on the gurney with the sharp stench of the hospital in my nostrils. My clothes have been replaced by one of those damned hospital gowns and my butt is sticking to the warm vinyl gurney. My tongue is an evil-tasting, desiccated mass, my temples are throbbing in sync with my heartbeat and a burning pain smolders under one eye. I try to rub my eye and find that my hands are tied down, so I start yelling!

A nurse arrives to calm me, sponging my sore face with a damp cloth.

"You've been the victim of an assault." No shit, Sherlock! "You're going to be okay. We've just restrained you so you can't hurt yourself."

"Uncle Amos! Danny!"

"Mr. Merkel is fine. He was shot, but it's not serious. He's recovering." She hesitates. "Your uncle is in surgery."

"Is he…"

"We don't know. The doctor will come and talk to you when we know something. Meanwhile, you need to rest. You've had a terrible shock."

You got that right, lady!

"If you promise not to try to get up, I'll untie your hands."

What choice do I have? "I promise."

She releases the restraints. I touch my eye. I can feel the stiches.

"Have you got a mirror?"

"Don't worry, you're still beautiful," she smiles. "It's just a little cut. Shouldn't even leave a scar."

"I'd still like to see."

She drops one of the rails on the gurney. "There's a mirror in the rest room," she says.

I slide off the gurney and almost fall when my bare feet hit the icy floor. The nurse supports me.

"Let me help you. You can go to the bathroom, and then to bed."

My room is only a few steps down the hall. The nurse walks me inside and up to the bathroom door. "Do you need help?" she asks.

"No, I've got this."

I make a beeline for the mirror. There's a little cut under my eye about an inch long – I a couple of stiches along its length, and a fine purple color is developing around it. Great. A stripper with a black eye. That will attract the right kind of fans!

I go back outside where the nurse has turned down the bed and dropped the rail.

"Can I see Danny?" I ask her.

Stripper!

"Maybe tomorrow. Doctor would like you to get some sleep."

"Can I call my roommate and let her know where I am? She'll worry."

"That you can do."

She hands me my cell and I call the land line at the townhouse – I haven't gotten Lupe's cell number yet. It rings and rings. I'll bet she's afraid to pick up. The machine kicks in. I wait for the beep, then, "Lupe, pick up if you're there. It's Nattie." She does so.

I make a snap decision and tell her simply that I'm not coming home tonight, and that she shouldn't worry. I don't want to get into the complexity of the situation with her right now. After I hang up, the nurse offers me a little white cup containing a couple of pills.

"These will help you relax."

"I don't want to go to sleep until I know how my Uncle is."

"You can't do anything for him and losing sleep won't help him. I promise that someone will give you a report when you wake up."

I know she's right. I take the pills and let her help me into bed.

****

It's like I'm under water, clawing my way to the surface from the depths. Darkness gradually transitions into light. My other senses become active as well – the sheets chafe my back, and pain stabs the back of my right hand. I hear the rumble of a cart, glass clinks and a strong medicinal odor reminds me where I am. I search for the source of the pain – it's an i.v. needle.

The hospital! Uncle Amos!

I struggle to rise. They haven't tied me down, but the rails on the bed are up, so it's almost impossible for me to get out of it. A momentary wave of anxiety courses through me, then I notice the call button hanging on the rail. I push it and lie back.

In a moment, the nurse arrives. She's a different one than last night – a large, chubby black woman wearing bright pink scrubs.

"How are we feeling this morning?" she smiles.

151

I stifle a sarcastic reply about our collective well-being. "Fine, I guess. Is there any news about my uncle? Amos Murdoch? He was shot yesterday."

Her smile fades, and fear explodes in my belly.

"Wait a few minutes and I'll see if there's any news."

It's a damn sight longer than a few minutes before Dr. Chowdhury arrives. Her expression is grave. I brace myself for the worst.

"Your uncle is the luckiest man I've met in a while," she begins.

My bladder actually releases and I wet the bed!

She doesn't notice. "He was in surgery for most of last night," she goes on. "Three of the bullets went into the mattress. Only one hit him, and not in a vital spot." She pauses. "But the news is not all good."

She's obviously waiting for me to ask. "What's wrong?"

"The bullet impacted a lumbar vertebra and shattered it. It's very likely that he'll never walk again." She lets that sink in.

The enormity overwhelms me. Sure, Uncle Amos has been overweight and slow ever since I've known him, but at the same time, he's always been very active. He was a marine in his younger days, then he ran the detective agency solo for many years. I just can't picture him as an invalid!

"We've had to put him back in the coma, and back in ICU," she goes on. "He's lost a great deal of blood that he didn't have to lose because of his earlier injury."

"When do you think he'll come out of it?"

"To be frank with you, there's no telling if he'll come out of it at all. He's taken a great deal of punishment for his age and infirmities."

An ominous thought intrudes. "Is he being guarded? I mean, this is the second time somebody has tried to kill him."

"We've reported the incident to the police, of course," she replies. "However, there's no further security as yet beyond that already implemented for ICU. You know that we carefully control access there. That's probably why the assailant waited until your uncle was moved downstairs, where the security is laxer."

I don't like this one bit! "Is your security sufficient to stop someone from shooting his way in? Somebody obviously wants Uncle Amos dead!"

"It's out of my hands, Miss McMasters. I can and will talk to the hospital director about it. You should talk to the police, as well."

Damn straight! This argument is going nowhere, so I change tack. "How is Danny?"

"Mr. Merkel is fine. He was shot in the leg and it just grazed the muscle. We're releasing him, and you, later this morning."

"Can I see him before that?" I don't want him to run out on me before I have a chance to talk to him.

"I'll see what I can do. Have your breakfast first."

I don't want fucking breakfast, lady! I want to find the son of a bitch who shot my uncle!

She leaves and I buzz for the nurse to tell her about the bed. She's all sweetness and light, but I sense that she's a little p.o.'d about it. She lets the rail down and tells me I can go to the bathroom and clean myself, and that she'll bring me a clean gown.

"Can I go see Danny Merkel after I get cleaned up?"

"I don't see why not."

She knocks on the bathroom door to hand me another gown, but I've already found my clothes, so I put those on instead. I'm tempted to take the i.v. out of my hand, but I know that would just piss them off and they might even feel the need to reinsert it, which would piss me off.

I go out to the nurses' station and ask for Danny's room number. He gives it to me, so I wander about a bit before finding it. The door is partly shut, so I knock and push it open after I hear, "Come in."

Danny is standing next to the bed, wearing nothing but a pair of cargo pants. God, the man is hot! His upper body looks like a bodybuilder's, with those six-pack abs. He picks up his t-shirt and slips it over his head, giving me a great view of his impressive deltoids. He turns towards me, and his face hardens. Still not forgiven, I see.

"I've heard about Amos," he says. "I'm sorry, Nattie."

"Do you know that they didn't put a guard on him?"

153

His eyes widen. "They've been pinching pennies in the police department for a while now." he says. "They're probably relying on hospital security, which is pretty tight."

I don't believe this - even ex-cops stick together! I try not to shout. "Somebody totally wants him dead, Danny. Maybe enough to take a lot of other people with him."

"Maybe I'd better talk to Kidd," Danny says hesitantly.

"Do you think it will do any good?"

"I don't know."

"Well, maybe now you'll get why I'm doing what I am. I can't just sit still and take it. I'm sure Judd Horaz is behind this. I just have to prove it."

He looks like he doesn't want to, but he finally asks, "Why do you think that?"

I can't help but throw a barb. "Because, unlike some other people, I've been investigating. I found out that Judd and Becca had a history. She went for a job at the club, and somehow ended up cutting Judd pretty good. He's got a scar on his face to show for it. She had one on her hand. So he had a reason to want her dead."

"Judd probably had reason to want Robyn Carlson dead too," I go on. "She likely found evidence that he was dealing drugs or worse, and he got to her before she could tell Kidd. Then, when Uncle Amos came snooping around, he was next. Judd's bartender Valery is a real piece of work. I could see him stabbing Uncle Amos, easy."

"What about Blackie O'Halloran?"

"I haven't figured out where he fits in yet. Somehow Becca discovered he was her grandfather. Maybe she used an online genealogy site, though I couldn't find any evidence of it on her computer. Or maybe Judd started looking into her background after she cut him, and he found out. Blackie's death would have been worth a lot of money to the right people."

"I don't know if Judd killed Becca himself or had it done." I finish grimly. "But I could see him cutting her up like that, or having someone else do it, and enjoying it."

He looks dubious. "Even if you're right, how would you prove it?"

154

"I'm still working on that."

My nurse comes into the room. "Good. You're both here," she says. "Doctor Chowdhury has released both of you. Hospital policy requires us to escort you to the lobby, so wait here and we'll bring a couple of wheelchairs."

Unbidden, the image of Uncle Amos hunched in a wheelchair flashes into in my head. I can feel the tears welling up, despite my effort to suppress them.

"Nattie, don't," says Danny, moving to embrace me. I glare at him with my arms ramrod-straight at my sides. He backs off with a diffident, "Sorry."

We sit in the chairs and the nurses remove the i.v.s, thank God! Then they wheel us down to the hospital entrance. I head for the garage without acknowledging Danny. I have somewhere to be.

****

Thanks to a former "friend", I have a connection to a street gang called the Urban Legends. They totally owe me a favor. Now it's time to collect.

Later that afternoon, I exit my car on the periphery of a downtown square. I make sure to put fifty cents in the meter, no doubt drawing the ire of the meter maid hovering nearby. There's a faint smell of excrement as I enter the park – I'm not totally sure if it's canine or human. A squirrel darts out of the bushes and runs across the path, then I spot a naked tail and realize it's no squirrel! Many of the benches are occupied by the homeless people that the city has decided to tolerate.

I'm dressed somewhat sedately in jeans and a windbreaker with my long blonde hair jammed under a ballcap, but I still get requests for handouts, which I ignore. I'm don't mind helping the unfortunate, but I know that if I'm seen giving something to anyone, they'll all descend on me like a summer storm.

The guy I'm looking for is occupying a bench near the park's center, just where he said he'd be. He's a big black dude who looks like he could play tight end for State. Bling glistens against his black turtleneck. None of the benches near him are occupied, although the remnants of newspapers and empty wine bottles show they used to be. LeBrowne Ellis is the current president of the Urban Legends and he commands respect.

"S'up, girl?" he greets me as I approach.

I sit down next to him. I skip the preliminaries.

"I'm looking for some information about a .22 magnum semiauto pistol.

"Dass a ho's gun or a faggot's," he says. Politically correct, he ain't! I smile at his street vernacular. I happen to know that LeBrowne has an M.B.A. from one of the better schools in the state.

I need to be cagey. "Well, I'm a girl. Can you get me one?"

"I can get anything. Could take some time, though."

"Have you had one before?"

"A while back."

"Remember who you sold it to?"

He grins at me, showing a large gold tooth. "Now, my bidness depends on con-fi-denti-ality," he stretches the last word out. "Ain't gonna have no customers if I tell anybody who axes who they are!"

"I'm not just anybody."

"No, you ain't," he agrees. "But I tell you and we're square, a'ite?"

"I guess."

"A'ite?"

"All right!"

"I sold it to a hooker, name of Allie."

"And where do I find this Allie?"

He grins again. "Don't rightly know where they dumped the body," he says.

I've been had! "She's dead! How?"

His grin is broader now. "Somebody cut her up."

"Cops catch him?"

"Nuh-uhh. Cops don't pay a lot of attention when a hooker gets it."

Don't I know it!

"Who can I talk to that might have known her?"

"I dunno. Maybe some of the poontang down at that strip joint by State. She worked there some."

156

Stripper!

"The Kitten Club!"

"Dass the one."

I hesitate before asking another question. He's made it obvious that he's only going to answer me literally.

"Anybody in the market for one of those pistols now?"

That grin is getting annoying. "You are," he smirks.

"You know what I mean!"

"A'ite, but this time, you owe me!"

"If the info's worthwhile!"

"Dass for you to say. But you still owe me."

I grit my teeth. "Give it to me."

"Another stripper asked me about one a couple weeks ago."

"She got a name?"

"She wouldn't tell me." He raises a finger. "But I found out anyway. I likes to know who I doon bidness with."

I just wait. Damned if I'll ask him again!

"It was Robyn. Robyn Carlson."

Holy shit! "Did you get her one?"

"Yep. She picked them up a few days later."

"Them?"

"Yep. Two of 'em."

So Robyn bought two illegal .22 magnum pistols, then disappeared! Folks, this is no coincidence!

"You still want one?"

I think about it. Do you really want to commit a felony, Nattie?

"How much?" I ask.

"One large."

"Too steep for me."

"Seven fiddy."

"Eight fifty, and you owe me," I say.

Now why the hell did I just do that?

"Done," he says? "I'll catch up with you at the club."

How in the hell does he know that I'm there? I ask him as much.

"You don't think I know things? Dis is my hood!"

"I just don't picture you as a guy that hangs around strip clubs."

"And I don't see you as a 'ho that strips in one. But you're doin' it. Howcum? Money tight?"

I hesitate. I could totally blow everything here, but I'm getting absolutely no where finding the guy that hurt Uncle Amos.

"My uncle Amos Murdock was down there on a case a while ago, and somebody stabbed him. I'd like to find out who did that."

"What case?"

"I'm not sure. He didn't say."

"Does it have anything to do with that piece you're so interested in?"

"I think so. He didn't die from the stabbing, so somebody shot him at University hospital yesterday. With a .22 magnum. I was there."

LeBrowne purses his lips in a silent whistle. "Listen, this will make us even again after you pay for that piece. Word is that the dude who uses that .22 mag is real, bad, ass." He deliberately separates the last three words for emphasis.

My heart leaps! "So you know who he is!"

"No'm. But I hear he's got him a url."

"A url?"

"Dass right. You want somebody whacked, you can go there. Set it up all online. Pay him in bitcoin."

"Why didn't you tell me this to begin with?"

"You didn't ax. All you axed me was if I could get you a piece."

"Do you know the url?"

"Nope. The Legends take care of they own bidness. They don't hire it out."

"Can you find out?"

"Better make that one large for the gun and the 411."

Damn it! "OK, done. You let me know ASAP." I hesitate – I don't know whether it's a good idea to ask him this or not. "The Legends do any business with Judd Horaz?"

"I toll you before – I don't talk about who the Legends do bidness with."

"It's just that I don't want to step on your toes if you're selling drugs to Judd."

"Ain't sellin' no drugs to nobody," he says facetiously. "Way I hear it, Judd don't need nobody sellin' him no drugs nohow."

"Meaning?"

"Judd sells enough of his own."

"Bull! Using drugs in the club will get you thrown out faster than anything!"

"He ain't no retailer, dass for sure."

Suddenly, it clicks into place. Judd's a wholesaler! That's why he's so hard-ass about drugs in the club! He doesn't want to draw narcs.

I get no propositions as I leave the park – either word has gotten around that I'm no soft touch or it's been noticed with whom I met. Either way, no problem.

Chapter 23.

On the way back to the townhouse, I think about how much to share with Lupe. I know that she's way too polite to pry, but as my roomie, I think she has a right to know at least some of it.

Turns out that it's taken out of my hands. I'm back about ten minutes when the door chime sounds. I check the peep hole. Danny!

He's somewhat disheveled and still wearing the clothes from the hospital this morning. I wonder whether he's been home.

"We need to talk," he says. I don't immediately move back to let him enter.

"Oh, do we now?"

His expression is somewhere between apologetic and pissed. I can see that he's trying to be nice, and that pisses me off.

"Look, I've thought about it, and maybe I shouldn't have said some of the things I did."

Maybe? Really?

"Please let me come in." That actually sounded polite, so I back off and wave him in.

I follow him into the great room. He stops abruptly. Lupe and Eduardo are on the sofa, playing a game on my tablet.

Danny turns to leave. "I'm sorry," he says. "You have company. I should have called."

"They're not company, Danny. Lupe is my roommate." That gets a raised eyebrow. I make introductions.

"We can go to my room," Lupe says, getting up from the sofa.

I don't see any reason to deny her the comfort of the great room. It's her home too.

"No, Lupe, please stay."

I offer Danny a drink.

"I'll take a beer, but no boilermakers, please."

Stripper!

I go to the kitchen to get it. I reach for one for myself, but then I remember my prescription, and I get a soda instead.

I let Danny have the easy chair and settle on the beanbag.

"I've been thinking about what you said," he begins haltingly. "About the cops, I mean, and I think you might be right."

"Right about what?"

"Right about that they aren't taking this thing with Amos seriously."

"You didn't seem to think so when we were talking in the hospital this morning."

He takes a swig of his beer out of the bottle. His tone and demeanor tell me this is hard for him.

"Look, I'll admit that I got angry with you when you took a job in that place," he says. "After what happened, I thought we had something going on, but I just can't condone your stripping."

Who the hell are you to condone anything that I do, Danny boy? Then I realize that part of what attracted me to him in the first place was his strong sense of ethics. Be careful of what you wish for...

"I talked to Kidd about a guard for Amos," Danny goes on. "He said that the Lieutenant thinks that hospital security is adequate. They did tell the hospital not to release anything about Amos' condition to anyone but you, so that's something. But they're not gonna assign a uni to guard him."

"Why would they not do that!" I explode. "It's obvious that Uncle Amos can identify this guy. And it's definitely the same guy who killed Blackie. He's a pro - Kidd said so. He's not going to stop trying!"

Maybe it was a bad idea to let Lupe stay - her face is as white as the carpet. Eduardo has picked up on his sister's apprehension and looks scared too. I realize that I've haven't told her anything about what happened at the hospital, so I do now.

"It's terrible what happened to your uncle," is her reaction. "You are right to try and find the bad guy who hurt him."

Now I'm glad I let her stay.

"Lupe's right," Danny says. "I still don't agree with how you're going about it, but I think the cops are blowing it off, and I might know why."

Now it's my turn to raise an eyebrow.

"Remember on our first date, you asked me why I quit the force?"

"You told me that some things went down that you couldn't square yourself with. But you didn't say what."

"That's right. After I was in the department for a few months, it became apparent that there were some cases that just weren't being investigated like they should be. I mentioned it to a few people and was told that investigation is the detectives' prerogative. I was just a uni, so I should butt out."

He takes another swig of beer. "Well, I tried to butt out. I learned in the Corps that everything doesn't always get done the way it should, and that pointing out your superiors' deficiencies was not the way to get promoted."

"Sometimes getting promoted isn't the most important thing," I say.

"You're right, but on the other hand, it's hard to make a difference if you're never given the power to do so. Anyway, I started to see a pattern in the cases that were getting short shrift. Many involved excessive force claims against cops. Sometimes cops can be damned cold if they think that a bad guy hasn't gotten what's coming to him, and they like to deliver a little street justice."

"So if you were keeping your head down about this stuff, why'd you quit?" I ask him.

He looks at Lupe and Eduardo with an uneasy expression on his face, then back at me.

I can tell that he totally doesn't want to talk about this. "Maybe we'd better go to my room," I say.

Lupe says, "No, Nattie. Eduardo should have a nap. I'll take him upstairs."

This time, I let her go. Danny and I are silent until they're gone.

"This goes no further than this room," he says. I nod.

"There was a shooting involving me and my partner. We were busting online hookers. One of us would make a date with a girl, then we'd meet her where she told us. Once money changed hands, we'd bust her."

What a waste of the taxpayers' money! "Isn't that entrapment?"

162

"Sometimes," Danny agrees. "But it really didn't matter. We'd carry her downtown and lock her up. That would kill her business for the night. If we could make a case, we would - if not, we'd cut her loose until the next time. At least she'd worry every time she got an email from a john. But anyway," he continues, "one night we go to this motel. Josh goes in with the girl. I'm outside as backup when I hear the shot. I bust in and find him standing over her with a smoking gun and she's stone dead. She has a pistol next to her."

"That doesn't make sense," is my first reaction.

"You're right," he concurs. "Josh claimed she drew on him when he tried to arrest her. But why would a hooker risk getting shot just because she was being busted? It happens all the time – it's a cost of doing business. What's more, the pistol was a Glock 17. That's not a woman's weapon, if you know what I mean."

"Not really." What a sexist!

"It's a full-sized gun, not a little compact. She was wearing shorts and a tank top – I don't know where she'd even have had it."

Suddenly I get it. "You think he shot her on purpose!"

Danny nods. "Some cops carry a gun that they've confiscated and never turned in. The serial number is usually filed off. If the cop is involved in a dicey shooting, he just drops the burner and everything is suddenly okay."

"You think that's what Josh did?"

His grim look tells me that's exactly what he thinks.

"So what did you do about it?"

"Josh wanted me to say I saw her with the gun. That would have been the end of it."

"Even though she was wearing shorts and a tank top?"

"Yeah. Not even IA wanted this to look like anything but a clean shoot."

"So what did you do?"

"I told IA the god's truth. That I was outside when the shot was fired and that I saw the gun on the floor next to the girl when I entered. When they asked me if I thought it was a clean shoot, I said that I couldn't say, because I didn't see it."

Relief washes over me. "I'll bet that didn't make Josh happy."

"Nuh-uhh. They suspended him while they investigated. But the shoot came back clean anyway."

"Howcum?"

"Because they didn't have any direct evidence that it wasn't, and Josh had friends high up. He was a lot more willing to overlook certain things than I was."

"So what happened to you?"

"Well, they couldn't do anything to me administratively for telling the truth, but naturally, Josh put in for a new partner. He bad-mouthed me all over – said I didn't have his six. I got labelled as a rat. Nobody wanted to work with me, and nobody would back me up. The best thing for everybody was for me to quit the job."

"Why do you think he shot her?"

"I think he was getting some from her on the side. Maybe she was threatening to rat on him. Josh has a wife and a kid, and his wife's pretty straight-laced. If the hooker could prove he had sex with her, the best that would happen is that he'd have to resign. He could even go to prison. So it made sense for him to set her up and shoot her."

"You think she could have proved he was screwing her?"

His sour expression lets me know that he doesn't appreciate my blunt language. "Ask Monica Lewinsky. All it would have taken is a biological sample."

I shouldn't, but I can't resist. "You mean a sample of his cum on her clothes." He blushes and doesn't answer. I'm sorry I said it, but I can't bring myself to say so. I ask instead, "So what does all of this have to do with Uncle Amos?"

"A lot of the excessive force by officers was selective. They cracked down on some hookers and drug dealers, but not others. It was obvious that some people in the upper echelons were turning a blind eye to certain people's criminal activity and even worse, helping them out by cracking down on the competition. I think my ex-partner Josh was in bed with these guys and I wasn't, and that's why he got a bye and I got the shaft."

"And Uncle Amos?"

164

"Was probably assaulted by somebody that the cops have been protecting. Like Judd maybe." Danny says.

"Which is why they're not falling all over themselves to provide Uncle Amos a bodyguard.

Danny nods somberly.

A bothersome thought intrudes. "Then what about Robyn Carlson?" I ask. "She was trying to get the goods on Judd."

"And look what happened. I'll tell you something else. When I was in the department, I knew of Leon Kidd. He had a rep as a straight arrow. Some people would have been really happy to see him gone, but it's not easy to get rid of a senior officer, especially a minority. But this Carlson affair might just do it since he was her handler."

"And you're just going to let all of this go?" I ask him.

He holds his arms out in supplication. "I can't prove a damn thing. What would you have me do?"

He's obviously distressed. No point in my rubbing salt into the wound. "All right, I get that you can't right every wrong in the world, but maybe you can make up for it by helping me get the goods on Judd."

"How?"

I tell him about Judd's trip to Mexico, and my plan to break into his office with the magnet. The look on his face tells me that he's not thrilled, but I press on. "You could help me get past Valery and the bartenders."

"How?" he says again.

I tell him the plan I've cooked up while we've been talking. His look becomes even more disbelieving.

"It's dangerous as hell," he says. "What if you get caught?"

"If you do your job, that won't happen."

He tries again. "Just because you're not a cop doesn't mean you can do a warrantless search. Technically, you'll be guilty of burglary."

"If I don't get caught, there'll be no charges."

"Even if you find something, the cops can't use it because it was obtained illegally."

"How is what I'm proposing different than what Robyn Carlson was doing?"

Kidd probably had warrants in place before she ever had a job there," Danny says.

"If I find anything, I can always phone in an anonymous tip or something. Then they can get a warrant."

"You need evidence for a warrant, not an anonymous tip. You could screw up an ongoing investigation."

"I thought you said that there was no investigation," I say.

His expression tells me I scored a hit.

"Let me sleep on it," he says after a moment.

Chapter 24.

Afﬁter Danny's gone, I go up to tell Lupe it's safe to come downstairs. Her door is closed, so I knock gently. She opens it part way, then holds a finger to her lips. She swings it fully open. Eduardo is on her bed, sound asleep. Her face radiates love for that little boy, and I feel a tightness in my throat and a slight pain in the center of my chest as I look at her. She slides out into the hallway and softly closes the door.

We don't speak until we're back in the great room.

"I'm sorry that you had to go upstairs, Lupe. I want you to know that I consider this your home as well as mine. You shouldn't always have to make way for me."

"*De nada*," she says dismissively. "I know you would do it for me. Besides, is good that *el niño* get a nap." Her expression becomes one of concern. "I hope you will not get into trouble messing with Judd. He is a bad man."

"Yes he is, and I'm sure he's responsible for what happened to my uncle. I'm so glad that you don't have to go back and work there anymore."

"I am too," she says. "I hope you don't mind, but I go shopping while you were out. I can make us some dinner then you can go to the club."

I don't think about it very long. "I'm not going to the club tonight, Lupe. The last few days have wiped me out."

"Then I will fix us a nice dinner." Lupe heads for the kitchen.

It is not long before the townhouse is permeated with the rich, deep scent of Mexico – the sharp fragrance of chilies and other spices, underscored by the sweet earthy odor of corn and the homey smell of simmering chicken. I have all I can do not to go charging in there, but I want to give Lupe her space. I know she is proud of her cooking and that she will enjoy surprising me with her culinary creation. I only hope that she doesn't put so much weight on me that I have to stop dancing at the club before I can nail Judd. I resolve to ask her how she keeps her figure – Lupe is heftier than I am, but she is by no means fat.

Music begins to play – my ringtone. The screen brightens as I pick it up. Rebecca Feiner.

Oh shit!

I briefly consider letting it go to voicemail, but I realize that's a bad idea. My short association with this gracious lady has done much for me. I tap the icon to talk to her.

"Hello, Rebecca."

"Hello, Natalie. How are you?" There's no impatience or annoyance in her voice at all. Just concern.

"I'm okay. I'm sorry I've missed our appointments. The last few weeks have been rough."

"All the more reason to be assiduous about your treatment, Natalie. What's been going on?"

I glance towards the kitchen. Lupe is working industriously, paying no attention to me.

I briefly summarize the events of the last couple of weeks, leaving out my new employment situation. That I'd rather discuss in person.

"Oh my God!" says Rebecca, after I tell her about the shooting at the hospital. "Are you all right? How is your uncle?"

"Not good." I don't want to get into details. "I'm getting daily updates."

"How about your sexual orientation? Any progress?"

I glance at Lupe. "I'm working on it."

"Listen, I can understand if you don't want to come in until next week," Rebecca says, "But don't you dare try to get through this by yourself. Do you have anyone that you can talk to?"

"Not really," I say.

"I'm texting you my home number," Rebecca says. "If you need me, call me! I don't care what time it is. And call me immediately if anything happens to your uncle."

"I will," I tell her, and mean it.

"I'm setting you up for ten a.m. on Monday. Call me if something comes up and you can't make it. I mean it, Natalie!"

Stripper!

"I will do my best to be there, Rebecca, and I'll call you if I can't." My voice breaks suddenly. "I really want to thank you for all…"

"It's my job, Natalie, and I'm glad to help you. See you on Monday." The phone goes silent, then chings for her text.

"Natalie," Lupe calls. "Could you please wake Eduardo, and tell him to wash his hands and face and come to dinner?"

I go upstairs to Lupe's room. It's dark inside because she's pulled the curtains. The room has that lived-in smell – a muddle of body odor, perfume, food scents and other things – it's Lupe's scent and it's oddly comforting. I walk over to the small lump in her bed. Eduardo's dark, curly locks are barely peeping out of the covers. He's turned his head so his nostrils are free of the blankets, and I can just hear the low buzz of his childish snores. I smile. Motherhood has never been as aspiration of mine, but the sight of that little boy stirs something primal in me, something that wants to protect and nurture, and keep him from harm. I reach down and ruffle his hair. Deep in the slumber of his innocence, he never moves. I reach under the covers and give him a shake. His dark brown eyes pop open, and he smiles when he sees me. Nothing makes you feel more special than a little boy smiling at you.

He gives me some trouble about washing his hands as a boy should, but soon we're downstairs chowing down on Lupe's fabulous dinner – chicken enchiladas with red sauce, rice, beans and salad with guacamole. I'm very glad I decided not to go to club tonight – I doubt that I could do much pole dancing after a meal like this!

Lupe wants to clean the kitchen too but I won't let her. She's so eager to please me that it would be easy to treat her like a servant. I get Eduardo to help instead, letting him put the dishes in the dishwasher as I rinse them. As we work, I reflect that it's been a long time since I've done anything like this. After dad died, it was just me and mom, and she worked two jobs just to keep us in the house so we rarely had meals together. I can feel myself smiling again. I totally think that having Lupe and Eduardo move in here was the best thing I could have done.

When we're finished, Lupe gives Eduardo the remote and parks him in front of the TV.

"Want to take those pictures for the website?" I ask her. She nods enthusiastically.

169

We go to my room and raid Becca's clothes. Lupe is somewhat heftier than Becca and me, but I don't think tight clothing will be a problem for the kind of pictures we want to take. Lupe picks out three or four outfits and we go up to the studio.

While Lupe changes, I fire up the lights and the computer. I'm going to use the wall-mounted web cams and the green screen to take the pix so potential clients can get a good idea of what they're buying. I think about posting a short video, but then decide against it – don't want to give them too much for free. Just enough to whet the appetite.

Finally I'm ready and so is Lupe. She's chosen a deep red baby doll nightie with frills that ties in the front, and a pair of shiny black heels. She's not wearing a bra, but I do catch a glimpse of a matching bikini bottom. The vivid red of the chemise dramatically sets off her mocha skin and black hair. That familiar tingling awakens.

"What do you want to do first?" I ask her.

She moves to a pole in front of the green screen. "I'll do a pole dance," she says. "It's what I know."

I pull up the control panel for the green screen and select the nightclub scene I used for that first dance with Bobby. It's amazing – on the screen, it really does look as if Lupe's in a cabaret. I click an icon labelled with a couple of musical notes and select a slow, jazz trumpet piece, which begins wailing from the hidden speakers. "That should put you in the mood," I tell her "You can start anytime."

I focus on the screen while Lupe dances behind me. She begins by embracing the pole and slowly rubbing it between her breasts. She arches her back and throws her head back, pumping her chest towards the camera. I get a couple of wide shots, then zoom in for a close-up of her bosom.

I widen out the view just in time to catch her mounting the pole. She grips it over her head with both hands and swings upward, scissoring the pole with her legs. She slowly extends her upper body backwards, letting her curly ebon tresses cascade down. The nightie, a little too small, comes undone at the tie across her breasts. The harsh lights accentuate her dark brown nipples.

She slowly spreads her legs to their fullest extent. Now she's welded the pole only by the strength of her arms and the pressure on her crotch. She begins to spin, then releases one hand and gracefully extends the arm back over her head.

Stripper!

I'm amazed and aroused simultaneously –no way I could do that move without falling! She uses her free hand to undo the tie at the waist. Now her entire upper body is displayed. I'm clicking the mouse frantically taking as many pictures as I can.

She gracefully flips herself forward and the nightie drops off her shoulders as her feet touch the floor. It lands in a heap. Now it's apparent that the red bottom is only a thong, held on by ties on her hips.

She's back on the pole again for another spin, and this time the free hand reaches for the tie on her uppermost hip. The teeny scrap of cloth flutters down, exposing the dark triangle between her legs. My mouse clicks have become maniacal, because I'm doing everything I can just to stay in that chair!

She flips forward again and the thong slithers down her leg to join the nightie. Nude now except for her heels, she begins making love to the pole again, which glistens with her bodily fluids.

She remounts the pole and flips her body completely over so her long hair brushes the floor. Her legs are totally spread-eagled – it's impossible to know what's keeping her on that pole as she slowly revolves. She stays there for what seems like forever before she pivots and lands gracefully on the floor.

I turn away from the screen and see her standing there, shimmering with a thin sheen of sweat. She's making an obvious effort not to pant.

"Did you get all the pictures we need?" she says in a breathy voice.

I don't even think as I pop out of the chair. Her overpowering musk takes my breath away as our tongues meet and we tumble onto the bed.

I end up on the bottom. She never stops kissing me as she tears at my clothes, and I help her just as enthusiastically. Finally, we're both nude. I push her shoulders to get her off my chest because I can hardly breathe. She ends up sitting upright on my hips. Her face is radiant and her nipples are rampant. She begins rotating her hips and I thrust mine up to meet her. She tweaks my nipples and I cover hers with my hands.

The pressure in my crotch is building, but it's frustratingly slow. She must think so too, because she rolls sideways, pulling me on top of her, then turns me around to face her feet. She grips my upper thighs and pulls my hips to her mouth and I fall forward between her legs. I know what to do!

I wake up in that position sometime later. I roll off of Lupe, then turn around to crawl up into the crook of her arm. She enfolds me and we spend quite a while just petting, kissing gently and gazing into each other's eyes.

An unwanted thought intrudes. "Lupe, I shouldn't have. Especially after what Judd did."

"You did exactly right, *cariño*," she says. "Especially after what Judd did."

I've always wondered what real love feels like. All my life I've wanted the fireworks, an overwhelming feeling of ecstasy that I could lose myself in, but it's never happened for me. Not with Michael, Danny or any other lover. I don't feel it now, either.

What I do feel is intense contentment - a sensation of utter rightness that I've never experienced before. No worry, no fear, and no sense of want. I feel whole and complete for the first time in my life.

OMG, I think I'm in love! With a stripper!

Chapter 25.

It's Wednesday evening. I'm at the club, but I'm not dancing. I'm sitting at the bar, dressed in jeans, a t-shirt, a ballcap and sunglasses, drinking an expensive Corona. The sunglasses hide the shiner I got from the gunman, which has blossomed. It's now a radiant dark purple with tinges of green at the edges and has migrated halfway down my cheek. It would be way hard to completely hide it with cosmetics and when I start sweating under those hot lights, it wouldn't take long to come to light. Some guys might think a nude dancer with a shiner is sexy, but those are not who I want to give lap dances to.

I check in with Nan because it has been a few days since I danced. The shiner is a convenient excuse for staying off stage, and I don't go into the details. She doesn't ask. The hospital shooting did make the local news, but strippers are not news junkies and nobody mentions it. I tell Nan that I just want to make an appearance so my fans know that I'm still around, and she says she thinks it's a good idea. She doesn't mention Lupe's absence. She's probably used to strippers coming and going.

I'm sitting at the bar near to the door to Judd's office. Because I normally wear a belt pouch, I'm carrying one of Becca's purses, which contains a rather large magnet.

Valery is behind the bar with a State kid. The crowd is good for midweek, but it's far from a packed house. The bartenders are working steadily but not frantically. They've got plenty of time to watch the crowd and the dancers.

I glance at the runways. Annie and Summer are writhing on adjacent poles on the stage nearest the bar, surrounded by their little coterie. One of them is Danny. He's pulled a chair right up next to where Annie is dancing and gazing up at her with lust in his eyes. He's acting like he's very drunk.

It's a club rule that a customer may not touch a dancer on a runway unless he gives her money and she initiates the contact. He has to keep his arms behind him for a kiss. Another rule is that no customer may go up on a runway for any reason. Violating either rule gets the offender ejected.

I can't hear him over the music, but it's obvious that Danny is chatting up the dancers. He gets up from his chair and reaches out for Summer, who spins to put the pole between herself and him. Seeing that he's offering no cash, she shakes her head vigorously. Since he can't reach her from where he's standing, he climbs up on his chair and puts a foot on the stage. Now Summer has let go of the pole and is backing away from him, her hands out to push him back if he gets too close.

The two tight ends rocket from their stools on the periphery of the room and effortlessly glide towards Danny like they've done a thousand times before. Danny's still on the stage – his gestures indicate that he's drunkenly trying to reason with Summer, who wants no part of him. One of the bouncers vaults onto the stage and grabs Danny by the shoulders. Danny shrugs him off. The bouncer cocks a fist and launches it at Danny's jaw. Danny pirouettes like a ballet dancer and interposes a perfect block with his left, redirecting the punch over his shoulder, then follows up with a devastating right to the gut. The shock on the frat boy's face is comical as he drops to the stage with his hands around his middle.

Now the second bouncer is on the stage and being much more careful than his companion since he's been warned. The two fighters are turning in a tight circle and Danny has his open hands raised in a martial arts posture. The tight end feints left and steps in with a right. Danny catches the punch in both hands, locks the wrist and elbow and spins from the hips, launching his unfortunate opponent out into the crowd, where he annihilates a table on landing.

That's all it takes. The guys at the table destroyed by the human missile come up swinging, and the fight spreads like fire ants after somebody kicks the hill. Valery and the other bartender draw saps from under the bar and wade into the melee. Now is my chance!

It's only two steps from my seat to the metal door. I yank on the handle. Shit! It stays closed, as solid as if welded. My heart sinks – this little foray could be over before it starts. Then I remember something. I step behind the bar and feel underneath it near the end. My finger finds a button, and I push it. Back at the door, I grab the handle and pull. It opens so easily that I stumble backwards. In a nanosecond I'm in the hallway. The door shuts and that infernal music diminishes to a dull thumping.

I really hope that Danny can survive without getting beaten too badly. I have to confess that a thrill went through me when I saw how easily he handled those bouncers on the stage, both of whom were considerably larger than him. Marine training rocks. I totally owe him for this!

174

Stripper!

I move down the hallway to Judd's office door. I try the handle and it moves downward, but when I tug on it, of course it's locked. I remove a package wrapped in a washcloth that's a little smaller than a playing card pack from my purse. Inside is an incredibly powerful magnet made of a rare earth metal. The website said that these magnets are brittle, and they recommended wrapping it up so it doesn't chip. Such magnets are also dangerous – I've got a small bruise on my hand because I let it get too near another piece of metal and got a painful pinch. I'm lucky it wasn't a crushed finger. I also left my cellphone in the car to keep it away from the magnet.

I prop one end of the magnet against the lock, being very careful to keep my fingers out of the way and let the other end rest against the wooden door. I'm so glad the door is not metal like the one outside in the club – if it was, I'd never be able to remove the magnet.

I put my hand on the door handle. The website that showed me how to do this said that it doesn't work on all push-button locks, and that some locks it used to work on were upgraded to secure them against this technique. Please God it works on this one! I hold my breath and push down on the handle, then pull it towards me. The door swings silently open, and the woody tobacco aroma of Judd's office flows over me.

It's dark in the office. I try to remove the magnet, but it doesn't come off. Yikes, that thing is strong! I grab it with both hands and heave, and it releases, nearly pinching my fingers as it tries to lock itself back on. I get it far enough away so I can handle it, then put it back in my purse. I prop the door with the purse against to keep it from closing fully, then I step into the office. The light pops on! I smile. Judd and I have the same technology.

I hunt for a switch, because if Judd's lights are like mine, they'll go out in a minute if the switch isn't thrown. I find and click it, then remove my purse from the doorway and let the door fully close. As the silence envelops me, I finally feel somewhat secure.

The office looks much as it did during my audition, with its ostentatious oriental motif. My eyes are immediately drawn to the tapestry behind the desk that depicts the Japanese lesbians. It reminds me that the last time I was here, I still thought I was straight. That's all changed now. I close my eyes to get myself back on task.

I'm not totally sure what I'm looking for, but the desk seems like the best bet. Naturally, the drawers are locked. I jiggle the mouse and a green and fuchsia screen that mirrors the sign on the roof springs to life. Nothing like a brand, is there, Judd? I left click and get a username/password screen.

Shit. What did you expect, Nattie, that he'd have it all booted up for you with the incriminating page on top?

I pull out the lockpicks from the 3M office and select a short, fine one to work on the middle drawer. If I can open that one, all the rest will usually unlock.

I work for about ten minutes. No luck. The inside of that lock feels as smooth as the inside of a beer bottle. Shit! I bang the drawer in frustration, hurting my hand. Some detective!

I look about the room in frustration and my eyes light on the lascivious tapestry behind the desk again. The naked girls smile, mocking me. Then I notice it's hanging on rings, like a shower curtain. Why?

I slide the tapestry sideways, revealing a wooden door. It has pushbutton lock like the one outside. In a moment the magnet is on the lock, and the door opens. The light in the room behind it flashes on and the smell of incense washes over me.

It's a bedroom, done in the same tacky Eastern style as the office. I shudder, not because I expect to find a girl in a box under the bed, but because I know what was done to my Lupe on that bed. I could kill Judd without a thought right now!

The room is furnished sparsely, with the large bed dominating it. There's a chest of drawers on the wall across from the foot of the bed, with a large, flat screen TV on top.

I'm not sure why I push the button to turn on the TV, but when it springs to life, instead of a mundane TV program, the screen displays a rectangle containing about two dozen little square boxes. Closer inspection reveals that each box is a shot of the club floor from a different angle. There are views of the bar, the runways, the tables and the inside of the lap dance alcoves. The girls' locker room and the shower room are there too. Just can't get enough, can you, Judd?

I touch a rectangle that shows the club floor and the runways from the parking lot entrance. It expands to fill the entire 60" screen. It looks like the fight is still in full swing. I look for Danny, and I spot him making his way toward the exit.

Stripper!

Suddenly, Valery is in front of him. He's probably identified Danny as responsible for the fracas. Danny assumes a fighting stance with one foot forward and the other back. Valery's hand chops down at Danny's head like he is throwing something and Danny's left blocks it, forearm to forearm, then slithers up to Valery's wrist and locks on.

I touch the screen again and it goes back to the little squares. I scan quickly and chose a perspective that gives me a closer view.

Danny now has Valery's left hand in a wristlock and is bending the arm at an impossible angle. I see a small, dark object fall to the floor from Valery's hand. A sap!

Danny suddenly reverses the hold to bring the arm upwards, then releases it, throwing Valery onto the floor on his back. Or so he thinks. Valery somehow gets his arms behind him and pops back to his feet like he's on springs. It's obvious that Danny wasn't expecting that because Valery pastes him full on the jaw with a wicked left.

Danny staggers, but manages to get a block against the second left. He'd have probably been gone if he hadn't. For the next fifteen or twenty seconds, Valery throws a flurry of left jabs at the beleaguered Danny, who blocks every one, albeit with difficulty. It's obvious that that bartender has some serious skills! But why is he fighting with one hand?

Oh no! Valery throws one more punch and Danny falls over backwards! Valery rears a leg for a finishing kick, but Danny sweeps his other leg out from under him while lying on the floor. That's when I realize that Valery's last punch never landed.

This time it's Danny who pops back up like a kid's toy. He clears the supine Valery with a leap and books it for the door to the parking lot.

I follow Danny's progress by tapping the screen to switch to another camera. My eye catches a view of the hallway outside of Judd's office, and the door at the end opens and somebody enters. I expand the square. It's Bobby, heading for the office door! It's a good thing that I removed the magnet and locked it.

Bobby stops at the door and I see him punching buttons. WTF? He's opening the door!

Horrified, I look at the bedroom door. It's closed, but the tapestry is still retracted and the magnet is on the lock. I'm trapped!

177

The door opens and Bobby is staring at me.

"Kira, you idiot! Get out of here! Judd's got the place alarmed and cameras all over everywhere! He'll know you're in here!"

A loud THUNK! sounds from the outer office.

"Oh shit!" Bobby says. "He's locked the door! We can't get out!"

"But he's in Mexico!"

Bobby gives me a disgusted look. "Haven't you ever heard of a smartphone? He's probably calling Valery right now!"

My gaze returns to the TV. The outer hallway is still empty. I tap the screen and bring up the club floor. The fight looks all but over. Danny got away! But Valery is on his phone.

"We've got to get out of here!"

I push past Bobby, back into the outer office. I'm looking for any way to barricade the door to buy us just a little more time. I spot the chair that Judd sat in while I stripped for him. I move quickly towards it, trip over something and fall flat on my face!

I come up seeing stars and with a throbbing nose. I wipe my face and my hand comes away bloody. Great. I'm going to look like a Roller Derby poster girl before this is over!

WTF did I trip over? I'm standing on the large oriental rug on the burgundy shag carpet in the center of the room. A nude oriental man with an impossibly long penis leers at me as he mounts a rotund lady from the rear. Her butt is prominent, because it's raised from the floor by something underneath the rug that I tripped over. I remember I tripped over it before when I was auditioning for Judd. Hope glimmers.

"Bobby! Help me move the rug!" He's standing there with a deer-in-the-headlights look.

I grab a corner of the rug and pull it back and up. It moves, but it's heavy and unwieldy.

"Bobby! Help!"

This time he moves. He grabs the other corner and we fold the rug back on itself, revealing a wooden floor. And a trap door. This place has a cellar!

178

Stripper!

The trap door is raised about an inch off the floor, which is why I tripped over it. There's a handle on one side that folds down into a niche cut in the door's surface. I grab it and pull. Christ! It's heavy!

"Bobby! A little help here!"

Both of us can't get a grip on the handle because it's too small, but I've raised the door up just enough so Bobby can get his fingers underneath. We heave, and the door moves up to a vertical position.

A metal rod attached to the bottom of the door swings beneath it. Instantly, I see what it's for.

"Bobby! Can you hold the door by yourself for a sec?"

"I think so."

"Okay, I'm letting go."

I do so, and grab the metal rod, looking for the place where it goes. There! A round hole on the floor along on edge of the door, a little larger in diameter than the rod. I ease the rod into it.

"Now let it go easy."

Bobby does so, and the weight of the door forces the rod further into the hole, propping the door open.

I look around for my purse and realize that it's still in the bedroom. I run back in to get it.

I check out the TV. The bouncers and the bartenders are rounding up the patrons and ushering them towards the parking lot. Probably closing for the night to clean up the mess. I bring up the outer hallway and see that it is still clear. I don't know if Judd has called his lackeys yet or not. There's no hurry. He's got us locked in here. Or so he thinks.

OMG! What if he's still watching? He'll see that the cellar door is open. Time to move, Nattie!

I go back to the outer office, removing my flashlight from my purse. I didn't come in here totally unprepared. I turn it on and a solid bar of white light leaps across the room.

I move to the basement entrance, twisting the front of the flashlight to widen the beam. I shine it into the cellar. There's a flight of wooden steps that begins

179

on the side of the entry opposite the door hinges. You can close the door by disengaging the rod and lowering it as you go down.

I look at Bobby, who's still freaked AF. "You know if we can get out this way?"

He shakes his head.

"Snap out of it, Bobby! Is that no we can't, or you don't know?"

"I don't know!" he says.

"Well, we've got nothing to lose."

I retrieve my magnet and put it back in my purse, then redirect the light into the cellar.

"You go first," I tell Bobby. "I'll hold the light for you."

"No way! There could be spiders and everything down there!"

What a wuss! "Would you rather hang out here waiting for Judd's studs to come and get us?" He looks like he's going to cry!

"You go first," he says, "Then I'll come down. You can hold the light from down there."

I shake my head in frustration. There's no way I'm going to get that candy ass to go first. I move over to the lip of the entryway. The cone of light illuminates the stairs, but the darkness outside of it is absolute. I take the first step, dreading what I'm going to find.

Chapter 26.

T he chill of the basement causes my skin to tighten, making my face feel like a mask. It stinks of ancient insects and mold like all basements, but other odors are intermingled. It takes me a moment to identify them. Booze, wood smoke – and bleach!

The floor is concrete, and covered with sawdust, which is obviously the source of the moldy odor. The cone of light gradually illuminates the chamber as I make my way down the stairs. It looks to be one cavernous room that runs underneath the entire club. The ceiling is constructed of wide boards held up by square posts that are easily a foot in diameter. They're regularly spaced about ten feet apart on all sides. The light causes a pattern of shadows to dance on the floor, giving the place the atmosphere of a bizarre, otherworldly forest.

I reach the bottom of the stairs and shine the light around to make sure that I'm alone. I'm about fifteen feet below street level. The light picks out a concrete wall about twenty feet from the base of the stairs. Cartons, crates and kegs are stacked everywhere and make it hard to tell just how big this place is.

I catch a glint of metal and shine the light on one of the posts. WTF? A big ass hook is mounted on one side near the top of the post. I shine the light around some more and find a couple of other posts similarly equipped.

THUNK!

OMG! You didn't! I flash my light up the stairs.

You did! Bobby you motherfucker! You dropped the goddam door!

I tear back up the stairs, the light bobbing crazily. I push against the bottom of the door with my hand, but it might as well be a wall. I try to push with both hands but I can't with the light. I set it down on the steps so it shines off into the basement, then I reach up with both hands and strain. Nothing! I pound the heels of my hands against the bottom of the door. I get nothing but splinters for my trouble, and it hardly even makes any noise. I take a step up so I can use my legs for leverage and kick the light through the back of the step. It seems like it tumbles down in slow motion before it hits the floor with a sickening plastic CRACK! and winks out.

Shit! Shit shit, shit shit, shit shit, shit!

It's a cliché to say that you can't see your hand in front of your face, but that's the only apt description of the darkness in here. There are no windows, and the place is so solidly built that not a wink of light comes from upstairs or outside. Panic explodes in my chest – I'm breathing in short, rapid gasps. My face is starting to tingle and my head is beginning to swirl. I've had this feeling before! I'm hyperventilating!

When I was a kid, a playmate thought it would be funny to lock me in an old refrigerator. I screamed and pounded the door, then hyperventilated and passed out. I came to in my mother's arms. Later I found out that my friend had tried to release me, but the door was old style with the latch in the handle and he couldn't get it open. Luckily, he was able to get my mom to come before my air ran out. I'll never forget that feeling – it's like the breath is being sucked out of you and you're dissolving into the darkness.

I know I have to get control of myself before I pass out. I make a deliberate effort to slow my breathing. Think of something pleasant, Nattie! An image my fingernails digging into Bobby's eyes flashes into my head, but it seems to just make my breathing faster. Then I think of Lupe's umber eyes, gazing into mine as we lay together, kissing and petting. If I don't get myself out of here, I'll never see her again. My breathing comes under control.

I've sunk down onto the steps and I'm gripping one so hard my hands hurt, to avoid falling backwards off the staircase. I slowly ease the pressure and crawl down the steps like I'm going down a ladder. My feet touch the concrete and I collapse onto the dirty floor. I sluggishly pull myself into a sitting position.

Think, Nattie!

First order of business is to find my flashlight. That crack I heard when it hit doesn't bode well, but I've dropped a flashlight before and had it go out, only to have it come on again after a second rap. If I can make it work, I can find a light switch.

Because of how it fell, I know that the flashlight must be behind the stairs. I touch the stairs, then hold on as I move around and under. I crawl forward, sweeping my hands back and forth. The floor is like cold sandpaper and I swear I can feel things crawling in the sawdust. Don't black widows live in places like this? Stop it, Nattie!

As careful as I am about covering all of the space in front of me with my sweeping hands, I miss the goddam flashlight anyway. I know because I find it with my knee. There's another sickening crack as my weight comes down on it.

Stripper!

I hold back tears as I work the switch. That fucking flashlight is as dead as a hunk of meat hanging on one of those goddam hooks. I bang it on the concrete floor to no avail, then slam it harder and harder until the plastic splits again and there's a sharp stab in my hand. The pain and the warm wetness running on my palm brings me to my senses. I'll never get out of here if I don't keep my shit together!

I take stock again. It's obvious that this basement is used to store booze and beer. These things come in from outside. Does this basement have an exit to the outside? Where would it be? Along one of the walls! So all I need to do is crawl to a wall, then follow it until I come to the exit. I'm proud of myself!

Abruptly, I remember Jesse propping his feet on the slanted basement door next to club entrance. Which wall would that be?

I envision the club in my mind's eye. You walk in the door, turn right towards the bar. You go into the hallway to Judd's office, and turn right at the end toward the door. You go through the door and straight to his desk, trip over the trap door under the carpet. The trap door opens parallel to the wall where the office door is, and the stairs run downward from the other side in the same direction. Do a one-eighty to get under the stairs. Then the outside basement door is on the wall to the left. Now I am totally proud of myself!

Even though it's possible that creepy-crawlies inhabit the sawdust, I decide it's better to be on my hands and knees than to walk upright – no chance that I'll trip and fall over something I can't see.

I crawl slowly, resisting the urge to move as quickly as possible. My hand contacts something hard and cold – metal. It's a thin tube with a wheel on the bottom and a large, hemispherical piece on top. The top is open. I reach inside and feel grit or dirt. I remove my hands and the smell of wood smoke becomes almost overpowering. Ashes. It's a grill!

What did Kidd say about Becca being tortured? She had multiple burns. Hooks on the columns. A charcoal brazier. I suddenly realize that it was in this basement where Becca was raped, tortured and killed. And Judd did it, or ordered it done and watched it happen, all because she cut him!

I push past the grill, crawling faster. Soon I bark my fingers on a rough stone wall. Now which is the door? I replay the exercise of getting into Judd's office in my head. Right! I have to turn right.

I stand and sidle along the wall, feeling constantly with both hands. The texture changes from stone to rough wood. The tears well up. I found it! A door! I drop my hands to waist level where the handle should be, find it, pull. It doesn't budge! I yank harder. Nothing!

"No, no, no, no, NO!"

I'm hauling on that door handle with my whole body, swinging back and forth like a kid on some horrific playground apparatus. The door still doesn't open. Finally, I crumple to the floor in a heap, sobs rising from my guts to my throat. I'm going to end up like Becca. I just know it!

Gradually the sobs cease, and I get my breathing under control again. There's got to be a way out of here! I grab the door to get to my feet again when I feel a piece of metal about a foot above the floor. It's round, as thick as my fuck-you finger and six inches long. It runs from the door to the wall, and there's a ninety-degree bend at the end on the door, pointing toward the floor. It's a latch!

I grip the downward-pointing bar with my fingers and try to pry it up and away from the door. I can't! Panic begins to rise in my gorge again and I force it back down. Don't freak Nattie, think! I reach into my pocket for the Swiss Army knife that my dad gave me. I open the large blade and wiggle it underneath the handle between the metal and the wood, then use the blade as a lever to raise the latch off the door's surface. It's coming now! It's moved enough so I can get my fingers underneath. I pull the latch so the handle is perpendicular to the door, then yank to slide it back. It resists, then grates back with a loud scarping sound. It's open!

I'm on that handle like a cat on a mouse and I pull hard. Dammit! It still won't open! Of course it won't you idiot, because there's a second latch on top. I make quick work of that one with the knife, yank again and nearly go ass-over-teakettle as the door pops open. I step into the opening and almost fall up the stairs. I put the knife back in my pocket, then walk up the short flight of stairs and make contact with the angled doors with my hands. They're held shut on the inside with a bar in brackets that spans both doors. I lift it out and toss it on the stairs where it lands with a clang, then put one hand on either door and push for all I'm worth. The doors move up and fall sideways. I'm immersed in the warm night air and the smells of beer, pot and pee. That parking lot never smelled so good!

It's a scene of minor mayhem. Customers, half-naked and mostly naked women are milling about under the scintillating pink and green glare. My primal instincts tell me there's safety in the herd, so I pop out of the basement and run into the crowd. My eye catches Valery, who still looks a little worse for his encounter with Danny, but he doesn't appear to notice me. Yet. I move deeper into the crowd looking for Danny, but he's nowhere to be found. I don't see Bobby either, which is a good thing. For him!

Valery notices the basement doors and closes them, then scans the crowd. He's not stupid. He's looking for me! I move further toward the back of the parking lot where my car is. I get inside and hunker down.

There's a high board fence facing the streets on either side of the parking lot (some patrons don't want just anybody to see their cars parked here), with a ten-foot opening so cars can get in and out, but nobody's going anywhere right now because of the crowd.

Valery is waving his arms and saying something that I can't hear because my windows are shut. I give the ignition a single click, then hit the button so the passenger window whirrs down.

"...closed for tonight," he's saying. "Everybody go to your cars and we'll get you outta here. Come back tomorrow. There'll be no cover charge!" A half-hearted cheer goes up from the crowd.

Everyone goes to their vehicle and engines fire up. The sweet smell of exhaust fills the air. The bartenders and bouncers are directing traffic to get the cars out on the street in an orderly manner. I'm at the back of the lot, so I'll be one of the last to leave.

As the lot empties, I watch out my back window. OMG! As each car reaches the exit, Valery stops it and shines a light inside. He's really hunting me!

I can't chance the queue. If he sees me and there are cars in front of me, I'll have nowhere to go.

There's an identical gap between the board fence and the building on the other side of the lot, but it's blocked by a chain-link gate. Just maybe…

I start the car, step on the clutch and drop it into reverse. I back out of the parking spot, then turn towards the locked gate, ostensibly to get to the end of the line of exiting cars. I pop it into first and creep forward, waiting until I have an unobstructed line to the gate. I pray that I'll be able to build up enough momentum to break through that gate in such a short distance.

There! Nothing between me and freedom but that gate! I resist the urge to stomp the pedal to the floor – don't need to stall out now! The car accelerates slowly, then I hit the gate, push on it, it doesn't give! I pound the clutch and pop it into second, then floor it. The engine screams and the gate collapses. Something hits my driver's side window, showering me with glass. Now I'm on the street, racing madly at a phone pole. I jerk the wheel and run down the sidewalk a few yards, gritting my teeth at the horrible sound of the Z-car sideswiping a concrete building. Wonderful. Now my car matches my face!

I wrestle the car back into the street and stomp the brake and the clutch to make a two-wheeled turn onto Lee. A car horn blares in a scolding tone. Thank Christ he had room to slow down! Then I'm accelerating up Lee. I scream a cheer out my shattered window. Freedom!

Chapter 27.

It's Thursday morning. The day after my Hollywood-like escape from the jaws of death. I'm sitting in the malodorous interrogation room at the cop shop that I've occupied before. Detective Kidd is on the other side of table, glaring. He doesn't look much like a sweet old uncle now.

I was rudely awakened at 6:30 a.m. by a loud pounding on the door. As I crossed the great room, I heard the shouts of "Police! Open the door Ms. McMasters!"

At least the officers gave me time to dress before arresting me. Poor Lupe awoke when I did and became nearly hysterical as I was hauled away. It can be a lot different when the police take you away where she came from.

I was fingerprinted, photographed and booked at headquarters before being placed in this room. Kidd showed up a few minutes later.

"You're a lucky lady, Ms. McMasters," is Kidd's opening salvo. "The Kitten Club has declined to press charges for breaking and entering and burglary, but they are pursuing willful destruction of property in regard to the damage to their chain-link fence. We'll add reckless driving to that for the damage done to the building next door. Oh, and Mr. Didier has also asked me to tell you that you are fired." He pauses to let that sink in. "What the hell did you think you were doing?"

Shut up, Nattie! Don't say a word! "What you wouldn't do, Detective! Investigating the attack on my uncle, and my best friend's murder!"

His anger is palpable. "What you've likely accomplished is to make it impossible for us to investigate anything."

"Bullshit! There hasn't been a cop in that club since Robyn Carlson. I wonder how she'd feel about your so-called investigation?"

Kidd struggles for control. Maybe I've gone too far. Again. He gets hold of himself, then says, "I understand that you're distressed by recent events. I did you the favor of having you arrested early enough so that you can have your bond hearing before lunch. You wouldn't have to spend the night in jail." He hesitates, then continues, "But we can always lose your paperwork for an hour or two so you can't make it until tomorrow."

187

Time to suck it up, Nattie. "I'm sorry, Detective. You're right. I have been under a lot of stress lately. I've even been diagnosed with PTSD. I'll pay for the damage."

His expression softens. "Just because bad things have happened to you doesn't exempt you from obeying the law, or me from enforcing it. I didn't know about the PTSD. Make sure you mention that to the judge, as well as your willingness to pay for the damage."

Kidd indicates the phone on the table, which he brought in with him. "You'd better call your lawyer and tell him to send somebody to meet you at the bond hearing. The judge will delay until you have a representative present. There are usually plenty of people to process, so if your number comes up before your attorney gets there, she'll move on to somebody else."

He slides his chair back and rises to leave. He turns at the doorway for one last remark. "Whether you know it or not, it's a good thing that you're out of that place. Now stay out and let us do our job." He turns to leave.

"You figured out yet that Becca was killed in the club basement?" That stops him in his tracks. "And what about a police guard for Uncle Amos? Don't you think if the shooter came back once, he might come back again?"

"Even if you have evidence that what you say is true, it would likely be excluded by a judge because it was gained unlawfully." Kidd replies. "And I've already talked to the Captain about a guard for your Uncle. There should be somebody there this afternoon."

"I found a charcoal grill in the basement," I tell him. "You told me Becca had burns."

"Yes, I did. But isn't it just as likely that the grill is there so they can cook hotdogs in the parking lot?"

"Sure. And I suppose that they hang the strings of hot dogs on the hooks on the basement support columns?"

He surveys me with a glum expression. "Natalie, I like you, I really do. You're intelligent, you have spunk and you seem to have more principles than most young people do these days. You might even make a good cop someday. And you've been through a lot, which might have contributed to the stupid choices you've made lately. Now it's time to back off. We can probably smooth this over so you don't get kicked out of school and ruin your chances for a career. But if you're back here again for something similar, then all bets are off. You could even go to jail. Now tell me who that will help?"

I don't have an answer for him.

I call Gary and he tells me that either he or a surrogate will meet me at the courthouse. I'm left to meditate on my sins for about an hour before a matron comes in to escort me to court.

Even though the courthouse is just a couple of blocks away, I get another ride in a patrol car in handcuffs. Thankfully, the manacles are removed after we get into the courtroom. It's a depressing place - a contemporary windowless, airless, room full of the sour smell of too many people cooped up for too long. It has a low ceiling that's textured with sound baffling blocks, which makes the room seem to close in on you. The judge is already there, dealing with other unfortunates. The matron sits me in the first row behind the railing that separates the attorneys' tables from the rest of the courtroom. I look around and spy Gary in the crowd. He gives me an unobtrusive nod.

It's about an hour before my case is called. Being here is an eye-opening experience. There are the usual prostitutes, drug dealers and petty thieves, but some other sorry characters stand out. There's a guy who put his wife in the hospital by beating her with a cast iron frying pan because he didn't like the dinner she made him. Thankfully, the judge denies him bond. There's a woman who was so drunk that she didn't even realize that she'd run down a teenager riding his bike to work early this morning while it was still dark. A traffic cam caught the incident and the cops even found part of the kid's bike on her front bumper while the car was parked in her driveway. She doesn't get bond either. She's remanded to a hospital for detox instead.

Finally, my name comes up. A bailiff opens the gate and signals me to rise. Gary meets me and we sit at the defendant's table. The enormity of my circumstances is beginning to sink in. Someday, I want to be doing for others what Gary is doing for me. This situation has the potential to make that impossible.

The judge reads the charges, then asks the prosecutor for a brief summary of my offenses. She complies and actually gives a pretty impartial narrative of my actions. The judge asks the prosecutor if I'm a danger to the community or a flight risk.

"Your honor," she says, "Due to Ms. McMaster's extremely reckless behavior, we think it's possible that she might pose a danger to the community."

I start to leap to my feet, but Gary's hand on my shoulder prevents it. "Tell me," he mouths silently, the inclines his head so I can whisper in his ear.

I tell him that I have PTSD and am under a doctor's care. He dutifully rises and repeats this to the judge. I pluck his sleeve. "Tell her I'll pay for the damage."

"My client is also willing to make restitution for any damage she may have caused," Gary says.

The judge regards me gravely. "Miss McMasters," she says, "that you've sought treatment is certainly a point in your favor, but your recent actions lead me to question the effectiveness of that treatment."

OMG! Is she going to put me in jail!

A voice pipes up from the back of the room. "Your honor, may I speak?"

It's Kidd! When did he get here?

"Go ahead, Detective Kidd," the judge says.

"I know Ms. McMasters personally and I'm willing to assure you that she is not a danger to the community."

Oh man, I owe him big time!

"Very well," the judge says, "Bond is set at fifty thousand dollars. Does the accused have the means to make this bond?"

Fifty thousand! Is she kidding?

Another voice from the courtroom.

"I'll post her bond, your honor."

Bobby?

I twist around so I can see him. He's wearing a white dress shirt, a thin black tie and a hideous sport coat. No pink t-shirt. No wonder I didn't spot him! He's also sporting a black eye to rival mine.

I tell Gary, "No, I have money, I'll post it myself."

190

Stripper!

The judge raps her gavel to signal that she's going to proceed to the next case.

It turns out that I only have to write a check for five of the 50K. Gary tells me that I'll have another court date in about a month to six weeks to ensure that I have a lawyer of record, then again about six months after that to enter a plea. Of course, negotiations with the D.A. can go on during that time.

"Willful damage to property is either a felony or a misdemeanor depending on the value of the property," Gary tells me. "The damage you did to the gate is right on the cusp. The damage to the building next door wasn't structural, so a repainting should suffice. If you plead *nolo contendre* and pay for the damage, I feel sure we can plead it down to a misdemeanor and avoid jail time."

"What about the reckless driving? Will I lose my license?

"How many points do you have?"

"None, that I know of."

"Then you should be fine. Just don't get a speeding ticket or anything worse in the next three years."

"Will I get my money back?"

"You will if you make all your required court appearances, even if you're convicted."

"And what about school?"

"You'll have to take that up with them. The fact that you're receiving treatment through the University will doubtless weigh in your favor. Just stay out of trouble for the next few years and you should be okay."

Stay out of trouble for the next few years? How 'bout the next few days?

Gary leaves me on the courthouse steps. As soon as he walks away, Bobby appears at my elbow.

"You should have let me pay your bond, Kira."

"Don't call me that anymore! My name's Natalie."

"Sorry. It's how I think of you."

I indicate his multihued face. "What happened to you?"

"I'll bet you're wondering why I shut you up in that basement."

No shit, Bobby.

"It was because I didn't want you to get hurt if Valery and his goons came into Judd's office. It worked."

"It only worked because I didn't pass out in the dark in that horrible basement!"

"You had a flashlight!"

I give him a brief synopsis of my adventures in the basement.

"Why didn't you use the flashlight on your cell phone after you broke the other one?"

"I left my cell in my car to keep it from being destroyed by the magnet."

"Cell phones aren't like computers. A magnet won't hurt them."

"Really? Then I went through that hell in the dark for nothing?"

"Hey, don't feel bad. You didn't know."

I point at his eye. "So you took my beating for me?"

"Kinda. I told Valery that you didn't break in to Judd's office. I let you in."

"And why would you do that?"

"Because you were gonna help me run checks on Judd's computer system. I'm his IT guy, you know."

The light dawns! "That's why you knew the code to the door!" And you saved me from a burglary charge!" Despite myself, I'm starting to feel a little gratitude towards Bobby.

"Uh-huh. Juddo doesn't like me to be in his office while he's there, so he gave me the code so I can work while he's away." He pauses, then continues. "As soon as I saw Merkel on the stage, I knew what you did. I also figured that you didn't know that Judd had alarms and a surveillance system that he could access in Mexico. I hustled down there to save your ass just as soon as I could get around the fight."

"Is that when that happened?" I indicate his black eye again.

"Nope," Bobby grins. "Valery gave it to me later to remind me that I bring nobody into the inner sanctum without his or Judd's permission. Actually, I think he was mad that your boyfriend beat him up and he wanted somebody to hit. I was handy."

"Danny's not my boyfriend." Now why would I tell him that?

His grin gets even bigger. "That's good to hear."

"Did they ban you from the club, too?"

"No way! I spend way too fucking much money in there."

A troubling thought occurs to me. "Won't Judd know I broke into the office when he sees the surveillance footage?"

"Nope," he grins. "I erased it." A beat, then, "So what do we do now?"

What's this we shit, Bobby?

"I hear you've been canned," he goes on. "You'll need a man on the inside to continue your investigation. I can be your secret agent!"

Secret agent? Is he for real? I stifle the "No fucking way!" before it comes out. The little perv has got a point. Both Danny and I are now *persona non-grata* at the club. The only other alternative is to trust Kidd and the cops to continue the investigation. I might just trust Kidd because of Robin, but after what Danny told me, I know I can't trust the police department worth a damn.

"Let me think about it." I tell Bobby.

"You need a ride home?" he asks.

Shit. I could call Lupe, but she was so distraught when the cops arrested me that I'm afraid she'll wreck on the way. "I guess so."

"Great! I'm your man!"

Not hardly, Bobby.

He chatters incessantly on the drive to the townhouse. What is it about this guy that so completely turns me off? It's obvious that he's harmless, and he's way smitten with me. He's a total wuss, but he put himself in physical danger to protect me, and I owe him for that. I've been intimate with him in the sense that I've given him a bunch of lap dances, all of which he's paid for, in addition to the online performances. And he was willing to bail me out of jail. Is he really such a bad guy?

No, he's not a bad guy, he's just a sorry meth head. And that's what I can't seem to get past.

We pull into my parking lot next to the Z-car. The passenger side is almost completely destroyed. Seeing it brings tears to my eyes.

Bobby notices. "Hey, don't," he says.

"I'm sorry. It was Becca's, and she was so proud of it. Now look what I've done to it!"

"It's just a car, Nattie. A little body work and you'll never notice. Well, maybe more than a little."

I look at him and he's smiling. Was that a joke to cheer me up?

"Thanks for the lift." I get out of the car. "Oh, by the way, Lupe and I have those pictures for her website."

His grin is now huge. "Great! Just make sure your computer is turned on and I'll get in and set things up remotely. It should be ready in a couple days. I'll call you. Maybe I can be her first customer."

I watch him drive off, then I open the townhouse door. The aromas of Mexican cooking assault my senses. Lupe is in the kitchen amidst a massive assemblage of pots and pans.

She shrieks my name when she sees me, dropping a stainless-steel bowl on the floor with a dreadful clatter. She bolts across the room and gathers me into her arms, blubbering and kissing me. I return the hug and kisses. Damn, it's nice to have somebody who's worried about you to come home to!

When we get all settled down, she tells me that she's made a *fiesta* meal to welcome me home. Apparently, when Lupe gets stressed, she cooks. If I want to keep my figure, I'll have to keep her calm.

There's another thing, she says, but she won't tell me. Instead, she takes my hand and leads me to the spiral staircase, puts a finger to her lips and beckons me to follow. We go down the hall to Eduardo's room (she's moved in with me), shushes me again, then silently cracks the door. She motions me to look inside.

Stripper!

Eduardo is on the bed, sleeping as only a little boy can, with a ball of fur curled up next to his cheek. Xin Niu has finally come around! That cat has no idea how grateful she's made me – I was totally worried that she would never tolerate Eduardo and that her life would be miserable as long as he was here. Now I'm hoping that he will be here for quite a long time because I surely don't want Lupe to leave. But it's important to me that Xin Niu is happy, too. She's the most tangible part of Becca that I have left.

Chapter 28.

After the ordeal of my arrest, I spend the rest of the day at home with Lupe and Eduardo. Now that Xin Niu has taken to him, Eduardo can't get rid of her – she follows him everywhere and yowls plaintively if he's not playing with her or holding her. The three of us stuff ourselves with tamales and salad, then after Eduardo and I clean the kitchen, we retire to the great room to watch TV.

Our program choices are largely governed by Eduardo. He loves animal shows, and the fact that they're in English doesn't bother him. He's actually picking up some words and phrases from the shows and the commercials. I tell Lupe that we really have to work on getting him into school this fall.

I can't remember the last time I've spent an evening just sitting in front of the TV. Almost overnight, Lupe and Eduardo have become my family, and this domestic experience makes me realize how much I've missed this. When I was living with Fields and Kwan, our lives were separate and only rarely did we even have a meal together. If we watched TV, it was only a program here and there, not an entire evening's worth. I really haven't had much of a family since I was fifteen. It's way nice to have one again.

Before I know it, it's ten o'clock. Eduardo is asleep on the couch with Xin Niu and Lupe and I are cuddling on the beanbag.

"I should get him to bed," she says.

"Go ahead. I'm going to watch the news, then turn in myself. It's been a totally stressful day."

She takes the remote from Eduardo and flips it to me before she gently wakes him to get him upstairs. I punch in the number for the local news channel.

"… a fire alarm in the ICU at University Hospital. The attack apparently occurred as the patients were being evacuated. An unidentified city policeman has been shot and is in surgery at this hour. No report on his condition has been received from the hospital as yet. It is unknown whether any hospital personnel or patients were injured in the attack, or whether this attack is connected with the one that occurred on Monday. No one has claimed responsibility…"

Stripper!

OMG! Uncle Amos! I rocket off the beanbag, grab the phone and frantically punch in the hospital number. Busy! Shit! I try again. Same result.

"Lupe, I'm going to the hospital," I shout as I grab my pouch and head out the door.

The Z-car is in wretched shape, but drivable. I try to keep Gary's earlier admonition about further moving violations in mind as I head for the freeway – what I want to do is floor it. I try not to run scenarios in my head as I drive. The news said that a cop was shot. That was likely the officer protecting Uncle Amos. If Uncle had been shot too, they would've said so, right?

Traffic backs up after I get off the hospital exit and I soon see why. The place is cordoned off and the cops are stopping every car at the parking garage entrance. Many don't get in.

It's a righteous fifteen minutes before I get to the head of the line. The cop looks in the driver's window.

"License and registration, please."

"Look, my name is Natalie McMasters…"

"License and registration."

I grit my teeth, dig my license out of my pouch and the registration out of the glove compartment. There's no arguing with these fools. I hand them over.

"The license and registration don't match, Miss. Who is Rebecca Chapman?"

I try not to yell. "Please, officer. My uncle is in ICU. He's the one you guys were protecting. I need to know he's O.K."

The cop indicates a driveway to the right. "Please pull over there." He hands my license and registration to another officer, who follows me over to a parking space.

I throw the car in park and kill the engine, then start to exit, but an officer puts his hand on the door. "Please remain in the vehicle, Miss."

"Please, I need to get inside and find out about my uncle. If you'll just call Detective Kidd, he'll vouch for me."

The officer suddenly turns cold. "How do you know Detective Kidd?"

Of course, I say the stupidest thing possible. "Well, he had me arrested earlier today…"

"Miss, get out of the vehicle, and keep your hands in sight."

He makes me put my hands-on top of the car and stay there until he can get a female officer to come and pat me down. She brings my arms behind me and puts me in handcuffs for the third time that day. All the while I'm yammering on about Uncle Amos, Detective Kidd and the goddamned unfairness of it all (yes, my resolve to behave myself has finally evaporated), but it falls on deaf ears.

It's another ten minutes before a sergeant shows up and I'm loaded into the back of a squad car.

"Take her downtown until we can get somebody to check her out," the sergeant says to the driver.

Downtown? Downtown! Oh fuck no! "I'm Natalie McMasters! My uncle is in the ICU! He's the one they were trying to kill!"

The sergeant gives me a frigid stare. "I know who you are," he says. "Take her and lock her ass up when you get there."

The car drives off towards the parking lot exit. I sit in the back seat, stunned, resisting the impulse to curl into the fetal position. Why have they arrested me? For trying to get into the hospital to see my uncle? I have a horrible feeling that this time, I'm not going to get out of custody so easily.

The car stops at the exit. The driver opens the window and another officer leans in. I notice the silver bar on his collar.

"What's up, Evans?" he addresses the driver.

"Taking this one downtown for processing…"

"Lieutenant! Please get Detective Kidd! He'll tell you who I am! Please!"

The lieutenant looks at me strangely. "Detective Kidd is still in surgery," he says.

Surgery? OMG! Kidd was the one protecting Uncle Amos?

I force my voice down a couple of octaves. "I didn't know that Detective Kidd was the one guarding my uncle. He was shot? How is he?"

"We don't know yet," he says. "Who is your uncle?"

"Amos Murdoch. He's the one that Detective Kidd was guarding. Please, Lieutenant, I just want to go inside and find out how Kidd and my uncle are doing."

Something in my voice must have finally gotten to him.

"Who told you to take her downtown?" he asks the driver.

"Sergeant Russell. He said he knew who she was. Thought he meant that there was something off about her."

The lieutenant gets a stern look on his face, then opens the door to the back seat. "Get out, Miss McMasters," he says.

Shit, he knows my name? I do as I'm told.

"Turn around." He removes the cuffs.

"Now get back in and we'll give you a ride over to the main entrance. Nobody gets in or out of the hospital right now without authorization."

I don't know what's going on with the cops around here, but I don't ask questions. I get back in the car and the officer drives me to the main entrance, where there's a heavy police presence. Unrepentantly, I think that there'll be no problem getting protection for Uncle Amos now.

Once inside, my security badge gets me past the remaining checkpoints and up to ICU. I'm grateful to find out that Uncle Amos has not been harmed further. Apparently Kidd was able to drive off the attacker before that could happen, but he unfortunately collapsed before he could give chase. Nobody knows whether he wounded the attacker.

I call Lupe to let know that everything's okay, then settle in. I'm not going anywhere until there's another guard on Uncle Amos.

I must have fallen asleep in that uncomfortable metal chair because the next thing I know, someone is shaking my shoulder. Danny!

"You had your phone switched off," he accuses. "I called your place and Lupe told me you were here," he says. "I didn't think they were ever going to let me in."

I don't remember switching off my phone.

"You heard about Kidd?" I ask him.

He nods. "They tell me he'll be up here in a little while. As a patient."

I look intently at Danny, then get up and hug him. He doesn't know how to respond – he leaves his arms hanging at his sides.

"Damn it!" I say. "We have to get this motherfucker!"

He finally gives me a light embrace, and I hold him tighter and burrow into his chest, crying. I totally need the human contact right now. He hesitantly strokes my hair to comfort me.

It's a few minutes before I'm cried out. I push back from him, but now he doesn't want to let me go.

"One thing that bothers me," I say. "Why was a Detective Lieutenant standing guard over Uncle Amos? You'd think they'd have the grunts do that."

"I'll bet he was doing it on his own time, too." Danny replies. "The Captain probably told Kidd that he wasn't going to supply a guard."

"Kidd did tell me this morning that a guard would be posted. He just didn't say it was going to be him." A pause. "It's scary to think that Judd has that much power, even when he's away."

"Well, I don't think we have to worry about that anymore," he says. "The cops have this place locked down tighter than the penitentiary and it's likely to stay that way until this asshole is caught. Finally the cops have a stake in this thing. Kidd is one of their own."

"Wasn't Robin? That didn't seem to make much of a difference."

"You're right, but her disappearance didn't get the publicity that this is getting. Kidd may have had enemies on the force, but no cop can afford to let an incident like this go unchallenged. It would be open season on us if we did."

He's still got his arms around me. "We?" I say. "Us?"

He drops his arms. After a second, he says, "It's hard to let go. I used to be one, you know."

I give him another hug. "I know."

I tell him about the incident in the parking lot. "It was weird. It seems like that sergeant had it in for me for some reason. He said that he knew who I was, and that they should lock me up."

"Did you know him?" Danny asks.

"Nope. The driver said he was Sergeant Russell."

Danny gets a queer look. "Are you sure?"

"I heard him as clearly as I hear you. What's wrong?"

"Josh Russell was my partner when I was on the force. And he wasn't a sergeant then."

"He was the one who shot…"

Danny puts a finger to his lips, and nods.

"What's going on here?" I ask Danny.

"I'm not sure," Danny says. "But let's not talk about it here."

I start to protest, then think better of it. Danny did say that he thought some cops might be protecting certain drug dealers. That could explain a lot of things. Like how Judd could operate as a drug wholesaler with impunity. And maybe how Judd knew that Robyn was a cop, and had Valery take care of her.

We hang around for another couple of hours until a uniformed officer arrives. In the meantime, Kidd is brought up. There's another uni outside of his unit, but he's apparently been told who we are because he gives us no trouble about paying our respects. Kidd looks shrunken and old in that bed – even though I know that a hospital is a place of healing, I'll never be totally comfortable in one again.

The sun is rising when we decide to leave. We have to go through a couple of checkpoints to get outside, and there's a minor row when they want to confiscate our I.D. badges. I fight it, because I totally don't want to spend twenty minutes getting another one every time I come back to see Uncle Amos. Luckily, the lieutenant who helped me earlier is in earshot, and he comes over and tells them to back off.

We're in the parking lot, getting ready to go to our respective cars, when Danny says, "Nattie. Please let the cops take it from here. I don't want to see you get in any more trouble than you're already in."

The look on his face scares me. I totally remember what he said about one-night stands. I think I'm going to have to tell him about Lupe way soon.

Chapter 29.

L upe is (guess what?) fixing breakfast when I get home. She greets me with another of her flying hugs.

I turn down her high-octane coffee, which makes her sad, but I've got to get some sleep. I do agree to breakfast - one of last night's tamales with a fried egg on top.

After breakfast, I hit the sack. I swear to God I'm asleep before my head hits the pillow.

I'm awakened by Lupe gently shaking me.

"Bobby's here. He say that the website is ready. He wants to show us."

"What time is it?" I ask peevishly.

"After one. You sleep all morning."

"Give me ten minutes. And I could sure use a cup of that coffee of yours, now."

A quick trip to the bathroom to throw some water on my face works wonders, but I realize that it will take much longer to make myself presentable. Oh, what the hell! I've got a black eye, and it's just Bobby. I brush the worst of the tangles out of my hair and pull on a t-shirt and cut-offs.

He's on the couch, playing on the tablet with Eduardo. Funny – I never figured Bobby as one for kids.

Lupe brings me a cup of that glorious coffee, which I'm already addicted to. We leave Eduardo on the couch, thoroughly engrossed in his new game, and head up to the studio.

Bobby immediately assumes the driver's seat at the computer and logs in. He brings up the home page of the new website.

Wow! The banner header is Casa Carmella, and it's over a full page shot of Lupe wrapped around the pole. Enough of her is visible so there's no doubt what kind of site this is, but not so much that someone viewing it won't be looking for more.

Stripper!

"If you navigate here from a search engine, you'll get the standard page that says you have to be eighteen or older to enter." Bobby says. "But I've put in a cookie so it doesn't come up again after you've clicked in once."

"It's really well-designed and easy to use," he goes on. "You got your secure payment options by credit card, wire transfer and bitcoin. The site also automatically tracks anybody who accesses it back to their IP, unless they're on Tor of course, and you can send teasers to them periodically to entice them in. I'm also going to strongly recommend that Carmella set up other social media accounts to look for new clients. You can even use sites like Facebook that don't allow nude pictures. You just use that site to get the guys interested, then take it off FB with a different contact method."

He's really got this all thought out.

"And I had this really great idea!" Oh, oh! Now what, Bobby?

"I think that Kira Foxxx should give one last, free performance. We can stream it live to all your loyal fans who sign up, and you can use it to introduce Carmella. Give her a running start, so to speak."

I start to say, hell no, but then I reconsider. It's actually not a bad idea. I may be on my way out of the stripping business, but it looks like Lupe's going to be doing it for a while, at least until she can get training that will lead to another job.

"OK, Bobby. I have no idea how to set something like that up, so I guess you'll have to do it." He's now wearing the mother of all shit-eating grins.

He takes us through the rest of the site, which mostly has the same structure as the old Kira Foxxx site. I realize that I've got a lot of work to do to train Lupe to run this by herself.

Finally, we're done. Bobby logs off and shuts down and Lupe goes downstairs to check on Eduardo.

I don't want to do this, but I have to.

"Hey Bobby. Stay a minute, will you. There's something I want to talk to you about."

His eyes immediately flicker to the heart-shaped bed. What a one-track mind!

"Not that." His face falls. "Did you really mean it when you said that you would be my secret agent at the club?"

"Fucking A!"

"Well, I've got a plan." I take a deep breath. I'm really letting the cat out of the bag. "I'm pretty sure that Valery killed Becca and tried to kill me."

He looks interested. "What makes you think so?"

"He's way sus! He's got a bad arm, for one thing. And he damn near took Danny down in a fight even with that bad arm, and Danny is an ex-Marine. But I've thought of a way to prove it."

"The cops have a sample of the killer's DNA from the blood he left here," I go on. "I need you to get me sample of Valery's DNA. I can give it to the cops and let them run it. If it's a match, we've got him!"

"I dunno…"

Don't wimp out on me now, you little wuss! "C'mon! It's a killer plan!"

"But how am I gonna do that without him knowing it? Valery is one scary dude! I don't want another one of these." He indicates his eye.

"Get creative, Bobby! Buy him a beer to apologize for letting me in the office and steal the bottle. You'll think of something. You're obviously a bright guy."

"But it will only be my word that the sample came from Valery. And there's no way I'll testify against him."

That seems an odd thing for him to say. "What are you, a lawyer?"

"I know that you can't use evidence against somebody in court unless you get it legally and you can prove that it came from where you said it did. If the cops find drugs in my car, they can't necessarily prove the drugs are mine."

"I've thought about that. This won't be evidence for court – it will just be a way to let the cops know who he is. Remember, he's shot a cop now. Once they know it's him, they won't rest until they bring him down."

"What do you mean, he's shot a cop?"

He doesn't know? It's been all over the news. I tell him about the attack on the hospital, and about Kidd and Uncle Amos.

"Wow, I didn't realize that he was after Mr. Murdoch, too. I wonder why?"

"I think Uncle found out something at the club that he shouldn't have. And Judd sicced Valery on him. When Uncle Amos wakes up, I hope he can tell us who hurt him. But we don't know when that will be, and there's no guarantee that he even knows."

Bobby looks as serious as I've ever seen him. Finally he says. "OK, Kira. I'll give it a try. For you."

I'm so happy that I don't even scold him for calling me Kira. I just hope that he can pull it off without getting himself hurt or killed.

Later, after Bobby's gone and Eduardo's down for his nap, I bring Lupe back upstairs to begin her education. Using the website is relatively simple, but she also must know how to verify payments, set up the green screen and control the various cameras while she's performing. After I explain all of this to her, she looks glum.

"Oh *cariño*," she says. "I did not know this was so complicated! I am afraid I will never learn!"

I try to reassure her. "Yes, you will. I will be here to help you before you have to do it on your own."

Before he left, Bobby asked me to give him a time frame for the launch of Carmella's website. I told him a couple of weeks, but he said the sooner the better, because more and more of Kira's fans would vanish every day. I know he's right, but I'm nervous because that doesn't give us a lot of time to get an act together.

"Don't worry, *cariño*." Lupe says. "Just tell Bobby to set it up whenever. I'm sure we'll think of something." Now who's reassuring who?

My phone plays the ringtone for an unknown caller. I look at the screen – no caller ID, just a phone number.

"Hello?"

"I gots that piece," a black voice says. "Meet me in two hours where we met last time and bring the cheese." The phone goes dead.

What did Kidd tell me yesterday about staying out of trouble? So let's go buy an illegal gun from a gang-banger in a public park. Got a death wish, Nattie?

I make some banal excuse to Lupe about an errand and head to the bank. Becca left me well off, but it's not gonna last if I keep spending it like I have in the last few days – five large for bail and another for the gun. I get it in hundreds so I can just tuck it in my pouch and pass it unobtrusively to LeBrowne.

He's already there when I get to the park. The park is fairly empty in late afternoon, but I'm sure that I passed a couple of LeBrowne's hoods on the way in, probably lookouts to ensure our transaction doesn't draw unwanted attention. They probably evicted the resident homeless population as well.

The man himself is occupying the usual bench, all laid back and enjoying the early summer air. There's a shopping bag next to him. Victoria's Secret. Cute, LeBrowne.

"S'up?"

I sit next to him with the shopping bag between us. Inside is a package encased in pink gift wrap with a frilly white bow all the way around.

"What this?"

"Watchoo think?"

"I'm not gonna give you a grand so I can get home and find a nightie."

"Hey, word is bond. It's what you axed for."

Okay, so it would be way stupid to be seen handing me a gun box in a public park. I get that. I use my Swiss Army knife to slit the wrapping paper with the package still in the bag. I can see the black plastic inside. I heft the bag. The weight's right.

I trade the knife for the folded bills. "There better be a gun in that box," I tell him.

He favors me with his golden grin. "You axed for a deuce deuce, you gots a deuce deuce. You needs to get you own ammo though."

I slip him the bills and he drops them in his vest pocket without counting.

"You have something else for me?"

"It's thorough. In the box."

"The url?"

He nods.

"Then I guess we're done."

"Pleasure."

Stripper!

I pick up the Victoria's Secret bag and head to my car. Unless a cop saw the transaction go down, he wouldn't look twice at me now. LeBrowne is not dumb.

I stop by Wal-Mart and pick up a hundred rounds of .22 magnum ammo. The bullets look ridiculously tiny to entrust my life to.

When I get back to the townhouse, Lupe is in the kitchen. I give her a quick "Hi" and head up to the studio.

I lock the door. I don't want Lupe walking in on me right now.

I'm really ambivalent. Why did I do this? The cops confiscated Becca's gun after I shot the killer with it. I can't buy another handgun legally or get a carry permit until my next birthday. Uncle Amos has pistols at the 3M office, but if I'm caught with one, I'll get him in trouble. I'm between a rock and a hard place. If Becca had her pistol when the bad guy grabbed her, she might be alive. I'm not sure that this asshole is after me, but PTSD notwithstanding, I don't know that he isn't, either. I need every edge I can get. I'd rather go to jail for an illegal gun than end up like Becca.

I take the box out of the bag and remove the paper. Inside is a standard black plastic gun box with a built-in handle. Two plastic flaps that lock down over a lip that runs around the bottom of the lid keep it closed. I take a deep breath, flip them up and open the box.

Word is bond. A black pistol is inside, securely nestled in a matching foam rubber cut-out. Another cut-out holds a magazine.

The pistol is half again as large as Becca's little 9mm, but I think it will still fit in my pouch. It's feather-light, dead black with a deeply textured grip and has a rail on the bottom of the muzzle for mounting a laser or a light. The front and rear sights glow green and orange, respectively, because they have little fiber optics inserted for low light target acquisition. There's another magazine in the pistol. The magazine release is not in the usual place on the grip. After a little hunting, I find it at the very bottom of the grip where the magazine goes in. I pop out the mag, then work the action and lock back the slide to ensure that that the gun is clear. Unlike Becca's pistol, the slide on this one is very easy to work - it doesn't need a heavy spring to compensate for a heavy load like a 9mm. I think I'm going to like this pistol.

I break out my ammo and the gun cleaning kit that I bought at Wal-Mart. Uncle Amos' voice echoes in my head. "Always clean and oil a new gun before you fire it." I'm not sure how to disassemble this weapon, so I look for instructions. The foam rubber insert in the lid is removable and the owner's manual is behind it. There's also a little yellow card that tells you what kind of ammo to use. There's something written on the back.

http://aooeeu7wqpnkn14x.onion/

The url! But what is this onion shit?

I'm tempted to boot up the PC and try it, but another thing Uncle Amos taught me is not to get distracted when you're messing with a gun.

The pistol disassembly is fairly standard and I have it cleaned, oiled and reassembled in a few minutes.

I load the mags. Holy shit! I put round after round into one. How much ammo does this thing hold? I've lost count, so I just keep going until it becomes too hard to put in another cartridge, then count the empty spaces in my ammo box. 26 rounds! I check the owner's manual and it tells me that the mag capacity is 30 rounds. It also outlines a specific procedure for loading the magazine so the weapon doesn't jam. Way to go Nattie. Read the damn direction afterwards, not before! I sigh and unload all those rounds, then reload it properly. This time the magazine does accommodate all 30 rounds.

I pop the loaded mag into the grip and close the slide to chamber a round. All that ammo has made the pistol somewhat heavier, but not excessively.

I engage the safety and slide the pistol into its own compartment in my pouch, then load the second mag and put it in the other compartment with my wallet and my other things. With 60 rounds of ammo, I can fight a small war.

Now that the pistol is secure, I quickly boot up the PC and type in the url I got from LeBrowne.

<Server not found>

I type it again and get the same result. Did LeBrowne give me a phony url?

I vacillate about telling Lupe about the pistol, but I figure I'd better since it's in her house. I'm also going to have to make damn sure that Eduardo can't get to my pouch.

I go to the top of the circular staircase and call down to her.

"Lupe, can you come up here for a minute, please?"

When she does, I motion her to follow me into the studio, then close and lock the door again.

"I have something to show you, and I don't want you to freak out." I open the pouch and take out the gun. "I got this when I went out."

She looks at me strangely, then says, "Good. I feel much better that you are safe."

"I want you know that I'm not supposed to have it. I could get in trouble. It's illegal."

She shrugs. "I am illegal. I can get in trouble for just being here. The law is only the law. It isn't always what's right. What's right is that you can protect us now from the bad man who killed your friend and hurt your uncle."

And I was worried that she'd freak out? God, I love this woman!

Chapter 30.

For the most part, Saturday is quiet. We sleep in as late as Eduardo and Xin Niu will allow – we don't have much choice when those two end up in bed with us. Lupe prepares one of her familiar, stunning brunches, during which I suck down not one but two cups of her potent *café de olla*. Afterwards, I'm a bundle of nervous energy.

Just before noon, Bobby calls.

"Hi, Kira! I've got great news! I've got yours and Lupe's performance set up for tomorrow night. Eight o'clock. I didn't do it for tonight because Saturday is the biggest night at the clubs and I thought you shouldn't have the competition. Oh and by the way, I'm sorry you missed the twerking contest at the club last night. It was awesome! I'm sure you would have won if you were there!"

My God, Bobby, STFU! You're going on like you're on meth or something.

"I guess that's okay – the performance, I mean. Do we have to do anything special with the computer?"

"Nope. I'll log on and call you on Kira's line a little before eight. You just set up things as per normal and do your dance. I'll handle the broadcast remotely. With luck, we should have nearly a hundred people watching! That should get Lupe off to a great start. You should do a little speech or something to tell them you're retiring and there's going to be a changing of the guard."

"OK. We'll have it together by then."

"Can't wait! Bye!"

I think of something else. "Hey Bobby, don't hang up! I have another question."

"What is it?"

"What can you tell me about a url that ends in dot onion?"

"Where did you get that?" When I don't answer, he goes on, "What's the url?"

"It's a bunch of gobbledygook. I can't remember it – letters and numbers that don't make any sense. But it ends in dot onion. I tried it on my PC and didn't get anything."

"You wouldn't." he tells me. "It's a darknet url. You have to use the Tor browser. I installed it on the PC in Mr. Murdoch's office."

"OK, I can try it there."

"I'd better help you with that," he says. "The darknet is no place for a user to be messin'."

I don't need his nose in all my business "I'll be fine."

"I hope so. Don't blame me if you get hacked." He hangs up.

I suggest to Lupe that we go upstairs and talk about tomorrow night. We set Eduardo up on the PS4 with a game that'll keep him occupied for hours.

"Have you ever danced on a pole with another girl," Lupe asks.

"Nope. The first time I pole danced ever was at the club. Have you danced with another girl?"

"Sure! We would do it sometimes at the club when we got bored. Not too much, though, 'cause you make less money when you have to split it. I can show you some moves."

She shows me the moves for the next hour. Lupe is really an incredible artist on the pole. She shows me some things I'm just not physically capable of doing. She tells me that the weaker dancer should be above the stronger one on the pole, because the weaker girl can actually rest on her partner's body if she has to. At one point, I'm standing with both feet on Lupe's torso, who is supine beneath me, holding on to the pole with just her legs. It's almost like standing on the floor. She tells me to shimmy back and forth on the pole and I do it, amazed that she doesn't fall to the floor and spill both of us.

By the time we're done, we have a strategy for our *pas de deux* tomorrow night. Our audience will be in for a treat!

Naturally, we end up in the big bed.

We shower together and go back downstairs where Eduardo is still engrossed in his game. What did parents do before they had these things to babysit?

211

It's midafternoon, and I'm still throbbing with energy. Lupe is content to lie around and watch TV with Eduardo, but not me. I decide to go check up on Uncle Amos, then to the 3M office to see about that website.

The hospital is depressing. I have to leave my pouch in the car because the pistol and the spare magazine are inside, and there's a metal detector at the hospital entrance. I feel naked walking across the parking lot without it.

Uncle is no better, no worse, and the prognosis is the same for Detective Kidd. The only positive thing is that there are now two uniformed officers on duty around the clock.

When I pull into the 3M parking lot, Danny's car is there. Shit! Do I want to bring him in on this? He's going to want to know where I got the url, and I don't want to tell him about LeBrowne. OTOH, Danny was a big help getting me into Judd's office. It's not his fault that very little came out of it. And the experience taught me it's better to have a partner than to go it alone.

I go in. Danny is sitting in front of the computer, so engrossed that he doesn't hear me enter.

"Hey. Whatcha up to?" He jumps like he got caught watching porn, but I can see that it's only email on the screen.

"Oh, hi Nattie. Just checking to see we got any jobs. It's been really dead since Amos got hurt. He always knew who to call at the insurance companies and the bigger agencies to scare up work, but he hadn't got around to sharing that with me yet."

"Is there anything?"

"Not really. And I'm worried. There's enough to keep the lights on this month, but I'm not so sure about next. How's Amos? Any change?"

"Nope." I hesitate, then I decide to tell him. "Look, I've got something that might help us find out who did this to him. But I'm telling you up front not to ask me where I got it, because I'm not going to tell you and I don't want to fight about it."

"Fine." The look on his face tells me it's not.

I move the chair from the other desk over next to his. "Push over and let me drive."

212

Stripper!

He complies grudgingly. In a few seconds I locate the bright green Tor icon. I click it and the homepage pops up. It has a drawing of an onion on it!

I take the yellow card out of my pouch, cupping it in my hand so Danny can't see the ammo info on the back. I laboriously type in the complex url and click the curly arrow.

The screen goes black. After a few seconds, a picture pops up. A Guy Fawkes mask! The mask moves right, and a second picture coalesces on the screen. It's a black-and-white photo of a bunch of men in old-timey clothes, standing between two vintage cars in front of an old brick building. Looks to be the 1920s or 30s. Garish pink words that match the cheeks and lips of the mask slowly fade in at the top of the screen.

2122 North Clark Street

"What is this?" says Danny.

The photo fades out, and another fades in. It's another black-and-white photo of three, no, four, no, six men laying in front of a wall. They look dead. Are those black pools beneath them blood?

A pink box with black letters fades in.

ENTER PASSWORD

Shit!

"What's at 2122 North Clark Street?" Danny asks.

I bring up Google and type in the address. A click brings up a list of websites that refer to the St. Valentine's Day Massacre.

The St. Valentine's Day Massacre was one of the most notorious murders for hire. It occurred at 10:30 a.m. on February 14, 1929. Seven members of George "Bugs" Moran's gang were murdered at a garage at 2122 North Clark Street on Chicago's North Side. They were gunned down against a wall with Thompson submachine guns by four men who were allegedly hired by Al Capone. Two of the shooters wore policemen's uniforms and they led the other shooters out of the garage at gunpoint after the massacre.

The computer chimes and the little box that signals new mail flashes briefly on the screen. The subject line of the new mail is Password.

No! Could it be?

213

I go to the mail app and open the email at the top of the queue. The email is from 2122 North Clark Street. It runs:

This password is good for 1 hour.

Q%^ll68795xX90hjkQ!

That's a password? I swipe it with the cursor, right click to copy it, then hit the tab to take me back to 2122 North Clark Street and paste it in the box, where it produces a line of asterisks. I click the ENTER button.

Everything but the Guy Fawkes mask disappears from the screen, and the following list comes up in vibrant pink letters.

<u>Me</u>

<u>My Work</u>

<u>Hire Me</u>

With much trepidation, I click <u>Me</u>.

> Hi! I'm sure you've found your way here because you've got someone in your life who is getting in your way, making you thoroughly miserable, or just being a general pain in the ass! Never fear, you've come to right place! I don't care if it's your spouse or boss, a business rival or even somebody who just pisses you off. For a reasonable fee, I can solve that problem. You can pay me by bank draft, credit card, or bitcoin. If you want your life and your freedom back, it's easy. Just click on <u>Hire Me</u> and follow the simple instructions. You can also see samples of <u>My Work</u>. You'll be glad you did!

I click <u>My Work</u> and a slide show starts. It's a catalog of cadavers. Men and women, young, middle-aged, old. The slides fade in and out, each one on the screen for a few seconds. Each slowly zooms in on the dead face. There are no visible signs of violence on most of the bodies. I lose count of the victims. I

214

want to shut it down but I just can't – it has a morbid fascination that seeps into my soul. Then a person that I know pops up.

Blackie O'Halloran!

It's a color shot of my hallway with Blackie on the white shag carpet in a pool of blood. His face fills the screen so there's no doubt as to his identity. I can't believe that this psycho took the time to snap pictures while I was back cowering behind the bed.

Then I see myself appear on the screen. Beside me, Danny gasps.

Becca!

Unlike all of the other victims, she's nude. One of her breasts is gone and many more cuts and weals cover her body. A wound in her lower abdomen gapes obscenely above a large pool of blood between her legs. The picture zooms in and out, showcasing the details of the various mutilations.

Danny reaches over and kills the PC. The screen goes dark.

"You don't need to see that," he says.

I spin in the swivel chair and slap him across the face just as hard as I can. His shocked look is profound.

"Don't you ever do anything like that again!" I hiss.

I turn back to the computer and reboot. It takes a couple of minutes to navigate back to the website and the password box.

I open email app to recopy the password.

The email is gone!

How can that be? I didn't delete it! I check the trash anyway, then run a search for 2122 Clark Street. Nothing! I wheel on Danny again, who's still sitting there gobsmacked.

"Do you see what you've done!"

"I'm sorry," he babbles.

"Sorry! You asshole! We've just lost the best lead that we ever had to find Becca's killer!"

"I've got a pretty good memory," Danny says "Maybe I can remember the password."

I push over and let him get to the keyboard, then watch his fingers as he types it in. I remember it had a Q at the beginning and a Q with an exclamation point at the end, but that's all. Danny finishes typing, then clicks the enter button.

Nothing.

"Let me try again."

Still nothing.

He tries one more time.

A message in those vibrant pink letters appears on the screen.

"Try it again and I'll wipe your hard drive, asshole!"

It as if an electric current courses through me as I read those words.

Danny's lips are compressed so tightly they're almost invisible. "I'm sorry," he says again. "I didn't do that just because of you. I didn't know Becca. It looked like you were lying there all cut up. I couldn't stand it anymore."

Is that a tear running down his cheek?

"I was just starting to notice the background of that picture when you cut the computer off. I'm pretty sure that was taken in the basement of the Kitten Club. Do you remember seeing sawdust on the floor in the picture?"

"I'm sorry. I wasn't looking at the floor."

"Dammit!" I explode again. "If we could have copied that picture, it might have been enough for a warrant if we took it to the cops."

"I doubt it," Danny replies. "It could have been taken anywhere, or at least a judge would say so. Even if you or somebody claimed that they recognized the background."

Is he saying that just because he fucked up? No matter. What's done is done.

I look at my watch. It's after five – I should be getting home to Lupe soon.

"What do you think we should do now?" I ask Danny.

216

"I don't know. We should probably tell the cops about the website and the pictures. Maybe they can get somebody who's good with computers to hack into it and find out who runs it."

"The whole point of the dark net is anonymity," I tell him.

"What do you know about the dark net?"

"Not much," I admit, "but I have a friend who does. Maybe I should talk to him." Did I just call Bobby my friend?

"I still think we should tell the cops."

"Really? Who should we tell? Kidd is still in ICU with Uncle Amos. We don't even know who's working on this. And if we tell the cops, maybe it will get back to Judd. I'm sure he's got a few on his payroll."

"I want to tell them." I know that adamant tone. "Let me see that url again."

No way I'm giving you that yellow card, Jose. "I'll write it down for you."

I dig the card out of my pouch and copy the url on a piece of notepaper.

"Good luck with that," I say as I hand it to him.

Later, I'm in the Z-car heading home. Something's bothering me about that website and that final message. I'm trying to pinpoint it, but that terrible picture of Becca keeps intruding, obliterating everything else. I give it up for now. I just want to get home and hug Lupe real, real tight. Maybe it will come to me after a night's sleep.

Chapter 31.

S unday is a mellow day. After breakfast, we ensconce Eduardo in front of the PS, and Lupe and I go back to bed. We finally get up for lunch, then practice for tonight's performance in the studio. I can't do too much on the pole because I don't want to blow my muscles out. But I work some more with Lupe on the computer, the cameras and the hand-held controller, and she finally seems to be getting it.

Perversely, I'm a little sad that tonight will be my final performance. I was always somewhat ambivalent about the dancing. I unequivocally despised the kisses and the lap dances at the club, but I must confess that I was finally enjoying the attention of my audience when I was on the pole and I frankly got off on the sense of control. More than once, a guy came in who I knew had made up his mind that he wasn't going to tip me all night, and I would just work him until he did. It was a total rush when he finally tucked that bill into my thong! And I really enjoyed the online dancing because it was almost all in my head. I got just enough reinforcement from the client on the phone to keep it interesting and sexy and I didn't have to deal with the physical stuff.

I tell Lupe to prepare a light supper so we'll be ready. We spend an hour after dinner getting our wardrobe together, and I'm all tingly when we're dressed.

We're wearing matching gauzy, floor length gowns split up the front and back so we can get our legs around the pole. Mine is black to accent my blonde hair, and Lupe's is bright red to contrast with her dark brown tresses. Underneath are matching stockings and garters. You can't do a striptease if there's nothing to take off, right?

We're in the studio about twenty minutes early and I review the computer set-up with Lupe once again. I reassure her that I'll be controlling the cameras tonight.

Finally, everything's ready and the business phone is on its stand next to the PC. Lupe and I are on the divan where Becca performed for me. I'm as nervous as a teen-ager waiting to go on stage for the first time during the high school play. Lupe, on the other hand, is cool and collected as an experienced dancer should be. She takes my hand and looks into my eyes.

"Don't worry, *cariño*. You will do fine." She gives me a deep, soulful kiss.

Stripper!

I push her away. "Not now, or our audience will get a lot more than they expect."

The phone chimes.

"This is Kira."

"Hey, doll!" Bobby says. "You two ready for your big night?"

I bring the cameras on line, then tuck the small controller in the top of my stocking.

"We're ready when you are, Bobby."

"Okay. Before I bring everyone online, I want you to know that over a hundred people will be watching." OMG! "I've told them that the performance is free, but that any tips in appreciation will be gratefully accepted."

"That's great!" I say and mean it. We stand to make a lot of money here, and I'm going to give it all to Lupe, since she's lost her job.

"OK you guys, get ready! I'm bringing them on in ten, nine, eight..."

We each take a position on opposite sides the pole.

"... three, two, one, we're live!"

I touch a button on the controller that zooms the camera in on me. I can immediately tell which camera is on by the little green light beneath it. A glance at the PC monitor tells me it's working as it should.

I address the camera. "I want to say hi to all my loyal fans. I'm so glad you're here for my last performance! We'll make it a good one! And I want to introduce the beautiful lady who's taking over." I touch another button and a second camera zooms in on Lupe, who is blushing after my comment. "Please welcome Carmella Picante!"

Lupe takes a bow like the veteran performer that she is.

I zoom the camera back out so that both of us and the pole are visible on the screen. Another touch on a button darkens the room leaving a soft spotlight on the pole. The music swells. Tonight I've chosen a compilation of classical music and made it audible in the room as well as on line.

Each with one hand on the pole, we begin to circle slowly, keeping an equal distance between us. We gradually speed up, then we both grab the pole simultaneously with two hands. We raise our legs off the floor so we're spinning around the pole in sync, using the momentum that built up in our circle dance. We hook two legs together around the pole and extend the other leg fully – Lupe grabs on to my ankle and I on to hers. Now we're spread-eagled and slowly revolving, and the split gowns drape down, exposing our legs and other charms. As the spins slows to a stop, we gracefully drop back to the floor.

We begin the slow circle again. It is crucial that we do this between stints on the pole, especially for me. I just don't have Lupe's stamina.

I undo the tie on the front of my gown, then mount the pole and quickly shinny to the top, spinning as I go so the gown flares out like the tail of a comet. I undo my legs while still griping the pole with both hands and bend my torso to clamp my belly muscles tightly around it. Meanwhile, Lupe mounts beneath me and stands with her top leg crooked around the pole and other one fully extended, her bottom foot pressing hard as a second point of contact with the pole. She has undone her gown too. She drops one hand and extends her arm fully displaying her charms. I ease down to lie on her top leg and lean back, spreading my legs wide while still holding the pole with one hand. Now comes the tricky part. I let go of the pole completely –the only thing supporting me is Lupe's upper leg, which feels like an iron bar against my back. My gown falls away, exposing my torso but still clinging to my shoulders. We're still slowly revolving and I can feel Lupe trembling beneath me from the terrific exertion of supporting us both. She grips my ankles, holding my legs apart – now we're both supported on the pole only by the pressure of her leg and foot! She slowly rides down to the floor, taking me with her, before she alights and helps me up.

I step up behind her and pull her gown off her shoulders, letting it drop to the floor, then I turn around so she can do the same for me. Now we're both wearing nothing but stockings, garters and heels. I undo the straps on my heels and kick them off. We move to opposite sides of the pole, grip it with both hands, and lean towards each other for a kiss that doesn't quite happen – we've both agreed to no sex on camera. That's just for us.

We start our final circle dance. Three stints of this complexity on the pole is all I can handle. Faster and faster we go, then Lupe nods imperceptibly and we mount the pole simultaneously, climbing and spinning as we go. Lupe stops and leans backwards facing me, while I climb high enough to swing down and plant my feet on her belly. I let go with one hand and let her support all my weight. I kick out one leg and extend my arm in a triumphant pose.

Stripper!

I grab with both hands and twist myself around so my back is against the pole, then pivot so I'm facing downward. Right now, the only thing holding me on that pole is my legs – this is the hardest move I've ever done! I slowly slide down until I'm on top of Lupe, who is still facing upward. She smiles and winks to tell me that she's ready to accept my weight, so I let go completely and spread my arms and legs. She slowly rides both of us down to the floor. I dismount and help her to her feet, the turn and bow. I take Lupe by the shoulders and move behind her, presenting her to her audience then I step out of camera range, giving her the stage.

Lupe dances solo for another ten minutes, demonstrating incredible virtuosity. I have all I can do to keep from touching myself as I watch her – I don't want to spoil things for later. Finally, as the music reaches its climax, I work the control to fade out as she revolves around the pole in a star-shaped pose.

"That's it," I say to Bobby on the phone.

"You guys were great! Check your wallet."

I move to the pc and do so. OMG! That can't be right! A little over $9,000?

"You two should consider making these shows a regular thing, or at least you should come on for a guest appearance once in a while, Kira. Now how about a private show?"

Is he kidding? "Not tonight, Bobby. We're beat!"

"Okay, but you promised me privileges," he grouses.

"You'll get them. But not now."

I shut down the site and then the PC, automatically checking the wall-mounted cameras to verify that the little lights are dark. I then go over to Becca's toy chest and take out a toy. I turn to Lupe and pat it in my hand.

"You didn't think we were all done, did you?"

She smiles and comes to me.

Later, we're relaxing in bed, enjoying the afterglow. The lights are on, but turned down low, bathing the room is a warm, diffuse glow. Lupe is snoring softly – given her earlier exertions, it's no wonder that she's asleep.

I reflect upon the past few weeks, amazed at the unexpected turns of life. Some terrible things have happened to be sure, but some wonderful things too, chiefly, my relationship with Lupe. I never even suspected that I was a lesbian until I met Becca. Now I wonder if that was why I could never seem to have a lasting relationship with a guy. I look at Lupe lying next to me and reach over to ruffle her hair. She doesn't stir.

It's amazing. I never would have thought that the love of my life would be an illegal Mexican woman with an eight-year old brother!

My eyes wander upward. Shit! Is that a light on one of the cameras? I turned them off, I know I did! The PC too! I bounce out of bed and go to the PC. The little light next to the on/off switch is glowing, but it winks out as I approach.

WTF is going on? The answer hits me with the force of a bullet.

Bobby! He was watching us the whole time!

Chapter 32.

I'm horrified! Lupe and I spent an hour in intimate play after our performance. Were we being live-streamed? To how many guys? Was it even recorded? Is a video of our lovemaking now posted on a porn site, for anyone to see? I wouldn't for a second put it past Bobby to do just that – he'd call it privileges. I can't even!

I grab my phone and punch in his number. It rings and rings. Pick it up, you little shit! He doesn't answer. Now I'm sure it was him!

I resist the urge to get dressed and go hunting him. After all, what can I do? I don't deny that I'd get grim satisfaction from slapping the shit out of him, and that will likely occur in the near future. But if he has shared our encounter with others, it's done and can't be undone.

This is way different than dancing online, or in the club. I did those things because I wanted to, or out of a sense of duty, which is essentially the same thing. But the things I did with Lupe were private, an expression of our love. They weren't meant to be a vehicle for someone's entertainment.

Now I understand what it means to be violated!

I resolve to say nothing about this to Lupe. She has way enough on her plate as it is.

I'm still quite morose Monday morning. Lupe can't help but notice and tries to get me to tell her what's wrong.

"It's just everything, Lupe. I'm worried about Uncle Amos and Detective Kidd, I'm worried about you and Eduardo, I'm worried that I'll never get back into school and finish my degree and go on to law school like I planned."

"*Si tu mal tiene remedio, ¿de qué te apuras?; y si no, ¿de qué te preocupas?*"

"What? You know I don't speak Spanish."

"My *abuela* used to say it to me when I was a little girl and I thought everything was terrible. It means that things will work out as we want or they won't but worrying over them will not help in either case."

I squelch a sarcastic reply. She's just trying to make me feel better. I smile at her, but I notice that she's looking at me strangely.

"Natalie," she says. "I must tell you something."

Now she looks distressed!

"What is it? Lupe, what's wrong?"

"Now that we are *amantes*, I must tell you that I have lied to you."

"About what?"

"Eduardo. I tell you that he is my brother. He is not. He is my son."

Her son! "Why would you lie about that, Lupe? There is no shame in it."

"Yes, there is! In my country, it is a big sin to have a child with no husband. Even Eduardo does not know. He thinks I am his big sister."

"Who is his father?"

"I dunno. The men from the *cártel* used to come around. A girl could not say no. It is one of them."

She's crying now. I go to her and take her in my arms.

"Lupe, it's okay. You didn't do anything wrong. I still love you." She cries all the harder.

I feel thoroughly ashamed. It's totally obvious that I never knew real hardship. She was raped in Mexico, so she left to come here, just to get raped again by Judd.

After she calms down, I tell her, "We are going to get Eduardo into school and we're going to get you a good job that you can do with your clothes on. And you must tell Eduardo the truth, too. A boy should know who his Mama is. I don't care what you've done in the past. I only care about now, and I know that I love you."

"And I love you."

Now I'm crying too!

After breakfast, I return to the problem of Bobby. I've tried calling him a few more times, but he isn't picking up. He knows it's me. I want to confront him, but I realize that, other than the club, I have no idea where he is. I don't know

224

where he lives. I don't even know his last name. It occurs to me that paperwork at the 3M office about the work he did for Uncle Amos might have an address – I'm almost hundo p sure that he works out of his home.

My phone beeps. I check the screen.

A calendar reminder. Rebecca Feiner – 10 a.m. Today! Forgot again!

I throw on some clothes and tell Lupe I'll likely be gone for most of the day. The sight of my poor Z-car reminds me that I've got to find a body shop. I drive over to State.

It actually feels strange to be walking on campus. I've only been away a couple of weeks, but the changes in my life make it seem like an eternity. I feel like I have very little in common with the students who pass me by.

It's 10:06 when I arrive at the Counselling Center. I sign in and they call Rebecca. A minute later, she comes into the reception area.

"I was just getting ready to send out the dogs for you." Her brown eyes flash fire from the overhead lights. "I was sure you weren't going to show up."

She leads me back to her office and indicates the daybed.

"I'd rather have the chair if it's all the same," I tell her.

"Suit yourself." She takes a seat behind her desk. "What's been going on?"

Where to begin? I haven't told her about my stripping at the club, so I do. I recount my adventures over the last week or so, ending with my stint at the police station. One thing I hold back - the gun. The one that's in my pouch under the chair, on the gun-free campus.

"Very interesting." She says when I've finished. "I can't say that I think you chose the best way to deal with your uncle's assault, but what's done is done. You say that you're no longer working there?"

"No ma'am. They fired me when I wrecked their gate." Did I see a hint of a smile?

"Well, I think you should stay out of there. You're better than that. Now, regarding the criminal charges, we'll have to wait and see. If your attorney is right and you're charged with a misdemeanor, there shouldn't be any trouble with the University. A felony conviction would likely result in expulsion, but we can request a hearing with the Dean of Students to present mitigating circumstances.

The word 'expulsion' makes me wince.

"How about the dream?" she asks.

"It seems to be gone."

"Are you still taking your medicine?"

"Yes. Do you think I can stop?"

"You can cut back on it the same way that you increased the dosage to make the dream go away. If it returns, just go up on the dose again. And what about your sexual orientation?"

"I think I've got that under control." I tell her about my relationship with Lupe, leaving out that she's a stripper now working out of my house and an illegal immigrant. Thankfully, Rebecca doesn't pry.

"But there is one other thing." I go on to tell her about my tryst with Danny. "I feel bad about it. I'm not at all sure that I didn't take him to bed just to prove I wasn't a lesbian."

"Do you think there's anything wrong with being a lesbian?"

"I don't know. I was raised Catholic, so there's baggage. I guess when I asked Danny to sleep with me, I just wanted to be something, straight or gay, and to be sure of what I was. Does that make sense?"

"It makes very good sense, Natalie. Uncertainty is at the root of many problems with sexual orientation, even when one is relatively sure what their sexual orientation is."

"How so?"

"Many people are in relationships because they feel that have to be, not necessarily because they want to be. That's generally a prescription for failure."

"You know, I think it was that way with Michael and me. It felt good to tell people I was engaged. It made me feel important."

"And how about your relationship with Lupe?"

"Oh, that's way different. I love her."

Stripper!

"See? No hesitation. I think you've got something you need to hold on to."

I think about last night – about our sexual encounter being broadcast live on the Internet, but I don't say anything. She can tell I'm holding something back.

"Anything else you want to tell me, Natalie?"

I think fast. "I think Danny wants to get back together."

"Well, you'll just have to tell him that's not going to happen, and why. You owe him that much."

We spend another ten minutes in small talk before she releases me.

"Natalie, I think you're making fine progress. But I think it will be better for you if you give up your investigation into your uncle's assault and let the police do their job. Concentrate on your relationship with Lupe and in getting yourself in shape to come back to school in the fall."

Maybe she's right. But I know that this guy isn't going to give up on Uncle Amos until the cops take him down.

There's at least some good news at the hospital. Uncle Amos is the same, but Kidd is doing better and he's slated to be moved out of ICU.

"You're still going to maintain a guard on my uncle after Detective Kidd is moved," I ask the officer who told me.

"Yes, as far as I know. It's pretty obvious that your uncle was the target when Detective Kidd got shot."

I find Danny working at his desk when I come in to the office. He comes over to give me a big hug. I stiffen and don't return it.

He lets me go. "Still mad at me because I shut off the computer?" he asks.

"No."

"What's wrong, then?" He hesitates, then says, "You know, I was going to wait until Amos got better to ask you, but I was kind of hoping that maybe we could pick up where we left off."

I was afraid of this.

"No Danny, I don't think that's going to work."

"Why not?"

I remember what Rebecca said. "Because I'm in a relationship."

He looks dumbstruck. "Really? With who?" He gets a distressed look. "Not that Bobby guy?"

"No fucking way!" I have got to tell him. "It's Lupe."

"Lupe? Your roommate? She's a woman!"

No shit, Sherlock. Wait for it...

"Ohhh."

I don't know how he's taking it. He's not happy, to be sure. Do I sense disgust? I don't know, but it doesn't really matter. I feel like I owe him an explanation, though.

"Lupe and I weren't together when you and I hooked up," I tell him.

"When did you get together? Didn't our lovemaking mean anything to you?"

"Yes, it did. But I'm having some issues. I wasn't sure if I wasn't a lesbian. Now I know that I am."

"So you had sex with me to prove you weren't a lesbian?" Is he angry, or what?

I have to be honest. "Maybe. But I wouldn't have done it if I didn't have some feelings for you."

"What does that mean?"

Now I'm getting angry. "It means just what it sounds like! It means that I like you. It means that I thought we might have a future together. But then I met Lupe."

"So you just dropped me." It's a statement of fact.

"If I recall correctly, it was you who dropped me when you found out you couldn't control me," I tell him.

I know that look. He's getting ready to yell. But then he swallows it.

"OK, you've got me there. I did drop you when you started stripping. And you met Lupe at the club, right?"

"Right."

228

Stripper!

"OK. So I guess it was me that blew it."

Men! "Goddamn it Danny, nobody blew anything! Shit happens! Look, I don't want to fight with you. The fact is that I've realized that I'm in love with Lupe. And she loves me back. That doesn't mean that I don't think you're a good guy. And I want to work with you. I need you to help me find out who hurt Uncle Amos. And he'll need the both of us to keep this business from going under when he gets out of the hospital. If I've hurt you, I'm sorry. I didn't mean to. Can we get past this and work together, or not?"

He's quiet for a good thirty seconds. Finally, "Yeah, we can work together." Half of the tension goes out of the room. I expect it will be quite a while before the other half leaves.

"I'm trying to get an address for Bobby," I tell him.

"Why?"

"He did some work on my computer at home."

"Don't you have his phone number?"

I won't yell, I won't yell, I won't yell. "He's not picking up. I'm getting worried about him."

"Well let's see if we've got any paperwork with an address or another number." He rummages around on Uncle's desk for a minute. "Here you go. Oh damn, it's a PO box."

"He'll probably be at the club," I say, "but neither one of us better dare show our face there."

"You got that right."

I'm sure there's no way I'm gonna get the post office to give me an address to go with that box. Uncle Amos might could have, but he's not here. It's just another reminder of how much I've grown to depend on my uncle since I've come to State. I don't know what I'm going to do if I lose him. I also don't know how I'm going to tell him about Lupe. Uncle Amos loves three things – his country, his bible and food. I hope that he's going to understand.

Prior to leaving, I ask Danny if he knows a good body shop, and unsurprisingly, he does. I give them a call and they tell me I can swing by for an estimate this afternoon.

I'm a bit shell-shocked when I finish at the body shop. The only reason that the car is not a total loss is that it's relatively new. The technician advises me to replace it. Of course, I don't tell him that I won't be claiming insurance because of how the damage occurred. I know he's right about replacing it, but I don't know whether I can. Becca really loved that car.

It's nearly dinnertime when I finally get home. True to form, Lupe has it ready. She tells me that she's been playing with the cameras and thinks that she might be ready for a trial run to see if she can run her own performances. She also has several clients lined up for later this week.

Naturally I'm happy for her, but I'm worried too. I'd hate to think that she went through all that she did to spend her life as an online stripper. It's not right that someone so beautiful and proud should be reduced to dancing naked for men. She could be so much more. I've got to think of something to get her out of stripping!

An idea occurs to me, but I resist the impulse to blurt it out until I've looked into it. I don't want to get her hopes up.

After Eduardo and I are finished in the kitchen, Lupe wants to go upstairs for another session on the computer. We work steadily for a couple of hours, and I'm surprised and pleased how quickly she's getting it.

"I'll be there for your first performance of course," I tell her, "but I really don't think you're going to need me."

"I will always need you, *cariño*," she says, making me tear up.

The lights flicker. That's a signal that someone is ringing the doorbell downstairs. I wonder…

I run down to the front door and look through the peephole. It's Bobby!

Chapter 33.

I open the door. Bobby's wearing his usual pink t-shirt and carrying a shoulder bag.

"Hi Kira!"

As he starts to come in, I step out and bump him with my chest. He's bigger than me, but my action is unexpected and it causes him to step back. I pull the door shut and stand with my back against it.

"You're not welcome in my home." He favors me with his usual tweaker's stare.

"Whadido?"

"You know what you did!" His face still says *no comprende*. "Last night. After the performance. You turned the computer and the cameras back on."

"I didn't…"

"Don't you lie to me, you sorry son of a bitch! You watched me and Lupe! How many people did you show it to? Did you record it?"

Is that a flicker of anger I see in his eyes? It's hard to tell because his sketcher's expression doesn't flinch. But he finally cops.

"Hey, I didn't mean anything. Nobody else was there. Just me." He grins. "I thought I'd catch you changing clothes or something."

My voice starts quietly and gets louder with each word. "Don't. You. Ever. Do anything like that again!" He recoils from the fury in those last words.

"Kira…"

"Don't call me that!"

"Natalie, then. I'm sorry. I shouldn't have. I know that now." He looks like he's going to cry. "I have a problem. With sex. I can't help it."

I'm still mad as fire, but his words take me aback. Hell, yes, he has a problem with sex, sitting in that seedy club until closing seven nights a week, then going home to get more online. It's a positive thing for him if he's finally realized it.

He reaches into the bag he's carrying and comes out with a Ziploc bag. An object inside gleams green in the streetlight. A beer bottle!

"Is that…" I ask him.

"I did like you told me, Ki…, ah, Natalie. I bought Valery a beer and I stole the bottle when he wasn't looking." He smiles pitifully. "Am I forgiven?"

"Not by a damn sight!" I snap at him, snatching the bottle away. "I still have a mind to trash that computer and get another one that you've never laid hands on."

"Oh, that wouldn't make any difference," he says stupidly. "I could get into any computer you'd get in only a few minutes." A horrified look crosses his face as he realizes what he's just told me. "But I wouldn't do that! I promise! Please don't stop being my friend!"

We were never friends, you pathetic asshole! But you've just done me a huge favor.

"OK, I'll trust you one more time," I tell him. "But if I ever find out that you've done something like this again…" I leave the threat unfinished.

His smile is pitiful. He reaches to take my hand and I slap him away. "You've made me so happy," he says. "I'll be good, I promise. Can I please come inside for a few minutes?"

I start to refuse, then I think better of it. "Only for a few minutes."

We go inside. Lupe has put Eduardo to bed and come back downstairs. She's dressed in her usual long t-shirt, which hangs to her knees. It does little to hide her womanly charms.

"I have my first job," she smiles. "A man wants me to dance for him tomorrow night."

"That's great, Lupe!" I say.

"Awesome!" Bobby echoes me.

"I am going to get a beer before bedtime," I say to her. "Would you like one?"

232

Stripper!

"Yes!" Bobby says.

"I didn't ask you." I tell him.

"Don't be that way," he says. "I said I'm sorry."

"Sorry for what," Lupe asks.

"For showing up at this hour," I tell her before Bobby can get a word in. I haven't told her that he watched our love-making last night, and now is definitely not the time. Bobby better not say anything either! I favor him with a glare to shut him up.

I go into the kitchen and put the Ziploc bag on the table. I get two beers out of the fridge. Beads of moisture glisten on the outside of the emerald bottles, making them slippery. I wipe them down with a dishtowel and put them on a tray. I decide to pour a shot of Turkey for myself.

When I come back to the living room, I find that Bobby has taken the easy chair. Lupe is on the couch in front of the low table. I join her there.

"What about me?" Bobby says, eyeing the drinks.

"What about you?" He's starting to piss me off again.

I down my shot and drain off a third of the Heinie to chase it down. Bobby looks like he's settling in for the night.

"Bobby, I've got an early day tomorrow and I've got to get to bed."

"Don't let me stop you. I'm sure your roomie and I can find something to do," he leers.

I look him right in the eye. Is it my imagination, or has that tweaker's haze vanished? I notice he's ogling Lupe, and a flush of jealousy, followed by fury, rises in my gorge. It's a struggle not to cuss him out.

"So you two are an item now, is that right?" Bobby continues.

Yeah, you would know after your little peep show last night, wouldn't you. "That's really none of your business," I tell him.

"C'mon, I think it's cute! Might add some spice to your dual performances."

"There aren't going to be any more dual performances." I say emphatically. "This is Lupe's gig now. I'm out of the business."

"That's a shame." Is that disappointment or anger I detect in his voice? "Natalie, I have something I want to ask you," he says.

"What's that?"

"In private."

You've got to be kidding! "Lupe lives here. She's not leaving."

"It's okay," Lupe says. "I was going to bed anyhow." She gets up and takes her beer with her to our bedroom.

"That was crass, Bobby. But what else should I expect from you?"

"Don't be that way," he says again. "This is important." He pauses, then asks, "Are you and Lupe really in a relationship? Or were you guys just fooling around last night?"

Now he's really making me mad. "I told you that's none of your damn business!"

"But it is kinda. What I wanted to ask you is if you wanted to have a relationship with me."

WTF? Did I hear him right? I'm speechless!

"Listen to me before you say no," he says. "I've never met anyone like you before, Natalie. I think you're just the girl I've been looking for. If you'll be my girl, I promise I'll quit the club. I'll get rid of all of my porn, and I'll stay off the Internet porn sites. It would be just me and you. Maybe we could even go away and start a family."

Holy shit! I have to be really careful. My instinct is to slam him, but I'd better not.

"Bobby, I'm flattered." Not! "I really am. But I'm sorry. Lupe and I are in love. We're a couple. It doesn't mean that you and I can't be friends, but I'm committed to her."

He's not taking this well at all. His usual dumb look has definitely vanished, replaced by a furious glare.

"So you're going to dis me for some dyke? A stripper?"

What did he just say? "Don't you dare call her that!" I spring to my feet. "We're done, Bobby! Get the fuck out of here and don't come back!"

Stripper!

He comes out of the chair with his arms at his sides and his hands clenched into fists. "And what if I don't?"

Shit! The pistol is in the closet in our bedroom, and this guy looks like he's ready to light into me. He's no heavyweight, but I'm sure he could do some damage. There's a little kid upstairs. I've got to defuse this!

"Look, I don't want any trouble. I'm sure you're just tired or something." God, that's lame! "Just go home and we'll talk about this later." The hell we will!

He takes a step towards me. The look on his face is frightening. I think I'm in serious trouble!

"I'll call the cops. Don't make me!"

"You touch that phone and you'll regret it!" He grates, then he charges me!

I get my hands up and go for his eyes as he reaches me. He grabs my wrists in time to avoid being blinded, but my nails make a weal of scarlet down both cheeks. He pushes my hands away from his face and I can't stop him – he's too strong. He pushes me back towards the sofa. I thrust a knee at his groin and miss, hitting his thigh instead. He bears me down on the couch and holds me there with his weight.

His eyes shine brightly, furious and terrifying. "I'll make you understand! I love you! I want you!"

"You let her go or you'll regret it, *cabrón*!"

Lupe is standing in the bedroom door with the pistol trained on Bobby! She's in her nightie, and her fierce expression and flashing Latin eyes convince me that she'll shoot him in a heartbeat if he doesn't do as she says. I sure as hell hope she doesn't shoot me instead!

Apparently, she's convinced him as well.

"Okay, okay, let's not get all wonky here! I was just kidding!" His sketcher's demeanor is back. He lets go of my wrists and backs off. I can already see bruises beginning to form.

Kidding my ass! That motherfucker was as serious as Lupe is.

"Get out Bobby! Don't ever come back! And you can forget about working for 3M, too."

"But I was never paid!" he whines.

"Send us a fucking bill. You know the address. But don't ever let me see you again."

He looks at Lupe once more as if to convince himself that she's there. Then he goes to the door and leaves, slamming it behind him.

I tear across to the door, throw the deadbolt and put on the chain. Lupe is still standing in the bedroom door with the pistol. Now she looks scared. She has her finger on the trigger and the gun trained on me!

"He's gone, sweetie. Take your finger off the trigger and point the gun at the floor."

She does so, and I take the pistol from her. The safety is engaged. She wasn't going to shoot anybody with that.

She's shaking now. "What just happened?"

I tell her about what he did last night. "I didn't realize that he had those feelings for me," I conclude. "He wanted me to be with him instead of you. When I told him that wasn't going to happen, he went nuts! I'm glad you were here."

I get us another round of drinks to help us sleep. I hope to hell Bobby stays away – we would have been in a world of hurt if Lupe shot him with an illegal gun.

"Are you coming to bed?" she asks me when she finishes her beer.

"In a few minutes. You go warm it up for me."

After she's gone, I go into the bathroom to clean myself up. Then I ring Danny even though it's late. He doesn't answer, but his voicemail kicks in.

"This is Danny. You caught me at a bad time. Leave a message and I'll get back to you as soon as I can."

"Hey, it's Nattie. Can you come by here tomorrow? I need to talk with you."

Hearing his voice makes me sad. I wouldn't have slept with him if I didn't like him. I guess I miss him and I'm sad for what might have been. Is that okay? Can I miss him and still be in love with Lupe? I remember what Rebecca said.

"What you're feeling is what you're feeling. Period. Feel it. Don't judge it."

Stripper!

I sigh and go off to bed with the woman I love.

Danny calls first thing in the morning. I let it go to voicemail.

"Got your call last night. I'll swing by there in a half hour or so on my way to the office."

In a half hour or so? The clock says it's a little before seven. Marines! I'll have to hustle if I'm going to be decent when he gets here.

There's a knock on the door at seven thirty on the dot. I'm sure it's Danny, but I check the peephole anyway. Then I open the door and let him in.

He immediately spies the bruises on my wrists. "What have you been into, Nattie?"

"I don't want to talk about it." He must be getting to know me, because he doesn't argue.

"What did you have to show me?"

I get the bag that Bobby brought from the kitchen. "I might have the DNA of the man who killed Blackie, stabbed Uncle Amos and shot Detective Kidd. I kept a swatch of the carpet that had the blood of the man who killed Blackie on it. Do you know how to get it tested so it can be matched against the blood from my hallway?"

He takes the bag and looks inside, then regards me quizzically. "This isn't evidence…"

"Yes it is. If we get a match, I can testify where it came from."

Danny still looks skeptical. "There's a private lab in town where we used to send our samples when the police lab got jammed. I can take it there, I guess."

"Tell them to hurry." A pause. "I'm going to see Uncle this morning."

"I'll be at the office. Call me if there's news."

"I will."

After he leaves, I grab a quick breakfast. Lupe is still out and I let her sleep. She had a rough night.

It's almost ten when I get to the hospital. Kidd has been moved downstairs. A policewoman occupies a chair outside of Uncle Amos' room. His condition hasn't changed, so I just give him a quick peck on the forehead and go see Kidd.

237

It's easy to find his room, because there's an officer on duty outside. He rises to block my way as I approach the door.

"Sorry Miss, this room is restricted."

I hold out my I.D. badge to him. "I'm Natalie McMasters. Detective Kidd is my friend. He was shot protecting my uncle."

The cop examines my badge, then consults a clipboard. "OK, you can go in."

When I enter, Kidd is awake. He doesn't look good. His normally brown skin has a greyish tinge. He's lost weight, as evidenced by his hollow cheeks and prominent facial bones. He has no visible wounds, but that doesn't mean he wasn't badly hurt.

"Hi Natalie. How is your uncle?"

"The same, I'm afraid. Look, I want to thank you…"

He cuts me off. "I don't expect thanks for doing my job. I'm glad I was able to save him from further harm."

The nurse enters, takes one look at Kidd, then says to me, "Miss, I think you'll have to leave now. I'm going to give the detective a sedative so he can get some rest."

"OK." I tell her. I address Kidd again. "I come in every day to check on Uncle Amos, and I'll drop by to see you for as long as you're here."

"Which won't be long," he responds. I hope not.

As I'm making my way across the parking lot to the Z-car, my cell chirps. It's Lupe.

"What's going on, girl?"

"Nattie, I gotta problem! I went to turn on the computer to practice for tonight and it won't work."

"What won't work? What's it doing?"

"Nothing! It's beeping and I gotta black screen that says something about a missing operating system and the hard drive not detected."

WTF? "That doesn't sound good. Did you turn it off and back on again?"

"Yep, a coupla times. Does the same thing every time."

238

Stripper!

Shit! We do not need this right now. Lupe's first solo performance is tonight. I can't even call Bobby to help us fix... Bobby! Did that motherfucker do what I think he did?

There's one of those computer superstores not far from here that has a walk-in help desk. I head over there. After some waiting, I tell the guy at the counter what Lupe told me.

He whistles. "I hope you had everything backed up to the cloud," he says. "It sounds like your hard drive was wiped."

Yep. Bobby got even, all right. And no, nothing was backed up.

I decide to go by 3M to give Danny a report on Uncle Amos and ensure that the DNA samples went where they needed to go. I find him swearing at the computer. I see the black screen.

He turns on me like a rabid dog. "What's wrong with this thing?" Why do men always assume that we women know why things don't work?

Unfortunately, in this case I do know. I tell him about my altercation with Bobby.

"He won't get away with this," Danny snarls.

"He won't have left tracks. You'll never prove it was him."

"Maybe not. But I can sure track the little fucker down and whip his ass."

That's the last thing I want right now. "Please let it go. We have enough problems with Uncle Amos in the hospital. We don't need you in jail for assault. Besides, we don't even know where to find him."

"In case you haven't noticed, I'm a detective, Nattie. I'll find him."

"Please let me take care of Bobby."

"You haven't done a great job of that so far."

He's got me there.

"Just let me know when those DNA results come back. Call 'em and tell 'em we'll pay extra for a rush."

I've had about enough for one day. "I'm going home. Please don't go hunting Bobby. I promise I'll take care of him."

He doesn't say anything.

"Danny…"

"Okay, I won't go hunting Bobby. Today. But I want this thing fixed. If he did it, he can undo it."

Not necessarily. But I don't say that to Danny.

I can't wait to get back home. Did I say home? You know, the townhouse is finally starting to feel like home since Lupe came to live here.

It seems like forever before I pull into my space in the parking lot nest to Lupe's car. She's parked in the visitor space. I keep forgetting to go the office to get her assigned her own space now that she's living here.

As I get out of the car, something seems wrong. Approaching the door, I see that it's ajar.

A bolt of fear lances through me!

Chapter 34.

I push the door open. The place is silent as a cemetery. Where is Xin Niu?

"Lupe!"

No answer.

"Lupe! Eduardo!

No answer.

There's a piece of paper folded like a tent sitting on the bar between the kitchen and the great room.

If you want to see her again, come to the office at the club as soon as you get this. I don't have to tell you what happens if the cops show up.

It's not signed, but I know who's responsible.

Judd! And Valery!

I start to head for the car, then it hits me. *If you want to see her again.* Her, not them.

"Eduardo!"

There's not a lot of places to hide down here, and I check them all. No Eduardo.

I start going through the upstairs rooms. I find him and Xin Niu under the bed in the studio, both petrified.

"Un hombre del cartel con una pistola vinieron y llevaron a mi mamá."

Shit! "Eduardo, I don't speak Spanish. Can't you tell me in English?"

"Un hombre." He makes a gun with his hand. "Get Mama."

"What did the *hombre* look like?"

A blank look.

I had a year of Spanish as a freshman in high school. That was six years ago and I hated every second.

"*¿Cómo…*" Shit! How do you say face? "*¿Cómo la cara del hombre?*" I point to my face.

He spouts gibberish, and I shake my head.

He puts his finger under his right eye and draws a line down to his chin.

Valery!

Eduardo's presence is not something that Lupe shared at the club, so Valery had no idea that the kid was here. But the note suggests that he was looking for me. He'd have had no idea that Lupe was here either, until he walked in on her.

But why would Valery or Judd want me? I can think of only one reason. Judd finally found out that I broke into his office. But Bobby said he erased the tape. Suddenly I get it. He must've restored it. That little motherfucker!

Poor Lupe was in the wrong place at the wrong time. Thank God that Valery didn't get Eduardo!

I can't take the kid to the club – that would be worse than stupid. But I can't leave him here, either. Poor little guy is scared shitless.

I grab my phone and hit the speed dial. Come on, pick up!

"Hello, this is Kwaneshia."

"Kwan, hi! It's Nattie. I need a big favor."

I haven't talked to her for weeks, and now I'm asking for favors.

"What's wrong, Nattie?" She's obviously picked up on my anxiety.

"It's complicated, Kwan. Right now I need somebody to look after a little boy for a few hours."

"A little boy? What on earth have you been up to?"

"He's not mine, but his mother is a friend. She's not here right now and I've got to go somewhere I can't take him. Could you or Fields look after him for a little while?"

"I've got a class after supper, but Fields will be here. Let me ask her."

I hear her put down the phone. Oh, please, please, please, please, please…

"Fields says bring him over."

242

Stripper!

Yes! "Kwan, I love you and I'll pay you back, I promise."

I gather a few things that I think Eduardo might need and put them in a backpack. I check my pouch to make sure my pistol is inside, even though I know it is. I dangle my car keys in front of Eduardo.

"Eduardo, we're going to a friend's house where you're going to stay for a little while." I know he doesn't understand English, but he never will if it's not spoken to him.

He points at Xin Niu. "*El gato vendrá también.*"

"No, Xin Niu has to stay here and watch the house."

He's not happy, but he lets me lead him to the car. We chatter back and forth like the dudes on the Tower of Babel on the drive over, with about as much comprehension.

Nostalgia hits me as I pull into the driveway of my former residence and brings home again how much my life has changed in just a few short weeks. I'm dropping a little boy off at the babysitter's. Holy shit! A bolt of fear follows. His mother may be in deadly danger, and I have no freaking idea what I'm going to do about it. But I'm going to have to go over to that club and do something.

I have to stop myself from just walking right into the house as I used to. I don't live here anymore. I press the doorbell, and Kwan opens the door immediately, making me jump.

"And who is this?" Kwan says, indicating Eduardo.

I take him by the shoulders from behind. "This is Eduardo. He's my roommate's son. Eduardo, this is Kwaneshia. She's going to watch you for a little while."

"*Tiene un gato?*" asks Eduardo.

Before I can say anything, Kwan answers, "*No, no tenemos un gato, pero tenemos algunos leche y galletas. ¿Le gustaría a algunos?*"

Eduardo visibly brightens. "*Si, si!*" It had totally slipped my mind that Kwan grew up in a bilingual household.

I hand Kwan the bag with Eduardo's things. "I can't thank you and Fields enough for doing this," I say.

"*De nada.* But you owe us that housewarming!"

"Soon, I promise." I reach into my pocket and pull out a folded piece of paper, which I hand to Kwan. "I should be back in a couple hours. But If I'm not, please call Danny Merkel at this number and tell him I went to the club to see Judd."

Kwan looks at me apprehensively. "Are you in trouble?"

"No questions, Kwan, please? Just call Danny if I'm not back, OK?"

"Ok, but…"

"Thanks, Kwan." I cut her off. "I really owe you guys for this."

I'm back in the car. It's a short drive to the club. My insides are all bound up like an ice-crusted freezer. My plan is go into Judd's office with my gun in my hand, get Lupe, get outside and take off. I hope to hell that I don't have to shoot anybody, because I'm surely screwed if I do, but to save Lupe, I don't have the slightest doubt that I will shoot if I have to. Yes, you're right, it's a way stupid plan! But it's all I've got.

Instead of parking in the club lot (I know Judd has cameras there), I park on the side street off Lee a little ways from the club. It's about three-thirty in the afternoon, so the club is closed, but the chain-link gate is open and I can see cars in the lot. Judd's Beamer, Valery's Ford, a black Escalade with out-of-state plates and a nondescript Chevy sedan. Quite a party.

I step through the gate, and rather than walking straight across the lot to the entrance, I follow the perimeter of the board fence to the club wall, then walk along it to the door. I don't remember if the cameras have a blind spot along that route, but I do know that I would surely be on camera if I walked straight through the middle of the lot.

Jesse's stool is next to the door, but he's not. The door is closed – did they leave it unlocked? Yes!

The main room is shrouded in shadow, lit only by the utility lights. There might be a fair chance to get to the door by the bar without being seen by those in the office – at least that's where I assume everyone is. I try the door and it's locked (can't be lucky all the time), so I slide behind the bar where the button is. This is a good time to get my pistol ready. I check to see that the safety is engaged and shove the gun down the front of my pants, letting my shirt flop over it. My only real chance is surprise, which would be non-existent if I'm seen with a gun.

244

Stripper!

I push the button, open the door, and enter the hallway. As the door behind me closes, Judd's office door opens and Valery emerges, leering. Oh shit, they saw me coming! But did they see the gun?

"We wondered if you'd come, or leave Lupe to the wolves," he grins.

I don't react and walk straight to him like I was expecting him to meet me. He stands there grinning until I'm a few feet away, then turns to go inside. I yank the pistol out and click the safety.

I step in behind him and take in the situation in a glance.

Lupe is in a chair on the left side of the room. She looks terrified. Three big black dudes in gangbanger chic flank her. They're all looking at Judd's desk, which I can't fully see because Valery blocks my view.

Valery moves aside. Judd and a fourth gangbanger are standing on either side of a mostly naked woman on the desk, her legs splayed wide. A couple of the club bouncers are also watching, and one looks positively ill. WTF! The sleeves of Judd's bright yellow dress shirt are rolled up and his arms are bloody to the elbows! He's got a knife in one hand and what looks like a bloody white balloon in the other.

"Hi Natalie," Judd smirks, then the grin leaves his face as he sees the gun.

Valery notices the pistol at the same time. He charges me from three feet away.

I fire as fast as I can. I can't miss! I hit Valery in the chest, four, five, six times. He doesn't go down! He's got me – one hand on my shoulder rips my shirt and the other reaches for the gun. I can't let him get it! I draw it back into my body and keep firing -he's taking the rounds in the belly now. He goes limp and falls.

I train the gun on Judd who's standing there stupefied, like a fiendish caricature of a doctor.

The bangers next to Lupe are drawing guns. I don't think – I just zero in on one and shoot. My pistol has almost no recoil, so I hit him multiple times. A crimson flower appears in an eye socket and he drops.

A tremendous BOOM causes my ears to ring and something whips past my face. The other banger is holding an enormous silver automatic sideways, which he just fired at me. I put several rounds into his belly as he fires again, and he goes down.

"Enough!" I barely hear the shout. "Drop it or she dead!" The banger next to Judd has his pistol trained on Lupe!

I drop it. I can't take the chance!

The banger takes a couple steps towards me and backhands me with the pistol. I dodge enough to avoid the full force of the blow, but I feel my cheek tear and warm blood fills my mouth. I go down. Something goes CRACK inside as a boot slams into my ribs, and explosion of pain erupts in my torso. Stupidly, I worry whether my face will be permanently scarred.

"Not here, Royce," I hear Judd say. "There's enough to clean up already."

Royce is the dude who hit me. "She shot my homies, she got to pay!"

"She shot my man, too," Judd says. "You can take her with you when you go. I don't care what you do with her after that. Put her in a chair, Chris."

The bouncer called Chris hauls me off the floor by my hair and drags me over to the chair that Judd occupied the night I gave him the lap dance. As we go, my eyes are drawn inexorably to the grisly spectacle on Judd's desk. It's Kathie, dead as a dog on the side of the road, with her lower abdomen laid open like a frog on a dissecting board. Judd turns back to his work, pulling bloody balloons out of her and tossing them into a basin held by the other bouncer.

"I got to check that shit," says Royce.

"Suit yourself," says Judd, "but you'll find it's H with a little added fentanyl. You can cut it thirty to one, at least."

"Ten to one, more likely," Royce says. "I still got to check it out."

Judd withdraws a busted balloon from Kathie and says, "Here's the problem," as a chunk of red goo drops from the bottom of the balloon back into her torso. "Once that shit got into her system, she was as good as dead. Still think you need to test it, Royce?"

"Rat poison kill her ass too. I gots to test it."

"Suit yourself," says Judd again. He turns to Chris and the other bouncer. "Get this off of here. We'll put her in the basement until we can find a more permanent solution."

Stripper!

Speechless and horrified, I watch them fold back the rug and open the basement door as Bobby and I did only a few nights ago. One bouncer takes Kathie by the ankles and another by the arms, and they hoist her off the desk and carry her to the basement stairs.

"Don't get blood on the rug," Judd cautions.

They give her once beautiful body a quick swing and throw it into the hole in the floor. A momentary pause is followed by a dull thud.

"No sense bustin' a gut carryin' her down," one says. "She don't care."

Valery is dead too, as is Royce's hood who I shot in the eye. Judd's thugs toss them into the basement after Kathie. The other thug that I shot has his jacket balled up and is holding it over his gut to staunch the blood.

It's just starting to sink in that I've killed two people!

Meanwhile, Royce has set up a test tube rack, some bottles and a small scale on the now vacant desktop. He takes the balloon that split open inside of Kathie and removes a little bit of the contents, which he scrapes on to a piece of paper on the scale. When he's got the right amount, he carefully picks up the paper, rolls it into a spill and taps the contents into a tube with liquid already inside. He retrieves a dropper bottle and adds a couple of drops into the tube. The contents immediately darken. Royce smiles.

"Told you," said Judd. "That will be two hundred and fifty thousand dollars, please."

"This bag's ruint," says Royce, indicating the balloon that he took the sample from. "That will cost you fifty large."

Judd frowns, then acquiesces. "OK, but remember I gave you a deal."

I'm frantically looking for a way out. I know that if Royce takes me away, I'm dead, and I'm sure that Lupe is too. But even with two of Royce's guys out of commission, there's still Judd and his two goons, and Royce and his remaining man. Not good odds.

Royce grabs a gym bag from the floor, opens it and begins tossing stacks of cash on the desk. He counts aloud, "One, two, three… twennny two, twenny three."

He pulls out two more stacks and stuffs them in his pockets, then distastefully regards the bloody balloons on the desk.

247

"I should make you buy me a new bag," he tells Judd. He stuffs the drug containers into his bag and zips it up.

"I'm getting rid of a body for you," says Judd. "That should count for something."

Royce addresses his homie that I shot. "How're you?"

"I'm good. But I need a doc, soon." He doesn't look good.

Apparently Royce doesn't think so either. He pulls draws his pistol out and shoots his man twice.

"Two bodies," he tells Judd.

I didn't kill that man, but I might as well have.

Royce gestures at me with his pistol. "C'mon." he says. "We got bidness, you and me."

I'm tempted to say no, but he's just proved that he'll shoot somebody dead. I get up to go with him.

"You too," Royce says to Lupe.

"Nope," says Judd. "She's mine."

Damn it! I know he's going to kill her after he rapes her one more time. Oh Lupe, what did I get you into?

Royce puts his gun up and takes me by the arm. He squeezers hard enough to let me know just how much stronger he is.

"Let's go," he says. "You do right by me and I might just let you live."

Yeah, right.

I've got no choice, so I let him lead me out into the hall. His remaining man follows. The club is still dark. People will start showing up to open soon, but that will be way too late for Lupe and me.

Royce pushes the door to the parking lot open and shoves me out. A huge cop in tactical gear shoves an AR into Royce's face.

"Keep your hands in sight and get down on the ground. Miss, get over against the wall. You're safe now!"

Stripper!

I ignore his command and turn to go back inside. I see Royce's henchman drawing his pistol. I scream, "Watch out!" and hit the pavement.

The banger's gun explodes over my head. My ears close up and a high-pitched whine fills them. The answering automatic fire seems muted, likely because my hearing has been largely destroyed. The stupid banger goes down, his chest a mass of scarlet.

Another cop grabs me by the shoulder and hauls me to my feet. I see that Royce is also in a bloody heap on the pavement.

"My friend is in there! Judd will kill her!"

The cop shoves me against the wall of the club. Someone steps up next to me and takes me by the shoulders. It's Danny! He crushes me to his chest, keeping me from interfering with the SWAT team as they make their final preparations.

The cop who spoke to me makes a circle in the air with his hand and half a dozen SWAT guys charge into the club.

"No!" I scream. "He has cameras! He'll see you coming! He'll kill her!" I try to block their way, but Danny won't let me!

It's dead quiet for a moment, then I hear the faint rattle of automatic fire from inside.

Lupe!

Chapter 35.

I tip the bottle of ginger ale into the punch bowl on the bar and give it a swirl with the ladle to mix it with the other ingredients – lemon-line soda, sparkling cider and orange juice. Normally, there's no way I'd drink a mess like that, but there's a kid present, as well as the doctor who told me not to drink on the medication that she prescribed. So I think I'd better be good for once.

Lupe is stunning in Mexican formal attire – a frilly white blouse and long billowing skirt, with a red flower in her hair. I even broke down and raided Becca's wardrobe for a sequined top, a skirt and stockings for myself. I know that the effect is somewhat marred by the bandage on my cheek, held in place by a flexible strap that snaps behind my head and circles my face from the top of my head to my chin. I think it gives me an exotic, Asian look.

Kwan and Fields are finally here for my long-awaited housewarming. Detective Kidd is sitting in our best easy chair under strict instructions not to move except to go to the bathroom – everything else will be done for him. I even invited the girls from the club, but unsurprisingly, they didn't come. I guess that stripping requires that you maintain boundaries. It's a goddamn lonely life. I want no more of it.

There's one person who I really wish was here who isn't. Uncle Amos. I wanted to wait and have this housewarming when he was able to make it, but Dr. Chowdhury told me that she simply couldn't predict when, if ever, he would regain consciousness.

It's been a week since the raid. Judd is dead –when the cops caught him in his bloody shirtsleeves with a stack of corpses, the idiot tried to fight. His bouncers got caught in the crossfire too. Luckily, Lupe came out of the ordeal unscathed. I expected her to be traumatized, but she surprised me. It seems that she'd had similar experiences with the cartel in Mexico. However, she's grateful to be alive.

I'm grateful to be alive, too. I have Kwan to thank for that. After I left Eduardo with her, he gave her an earful in Spanish about what had happened to Lupe. Kwan decided not to wait a couple of hours to call Danny to tell him that I was rushing into a situation involving men with guns. Danny had the good sense to call Kidd at the hospital instead of calling the cops directly. Kidd, in turn, contacted police HQ and called in some favors to ensure that the right people knew about what was going down at the Kitten Club. That resulted in the timely SWAT raid that saved my bacon.

I can't forget that I killed two people. I don't really regret it –an old joke says that "he needed killin'" is an acceptable defense in some Southern courtrooms, and it certainly applies to Valery and the other guys I shot. I'm sure that Valery was the guy in the mask who killed Blackie and Becca, hurt Uncle Amos and damn near killed me. The DNA from the beer bottle confirmed it. Looks like Judd was running the assassination business at 2122 North Clark Street along with his drug business.

But I'm worried. I showed the cops Valery's note and told them I went to plead for Lupe's life. I can only hope that they take the evidence at face value and don't look into things too closely. A fight broke out over drugs and money and some people got shot – happens all the time. The cops probably found the .22, but it had been taken away from me and disappeared into the big pile of guns in the room. All of the witnesses except me and Lupe are dead. I know Lupe won't talk.

"I never saw anyone so brave as you," she said to me after we returned home. "I will love you always, *cariño*."

"And I will love you always, Lupe."

We fell into each other's arms, only to have to back off to make room for Eduardo to get into the group hug.

I ladle out the punch into plastic glasses on a tray and walk around handing them out – the perfect little hostess, that's me.

Rebecca is absolutely gorgeous in a one-piece white pants suit with a plunging neckline and a matching string of pearls that stands out starkly against her olive skin. She accepts a glass of punch from the tray.

"I'm glad to see that you're recovering nicely from your ordeal. Lupe is a lovely person. I wish the two of you much happiness."

I had a session with Rebecca a couple of days after the incident at the club and decided not to discuss the details. I think she knows there's something I'm not telling her but she hasn't pressed me.

Danny steps up beside Rebecca and takes a glass as well. It's painfully obvious that he can't take his eyes off her.

"Aren't you going to introduce me to your friend, Nattie?"

I'm a little put out by his forwardness, but I don't let it show. "This is Rebecca, Danny. She's my...".

"I'm one of Nattie's advisors at State, Danny," she says, slurring her words a little. Is she drunk? "She speaks highly of you. I'm pleased to meet you."

It's apparent that Danny wants me to butt out, so I take the tray over to Detective Kidd, who's talking to Kwan and Fields. As I hold the tray down low so Kidd can take a glass without rising from his chair, Eduardo, whose mouth is rimmed with salsa, runs up, snatches one and gulps it down. I raise the tray back out of his reach as he grabs for another.

"Hey, go easy, my man. You don't want to get sick on this mess."

He's got a hurt puppy look. Lupe grabs him by the scruff and rebukes him in Spanish, and he goes over to the sofa to pout.

I deliver the remaining glasses, making sure that everyone has gotten one. I drink half a glass myself. God, I'd love me a boilermaker instead of this sweet stuff!

Lupe goes to the kitchen to retrieve the hors d'oeuvres. As usual, there's enough for a block party. We'll be eating this stuff for a week! I go to help her.

As I come out with a tray of taquitos, I see Eduardo asleep on the sofa. Strange – he was a little ball of energy just five minutes ago.

Danny and Rebecca are over near the front door away from everyone else. He's still chatting her up with his back to me. Rebecca steps a little to side so his body doesn't block her and gives me a distressed look. WTF?

I start over there and suddenly stop. The tray I'm holding with one hand, waitress-style, has become unbalanced. I take another step and it feels like I just stepped off a curb. The tray falls on the white shag carpet splattering meat and sauce everywhere.

Danny grabs Rebecca's shoulder strap. She pushes him away and the strap breaks. Her top falls away revealing the skimpiest of lace bras. Danny reaches for her and she slaps him!

There's a crash from behind. I turn to see Fields on top of the living room table where she's fallen. The glass top is split in two. Lupe and Kwan are looking at her stupidly. I take another step to go help her and I feel myself going down.

I push myself up with my arms and try to get my feet underneath me, but it's no good – my legs are rubber. I can see that Kidd has fallen out of the easy chair and is also face down on the floor. WTF?

An impossibly tall and thin figure steps up beside me. His white Guy Fawkes mask mocks me. He's done this somehow! I try to take a punch at him and my face is buried in the carpet again.

A knee in my back expels my breath and my hands are jerked behind me. Something snakes around my wrists and tightens painfully. A spasm of agony shoots through my shoulders as he jerks me to my feet by my bound hands. That's the last thing I remember.

Chapter 36.

I'm drowning in a sea of fire. There's an unendurable burning in my neck and shoulders and I'm vaguely nauseated as I bob upon fiery waves. The fetor of brimstone is almost overpowering.

I open my eyes. The pain worsens. I see the source of the brimstone smell – a charcoal brazier full of glowing coals. The handles of tools protrude from it. I can feel the heat on my skin.

OMG! I'm nude! Nude and hanging with my arms suspended over my head – the source of my pain! The rest of the room comes slowly into focus. I know this place! It's the Kitten Club basement, lit only by that glowing brazier.

The last thing I remember is passing out at the party. It's obvious that I was roofied, but how? The punch? How could anyone have spiked that?

There's something else hanging on the other side of the brazier. I strain to see – it's another naked woman! No! No! It's Lupe!

She's appears unconscious, suspended by her arms as I am. Her chin rests on her breasts. Is that blood I see on her belly and legs? Is she dead? Who has done this? The guy in the mask?

"Good. You're awake!"

I know that voice!

He steps into view. OMG, he's naked too! He cuts a ridiculous figure, wearing a pair of hiking boots and socks up to his knees. That horrible mask hides his face and a bandage sheaths his right shoulder. He's got something in his hands. A riding crop?

He steps closer. I can see that he's rampant. He faces me, then removes the mask.

Bobby!

He extends the crop and lifts my chin, then trails it down over my breasts and belly. Gone is his thousand-yard stare and meth head demeanor, replaced by a fierce and scary intelligence. He leers at me as his eyes travel unimpeded over my body.

Stripper!

"Bobby, what do you think you're doing?"

"That should be obvious, Nattie," he smirks.

He turns his back on me and moves to Lupe. He places the crop under her chin and raises her head. It flops backward like a rag doll's.

"She should be awake too." he says. "She's faking!" He takes a step back and whips the crop across her breasts. The sickening CRACK! makes me jump, sending fresh waves of pain through my arms and back. Lupe screams! She was faking!

Bobby stands where he can see both of us, hanging like prize cuts of meat. "Good!" he says. "Now we can get started!"

My voice is broken and weak. "What are you going to do?"

"He's going to kill us, of course," Lupe says matter-of-factly. I can her the pain in her voice, but she's trying to hide it. A scarlet weal rapidly grows across her breasts.

"Yes I am!" Bobby says.

"Why, Bobby?" I ask him. "What have we done?"

He waves the riding crop at Lupe. "She's first, so you can watch. That fucking dyke took you away from me. Convinced you that you were queer, so she could have you instead. You should have come with me, like I asked you to!"

He pauses for a second, then says, "I killed Kira, you know. Got good money from killing that grandfather of hers. Before I did her, my work was always clean and quick. But I was afraid if I did her that way, the old man wouldn't show. So I brought her here and took my time. I knew that Blackie would have a shit fit and come out of hiding when he heard about what happened to his granddaughter."

I've got to keep the little asshole talking while I think of a way out of this! "How did you even know who she was? Blackie's granddaughter, I mean."

"Oh, I hacked her. Watched her dancing for other clients and she never knew. Then one day, I was messing around on her hard drive and found her genealogy results. Blackie O'Halloran's granddaughter! I knew people who would pay a fortune to whoever offed Blackie. So I did her in the worst way I could think of to get him to come looking for me. God, what a rush that was!"

"I was sorry afterwards though," he goes on. "I missed having her dance for me. But then I heard she was back. I knew that wasn't possible, but I had to check it out. And there you were!"

"Did Judd know you killed Becca in his basement?"

"Naw!" Bobby grins. "He was in Mexico buying drugs." Bobby waves an arm to indicate the basement. "I found Judd's little playroom down here months ago after I hacked his system. He liked to bring his business rivals here. I figured as long as he wasn't using it, he wouldn't care if I did. I shut down his alarms and cameras to make sure," he smirks.

"I liked Kira and I really liked you too," he continues. "You could have been sisters. I thought that maybe if I could get something going with you, I could retire from this business, maybe even raise a family. I have plenty of money, enough to take care of you for the rest of your life. I tried and tried, but you just wouldn't let me in."

Really? The thought makes me shudder!

"When you told me you were in love with that spic dyke, that was the last straw. So I decided to at least have some fun with the two of you."

He pauses, then says "I thought if I got rid of your uncle and showed you I loved you, you'd be my girl. I could tell by your lap dances and your kisses that you were coming on to me. I didn't know that this fucking dyke turned you queer until it was too late. She's ruined you!"

Keep him ranting, Nattie! If he's talking, he's not using those knives! "How did you drug the punch?"

"Easy! I've had your place bugged for months. There's a webcam and a mike in every room. I came in after the two of you went to sleep last night. There are pass keys all over the dark net. I laced most of the food in your fridge with the GHB because I didn't know what you'd be serving or who would eat what."

He goes over to Lupe and starts stabbing at her chest with the crop, starting her swinging. She can't help the moans that escape. I have to do something! But what?

I can't take my eyes off that brazier. He removes one of the implements from it. It's a long, thin knife, glowing orange. He shows it to me and says, "It's better if the knife is red hot because it cauterizes the wound as you cut. Makes it last longer!"

Stripper!

I try as hard as I can to block out the pain. "What makes you think that she ruined me?" I ask him.

"She turned you into a muff diver!" he says. "I saw you!"

Suddenly. I know what I have to do!

"That doesn't mean that I still don't want to get it on with a guy," I tell him.

He's taken aback a little. "What do you mean?"

"I can see now that I wasn't thinking clearly when I turned you down, Bobby. If you cut me down, I'll show you what I mean."

"Natalie, no!" Lupe shouts.

Bobby draws the hot knife across her thigh. I swear I can hear the flesh sizzle over her wail of anguish! Now she has another ugly weal three inches long, but little blood flows.

"C'mon, Bobby!" I yell. "You win! You want me, here's your chance! I'll do anything you want!"

He stands there holding the knife, staring at me. He's clearly torn.

"You're just saying that to save her."

"No, Bobby, I'm not. I've never seen you like this before – so strong! So in control! Can't you see you're turning me on?"

He approaches and holds the knife near my belly. I can feel the heat radiating from it.

"If I cut you down and find out you're lying, I'll make you scream for days."

"I'm not lying. Take me down and see!"

He disappears behind me. I feel a jerk on the rope that sends fresh waves of pain through my back and shoulders, then I'm face first on the basement floor with the smell of sawdust in my nostrils. My arms are still bound at the wrists, splayed out in front of me.

"Get on your knees!" he grates.

"Wait. I can't move my arms right now."

He grabs the ropes holding my wrists and hauls me upright. I let out a wail. I don't want to give him my pain to enjoy, but I can't help it! He gets me on my knees with my arms in front of me, then places himself inches from my face.

I know what to do. He holds the knife so close to my face that the heat burns my cheek. I try not to get sick. I hear Lupe in the background, continuously moaning no, no, no! He drops the knife on the floor and entangles his hands in my hair. The sharp stink of his sweat is gradually replaced by the smell of smoke.

"Shit!" He pushes me onto my back, snatches up the hot knife and stomps out the burning sawdust! I squirm out of his way so I don't get kicked!

Finally, he's got the fire out. He puts the knife back into the brazier and comes back to me.

I don't want a repeat of that last encounter, so I say, "C'mon Bobby, cut me loose. Let me show you a really good time!"

He's still got a disbelieving look on his face, but my submission must have convinced him I'm serious, because he goes away for a minute and returns with a folding knife. He snaps it open and slices through the rope holding my wrists.

When my arms are free, I say, "Give me a couple minutes to get the feeling back in my arms. Then we can do anything you want."

"Don't you move!" he says. He disappears into the shadows. I briefly consider bolting, but I'm so weak I know he could easily run me down – besides, there's no way I can leave Lupe alone with him. He comes back dragging a dirty tarpaulin.

"Put it there by the fire," I tell him. "I'm cold."

He does so, folding it over several times to provide a modicum of softness.

"Come over here," he says. "Lie down!"

I obey. It's not rape if I let him do it.

He stands over me for a minute, leering, then he comes at me. I stare at the ceiling, trying to make my mind a blank. It doesn't work.

His hands move from my shoulders to my throat as he pounds away. I grab his wrists to keep him from choking me and only partly succeed. I feel myself beginning to pass out as he groans and stops moving, releasing my neck. He lays there, spent.

258

Stripper!

After a while, I feel him coming alive again. He raises his head off my shoulder and looks down at me. His macabre face glows orange from the brazier's light, but instead of a smirk, his expression is tender! He grabs my shoulders and begins to move. I reach up and stop him.

"No, Bobby," I say gently. "Let me drive this time!"

He looks surprised, but then he smiles and rolls off. He holds out his hands and I reach for them, and he pulls me to my feet. Somehow I don't wince when the pain lances through my shoulders. He lies down on his back on the tarp. I lower myself and begin a slow, rhythmic movement.

I watch his face. At first, he's grinning like a jackass but as things progress, his expression becomes serious, almost stern. I'm moving faster now, and he reaches up and grabs my breasts. He closes his eyes. That's what I was waiting for!

I snatch the largest knife out of the brazier and drive it in just below his breastbone. His scream cuts through the air like a wailing siren, urgent and plaintive. His flesh hisses and spits as the blade disappears inside him and the black blood boils up around it. I tear myself off him, leaving the sizzling knife behind. He wraps both hands around the protruding blade to pull it out. A fresh scream echoes throughout the basement as his hands are seared on the hot metal!

I burn my own hands as I tip the glowing brazier on top of him, but I hardly feel it. The orange coals cascade across his chest and face like a string of ghastly Christmas lights. Shrieking constantly now, he tries to rise with the hot knife still transfixing him. Hot coals bounce and roll all over the sawdust-covered floor. Once again, wisps of smoke arise as the sawdust catches fire!

He's frantically trying to remove that terrible blade and get away from the burning coals, but the tarpaulin is beginning to catch! I look around desperately. His folding knife is on the floor where he dropped it. I scoop it up and run to Lupe. She's suspended like I was, with the end of the rope that holds her tied off to a hook embedded in a beam behind her. I cut the rope and she crumples to the floor like a broken puppet.

"Get up, Lupe, you've got to get up! I'm not strong enough to drag you out of here!"

Bobby is ten feet away, still screeching like a madman and flailing about behind a curtain of smoke and fire. He's finally gotten the knife out. He staggers towards us. His hair is nearly gone and I can see ugly black burns on his torso.

259

There's an open carton of whisky stacked next to the wall beside me. I grab a bottle by the neck and fling it at him. It misses, shattering on the floor in from of him. The liquor instantly catches and flares up blindingly. Bobby is transformed into a blazing, shrieking silhouette like something out of Dante's Inferno. I heave two more bottles into the pyre. Other stacked cardboard boxes and wooden crates ignite.

"Lupe, get up or we're going to die in here!"

Bobby staggers out of the flames. He comes at me, raising the knife above his head, but his hands are so badly burned that he drops it behind his back as it reaches its apex. It's only a short step forward to smash him in the face with another bottle of liquor. He collapses like a burning building. The illusion becomes complete as the pool of liquor he's lying in ignites.

Lupe is on her knees with her bound hands on the floor in front of her. I grab her by the armpits and heave! It must be the adrenalin, because I manage to get her on her feet.

The fire flares ever more brightly, illuminating areas formerly in shadow. I see the stairwell that goes up to Judd's office, but I know that the trap door is probably locked. I push Lupe towards the door that leads to parking lot.

We've got to get out of here before the fire gets to the rest of that booze!

The fumes are getting heavier. It's uncomfortably hot and hard to breathe and getting darker by the second. A sudden cough explodes from my mouth! By reflex, I inhale a lungful of the noxious atmosphere before I think to hold my breath.

I feel myself beginning to pass out as we bump into the rough stone wall. The air is so thick now that I'm not sure if we're at the door or not. OMG, if Bobby's locked it, we're done for! I keep a hand on Lupe and flail about with the other, looking for a latch. I feel a cool, slender piece of metal. I grab it and heave, push and the door flies open. The chill night air rushes inside and we're suddenly immersed in a smoky, orange luminescence. My back feels like it's on fire and my hair is ablaze! Hacking and choking, we totter out into the parking lot. Lupe tries to fall to the ground but I won't let her –I know we have to get far enough away from the club so we won't get cooked when the building becomes fully involved. Gritting my teeth against the burning pain on my back and head, I keep us moving until we're a goodly distance away, then fall to the ground on top of her.

Stripper!

Both of us are coughing and crying uncontrollably as we lay on the asphalt. The old building is really going up now. The screams emanating from the conflagration must be my imagination. Surely the club is not open, full of patrons, employees and dancers. I am the one who started that fire. I know that nothing could be alive in that hell!

The roof collapses and the green and fuchsia sign winks out for the last time, only to be replaced with towering flames and smoke. Nan! Shalyla! Summer and Annie! Shelby and Liz! How can I ever live with this?

Orange fades to black...

Chapter 37.

This party in the 3M office is a whole lot smaller than my housewarming. Danny is here and so is Leon Kidd. And Uncle Amos!

Uncle is sitting in his usual spot behind his desk, but his feet aren't on it. The wheelchair makes that impossible. His face is not plump anymore, and there's a wattle of loose skin under his chin that makes him look so very old. His grey hair has thinned so much that I can see patches of scalp underneath. It looks like he's wearing somebody else's clothes and, in a sense, he is, because he lost nearly seventy pounds during his months in a coma. But he is smiling!

"It's great to be back home, y'all," he says.

3M is still a going concern, largely thanks to Danny. While Uncle Amos was sick, he singlehandedly brought in work and did most of it the same way, spending many a sixteen-hour day on stakeout. I started helping out again after I got out of the hospital. But Danny and I realized that it was just too much for the two of us. We had to have help.

Uncle Amos picks up a placard with his name on it and bangs it on his desk like a gavel.

"All right, y'all. This here is an organizational meeting for the new 3M Detective Agency, Amos Murdoch, CEO, presiding. The main purpose of this meeting is to welcome our new partner. Leon Kidd!"

Kidd has a lot of the same issues with the city police department that Danny does. He stepped on a lot of toes when he ginned up that SWAT raid on the Kitten Club, enough so that his efficiency as a detective would be seriously impaired if he stayed on. And he had enough time in to retire. That made the decision to put in his papers that much easier.

"Y'all know that I won't be able to join you much in the field anymore." Uncle Amos says. "I guess it's about time that I held down a chair in the office, anyhow. So I'll be in charge of gettin' the work in the door, and y'all will be in charge of doin' it. Suits the hell out of me!"

Stripper!

"And there's one more thing. I've reorganized this bidness – it's no longer a sole proprietorship. It's now a partnership between me, Danny and Leon. And we have a trainee for the office help." He cocks an eyebrow at me.

Office help? He's got to be kidding!

"I don't know how much help I'll be," I say. "I'm going back to school in a month, and I've got a lot to make up. Maybe y'all better find some other office help." I try hard to keep the bitterness out of those last two words, but I don't think I was successful.

The doorbell rings.

"That couldn't have come at a better time," says Danny.

He disappears into the front of the house and returns in a minute, standing in the doorway to the reception room. There's someone behind him, but I can't see who it is.

"Since Nattie will be too busy to handle the office, I had an agency send over somebody else." He steps aside and waves the lady in.

It's a short, blonde, fortysomething woman. She's way cute!

"Mom? Mom!"

She hesitates for a moment, unsure of which way to go first, then she runs over to Uncle Amos in his wheelchair and gives him a big hug and a kiss. Can't blame her for that. Then she comes to do the same for me.

"What is this?" I ask her.

"Danny called me and told me about Amos, and what's been going on with you. I can't blame you for not telling me – I know that you've had a really rough time lately." She caresses the scar on my right cheek with a fingertip. "Your poor face! And your pretty hair is all gone!"

I've already had one operation to correct the damage from Royce's pistol-whipping. The plastic surgeon told me that she's confident that the scar can be removed entirely, but I have to heal more first. And hair grows back.

"It's okay, Mom. They can fix it. But what are you doing here?"

"Amos needs someone to help him get by now, so I've agreed to move in with him and act as his caretaker. And to provide the agency with office support."

"But what does that leave for me?"

Mom and Uncle Amos answer in unison. "Go back to school!"

This time I don't try to keep the bitterness out of my voice. "So after everything I've done, you're firing me?"

"Call it an extended leave of absence," says Uncle Amos. "I tole you before, Nattie. If you get yourself a law degree and decide that you want to come on with me, there's a place here for you. But you said it yourself. You don't need this job 'cause you've got your own money now. You've also got a lot of school to make up. And you don't want to spend your life struggling for every dime like me and your mom have had to do."

I was afraid of this. Uncle Amos found out that I was stripping at the club, and that I had gotten myself arrested when the news coverage about the fire came out. I really wasn't happy about being back in the media spotlight, and to say that Uncle wasn't thrilled about it is a gross understatement, but I think at least he understands why I did it. And that's why he's keeping me out of the field. The media didn't get hold of much about what happened in Judd's office either, except that I was somehow involved in taking down a drug ring, and nothing about what happened in that basement with Bobby came out. I had another call from Roderigo to tell my side of it, but I'll never do that.

"Well, I guess that's it then." I say and gather up my things to leave. "Mom, I'll call you. We'll have lunch. And you'll have to come by and meet my roommate and her son."

I haven't told Uncle Amos about me and Lupe either. He's old school and he wouldn't understand. I will tell Mom before she comes over, though.

Speaking of Lupe, since Bobby trashed our computers, Kira Foxxx and Carmella Picante are out a job too. That got us to thinking about a different career for Lupe. Our joint performance online made me realize what an exceptionally skilled pole dancer she really is, so I made some calls. She's now working as a contractor for several health clubs in the area as a pole dancing coach. I also contacted a group in the city that helps undocumented immigrants make a life for themselves in the U.S., and they've agreed to help her get a green card. And Eduardo starts school the same week that I do.

Bobby! It's still hard to believe that he was the assassin. I was so sure it was Valery! FWIW, the DNA on the bottle Bobby gave me came back to the blood found in the townhouse, but it's obvious that Bobby just gave me his own DNA and said it was Valery's. He probably hoped that cops would kill Valery, and he'd be off the hook. Bobby or Judd probably made Robyn for a cop, and Bobby got her to buy guns for him –it's the kind of thing that would appeal to his desire for control. I don't want to think so, but I'll bet Bobby had her in that basement, too. And of course, he hurt Uncle Amos.

Uncle Amos told me that he went to the club to look into Robyn's disappearance and spotted Bobby right off. He told him that he could forget about doing the website. Said Bobby had low moral character. He didn't know the half of it! So Bobby followed Uncle out to his car, whining for forgiveness, then shanked him.

Bobby was a real screw-up and a half-assed killer at best! Maybe it was all the meth. I'm not even sure that he really killed all of those people whose pictures were on his website – he was pretty much a pathological liar. He never told me how he ambushed Becca – for all I know, she just went with him because she knew him. He did manage to kill Blackie and Robyn, but he botched it badly with Uncle Amos - he couldn't even finish the job with two more tries! He must have been scared shitless that Uncle would finger him if he woke up!

And I still can't believe that Bobby thought I might love him! In his twisted little mind, he had us living in connubial bliss on an island somewhere. The shock of my outright rejection must've pushed him over the edge.

Am I ready to go back to being just a college student? I've done some terrible things, but they were necessary. I'm back on my medicine and the dreams have subsided again. I'm seeing Rebecca weekly, but I still haven't told her about the people I killed in Judd's office, or what happened in the basement. I don't know that I ever can. In a short time I've learned what I'm truly capable of, and some of it I don't like at all.

I've tried to block what happened in that basement out of my mind, but I just can't. I despise myself for having sex with that little pervert, but it was the only way I could think of to get him to take me down off that hook. I'm glad I burned that little motherfucker alive! I really am!

****

It's few weeks after the fire at the club. Lupe is on the sofa trying to read a kids' book to Eduardo to help both of them with English, but the little guy has punked out and is asleep on Mama's lap.

Now is as good a time as any for this conversation.

"Lupe, can I ask you something?"

"What is it, *cariño?*"

I don't really know how to even approach this, so I just blurt it out.

"You said that you were raped before Judd did it?"

"I said that it is not rape if I let him do it. And I did let him, so it was not rape."

"But Judd blackmailed you. He forced you. So did those cartel guys."

She shrugs. "I let them do it too, because I know if I fight, I get hurt worse. Sometimes there is just not a good choice. So you take the choice you got. You did that with Bobby and you saved us." She smiles. "You were very brave!"

"But I killed him! And I killed those other men in Judd's office!" That's the first time I've admitted that to anyone. I wanted to tell Rebecca, but I couldn't because she'd have to tell the cops.

"*Si*, and you did a very good thing. They deserved it for what they did."

I can't help it. I start to cry. Lupe opens her arms and says, "*Cariño*, come here."

She sidles over so I can sit next to her, then adjusts the sleeping boy so he's on both of our laps. She puts her arms around my neck and presses my face to her bosom, strokes my hair and kisses my ear. She holds me that way until the tears pass.

"My Nattie!" she says, "So strong, so brave and such a *niña pequeña*. You save us from those terrible men. Now you must let me save you."

I fall asleep in her arms.

-- The End –

Acknowledgements

I want to thank the following people who were instrumental in the completion and publication of *Stripper!*.

My beta readers Craig Chapman, Ilia Davidovich and Paul Crockett provided many helpful suggestions and encouraged me to see this project through.

I also want to thank my two oldest friends for sticking with me for decades. Peter J. Reilly and I met in high school and we have stayed in contact ever since. He graciously agreed to read and provide comments on *Stripper!*.

I am also grateful that I have reconnected with my oldest friend from grammar school, Paul Rusnak, who also read and commented on *Stripper!*.

A recurring theme throughout the Natalie McMasters series is love and friendship. I learned a lot of it from Pete and Paul.

About the Author

As a kid, I started reading mysteries with the Hardy Boys, Ken Holt and Rick Brant, then graduated to the classics by authors such as A. Conan Doyle, Erle Stanley Gardner, John Dickson Carr, and Rex Stout, to name a few. I have written fiction as a hobby all of my life, starting in marble-backed copybooks in grade school. I built a career as a technical and science writer and as an editor for nearly thirty years in academia, industry and government. Now that I'm truly on my own as a freelance science writer and editor, I'm excited to publish my own mystery series as well.

Follow me on Facebook at

https://www.facebook.com/3MDetectiveAgency/, on Twitter

@3Mdetective, Instagram at 3mdetective, Tumblr at

nataliemcmasters or email me at tom@3mdetectiveagency.com.

Be sure to visit the 3M Detective Agency website at

https://www.3mdetectiveagency.com/contact/

and subscribe to my newsletter to get all the news about Nattie

and the 3M gang.

Don't miss the next book in the Natalie McMasters series by

Thomas A. Burns, Jr.

Turn the page for a preview of Revenge!

REVENGE!

A Natalie McMasters Novel

By

Thomas A. Burns, Jr.

Chapter 1

When you kill someone, it changes you. Totally.

My name is Natalie McMasters. I'm twenty, short and blonde (OK, it's bleached), and I'm way cute. And I've already killed three people.

Two of them, I shot. The third one, I stabbed and burned to death. I killed them because they would have killed me and my gf Lupe if I hadn't. For a while, that justification allowed me to sleep at night. But then the nightmares returned.

"What are you not telling me, Nattie?" Rebecca asks me.

Dr. Rebecca Feiner is my shrink. Her high cheekbones, copper skin and slanted, nearly black eyes suggest she has native American blood. She wears her ebon hair in a bun at work, but I've seen her with it down, and it falls nearly to her waist in a smoky cascade. She's a thirtysomething, about five eight, and the white doctor's smock she's wearing does little to hide her buxom curves. She is absolutely one of the most gorgeous women that I've ever seen.

I'm lying on a stainless steel and black leather daybed in her office. The sickly-sweet aroma exuding from the vase of blue hyacinths on her desk overwhelms the old building musk. I intently scrutinize the flowers to avoid meeting her gaze. I've been seeing Rebecca since last year after my best friend was murdered and I decided to find her killer. I found him, all right.

"I'm concerned that we can't seem to get you off the Prazosin." Rebecca says. "Outwardly, it seems that you've gotten your life back on track. You're back in school. You're in a stable relationship with Lupe, whom you tell me you love very much. You're not working as a private detective or a stripper anymore, and no one's stalking you or trying to kill you. But every time we stop the Prazosin, the nightmares come back. So what are you not telling me? What happened to you after you were kidnapped?"

I'm still not meeting her gaze, and I know she notices. I force my eyes away from the flowers to her face.

"Nothing," I lie calmly. "The kidnapper took me and Lupe to the basement of the Kitten Club. He was going to rape both of us there. But before he could, a fire got started and burned the place down. I managed to get myself and Lupe out, but he died in the fire."

She fixes me with those dark eyes of hers. "Did he rape you, Nattie?"

"No." It's not rape if I let him do it. "I've told you everything that's been going on with me." Inside my head, I scream, I'm not telling you I've killed three people!

A frown mars Rebecca's elegant face.

"I can't help you if you won't be honest with me, Natalie."

She's gone from Nattie to Natalie. A bad sign.

"If he did rape you, there's no shame in that. It wasn't your fault. But you can't heal from it if you won't talk about it."

I fleetingly consider telling her that I seduced my kidnapper to gain our freedom, but I'm afraid of what else I might let slip if I open that can of worms. Like that I killed him while screwing him, for instance. "But I really have been honest with you," I say.

Her frown morphs into a glare and she closes her portfolio with an audible crack.

"Then I guess we're done for today," she snaps.

I know there's at least twenty minutes left in the session, but I don't say anything and neither does she. The silence becomes painfully acute as I get up to go.

I put my hand on the knob to open the door, then turn and say, "I guess I'll see you next week."

"Why bother? Coming here isn't going to do you any good if you won't tell me what's going on with you."

"So you're cancelling the session?"

"No. You're cancelling it. I'm just not going to allow you to lie there and stonewall me. If you can tell me the truth, come on in. But if you won't talk to me, I'll have to ask you to leave again."

The only other person besides me who knows what happened is Lupe, because she was there too. She knows what I did. But she'll never tell.

Rebecca's office is in the Counselling Center, on the old part of the State University campus. I've been a student at State for the last two-and-a-half years, studying pre-law. I've also been working for my Uncle Amos Murdoch while in school. Uncle Amos is the founder and proprietor of the 3M Detective Agency.

271

Most of his current business comes from dogging insurance scofflaws, waiting for them to do something for the camera that shows they're not hurt as badly as they say. He hired me as his assistant. The pay ain't great but the work ain't hard - most of the time I could study in the car while on stakeout. He even got me a private detective trainee's license from the state, of which I was prouder than I liked to let on.

In our last case, my good friend Becca was murdered and Uncle Amos was attacked and left for dead. Becca was an online exotic dancer who could have been my twin sister. I took her place to draw her killer to me and ended up working undercover in a local strip joint. I found the killer and broke up a major drug ring, but I also got a good case of PTSD in the process. That's why I'm still seeing Rebecca. When Uncle found out about the stripping, he fired me. He told me I could see about a job with him when I had my law degree if I still wanted one. I didn't know it when he hired me, but it was Uncle Amos' strong sense of family that was responsible for the job offer. That's also why he fired me when he had reason to believe I might get hurt working for him.

I go out of the front door of the Counselling Center on to a red brick porch that overlooks a sunken courtyard the size of a football field, rimmed with stately oaks and a border of multicolored chrysanthemums. It's nearly lunchtime on a gorgeous fall day. Even though the morning was chilly, it's now well over eighty because we're in the South, but the fresh autumn breeze keeps the humidity down so it's not as oppressive as it would be in the summer. I slip out of my hoodie and tie it around my waist.

Because Rebecca cut the session short, I've got some time to kill. My next class is on new campus, so I head that way.

As usual on a day like this, the courtyard is full of students. Some are passing through, going from one class to another or back to the dorm. Others are playing Frisbee, lolling about on the grass or on beach towels, sleeping, reading or snuggling. A flash of anger wells up in my chest. How dare they be so carefree?

I turn my back on them as I climb the concrete staircase that leads out of the courtyard. Why am I so angry? I did nothing wrong. Those men I killed were murderers, and would have surely killed me and Lupe if I hadn't stopped them. I have no reason to feel guilty. And I have little reason to fear arrest. The fire destroyed all of the evidence along with the strip club, so the chance that cops will ever trace anything to me is vanishingly small.

Why won't I tell Rebecca what happened? I've finally accepted that I was raped in that basement, even though I was the one who initiated the sex. I didn't do it for revenge, I only did it to stop that pervert from killing me and Lupe. Lupe and I have talked about what happened, and she told me that wasn't my fault. But I'm still ashamed I had to let him do it. Lupe was a victim of multiple rapes by cartel thugs when she lived in Mexico, but she seems to have put that behind her. Why can't I?

I come to the top of the stairs where a the street runs along a ridge, separating old campus from new. I look down into the cement courtyard in front of me, the so-called New Commons. It's ringed with contemporary concrete and steel buildings and the university logo, done in orange and blue bricks, stands out hideously in the center. I can't imagine two colors that go together less well. The New Commons is also full of people, but almost none of them are lollygagging. The concrete benches are not welcoming, and who wants to fall on the hard pavement chasing a stupid Frisbee?

I make my way to the library on the opposite side of the Commons, where there's a snack bar/coffee shop/cafeteria on the ground floor. I push open the glass door and the smells of old coffee, sour bread and greasy burgers slap me in the face. It's a good thing I'm not really hungry because I think I might catch something if I ate here, but it's a good place to kill time before my next class. I get me a plain black coffee and find an empty table in the back. I'm in no mood for company.

I pull out my phone and thumb the button. 11:09. Thirty-five minutes until class. I could use the time to study, but I'm just not in the mood.

I let my eyes drift around the spacious room. It's about half full – the lunch crowd is still in class. The buzz of conversation fills the air. The glass and stainless-steel tables are bolted to the floor so the students can't inflict chaos on the arrangement. Most of the tables are occupied by groups, but a few loners like me are scattered about. TV sets hang from brackets on the ceiling at regular intervals and scroll public service announcements – club meetings, special lectures, concerts and the like. My eyes are automatically drawn to a screen, against my will.

…National syndicated columnist George Markarious will be on campus to discuss the failure of the current U.S. economic policy to address the needs of…

The screen suddenly flickers and goes black, but only for a second. When it comes back on, I see two naked women, entwined on a bed, engaging in an enthusiastic sixty-nine. It doesn't seem to be a porn flick - the perspective doesn't change and the room on the screen is dimly lit, so it's difficult to make out details. There's something disturbingly familiar about it, though. Wait a minute, I know that heart-shaped bed…

The girl on top raises her head from between her partner's legs to take a breath, giving the camera a full view of her face. OMG! It's me!

Made in the USA
Middletown, DE
10 April 2023

28599778R00152